Rudyard Kipling

2 Books in 1

The Jungle Book
&
Kim

A Wilco Book
Outstanding works of universal interest

This Omnibus edition printed in 2007

ISBN NO.: 81-8252-297-8

Rudyard Kipling

The Jungle Book &
Kim

Complete and Unabridged

Published by
WILCO PUBLISHING HOUSE
33, Sri Saibaba Marg, Kalaghoda,
Mumbai – 400 023. INDIA
Tel: (91-22) 22041420 / 22842574
Fax: (91-22) 22041429
E mail: wilcos@vsnl.com

About The Author

RUDYARD KIPLING

(1865-1936)

Rudyard Kipling was born in India where his father was a teacher at Mumbai's J.J. School of Arts. In early childhood, young Kipling was exposed to the fascinating sounds and sights of India. This was to have deep impression on his writings, which he began when he was just 13.

His famous novels *Jungle Books* and *Captains Courageous* were written while he was in America. Apart from these, Kipling's balladic poems are equally acclaimed; among them, the 'Absent-minded Beggar' brought-in huge sums of money. The philanthropist Kipling however donated the entire proceeds to the benefit of British soldiers engaged in the Boer War. Later he lost his own son, John, in World War I, at the tender age of 18.

In 1907, Kipling became the first British author to get the Nobel Prize for literature. His autobiography *Something Of Myself* was published posthumously.

THE JUNGLE BOOK

CONTENTS

PREFACE

The demands made by a work of this nature upon the generosity of specialists are very numerous, and the Editor would be wanting in all title to the generous treatment he has received were he not willing to make the fullest possible acknowledgment of his indebtedness.

His thanks are due in the first place to the scholarly and accomplished Bahadur Shah, baggage elephant 174 on the Indian Register, who, with his amiable sister Pudmini, most courteously supplied the history of 'Toomai of the Elephants' and much of the information contained in 'Her Majesty's Servants'. The adventures of Mowgli were collected at various times and in various places from a multitude of informants, most of whom desire to preserve the strictest anonymity. Yet, at this distance, the Editor feels at liberty to thank a Hindu gentleman of the old rock, an esteemed resident of the upper slopes of Jakko, for his convincing if somewhat caustic estimate of the national characteristics of his caste – the Presbytes. Sahi, a savant of infinite research and industry, a member of the recently disbanded Seeonee Pack, and an artist well known at most of the local fairs of southern India, where his muzzled dance with his master attracts the youth, beauty, and culture of many villages, have contributed most valuable data on people, manners, and customs. These have been freely drawn upon, in the stories of 'Tiger! Tiger!', 'Kaa's Hunting', and 'Mowgli's Brothers'. For the outlines of 'Rikki-tikki-tavi' the Editor stands indebted to one of the leading herpetologists of upper India, a fearless and independent investigator who, resolving 'not to live but know', lately sacrificed his life through over-application to the study of our Eastern Thanatophidia. A happy accident of travel enabled the Editor, when a passenger on the 'Empress of India', to be of some slight assistance to a fellow-passenger. How richly his poor services were repaid, readers of *The White Seal* may judge for themselves

R.K.

1

Mowgli's Brothers

Now Chil the Kite brings home the night
    That Mang the Bat sets free –
The herds are shut in byre and hut,
    For loosed till dawn are we.
This is the hour of pride and power,
    Talon and tush and claw.
Oh, hear the call! – Good hunting all
    That keep the Jungle Law!

- *Night Song in the Jungle*

It was seven o'clock of a very warm evening in the Seeonee hills when Father Wolf woke up from his day's rest, scratched himself, yawned, and spread out his paws one after the other to get rid of the sleepy feeling in their tips. Mother Wolf lay with her big grey nose dropped across her four tumbling, squealing cubs, and the moon shone into the mouth of the cave where they all lived. "Augrh!" said Father Wolf, "it is time to hunt again." and he was going to spring downhill when a little shadow with a bushy tail crossed the threshold and whined: "Good luck go with you, O Chief of the Wolves; and good luck and strong white teeth go with the noble children, that they may never forget the hungry in this world."

It was the jackal – Tabaqui, the Dish-licker – and the wolves of India despise Tabaqui because he runs about making mischief, and telling tales, and eating rags and pieces of leather from the village rubbish-heaps. But they are afraid of him too, because

Tabaqui, more than anyone else in the Jungle, is apt to go mad, and then he forgets that he was ever afraid of anyone, and runs through the forest biting everything in his way. Even the tiger runs and hides when little Tabaqui goes mad, for madness is the most disgraceful thing that can overtake a wild creature. We call it hydrophobia, but they call it *dewanee* – the madness – and run.

"Enter, then, and look," said Father Wolf stiffly; "but there is no food here."

"For a wolf, no," said Tabaqui; "but for so mean a person as myself a dry bone is a good feast. Who are we, the *Gidur-log* [the Jackal People], to pick and choose?" He scuttled to the back of the cave, where he found the bone of a buck with some meat on it, and sat cracking the end merrily.

"All thanks for this good meal," he said, licking his lips. "How beautiful are the noble children! How large are their eyes! And so young too! Indeed, indeed, I might have remembered that the children of Kings are men from the beginning."

Now, Tabaqui knew as well as anyone else that there is nothing so unlucky as to compliment children to their faces; and it pleased him to see Mother and Father Wolf look uncomfortable.

Tabaqui sat still, rejoicing in the mischief that he had made: then he said spitefully:

"Shere Khan, the Big One, has shifted his hunting-grounds. He will hunt among these hills for the next moon, so he has told me."

Shere Khan was the tiger who lived near the Waingunga River, twenty miles away.

"He has no right!" Father Wolf began angrily – "By the Law of the Jungle he has no right to change his quarters without due warning. He will frighten every head of game within ten miles, and I – I have to kill for two, these days."

"His mother did not call him Lungri [the Lame One] for

nothing," said Mother Wolf quietly. "He has been lame in one foot from his birth. That is why he has only killed cattle. Now the villagers of the Waingunga are angry with him, and he has come here to make our villagers angry. They will scour the Jungle for him when he is far away, and we and our children must run when the grass is set alight. Indeed, we are very grateful to Shere Khan!"

"Shall I tell him of your gratitude?" said Tabaqui.

"Out!" snapped Father Wolf. "Out and hunt with thy master. Thou hast done harm enough for one night."

"I go," said Tabaqui quietly. "Ye can hear Shere Khan below in the thickets. I might have saved myself the message."

Father Wolf listened, and below in the valley that ran down to a little river, he heard the dry, angry, snarly, singsong whine of a tiger who has caught nothing and does not care if all the Jungle knows it.

"The fool!" said Father Wolf. "To begin a night's work with that noise! Does he think that our buck are like his fat Waingunga bullocks?"

"H'sh! It is neither bullock nor buck he hunts tonight," said Mother Wolf. "It is Man." The whine had changed to a sort of humming purr that seemed to come from every quarter of the compass. It was the noise that bewilders woodcutters and gypsies sleeping in the open, and makes them run sometimes into the very mouth of the tiger.

"Man!" said Father Wolf, showing all his white teeth. "Faugh! Are there not enough beetles and frogs in the tanks that he must eat Man, and on our ground too?"

The law of the Jungle, which never orders anything without a reason, forbids every beast to eat Man except when he is killing to show his children how to kill, and then he must hunt outside the hunting-grounds of his pack or tribe. The real reason for this is that man-killing means, sooner or later, the arrival of white men on elephants, with guns, and hundreds of brown men with gongs and rockets and torches. Then everybody in the Jungle suffers. The reason the beasts give among themselves is that Man is the weakest and most defenceless of all living things, and it is unsportsmanlike to touch him. They say too – and it is true – that man-eaters become mangy, and lose their teeth.

The purr grew louder, and ended in the full-throated "Aaarh!" of the tiger's charge.

Then there was a howl – an untigerish howl – from Shere Khan. "He has missed," said Mother Wolf. "What is it?"

Father Wolf ran out a few paces and heard Shere Khan muttering and mumbling savagely, as he tumbled about in the scrub.

"The fool has had no more sense than to jump at a woodcutter's camp-fire, and has burned his feet," said Father Wolf, with a grunt. "Tabaqui is with him."

"Something is coming uphill," said Mother Wolf, twitching one ear. "Get ready."

The bushes rustled a little in the thicket, and Father Wolf dropped with his haunches under him, ready for his leap. Then, if you had been watching, you would have seen the most wonderful thing in the world – the wolf checked in mid-spring. He made his bound before he saw what it was he was jumping at, and then he tried to stop himself. The result was that he shot up straight into the air for four or five feet, landing almost where he left ground.

"Man!" he snapped. "A man's cub. Look!"

Directly in front of him, holding on by a low branch, stood a naked brown baby who could just walk – as soft and as dimpled a little atom as ever came to a wolf's cave at night. He looked up into Father Wolf's face, and laughed.

"Is that a man's cub?" said Mother Wolf. "I have never seen one. Bring it here."

A wolf accustomed to moving his own cubs can, if necessary, mouth an egg without breaking it, and though Father Wolf's jaws closed right on the child's back not a tooth even scratched the skin, as he laid it down among the cubs.

"How little! How naked, and – how bold!" said Mother Wolf softly. The baby was pushing his way between the cubs to get close to the warm hide. *"Ahai!* He is taking his meal with the others. And so this is a man's cub. Now, was there ever a wolf that could boast of a man's cub among her children?"

"I have heard now and again of such a thing, but never in our Pack or in my time," said Father Wolf. "He is altogether without hair, and I could kill him with a touch of my foot. But see, he looks up and is not afraid."

The moonlight was blocked out of the mouth of the cave, for Shere Khan's great square head and shoulders were thrust into the entrance. Tabaqui, behind him, was squeaking: "My lord, my lord, it went in here!"

"Shere Khan does us great honour," said Father Wolf, but his eyes were very angry. "What does Shere Khan need?"

"My quarry. A man's cub went this way," said Shere Khan. "Its parents have run off. Give it to me."

Shere Khan had jumped at a woodcutter's camp-fire, as Father Wolf had said, and was furious from the pain of his burned feet. But Father Wolf knew that the mouth of the cave was too narrow for a tiger to come in by. Even where he was, Shere Khan's shoulders and forepaws were cramped for want of room, as a man's would be if he tried to fight in a barrel.

"The Wolves are a free people," said Father Wolf. "They take orders from the Head of the Pack, and not from any striped cattle-killer. The man's cub is ours – to kill if we choose."

"Ye choose and ye do not choose! What talk is this of choosing? By the bull that I killed, am I to stand nosing into your dog's den for my fair dues? It is I, Shere Khan, who speak!"

The tiger's roar filled the cave with thunder. Mother Wolf shook herself clear of the cubs and sprang forward, her eyes, like two green moons in the darkness, facing the blazing eyes of Shere Khan.

"And it is I, Raksha [The Demon], who answers. The man's cub is mine, Lungri – mine to me! He shall not be killed. He shall live to run with the Pack and to hunt with the Pack; and in the end, look you, hunter of little naked cub – frog-eater – fish-killer – he shall hunt *thee*! Now get hence, or by the Sambhur that I killed (I eat no starved cattle), back thou goest to thy mother, burned beast of the Jungle, lamer than ever thou camest into the world! Go!"

Father Wolf looked on amazed. He had almost forgotten the days when he won Mother Wolf in fair fight from five other wolves, when she ran in the Pack and was not called The Demon for compliment's sake. Shere Khan might have faced Father Wolf, but he could not stand up against Mother Wolf, for he knew that where he was she had all the advantage of the ground, and would fight to the death. So he backed out of the cave-mouth growling, and when he was clear he shouted –

"Each dog barks in his own yard! We will see what the Pack will say to this fostering of man-cubs. The cub is mine, and to my teeth he will come in the end, O bush-tailed thieves!"

Mother Wolf threw herself down panting among the cubs, and Father Wolf said to her gravely –

"Shere Khan speaks this much truth. The cub must be shown to the Pack. Wilt thou still keep him, Mother?"

"Keep him!" she gasped. "He came naked, by night, alone and very hungry; yet he was not afraid! Look, he has pushed one of my babes to one side already. And that lame butcher would have killed him and would have run off to the Waingunga while the villagers here hunted through all our lairs in revenge! Keep him? Assuredly I will keep him. Lie still, little frog. O thou Mowgli – for Mowgli the Frog I will call thee – the time will come when thou wilt hunt Shere Khan as he has hunted thee."

"But what will our Pack say?" said Father Wolf.

The Law of the Jungle lays down very clearly that any wolf may, when he marries, withdraw from the Pack he belongs to; but as soon as his cubs are old enough to stand on their feet he must bring them to the Pack Council, which is generally held once a month at full moon, in order that the other wolves may identify them. After that inspection the cubs are free to run where they please, and until they have killed their first buck no excuse is accepted if a grown wolf of the Pack kills one of them. The punishment is death where the murderer can be found; and if you think for a minute you will see that this must be so.

Father Wolf waited till his cubs could run a little, and then on the night of the Pack Meeting took them and Mowgli and Mother Wolf to the Council Rock – a hilltop covered with stones and boulders where a hundred wolves could hide. Akela, the great grey Lone Wolf who led all the Pack by strength and cunning, lay out at full length on his rock, and below him sat forty or more wolves of every size and colour, from badger-coloured veterans who could handle a buck alone, to young black three-year-olds who thought they could. The Lone Wolf had led them for a year now. He had fallen twice into a wolf-trap in his youth, and once he had been beaten and left for dead; so he knew the manners and customs of men. There was very little talking at the Rock. The cubs tumbled over each other in the centre of the circle where their mothers and fathers sat, and now and again a senior wolf would go quietly up to a cub, look at him carefully, and return to his place on noiseless feet. Sometimes a mother would push her cub far out into the moonlight, to be sure that he had not been overlooked. Akela from his rock would cry: "Ye know the Law – ye know the Law. Look well, O Wolves!" and the anxious mothers would take up the call: "Look – look well, O Wolves!"

At last – and Mother Wolf's neck-bristles lifted as the time came – Father Wolf pushed "Mowgli the Frog," as they called him, into the centre, where he sat laughing and playing with some pebbles that glistened in the moonlight.

Akela never raised his head from his paws, but went on with the monotonous cry: "Look well!" A muffled roar came up from behind the rocks – the voice of Shere Khan crying: "The cub is mine. Give him to me. What have the Free People to do with a man's cub?" Akela never even twitched his ears: all he said was: "Look well, O Wolves! What have the Free People to do with the orders of any save the Free People? Look well!"

There was a chorus of deep growls, and a young wolf in his fourth year flung back Shere Khan's question to Akela: "What have the Free People to do with a man's cub?" Now, the Law of the Jungle lays down that if there is any dispute as to the right of a cub to be accepted by the Pack, he must be spoken for by at least two members of the Pack who are not his father and mother.

"Who speaks for this cub?" said Akela. "Among the Free People who speaks?" There was no answer, and Mother Wolf got ready for what she knew would be her last fight, if things came to fighting.

Then the only other creature who is allowed at the Pack Council – Baloo, the sleepy brown bear who teaches the wolf-cubs the Law of the Jungle: old Baloo, who can come and go where he pleases because he eats only nuts and roots and honey – rose up on his hindquarters and grunted.

"The man's cub – the man's cub?" he said. "*I* speak for the man's cub. There is no harm in a man's cub. I have no gift of words, but I speak the truth. Let him run with the Pack, and be entered with the others. I myself will teach him."

"We need yet another," said Akela. "Baloo has spoken, and he is our teacher for the young cubs. Who speaks besides Baloo?"

A black shadow dropped down into the circle. It was Bagheera the Black Panther, inky black all over, but with the panther markings showing up in certain lights like the pattern of watered silk. Everybody knew Bagheera, and nobody cared to cross his path; for he was as cunning as Tabaqui, as bold as the wild buffalo, and as reckless as the wounded elephant. But he had a voice as soft as wild honey dripping from a tree, and a skin softer than down.

"O Akela, and ye the Free People," he purred, "I have no right in your assembly; but the Law of the Jungle says that if there is a doubt which is not a killing matter in regard to a new cub, the life of that cub may be bought at a price. And the Law does not say who may or may not pay that price. Am I right?"

"Good! good!" said the young wolves, who are always hungry. "Listen to Bagheera. The cub can be bought for a price. It is the Law."

"Knowing that I have no right to speak here, I ask your leave."

"Speak then," cried twenty voices.

"To kill a naked cub is shame. Besides, he may make better sport for you when he is grown. Baloo has spoken in his behalf. Now to Baloo's word I will add one bull, and a fat one, newly killed, not half a mile from here, if ye will accept the man's cub according to the Law. Is it difficult?"

There was a clamour of scores of voices, saying: "What matter? He will die in the winter rains. He will scorch in the sun. What harm can a naked frog do us? Let him run with the Pack. Where is the bull, Bagheera? Let him be accepted." And then came Akela's deep bay, crying: "Look well – look well, O Wolves!"

Mowgli was still deeply interested in the pebbles and he did not notice when the wolves came and looked at him one by one. At last they all went down the hill for the dead bull, and only Akela, Bagheera, Baloo, and Mowgli's own wolves were left. Shere Khan roared still in the night, for he was very angry that Mowgli had not been handed over to him.

"Ay, roar well," said Bagheera, under his whiskers; "for the time will come when this naked thing will make thee roar to another tune, or I know nothing of Man."

"It was well done," said Akela. "Men and their cubs are very wise. He may be a help in time."

"Truly, a help in time of need; for none can hope to lead the Pack for ever," said Bagheera.

Akela said nothing. He was thinking of the time that comes to every leader of every pack when his strength goes from him and he gets feebler and feebler, till at last he is killed by the wolves and a new leader comes up – to be killed in his turn.

"Take him away," he said to Father Wolf, "and train him as befits one of the Free People."

And that is how Mowgli was entered into the Seeonee Wolf Pack at the price of a bull and on Baloo's good word.

Now you must be content to skip ten or eleven whole years, and only guess at all the wonderful life that Mowgli led among the wolves, because if it were written out it would fill ever so many books. He grew up with the cubs, though they, of course, were grown wolves almost before he was a child, and Father Wolf taught him his business, and the meaning of things in the Jungle, till every rustle in the grass, every breath of the warm night air, every note of the owls above his head, every scratch of a bat's claws as it roosted for a while in a tree, and every splash of every little fish jumping in a pool, meant just as much to him as the work of his office means to a business man. When he was not learning, he sat out in the sun and slept, and ate and went to sleep again; when he felt dirty or hot he swam in the forest pools; and when he wanted honey (Baloo told him that honey and nuts were just as pleasant to eat as raw meat) he climbed up for it, and that Bagheera showed him how to do. Bagheera would lie out on a branch and call, "Come along, Little Brother," and at first Mowgli would cling like the sloth, but afterward he would fling himself through the branches almost as boldly as the grey ape. He took his place at the Council Rock, too, when the Pack met, and there he discovered that if he stared hard at any wolf, the wolf would be forced to drop his eyes, and so he used to stare for fun. At other times he would pick the long thorns out of the pads of his friends, for wolves suffer terribly from thorns and burrs in their coats. He would go down the hillside into the cultivated lands by night, and look very curiously at the villagers in their huts, but he had a mistrust of men because Bagheera showed him a square box with a drop-gate so cunningly hidden in the Jungle that he nearly walked into it, and told him that it was a trap. He loved better than anything else to go with Bagheera into the dark warm heart of the forest, to sleep all through the drowsy day, and at night to see how Bagheera did his killing. Bagheera killed right and left as he felt hungry, and so did Mowgli – with one exception. As soon as he was old enough to understand things, Bagheera told him that he must never touch cattle because he had been bought into the Pack at the price of a bull's life. "All the Jungle is thine," said Bagheera, "and thou canst kill everything that thou art strong enough to kill; but for the sake of the bull that bought thee thou must never kill or eat any cattle young or old. That is the Law of the Jungle." Mowgli obeyed faithfully.

And he grew and grew strong as a boy must grow who does not know that he is learning any lessons, and who has nothing in the world to think of except things to eat.

Mother Wolf told him once or twice that Shere Khan was not a creature to be trusted, and that some day he must kill Shere Khan; but though a young wolf would have remembered that advice every hour, Mowgli forgot it because he was only a boy – though he would have called himself a wolf if he had been able to speak in any human tongue.

Shere Khan was always crossing his path in the Jungle, for as Akela grew older and feebler the lame tiger had come to be great friends with the younger wolves of the Pack, who followed him for scraps, a thing that Akela would never have allowed if he had dared to push his authority to the proper bounds. Then Shere Khan would flatter them and wonder that such fine young hunters were content to be led by a dying wolf and a man's cub. "They tell me," Shere Khan would say, "that at Council ye dare not look him between the eyes"; and the young wolves would growl and bristle.

Bagheera, who had eyes and ears everywhere, knew something of this, and once or twice he told Mowgli in so many words that Shere Khan would kill him some day; and Mowgli would laugh and answer: "I have the Pack and I have thee; and Baloo, though he is so lazy, might strike a blow or two for my sake. Why should I be afraid?"

It was one very warm day that a new notion came to Bagheera – born of something that he had heard. Perhaps Ikki the Porcupine had told him; but he said to Mowgli when they were deep in the Jungle, as the boy lay with his head on Bagheera's beautiful black skin: "Little Brother, how often have I told thee that Shere Khan is thy enemy?"

"As many times as there are nuts on that palm," said Mowgli, who, naturally, could not count. "What of it? I am sleepy, Bagheera, and Shere Khan is all long tail and loud talk – like Mao, the Peacock."

"But this is no time for sleeping. Baloo knows it; I know it; the Pack know it; and even the foolish, foolish deer know. Tabaqui has told thee, too."

"Ho! ho!" said Mowgli. "Tabaqui came to me not long ago

with some rude talk that I was a naked man's cub and not fit to dig pig-nuts; but I caught Tabaqui by the tail and swung him twice against a palm tree to teach him better manners."

"That was foolishness; for though Tabaqui is a mischief-maker, he would have told thee of something that concerned thee closely. Open those eyes, Little Brother. Shere Khan dare not kill thee in the Jungle; but remember, Akela is very old, and soon the day comes when he cannot kill his buck, and then he will be leader no more. Many of the wolves that looked thee over when thou wast brought to the Council first are old too, and the young wolves believe, as Shere Khan has taught them, that a man-cub has no place with the Pack. In a little time thou wilt be a man."

"And what is a man that he should not run with his brothers?" said Mowgli. "I was born in the Jungle. I have obeyed the Law of the Jungle, and there is no wolf of ours from whose paws I have not pulled a thorn. Surely they are my brothers!"

Bagheera stretched himself at full length and half shut his eyes. "Little Brother," said he, "feel under my jaw."

Mowgli put up his strong brown hand, and just under Bagheera's silky chin, where the giant rolling muscles were all hid by the glossy hair, he came upon a little bald spot.

"There is no one in the Jungle that knows that I, Bagheera, carry that mark – the mark of the collar; and yet, Little Brother, I was born among men, and it was among men that my mother died – in the cages of the King's palace at Oodeypore. It was because of this that I paid the price for thee at the Council when thou wast a little naked cub. Yes, I too was born among men. I had never seen the Jungle. They fed me behind bars from an iron pan till one night I felt that I was Bagheera – the Panther – and no man's plaything, and I broke the silly lock with one blow of my paw and came away; and because I had learned the ways of men, I became more terrible in the Jungle than Shere Khan. Is it not so?"

"Yes," said Mowgli; "all the jungle fear Bagheera – all except Mowgli."

"Oh, *thou* art a man's cub," said the Black Panther, very tenderly; "and even as I returned to my Jungle, so thou must go back to men at last – to the men who are thy brothers – if thou art not killed in the Council."

"But why – but why should any wish to kill me?" said Mowgli.

"Look at me," said Bagheera; and Mowgli looked at him steadily between the eyes. The big panther turned his head away in half a minute.

"*That* is why," he said, shifting his paw on the leaves. "Not even I can look thee between the eyes, and I was born among men, and I love thee, Little Brother. The others they hate thee because their eyes cannot meet thine – because thou art wise – because thou hast pulled out thorns from their feet – because thou art a man."

"I did not know these things," said Mowgli sullenly; and he frowned under his heavy black eyebrows.

"What is the Law of the Jungle? Strike first and then give tongue. By thy very carelessness they know that thou art a man. But be wise. It is in my heart that when Akela misses his next kill – and at each hunt it costs him more to pin the buck – the Pack will turn against him and against thee. They will hold a Jungle Council at the Rock, and then – and then – I have it!" said Bagheera, leaping up. "Go thou down quickly to the men's huts in the valley, and take some of the Red Flower which they grow there, so that when the time comes thou mayest have even a stronger friend than I or Baloo or those of the Pack that love thee. Get the Red Flower."

By Red Flower Bagheera meant fire, only no creature in the Jungle will call fire by its proper name. Every beast lives in deadly fear of it, and invents a hundred ways of describing it.

"The Red Flower?" said Mowgli. "That grows outside their huts in the twilight. I will get some."

"There speaks the man's cub," said Bagheera proudly. "Remember that it grows in little pots. Get one swiftly, and keep it by thee for time of need."

"Good!" said Mowgli. "I go. But art thou sure, O my Bagheera" – he slipped his arm round the splendid neck and looked deep into the big eyes – "art thou sure that all this is Shere Khan's doing?"

"By the Broken Lock that freed me, I am sure, Little Brother."

"Then, by the Bull that bought me, I will pay Shere Khan full tale for this, and it may be a little over," said Mowgli; and he bounded away.

"That is a man. That is all a man," said Bagheera to himself, lying down again. "Oh, Shere Khan, never was a blacker hunting than that frog-hunt of thine ten years ago!"

Mowgli was far and far through the forest, running hard, and his heart was hot in him. He came to the cave as the evening mist rose, and drew breath, and looked down the valley. The cubs were out, but Mother Wolf, at the back of the cave, knew by his breathing that something was troubling her frog.

"What is it, Son?" she said.

"Some bat's chatter of Shere Khan," he called back. "I hunt among the ploughed fields tonight," and he plunged downward through the bushes, to the stream at the bottom of the valley. There he checked, for he heard the yell of the Pack hunting, heard the bellow of a hunted sambhur, and the snort as the buck turned at bay. Then there were wicked, bitter howls from the young wolves: "Akela! Akela! Let the Lone Wolf show his strength. Room for the leader of the Pack! Spring, Akela!"

The Lone Wolf must have sprung and missed his hold, for Mowgli heard the snap of his teeth and then a yelp as the sambhur knocked him over with his fore-foot.

He did not wait for anything more, but dashed on; and the yells grew fainter behind him as he ran into the croplands where the villagers lived.

"Bagheera spoke truth," he panted, as he nestled down in some cattle-fodder by the window of a hut. "Tomorrow is one day both for Akela and for me."

Then he pressed his face close to the window and watched the fire on the hearth. He saw the husbandman's wife get up and feed it in the night with black lumps; and when the morning came and the mists were all white and cold, he saw the man's child pick up a wicker pot plastered inside with earth, fill it with lumps of red-hot charcoal, put it under his blanket, and go out to tend the cows in the byre.

"Is that all?" said Mowgli. "If a cub can do it, there is nothing to fear"; so he strode round the corner and met the boy, took the pot, from his hand, and disappeared into the mist while the boy howled with fear.

"They are very like me," said Mowgli, blowing into the pot as he had seen the woman do. "This thing will die if I do not give it things to eat"; and he dropped twigs and dried bark on the red stuff. Half-way up the hill he met Bagheera with the morning dew shining like moonstones on his coat.

"Akela has missed," said the Panther. "They would have killed him last night, but they needed thee also. They were looking for thee on the hill."

"I was among the ploughed lands. I am ready. See!" Mowgli held up the fire-pot.

"Good! Now, I have seen men thrust a dry branch into that stuff, and presently the Red Flower blossomed at the end of it. Art thou not afraid?"

"No. Why should I fear? I remember now – if it is not a

dream – how, before I was a Wolf, I lay beside the Red Flower, and it was warm and pleasant."

All that day Mowgli sat in the cave tending his fire-pot and dipping dry branches into it to see how they looked. He found a branch that satisfied him, and in the evening when Tabaqui came to the cave and told him rudely enough that he was wanted at the Council Rock, he laughed till Tabaqui ran away. Then Mowgli went to the Council, still laughing.

Akela the Lone Wolf lay by the side of his rock as a sign that the leadership of the Pack was open, and Shere Khan with his following of scrap-fed wolves walked to and fro openly, being flattered. Bagheera lay close to Mowgli, and the fire-pot was between Mowgli's knees. When they were all gathered together, Shere Khan began to speak – a thing he would never have dared to do when Akela was in his prime.

"He has no right," whispered Bagheera. "Say so. He is a dog's son. He will be frightened."

Mowgli sprang to his feet. "Free People," he cried, "does Shere Khan lead the Pack? What has a tiger to do with our leadership?"

"Seeing that the leadership is yet open, and being asked to speak –" Shere Khan began.

"By whom?" said Mowgli. "Are we *all* jackals, to fawn on this cattle-butcher? The leadership of the Pack is with the Pack alone."

There were yells of "Silence, thou man's cub!" "Let him speak. He has kept our Law"; and at last the seniors of the Pack thundered: "Let the Dead Wolf speak." When a leader of the Pack has missed his kill, he is called the Dead Wolf as long as he lives, which is not long, as a rule.

Akela raised his old head wearily –

"Free People, and ye too, jackals of Shere Khan, for many

seasons I have led ye to and from the kill, and in all my time not one has been trapped or maimed. Now I have missed my kill. Ye know how that plot was made. Ye know how ye brought me up to an untried buck to make my weakness known. It was cleverly done. Your right is to kill me here on the Council Rock now. Therefore, I ask, who comes to make an end of the Lone Wolf? For it is my right, by the Law of the Jungle, that ye come one by one."

There was a long hush, for no single wolf cared to fight Akela to the death. Then Shere Khan roared: "Bah! What have we to do with this toothless fool? He is doomed to die! It is the man-cub who has lived too long. Free People, he was my meat from the first. Give him to me. I am weary of this man-wolf folly. He has troubled the Jungle for ten seasons. Give me the man-cub, or I will hunt here always, and not give you one bone. He is a man, a man's child, and from the marrow of my bones I hate him!"

Then more than half the Pack yelled: "A man! a man! What has a man to do with us? Let him go to his own place."

"And turn all the people of the villages against us?" clamoured Shere Khan. "No; give him to me. He is a man, and none of us can look him between the eyes."

Akela lifted his head again and said: "He has eaten our food. He has slept with us. He has driven game for us. He has broken no word of the Law of the Jungle."

"Also, I paid for him with a bull when he was accepted. The worth of a bull is little, but Bagheera's honour is something that he will perhaps fight for," said Bagheera, in his gentlest voice.

"A bull paid ten years ago!" the Pack snarled. "What do we care for bones ten years old?"

"Or for a pledge?" said Bagheera, his white teeth bared under his lip. "Well are ye called the Free People!"

"No man's cub can run with the people of the Jungle," howled Shere Khan. "Give him to me!"

"He is our brother in all but blood," Akela went on; "and ye would kill him here! In truth, I have lived too long. Some of ye are eaters of cattle, and of others I have heard that, under Shere Khan's teaching, ye go by dark night and snatch children from the villager's doorstep. Therefore I know ye to be cowards, and it is to cowards I speak. It is certain that I must die, and my life is of no worth, or I would offer that in the Man-cub's place. But for the sake of the Honour of the Pack – a little matter that by being without a leader ye have forgotten – I promise that if ye let the Man-cub go to his own place, I will not, when my time comes to die, bare one tooth against ye. I will die without fighting. That will at least save the Pack three lives. More I cannot do; but if ye will, I can save ye the shame that comes of killing a brother against whom there is no fault – a brother spoken for and bought into the Pack according to the Law of the Jungle."

"He is a man – a man – a man!" snarled the Pack; and most of the wolves began to gather round Shere Khan, whose tail was beginning to switch.

"Now the business is in thy hands," said Bagheera to Mowgli. "*We* can do no more except fight."

Mowgli stood upright – the fire-pot in his hands. Then he stretched out his arms, and yawned in the face of the Council; but he was furious with rage and sorrow, for, wolf-like, the wolves had never told him how they hated him. "Listen you!" he cried. "There is no need for this dog's jabber. Ye have told me so often tonight that I am a man (and indeed I would have been a wolf with you to my life's end), that I feel your words are true. So I do not call ye my brothers any more, but *sag* [dogs], as a man should. What ye will do, and what ye will not do, is not yours to say. That matter is with me; and that we may see the matter more plainly, I, the man, have brought here a little of the Red

Flower which ye, dogs, fear."

He flung the fire-pot on the ground, and some of the red coals lit a tuft of dried moss that flared up, as all the Council drew back in terror before the leaping flames.

Mowgli thrust his dead branch into the fire till the twigs lit and crackled, and whirled it above his head among the cowering wolves.

"Thou art the master," said Bagheera, in an undertone. "Save Akela from the death. He was ever thy friend."

Akela, the grim old wolf who had never asked for mercy in his life, gave one piteous look at Mowgli as the boy stood all naked, his long black hair tossing over his shoulders in the light of the blazing branch that made the shadows jump and quiver.

"Good!" said Mowgli, staring round slowly. "I see that ye are dogs. I go from you to my own people – if they be my own people. The Jungle is shut to me, and I must forget your talk and your companionship; but I will be more merciful than ye are. Because I was all but your brother in blood, I promise that when I am a man among men I will not betray ye to men as ye have betrayed me." He kicked the fire with his foot, and the sparks flew up. "There shall be no war between any of us and the Pack. But here is a debt to pay before I go." He strode forward to where Shere Khan sat blinking stupidly at the flames, and caught him by the tuft on his chin. Bagheera followed in case of accidents. "Up, dog!" Mowgli cried. "Up, when a man speaks, or I will set that coat ablaze!"

Shere Khan's ears lay flat back on his head, and he shut his eyes, for the blazing branch was very near.

"This cattle-killer said he would kill me in the Council because he had not killed me when I was a cub. Thus and thus, then, do we beat dogs when we are men. Stir a whisker, Lungri, and I ram the Red Flower down thy gullet!" He beat Shere Khan over the head with the branch, and the tiger whimpered and whined in an agony of fear.

"Pah! Singed jungle-cat – go now! But remember when next I come to the Council Rock, as a man should come, it will be with Shere Khan's hide on my head. For the rest, Akela goes free to live as he pleases. Ye will *not* kill him, because that is not my will. Nor do I think that ye will sit here any longer, lolling out your tongues as though ye were somebodies, instead of dogs whom I drive out – thus! Go!" The fire was burning furiously at the end of the branch, and Mowgli struck right and left round the circle, and the wolves ran howling with the sparks burning their fur. At last there were only Akela, Bagheera, and perhaps ten wolves that had taken Mowgli's part. Then something began to hurt Mowgli inside him, as he had never been hurt in his life before, and he caught his breath and sobbed, and the tears ran down his face.

"What is it? What is it?" he said. "I do not wish to leave the Jungle, and I do not know what this is. Am I dying, Bagheera?"

"No, Little Brother. Those are only tears such as men use," said Bagheera. "Now I know thou art a man, and a man's cub no longer. The Jungle is shut indeed to thee henceforward. Let them fall, Mowgli. They are only tears." So Mowgli sat and cried as though his heart would break; and he had never cried in all his life before.

"Now," he said, "I will go to men. But first I must say farewell to my mother"; and he went to the cave where she lived with Father Wolf, and he cried on her coat, while the four cubs howled miserably.

"Ye will not forget me?" said Mowgli.

"Never while we can follow a trail," said the cubs. "Come to the foot of the hill when thou art a man, and we will talk to thee; and we will come into the crop-lands to play with thee by night."

"Come soon!" said Father Wolf. "Oh, wise little frog, come again soon; for we be old, thy mother and I."

"Come soon," said Mother Wolf, "little naked son of mine; for, listen, child of man, I loved thee more than ever I loved my cubs."

"I will surely come," said Mowgli; "and when I come it will be to lay out Shere Khan's hide upon the Council Rock. Do not forget me! Tell them in the Jungle never to forget me!"

The dawn was beginning to break when Mowgli went down the hillside alone, to meet those mysterious things that are called men.

2

Hunting Song of the Seeonee Pack

AS THE dawn was breaking the Sambhur belled
Once, twice and again!
And a doe leaped up, and a doe leaped up
From the pond in the wood where the wild deer sup.
This I, scouting alone, beheld,
Once, twice and again!

As the dawn was breaking the Sambhur belled
Once, twice and again!
And a wolf stole back, and a wolf stole back
To carry the word to the waiting pack,
And we sought and we found and we bayed on his track

Once, twice and again!
As the dawn was breaking the Wolf Pack yelled
Once, twice and again!
Feet in the Jungle that leave no mark!
Eyes that can see in the dark – the dark!
Tongue – give tongue to it! Hark! Oh hark!
Once, twice and again!

3

Kaa's Hunting

HIS SPOTS are the joy of the Leopard: his horns are
the Buffalo's pride.
Be clean, for the strength of the hunter is known by
the gloss of his hide.
If ye find that the bullock can toss you, or the
heavy-browed Sambhur can gore;
Ye need not stop work to inform us: we knew it ten
seasons before.
Oppress not the cubs of the stranger, but hail them
as Sister and Brother,
For though they are little and fubsy, it may be the
Bear is their mother.
"There is none like to me!" says the Cub in the

pride of his earliest kill;
But the Jungle is large and the Cub he is small.
Let him think and be still.

Maxims of Baloo

All that is told here happened some time before Mowgli was turned out of the Seeonee Wolf Pack, or revenged himself on Shere Khan the tiger. It was in the days when Baloo was teaching him the Law of the Jungle. The big, serious, old brown bear was delighted to have so quick a pupil, for the young wolves will only learn as much of the Law of the Jungle as applies to their own pack and tribe, and run away as soon as they can repeat the Hunting Verse – "Feet that make no noise; eyes that can see in the dark; ears that can hear the winds in their lairs, and sharp white teeth, all these things are the marks of our brothers except Tabaqui the Jackal and the Hyaena whom we hate." But Mowgli, as a man-cub, had to learn a great deal more than this. Sometimes Bagheera, the Black Panther, would come lounging through the Jungle to see how his pet was getting on, and would purr with his head against a tree while Mowgli recited the day's lesson to Baloo. The boy could climb almost as well as he could swim, and swim almost as well as he could run; so Baloo, the Teacher of the Law, taught him the Wood and Water Laws; how to tell a rotten branch from a sound one; how to speak politely to the wild bees when he came upon a hive of them fifty feet above ground; what to say to Mang the Bat when he disturbed him in the branches at midday; and how to warn the water-snakes in the pools before he splashed down among them. None of the Jungle People like being disturbed, and all are very ready to fly at an intruder. Then, too, Mowgli was taught the Strangers' Hunting Call, which must be repeated aloud till it is answered, whenever one of the Jungle People hunts outside his own grounds. It means, translated: "Give me leave to hunt here because I am hungry;"

and the answer is; "Hunt then for food, but not for pleasure."

All this will show you how much Mowgli had to learn by heart, and he grew very tired of saying the same thing over a hundred times; but, as Baloo said to Bagheera, one day when Mowgli had been cuffed and run off in a temper: "A Man's-cub is a man's-cub, and he must learn *all* the Law of the Jungle."

"But think how small he is," said the Black Panther, who would have spoiled Mowgli if he had had his own way. "How can his little head carry all thy long talk?"

"Is there anything in the Jungle too little to be killed? No. That is why I teach him these things, and that is why I hit him, very softly, when he forgets."

"Softly! What dost thou know of softness, old Iron-feet?" Bagheera grunted. "His face is all bruised today by thy – softness. Ugh!"

"Better he should be bruised from head to foot by me who love him than that he should come to harm through ignorance," Baloo answered very earnestly. "I am now teaching him the Master Words of the Jungle that shall protect him with the birds and the Snake People, and all that hunt on four feet, except his own pack. He can now claim protection, if he will only remember the words, from all in the Jungle. Is not that worth a little beating?"

"Well, look to it then that thou dost not kill the Man-cub. He is no tree-trunk to sharpen thy blunt claws upon. But what are those Master Words? I am more likely to give help than to ask it" – Bagheera stretched out one paw and admired the steel-blue, ripping-chisel talons at the end of it – "still I should like to know."

"I will call Mowgli and he shall say them – if he will. Come, Little Brother!"

"My head is ringing like a bee-tree," said a sullen little voice over their heads, and Mowgli slid down a tree-trunk very angry and indignant, adding as he reached the ground: "I come for

Bagheera and not for *thee,* fat old Baloo!"

"That is all one to me," said Baloo, though he was hurt and grieved. "Tell Bagheera, then, the Master Words of the Jungle that I have taught thee this day."

"Master Words for which people?" said Mowgli, delighted to show off. "The Jungle has many tongues. *I* know them all."

"A little thou knowest, but not much. See, O Bagheera, they never thank their teacher. Not one small wolfling has ever come back to thank old Baloo for his teachings. Say the word for the Hunting People, then – great scholar."

"We be of one blood, ye and I," said Mowgli, giving the words the Bear accent which all the Hunting People use.

"Good. Now for the birds."

Mowgli repeated, with the Kite's whistle at the end of the sentence.

"Now for the Snake People," said Bagheera.

The answer was a perfectly indescribable hiss, and Mowgli kicked up his feet behind, clapped his hands together to applaud himself, and jumped on to Bagheera's back, where he sat sideways, drumming with his heels on the glossy skin and making the worst faces he could think of at Baloo.

"There – there! That was worth a little bruise," said the brown bear tenderly. "Some day thou wilt remember me." Then he turned aside to tell Bagheera how he had begged the Master Words from Hathi the Wild Elephant, who knows all about these things, and how Hathi had taken Mowgli down to a pool to get the Snake Word from a water-snake, because Baloo could not pronounce it, and how Mowgli was now reasonably safe against all accidents in the Jungle, because neither snake, bird, nor beast would hurt him.

"No one, then, is to be feared," Baloo wound up, patting his big furry stomach with pride.

"Except his own tribe," said Bagheera, under his breath; and then aloud to Mowgli: "Have a care for my ribs, Little Brother! What is all this dancing up and down?"

Mowgli had been trying to make himself heard by pulling at Bagheera's shoulder-fur and kicking hard. When the two listened to him he was shouting at the top of his voice: "And so I shall have a tribe of my own, and lead them through the branches all day long."

"What is this new folly, little dreamer of dreams?" said Bagheera.

"Yes, and throw branches and dirt at old Baloo," Mowgli went on. "They have promised me this. Ah!"

"Whoof!" Baloo's big paw scooped Mowgli off Bagheera's back, and as the boy lay between the big fore-paws he could see the Bear was angry.

"Mowgli," said Baloo, "thou hast been talking with the *Bandar-log* – the Monkey People."

Mowgli looked at Bagheera to see if the Panther was angry too, and Bagheera's eyes were as hard as jade stones.

"Thou hast been with the Monkey People the grey apes – the people without a Law – the eaters of everything. That is great shame."

"'When Baloo hurt my head," said Mowgli (he was still on his back), "I went away, and the grey apes came down from the trees and had pity on me. No one else cared." He snuffled a little.

"The pity of the Monkey People!" Baloo snorted. "The stillness of the mountain stream! The cool of the summer sun! And then, Man-cub?"

"And then, and then, they gave me nuts and pleasant things to eat, and they – they carried me in their arms up to the top of the trees and said I was their blood-brother except that I had no tail, and should be their leader someday."

"They have *no* leader," said Bagheera. "They lie. They have always lied."

"They were very kind and bade me come again. Why have I never been taken among the Monkey People? They stand on their feet as I do. They do not hit me with hard paws. They play all day. Let me get up! Bad Baloo, let me up! I will play with them again."

"Listen, Man-cub," said the Bear, and his voice rumbled like thunder on a hot night. "I have taught thee all the Law of the Jungle for all the peoples of the Jungle – except the Monkey Folk who live in the trees. They have no Law. They are outcasts. They have no speech of their own, but use the stolen words which they overhear when they listen, and peep, and wait up above in the branches. Their way is not our way. They are without leaders. They have no remembrance. They boast and chatter and pretend that they are a great people about to do great affairs in the Jungle, but the falling of a nut turns their minds to laughter and all is forgotten. We of the Jungle have no dealings with them. We do not drink where the monkeys drink; we do not go where the monkeys go; we do not hunt where they hunt; we do not die where they die. Hast thou ever heard me speak of the *Bandar-log,* till today?"

"No," said Mowgli in a whisper, for the forest was very still now Baloo had finished.

"The Jungle People put them out of their mouths and out of their minds. They are very many, evil, dirty, shameless, and they desire, if they have any fixed desire, to be noticed by the Jungle People. But we do *not* notice them even when they throw nuts and filth on our heads."

He had hardly spoken when a shower of nuts and twigs spattered down through the branches; and they could hear coughings and howlings and angry jumpings high up in the air among the thin branches.

"The Monkey People are forbidden," said Baloo, "forbidden to the Jungle People. Remember."

"Forbidden," said Bagheera; "but I still think Baloo should have warned thee against them."

"I – I? How was I to guess he would play with such dirt? The Monkey People! Faugh!"

A fresh shower came down on their heads and the two trotted away, taking Mowgli with them. What Baloo had said about the monkeys was perfectly true. They belonged to the tree-tops, and as beasts very seldom look up, there was no occasion for the monkeys and the Jungle People to cross each other's path. But whenever they found a sick wolf, or a wounded tiger, or bear, the monkeys would torment him, and would throw sticks and nuts at any beast for fun and in the hope of being noticed. Then they would howl and shriek senseless songs, and invite the Jungle People to climb up their trees and fight them, or would start furious battles over nothing among themselves, and leave the dead monkeys where the Jungle People could see them. They were always just going to have a leader, and laws and customs of their own, but they never did, because their memories would not hold over from day to day, and so they compromised things by making up a saying; "What the *Bandar-log* think now the Jungle will think later," and that comforted them a great deal. None of the beasts could reach them, but on the other hand none of the beasts would notice them, and that was why they were so pleased when Mowgli came to play with them, and they heard how angry Baloo was.

They never meant to do any more – the *Bandar-log* never mean anything at all; but one of them invented what seemed to him a brilliant idea, and he told all the others that Mowgli would be a useful person to keep in the tribe, because he could weave sticks together for protection from the wind; so, if they caught him, they could make him teach them. Of course Mowgli, as a woodcutter's child, inherited all sorts of instincts, and used to make little huts of fallen branches without thinking how he came to do it, and the Monkey People, watching in the trees, considered his play most wonderful. This time, they said, they were really going to have a leader and become the wisest people in the Jungle – so wise that everyone else would notice and envy them. Therefore they followed Baloo and Bagheera and Mowgli through the Jungle very quietly till it was time for the midday nap, and Mowgli, who was very much ashamed of himself, slept between the Panther and the Bear, resolving to have no more to do with the Monkey People.

The next thing he remembered was feeling hands on his legs and arms – hard, strong, little hands – and then a swash of branches in his face, and then he was staring down through the swaying boughs as Baloo woke the Jungle with his deep cries and Bagheera bounded up the trunk with every tooth bared. The *Bandar-log* howled with triumph and scuffled away to the upper branches where Bagheera dared not follow, shouting: "He has noticed us! Bagheera has noticed us. All the Jungle People admire us for our skill and our cunning." Then they began their flight; and the flight of the Monkey People through tree-land is one of the things nobody can describe. They have their regular roads and crossroads, up hills and down hills, all laid out from fifty to seventy or a hundred feet above ground, and by these they can travel even at night if necessary. Two of the strongest monkeys caught Mowgli under the arms and swung off with him through the tree-tops, twenty feet at a bound. Had they been alone they could have gone twice as fast, but the boy's weight held them back. Sick and giddy as Mowgli was he could not help enjoying the wild rush, though the glimpses of earth far down below frightened him, and the terrible check and jerk at the end of the swing over nothing but empty air brought his heart between his teeth. His escort would rush him up a tree till he felt the thinnest topmost branches crackle and bend under them, and then with a cough and a whoop would fling themselves into the air outward and downward, and bring up, hanging by their hands or their feet to the lower limbs of the next tree. Sometimes he could see for miles and miles across the still green Jungle, as a man on the top of a mast can see for miles across the sea, and then the branches and leaves would lash him across the face, and he and his two guards would be almost down to earth again. So, bounding and crashing and whooping and yelling, the whole tribe of *Bandar-log* swept along the tree-roads with Mowgli their prisoner.

For a time he was afraid of being dropped: then he grew angry but knew better than to struggle, and then he began to think. The first thing was to send back word to Baloo and Bagheera, for, at the pace the monkeys were going, he knew his friends would be left far behind. It was useless to look down, for he could only see the top-sides of the branches, so he stared upward and saw, far away in the blue, Chil the Kite balancing and wheeling as he kept watch over the jungle waiting for things to die. Chil saw that the monkeys were carrying something, and dropped a few hundred yards to find out whether their load was good to eat. He whistled with surprise when he saw Mowgli being dragged up to a tree-top and heard him give the Kite call for – "We be of one blood, thou and I." The waves of the branches closed over the boy, but Chil balanced away to the next tree in time to see the little brown face come up again. "Mark my trail," Mowgli shouted. "Tell Baloo of the Seeonee Pack and Bagheera of the Council Rock."

"In whose name, Brother?" Chil had never seen Mowgli before, though of course he had heard of him.

"Mowgli, the Frog. Man-cub they call me! Mark my tra-il!"

The last words were shrieked as he was being swung through the air, but Chil nodded and rose up till he looked no bigger than a speck of dust, and there he hung, watching with his telescope eyes the swaying of the tree-tops as Mowgli's escort whirled along.

"They never go far," he said with a chuckle. "They never do what they set out to do. Always pecking at new things are the *Bandar-log.* This time, if I have any eyesight, they have pecked down trouble for themselves, for Baloo is no fledgling and Bagheera can, as I know, kill more than goats."

So he rocked on his wings, his feet gathered up under him, and waited.

Meantime, Baloo and Bagheera were furious with rage and grief. Bagheera climbed as he had never climbed before, but the thin branches broke beneath his weight, and he slipped down, his claws full of bark.

"Why didst thou not warn the Man-cub?" he roared to poor Baloo, who had set off at a clumsy trot in the hope of overtaking the monkeys. "What was the use of half slaying him with blows if thou didst not warn him?"

"Haste! Oh haste! We – we may catch them yet!" Baloo panted.

"At that speed! It would not tire a wounded cow. Teacher of the Law – cub-beater – a mile of that rolling to and fro would burst thee open. Sit still and think! Make a plan. This is no time for chasing. They may drop him if we follow too close."

"*Arrula! Whoo!* They may have dropped him already, being tired of carrying him. Who can trust the *Bandar-log*? Put dead bats on my head! Give me black bones to eat! Roll me into the hives of the wild bees that I may be stung to death, and bury me with the Hyaena, for I am most miserable of bears! *Arulala! Wahooa!* Oh, Mowgli, Mowgli! Why did I not warn thee against the Monkey Folk instead of breaking thy head? Now perhaps I may have knocked the day's lesson out of his mind, and he will be alone in the Jungle without the Master Words."

Baloo clasped his paws over his ears and rolled to and fro

moaning.

"At least he gave me all the Words correctly a little time ago," said Bagheera impatiently. "Baloo, thou hast neither memory nor respect. What would the Jungle think if I, the Black Panther, curled myself up like Ikki the Porcupine, and howled?"

"What do I care what the Jungle thinks? He may be dead by now."

"Unless and until they drop him from the branches in sport, or kill him out of idleness, I have no fear for the Man-cub. He is wise and well taught, and above all he has the eyes that make the Jungle People afraid. But (and it is a great evil) he is in the power of the *Bandar-log,* and they, because they live in trees, have no fear of any of our people." Bagheera licked one forepaw thoughtfully.

"Fool that I am! Oh, fat, brown, root-digging fool that I am," said Baloo, un-curling himself with a jerk, "it is true what Hathi the Wild Elephant says: `*To each his own fear*'; and they, the *Bandar-log,* fear Kaa the Rock Snake. He can climb as well as they can. He steals the young monkeys in the night. The whisper of his name makes their wicked tails cold. Let us go to Kaa."

"What will he do for us? He is not of our tribe, being footless – and with most evil eyes," said Bagheera.

"He is very old and very cunning. Above all, he is always hungry," said Baloo hopefully. "Promise him many goats."

"He sleeps for a full month after he has once eaten. He may be asleep now, and even were he awake what if he would rather kill his own goats?" Bagheera, who did not know much about Kaa, was naturally suspicious.

"Then in that case, thou and I together, old hunter, might make him see reason." Here Baloo rubbed his faded brown shoulder against the Panther, and they went off to look for Kaa the Rock Python.

They found him stretched out on a warm ledge in the afternoon sun, admiring his beautiful new coat, for he had been in retirement for the last ten days, changing his skin, and now he was very splendid – darting his big blunt-nosed head along the ground, and twisting the thirty feet of his body into fantastic knots and curves, and licking his lips as he thought of his dinner to come.

"He has not eaten," said Baloo, with a grunt of relief, as soon as he saw the beautifully mottled brown-and-yellow jacket. "Be careful, Bagheera! He is always a little blind after he has changed his skin, and very quick to strike."

Kaa was not a poison-snake – in fact he rather despised the poison-snakes as cowards – but his strength lay in his hug, and when he had once lapped his huge coils round anybody there was no more to be said. "Good hunting!" cried Baloo, sitting up on his haunches. Like all snakes of his breed, Kaa was rather deaf, and did not hear the call at first. Then he curled up ready for any accident, his head lowered.

"Good hunting for us all!" he answered. "Oho, Baloo, what dost thou do here? Good hunting, Bagheera! One of us at least needs food. Is there any news of game afoot? A doe now, or even a young buck? I am as empty as a dried well."

"We are hunting," said Baloo carelessly. He knew that you must not hurry Kaa. He is too big.

"Give me permission to come with you," said Kaa. "A blow more or less is nothing to thee, Bagheera or Baloo, but I – I have to wait and wait for days in a wood-path and climb half a night on the mere chance of a young ape. Psshaw! The branches are not what they were when I was young. Rotten twigs and dry boughs are they all."

"Maybe thy great weight has something to do with the matter," said Baloo.

"I am a fair length – a fair length," said Kaa, with a little pride. "But for all that, it is the fault of this new-grown timber. I came very near to falling on my last hunt – very near indeed – and the noise of my slipping, for my tail was not tight wrapped around the tree, waked the *Bandar-log,* and they called me most evil names."

"Footless, yellow earthworm," said Bagheera under his whiskers, as though he were trying to remember something.

"Sssss! Have they ever called me *that*?" said Kaa.

"Something of that kind it was that they shouted to us last moon, but we never noticed them. They will say anything – even that thou hast lost all thy teeth, and wilt not face anything bigger than a kid, because (they are indeed shameless, these *Bandar-log*) – because thou art afraid of the he-goat's horns," Bagheera went on sweetly.

Now a snake, especially a wary old python like Kaa, very seldom shows that he is angry, but Baloo and Bagheera could see the big swallowing-muscles on either side of Kaa's throat ripple and bulge.

"The *Bandar-log* have shifted their grounds," he said quietly. "When I came up into the sun today I heard them whooping among the tree-tops."

"It – it is the *Bandar-log* that we follow now," said Baloo; but the words stuck in his throat, for that was the first time in his memory that one of the Jungle People had owned to being interested in the doings of the monkeys.

"Beyond doubt then it is no small thing that takes two such hunters – leaders in their own Jungle I am certain – on the trail of the *Bandar-log,*" Kaa replied courteously, as he swelled with curiosity.

"Indeed," Baloo began, "I am no more than the old and sometimes very foolish Teacher of the Law to the Seeonee wolf-cubs, and Bagheera here – ”

“Is Bagheera,” said the Black Panther, and his jaws shut with a snap, for he did not believe in being humble. “The trouble is this, Kaa. Those nut-stealers and pickers of palm-leaves have stolen away our Man-cub, of whom thou hast perhaps heard.”

“I heard some news from Ikki (his quills make him presumptuous) of a man-thing that was entered into a wolf-pack, but I did not believe. Ikki is full of stories half heard and very badly told.”

“But it is true. He is such a Man-cub as never was,” said Baloo. “The best and wisest and boldest of Man-cubs – my own pupil, who shall make the name of Baloo famous through all the jungles; and besides, I – we – love him, Kaa.”

“Tss! Tss!” said Kaa, shaking his head to and fro. “I also have known what love is. There are tales I could tell that – ”

“That need a clear night when we are all well fed to praise properly,” said Bagheera quickly. “Our Man-cub is in the hands of the *Bandar-log* now, and we know that of all the Jungle People they fear Kaa alone.”

“They fear me alone. They have good reason,” said Kaa. “Chattering, foolish, vain – vain, foolish, and chattering, are the monkeys. But a man-thing in their hands is in no good luck. They grow tired of the nuts they pick, and throw them down. They carry a branch half a day, meaning to do great things with it, and then they snap it in two. That man-thing is not to be envied. They called me also – ‘yellow fish,’ was it not?”

“Worm – worm – earthworm,” said Bagheera, “as well as other things which I cannot now say for shame.”

“We must remind them to speak well of their master. Aaa – ssh! We must help their wandering memories. Now, whither went they with the cub?”

“The Jungle alone knows. Toward the sunset, I believe,”

said Baloo. "We had thought that thou wouldst know, Kaa."

"I? How? I take them when they come in my way, but I do not hunt the *Bandar-log,* or frogs – or green scum on a water-hole, for that matter."

"Up, Up! Up, Up! Hillo! Illo! Illo, Look up, Baloo of the Seeonee Wolf Pack!"

Baloo looked up to see where the voice came from, and there was Chil the Kite, sweeping down with the sun shining on the upturned flanges of his wings. It was near Chil's bedtime, but he had ranged all over the Jungle looking for the Bear and had missed him in the thick foliage.

"What is it?" said Baloo.

"I have seen Mowgli among the *Bandar-log.* He bade me tell you. I watched. The *Bandar-log* have taken him beyond the river to the monkey city – to the Cold Lairs. They may stay there for a night, or ten nights, or an hour. I have told the bats to watch through the dark time. That is my message. Good hunting, all you below!"

"Full gorge and a deep sleep to you, Chil," cried Bagheera. "I will remember thee in my next kill, and put aside the head for thee alone, O best of kites!"

"It is nothing. It is nothing. The boy held the Master Word. I could have done no less," and Chil circled up again to his roost.

"He has not forgotten to use his tongue," said Baloo, with a chuckle of pride. "To think of one so young remembering the Master Word for the birds too while he was being pulled across-trees!"

"It was most firmly driven into him," said Bagheera. "But I am proud of him, and now we must go to the Cold Lairs."

They all knew where that place was, but few of the Jungle People ever went there, because what they called the Cold Lairs was an old deserted city, lost and buried in the Jungle, and beasts seldom use a place that men have once used. The wild boar will, but the hunting tribes do not. Besides, the monkeys lived there as much as they could be said to live anywhere, and no self-respecting animal would come within eyeshot of it except in times of drought, when the half-ruined tanks and reservoirs held a little water.

"It is half a night's journey – at full speed," said Bagheera, and Baloo looked very serious. "*I will* go as fast as I can," he said anxiously.

"We dare not wait for thee. Follow, Baloo. We must go on the quick-foot – Kaa and I."

"Feet or no feet, I can keep abreast of all thy four," said Kaa shortly. Baloo made one effort to hurry, but had to sit down panting, and so they left him to come on later, while Bagheera hurried forward, at the quick panther-canter. Kaa said nothing, but, strive as Bagheera might, the huge Rock Python held level with him. When they came to a hill-stream, Bagheera gained, because he bounded across while Kaa swam, his head and two feet of his neck clearing the water, but on level ground Kaa made up the distance.

"By the Broken Lock that freed me," said Bagheera, when twilight had fallen, "thou art no slow goer!"

"I am hungry," said Kaa. "Besides, they called me speckled frog."

"Worm – earthworm, and yellow to boot."

"All one. Let us go on," and Kaa seemed to pour himself along the ground, finding the shortest road with his steady eyes, and keeping to it.

In the Cold Lairs the Monkey People were not thinking of Mowgli's friends at all. They had brought the boy to the Lost City, and were very much pleased with themselves for the time. Mowgli had never seen an Indian city before, and though this was almost a heap of ruins it seemed very wonderful and splendid. Some king had built it long ago on a little hill. You could still trace the stone causeways that led up to the ruined gates where the last splinters of wood hung to the worn, rusted hinges. Trees had grown into and out of the walls; the battlements were tumbled down and decayed, and wild creepers hung out of the windows of the towers on the walls in bushy hanging clumps.

A great roofless palace crowned the hill, and the marble of the courtyards and the fountains was split, and stained with red and green, and the very cobblestones in the courtyard where the king's elephants used to live had been thrust up and apart by grasses and young trees. From the palace you could see the rows and rows of roofless houses that made up the city looking like empty honeycombs filled with blackness; the shapeless block of stone that had been an idol, in the square where four roads met; the pits and dimples at street-corners where the public wells once stood, and the shattered domes of temples with wild figs sprouting on their sides. The monkeys called the place their city, and pretended to despise the Jungle People because they lived in the forest. And yet they never knew what the buildings were made for nor how to use them. They would sit in circles on the hall of the king's council chamber, and scratch for fleas and pretend to be men; or they would run in and out of the roofless houses and collect pieces of plaster and old bricks in a corner, and forget where they had hidden them, and fight and cry in scuffling crowds, and then break off to play up and down the terraces of the king's garden, where they would shake the rose trees and the oranges in sport to see the fruit and flowers fall. They explored all the passages and dark tunnels in the palace and the hundreds of little dark rooms, but they never remembered what they had seen and what they had not; and so drifted about in ones and twos or crowds telling each other that they were doing as men did. They drank at the tanks and made the water all muddy, and then they fought over it, and then they would all rush together in mobs and shout: "There is no one in the Jungle so wise and good and clever and strong and gentle as the *Bandar-log*." Then all would begin again till they grew tired of the city and went back to the tree-tops, hoping the Jungle People would notice them.

Mowgli, who had been trained under the Law of the Jungle, did not like or understand this kind of life. The monkeys dragged him into the Cold Lairs late in the afternoon, and instead of going to sleep, as Mowgli would have done after a long journey, they joined hands and danced about and sang their foolish songs. One of the monkeys made a speech and told his companions that Mowgli's capture marked a new thing in the history of the *Bandar-log,* for Mowgli was going to show them how to weave sticks and canes together as a protection against rain and cold. Mowgli picked up some creepers and began to work them in and out, and the monkeys tried to imitate; but in a very few minutes they lost interest and began to pull their friends' tails or jump up and down on all fours, coughing.

"I wish to eat," said Mowgli. "I am a stranger in this part of the Jungle. Bring me food, or give me leave to hunt here."

Twenty or thirty monkeys bounded away to bring him nuts and wild pawpaws; but they fell to fighting on the road, and it was too much trouble to go back with what was left of the fruit. Mowgli was sore and angry as well as hungry, and he roamed through the empty city giving the Strangers' Hunting Call from time to time, but no one answered him, and Mowgli felt that he had reached a very bad place indeed. "All that Baloo has said about the *Bandar-log* is true," he thought to himself. "They have no Law, no Hunting Call, and no leaders – nothing but foolish words and little picking thievish hands. So if I am starved or killed here, it will be all my own fault. But I must try to return to my own Jungle. Baloo will surely beat me, but that is better than chasing silly rose-leaves with the *Bandar-log.*"

No sooner had he walked to the city wall than the monkeys pulled him back, telling him that he did not know how happy he was, and pinching him to make him grateful. He set his teeth and said nothing, but went with the shouting monkeys to a terrace above the red sandstone reservoirs that were half-full of rain-water. There was a ruined summerhouse of white marble in the centre of the terrace, built for queens dead a hundred years ago. The domed roof had half fallen in and blocked up the underground passage from the palace by which the queens used to enter; but the walls were made of screens of marble tracery – beautiful milk-white fretwork, set with agates and cornelians and jasper and lapis lazuli, and as the moon came up behind the hill it shone through the open-work, casting shadows on the ground like black velvet embroidery. Sore, sleepy, and hungry as he was, Mowgli could not help laughing when the *Bandar-log* began, twenty at a time, to tell him how great and wise and strong and gentle they were, and how foolish he was to wish to leave them. "We are great. We are free. We are wonderful. We are the most wonderful people in all the Jungle! We all say so, and so it must be true," they shouted. "Now, as you are a new listener and can carry our words back to the Jungle People so that they may notice us in future, we will tell you all about our most excellent selves." Mowgli made no objection, and the monkeys gathered by hundreds and hundreds on the terrace to listen to their own speakers singing the praises of the *Bandar-log,* and whenever a speaker stopped for want of breath they would all shout together: "This is true; we all say so." Mowgli nodded and blinked, and said "Yes" when they asked him a question, and his head spun with the noise. "Tabaqui the Jackal must have bitten all these people," he said to himself, "and now they have madness. Certainly this *is dewanee,* the madness. Do they never go to sleep? Now there is a cloud coming to cover that moon. If it were only a big enough cloud I might try to run away in the darkness. But I am tired."

That same cloud was being watched by two good friends in the ruined ditch below the city wall, for Bagheera and Kaa, knowing well how dangerous the Monkey People were in large numbers, did not wish to run any risks. The monkeys never fight unless they are a hundred to one, and few in the Jungle care for those odds.

"I will go to the west wall," Kaa whispered, "and come down swiftly with the slope of the ground in my favour. They will not throw themselves upon *my* back in their hundreds, but –"

"I know it," said Bagheera. "Would that Baloo were here; but we must do what we can. When that cloud covers the moon I shall go to the terrace. They hold some sort of council there over the boy."

"Good hunting!" said Kaa grimly, and glided away to the west wall. That happened to be the least ruined of any, and the big snake was delayed a while before he could find a way up the stones. The cloud hid the moon, and as Mowgli wondered what would come next he heard Bagheera's light feet on the terrace. The Black Panther had raced up the slope almost without a sound and was striking – he knew better than to waste time in biting – right and left among the monkeys, who were seated round Mowgli in circles fifty and sixty deep. There was a howl of fright and rage, and then as Bagheera tripped on the rolling kicking bodies beneath him, a monkey shouted: "There is only one here! Kill him! Kill." A scuffling mass of monkeys, biting, scratching, tearing, and pulling, closed over Bagheera, while five or six laid hold of Mowgli, dragged him up the wall of the summerhouse and pushed him through the hole of the broken dome. A man-trained boy would have been badly bruised, for the fall was a good fifteen feet, but Mowgli fell as Baloo had taught him to fall, and landed on his feet.

"Stay there," shouted the monkeys, "till we have killed thy friends, and later we will play with thee – if the Poison People leave thee alive."

"We be of one blood, ye and I," said Mowgli, quickly giving the Snake's Call. He could hear rustling and hissing in the rubbish all round him and gave the Call a second time, to make sure.

"Even ssso! Down hoods all!" said half a dozen low voices (every ruin in India becomes sooner or later a dwelling-place of snakes, and the old summerhouse was alive with cobras). "Stand still, Little Brother, for thy feet may do us harm."

Mowgli stood as quietly as he could, peering through the open-work and listening to the furious din of the fight round the Black Panther – the yells and chatterings and scufflings, and Bagheera's deep, hoarse cough as he backed and bucked and twisted and plunged under the heaps of his enemies. For the first time since he was born, Bagheera was fighting for his life.

"Baloo must be at hand; Bagheera would not have come alone," Mowgli thought; and then he called aloud: "To the tank, Bagheera! Roll to the water-tank. Roll and plunge! Get to the water!"

Bagheera heard, and the cry that told him Mowgli was safe gave him new courage. He worked his way desperately, inch by inch, straight for the reservoirs, halting in silence. Then from the ruined wall nearest the Jungle rose up the rumbling war shout of Baloo. The old Bear had done his best, but he could not come before. "Bagheera," he shouted, "I am here. I climb! I haste! *Ahuwora!* The stones slip under my feet! Wait my coming, O most infamous *Bandar-log*!" He panted up the terrace only to disappear to the head in a wave of monkeys, but he threw himself squarely on his haunches, and, spreading out his fore-paws, hugged as many as he could hold, and then began to hit with a regular *bat-bat-bat,* like the flipping strokes of a paddle-wheel. A crash and a splash told Mowgli that Bagheera had fought his way to the tank where the monkeys could not follow. The Panther lay gasping for breath, his head just out of water, while the monkeys stood three deep on the red steps, dancing up and down with rage, ready to spring upon him from all sides if he came out to help Baloo. It was then that Bagheera lifted up his dripping chin, and in despair gave the Snake's Call for protection – "We be of one blood, ye and I " – for he believed that Kaa had turned tail at the last minute. Even Baloo, half smothered under the monkeys on the edge of the terrace, could not help chuckling as he heard the Black Panther asking for help.

Kaa had only just worked his way over the west wall, landing with a wrench that dislodged a coping-stone into the ditch. He had no intention of losing any advantage of the ground, and coiled and uncoiled himself once or twice, to be sure that every foot of his long body was in working order. All that while the fight with Baloo went on, and the monkeys yelled in the tank around Bagheera, and Mang the Bat, flying to and fro, carried the news of the great battle over the Jungle, till even Hathi the Wild Elephant trumpeted, and, far away, scattered bands of the Monkey Folk woke and came leaping along the tree-roads to help their comrades in the Cold Lairs, and the noise of the fight roused all the daybirds for miles round. Then Kaa came straight, quickly, and anxious to kill. The fighting-strength of a python is in the driving blow of his head backed by all the strength and weight of his body. If you can imagine a lance, or a battering-ram, or a hammer weighing nearly half a ton driven by a cool, quiet mind living in the handle of it, you can roughly imagine what Kaa was like when he fought. A python four or five feet long can knock a man down if he hits him fairly in the chest, and Kaa was thirty feet long, as you know. His first stroke was delivered into the heart of the crowd round Baloo – was sent home with shut mouth in silence, and there was no need of a second. The monkeys scattered with cries of – "Kaa! It is Kaa! Run! Run!"

Generations of monkeys had been scared into good behavior by the stories their elders told them of Kaa, the night-thief, who could slip along the branches as quietly as moss grows, and steal away the strongest monkey that ever lived; of old Kaa, who could make himself look so like a dead branch or a rotten stump that the wisest were deceived, till the branch caught them. Kaa was everything that the monkeys feared in the Jungle, for none of them knew the limits of his power, none of them could look him in the face, and none had ever come alive out of his hug. And so they ran, stammering with terror, to the walls and the roofs of the houses, and Baloo drew a deep breath of relief. His fur was much thicker than Bagheera's, but he had suffered sorely in the fight. Then Kaa opened his mouth for the first time and spoke one long hissing word, and the far-away monkeys, hurrying to the defence of the Cold Lairs, stayed where they were, cowering, till the loaded branches bent and crackled under them. The monkeys on the walls and the empty houses stopped their cries, and in the stillness that fell upon the city Mowgli heard Bagheera shaking his wet sides as he came up from the tank. Then the clamour broke out again. The monkeys leaped higher up the walls; they clung around the necks of the big stone idols and shrieked as they skipped along the battlements, while Mowgli, dancing in the summerhouse, put his eye to the screen-work and hooted owl-fashion between his front teeth, to show his derision and contempt.

"Get the Man-cub out of that trap; I can do no more," Bagheera gasped. "Let us take the Man-cub and go. They may attack again."

"They will not move till I order them. Stay you sssso!" Kaa hissed, and the city was silent once more. "I could not come before, Brother, but I *think* I heard thee call" – this was to Bagheera.

"I – I may have cried out in the battle," Bagheera answered. "Baloo, art thou hurt?"

"I am not sure that they did not pull me into a hundred little bearlings," said Baloo gravely, shaking one leg after the other.

"Wow! I am sore. Kaa, we owe thee, I think, our lives – Bagheera and I."

"No matter. Where is the Manling?"

"Here, in a trap. I cannot climb out," cried Mowgli. The curve of the broken dome was above his head.

"Take him away. He dances like Mao the Peacock. He will crush our young," said the cobras inside.

"Hah!" said Kaa, with a chuckle, "he has friends everywhere, this Manling. Stand back, Manling; and hide you, O Poison People. I break down the wall."

Kaa looked carefully till he found a discolored crack in the marble tracery showing a weak spot, made two or three light taps with his head to get the distance, and then lifting up six feet of his body clear of the ground, sent home half a dozen full-power smashing blows, nose-first. The screen-work broke and fell away in a cloud of dust and rubbish, and Mowgli leaped through the opening and flung himself between Baloo and Bagheera – an arm round each big neck.

"Art thou hurt?" said Baloo, hugging him softly.

"I am sore, hungry, and not a little bruised; but, oh, they have handled ye grievously, my Brothers! Ye bleed."

"Others also," said Bagheera, licking his lips and looking at the monkey-dead on the terrace and round the tank.

"It is nothing, it is nothing, if thou art safe, O my pride of all little frogs!" whimpered Baloo.

"Of that we shall judge later," said Bagheera, in a dry voice that Mowgli did not at all like. "But here is Kaa, to whom we owe the battle and thou owest thy life. Thank him according to our customs, Mowgli."

Mowgli turned and saw the great Python's head swaying a foot above his own.

"So this is the Manling," said Kaa. "Very soft is his skin, and he is not unlike the *Bandar-log*. Have a care, Manling, that I do not mistake thee for a monkey some twilight when I have newly changed my coat."

"We be one blood, thou and I," Mowgli answered. "I take my life from thee, tonight. My kill shall be thy kill if ever thou art hungry, O Kaa."

"All thanks, Little Brother," said Kaa, though his eyes twinkled. "And what may so bold a hunter kill? I ask that I may follow when next he goes abroad."

"I kill nothing – I am too little – but I drive goats toward such as can use them. When thou art empty come to me and see if I speak the truth. I have some skill in these" – he held out his hands – "and if ever thou art in a trap, I may pay the debt which I owe to thee, to Bagheera, and to Baloo, here. Good hunting to ye all, my masters."

"Well said," growled Baloo, for Mowgli had returned thanks very prettily. The python dropped his head lightly for a minute on Mowgli's shoulder. "A brave heart and a courteous tongue," said he. "They shall carry thee far through the Jungle, Manling. But now go hence quickly with thy friends. Go and sleep, for the moon sets, and what follows it is not well that thou shouldst see."

The moon was sinking behind the hills, and the lines of trembling monkeys huddled together on the walls and battlements looked like ragged, shaky fringes of things. Baloo went down to the tank for a drink, and Bagheera began to put his fur in order, as Kaa glided out into the centre of the terrace and brought his jaws together with a ringing snap that drew all the monkeys' eyes upon him.

"The moon sets," he said. "Is there yet light to see?"

From the walls came a moan like the wind in the tree-tops "We see, O Kaa."

"Good. Begins now the Dance – the Dance of the Hunger of Kaa. Sit still and watch."

He turned twice or thrice in a big circle, weaving his head from right to left. Then he began making loops and figures of eight with his body, and soft, oozy triangles that melted into squares and five-sided figures, and coiled mounds, never resting, never hurrying, and never stopping his low, humming song. It grew darker and darker, till at last the dragging, shifting coils disappeared, but they could hear the rustle of the scales.

Baloo and Bagheera stood still as stone, growling in their throats, their neck-hair bristling, and Mowgli watched and wondered.

"Bandar-log," said the voice of Kaa at last, "can ye stir foot or hand without my order? Speak!"

"Without thy order we cannot stir foot or hand, O Kaa!"

"Good! Come all one pace nearer to me."

The lines of the monkeys swayed forward helplessly, and Baloo and Bagheera took one stiff step forward with them.

"Nearer!" hissed Kaa, and they all moved again.

Mowgli laid his hands on Baloo and Bagheera to get them away, and the two great beasts started as though they had been waked from a dream.

"Keep thy hand on my shoulder," Bagheera whispered. "Keep it there, or I must go back – must go back to Kaa. *Aah!"*

"It is only old Kaa making circles on the dust," said Mowgli; "let us go;" and the three slipped off through a gap in the walls to the Jungle.

"Whoof!" said Baloo, when he stood under the still trees again. "Never more will I make an ally of Kaa," and he shook himself all over.

"He knows more than we," said Bagheera, trembling. "In a

little time, had I stayed, I should have walked down his throat."

"Many will walk by that road before the moon rises again," said Baloo. "He will have good hunting – after his own fashion."

"But what was the meaning of it all?" said Mowgli, who did not know anything of a python's powers of fascination. "I saw no more than a big snake making foolish circles till the dark came. And his nose was all sore. Ho! Ho!"

"Mowgli," said Bagheera angrily, "his nose was sore on *thy* account; as my ears and sides and paws, and Baloo's neck and shoulders are bitten on *thy* account. Neither Baloo nor Bagheera will be able to hunt with pleasure for many days."

"It is nothing," said Baloo; "we have the Man-cub again."

"True; but he has cost us heavily in time which might have been spent in good hunting, in wounds, in hair – I am half plucked along my back – and, last of all, in honour. For, remember, Mowgli, I, who am the Black Panther, was forced to call upon Kaa for protection, and Baloo and I were both made stupid as little birds by the Hunger Dance. All this, Man-cub, came of thy playing with the *Bandar-log.*"

"True; it is true," said Mowgli sorrowfully. "I am an evil Man-cub, and my stomach is sad in me."

"*Mf!* What says the Law of the Jungle, Baloo?"

Baloo did not wish to bring Mowgli into any more trouble, but he could not tamper with the Law, so he mumbled: "Sorrow never stays punishment. But remember, Bagheera, he is very little."

"I will remember; but he has done mischief, and blows must be dealt now. Mowgli, hast thou anything to say?"

"Nothing. I did wrong. Baloo and thou are wounded. It is just."

Bagheera gave him half a dozen love-taps; from a panther's point of view they would hardly have waked one of his own cubs, but for a seven-year-old boy they amounted to as severe a beating as you could wish to avoid. When it was all over Mowgli sneezed, and picked himself up without a word.

"Now," said Bagheera, "jump on my back, Little Brother, and we will go home."

One of the beauties of Jungle Law is that punishment settles all scores. There is no nagging afterward.

Mowgli laid his head down on Bagheera's back and slept so deeply that he never waked when he was put down by Mother Wolf's side in the home-cave.

4

Road Song of the Bandar-Log

HERE WE go in a flung festoon,
Half-way up to the jealous moon!
Don't you envy our pranceful bands?
Don't you wish you had extra hands?
Wouldn't you like if your tails were – *so* –
Curved in the shape of a Cupid's bow?
Now you're angry, but - never mind,
Brother, thy tail hangs down behind!

Here we sit in a branchy row,
Thinking of beautiful things we know;

Dreaming of deeds that we mean to do,
All complete, in a minute or two –
Something noble and grand and good,
Won by merely wishing we could.
Now we've forgotten, but never mind,
Brother, thy tail hangs down behind!

All the talk we ever have heard
Uttered by bat or beast or bird –
Hide or fin or scale or feather –
Jabber it quickly and all together!
Excellent! Wonderful! Once again!
Now we are talking just like men.

Let's pretend we are ... never mind,
Brother, thy tail hangs down behind!
This is the way of the Monkey - kind.

Then join our leaping lines that scumfish through the pines,
That rocket by where, light and high, the wild grape swings.
By the rubbish in our wake, and the noble noise we make,
Be sure, be sure, we're going to do some splendid things!

5

"Tiger! Tiger!"

WHAT OF the hunting, hunter bold?
Brother, the watch was long and cold.
What of the quarry ye went to kill?
Brother, he crops in the Jungle still.
Where is the power that made your pride?
Brother, it ebbs from my flank and side.
Where is the haste that ye hurry by?
Brother, I go to my lair-to die!

Now we must go back to the first tale. When Mowgli left the wolf's cave after the fight with the Pack at the Council Rock, he went down to the ploughed lands where the villagers lived, but he would not stop there because it was too near to the Jungle, and he knew that he had made at least one bad enemy at the Council. So he hurried on, keeping to the rough road that ran down the valley, and followed it at a steady jog-trot for nearly twenty miles, till he came to a country that he did not know. The valley opened out into a great plain dotted over with rocks and cut up by ravines. At one end stood a little village, and at the other the thick Jungle came down in a sweep to the grazing-grounds, and stopped there as though it had been cut off with a hoe. All over the plain, cattle and buffaloes were grazing, and when the little boys in charge of the herds saw Mowgli they shouted and ran away, and the yellow pariah dogs that hang about every Indian village barked. Mowgli walked on, for he was feeling hungry, and when he came to the village gate he saw the big thornbush that was drawn up before the gate at twilight, pushed to one side.

"Umph!" he said, for he had come across more than one such barricade in his night rambles after things to eat. "So men are afraid of the People of the Jungle here also." He sat down by the gate, and when a man came out he stood up, opened his mouth, and pointed down it to show that he wanted food. The man stared, and ran back up the one street of the village shouting for the priest, who was a big, fat man dressed in white, with a red-and -yellow mark on his forehead. The priest came to the gate, and with him at least a hundred people, who stared and talked and shouted and pointed at Mowgli.

"They have no manners, these Men Folk," said Mowgli to himself. "Only the grey ape would behave as they do." So he threw back his long hair and frowned at the crowd.

"What is there to be afraid of?" said the priest. "Look at the marks on his arms and legs. They are the bites of wolves. He is but a wolf-child run away from the Jungle."

Of course, in playing together, the cubs had often nipped Mowgli harder than they intended, and there were white scars all over his arms and legs. But he would have been the last person in the world to call these bites, for he knew what real biting meant.

"*Arre! Arre!*" said two or three women together. "To be bitten by wolves, poor child! He is a handsome boy. He has eyes like red fire. By my honour, Messua, he is not unlike thy boy that was taken by the tiger."

"Let me look," said a woman with heavy copper rings on her wrists and ankles, and she peered at Mowgli under the palm of her hand. "Indeed he is not. He is thinner, but he has the very look of my boy."

The priest was a clever man, and he knew that Messua was wife to the richest villager in the place. So he looked up at the sky for a minute, and said solemnly: "What the Jungle has taken the jungle has restored. Take the boy into thy house, my sister, and forget not to honour the priest who sees so far into the lives of men."

"By the Bull that bought me," said Mowgli to himself, "but all this talking is like another looking-over by the Pack! Well, if I am a man, a man I must become."

The crowd parted as the woman beckoned Mowgli to her hut, where there was a red-lacquered bedstead, a great earthen grain-chest with curious raised patterns on it, half a dozen copper cooking-pots, an image of a Hindu god in a little alcove, and on the wall a real looking-glass, such as they sell at the country fairs.

She gave him a long drink of milk and some bread, and then she laid her hand on his head and looked into his eyes; for she thought perhaps that he might be her real son come back from the Jungle where the tiger had taken him. So she said: "Nathoo, O Nathoo!" Mowgli did not show that he knew the name. "Dost thou not remember the day when I gave thee thy new shoes?" She touched his foot, and it was almost as hard as horn. "No," she said sorrowfully, "those feet have never worn shoes, but thou art very like my Nathoo, and thou shalt be my son."

Mowgli was uneasy, because he had never been under a roof before; but as he looked at the thatch, he saw that he could tear it out any time if he wanted to get away, and that the window had no fastenings. "What is the good of a man," he said to himself at last, "if he does not understand man's talk? Now I am as silly and dumb as a man would be with us in the Jungle. I must speak their talk."

It was not for fun that he had learned while he was with the wolves to imitate the challenge of bucks in the Jungle and the grunt of the little wild pig. So as soon as Messua pronounced a word Mowgli would imitate it almost perfectly, and before dark he had learned the names of many things in the hut.

There was a difficulty at bedtime, because Mowgli would

not sleep under anything that looked so like a panther-trap as that hut, and when they shut the door he went through the window. "Give him his will," said Messua's husband. "Remember he can never till now have slept on a bed. If he is indeed sent in the place of our son he will not run away."

So Mowgli stretched himself in some long, clean grass at the edge of the field, but before he had closed his eyes a soft grey nose poked him under the chin.

"Phew!" said Grey Brother (he was the eldest of Mother Wolf's cubs). "This is a poor reward for following thee twenty miles. Thou smellest of wood-smoke and cattle – altogether like a man already. Wake, Little Brother; I bring news."

"Are all well in the Jungle?" said Mowgli, hugging him.

"All except the wolves that were burned with the Red Flower. Now, listen. Shere Khan has gone away to hunt far off till his coat grows again, for he is badly singed. When he returns he swears that he will lay thy bones in the Waingunga."

"There are two words to that. I also have made a little promise. But news is always good. I am tired tonight – very tired with new things, Grey Brother – but bring me the news always."

"Thou wilt not forget that thou art a wolf? Men will not make thee forget?" said Grey Brother anxiously.

"Never. I will always remember that I love thee and all in our cave; but also I will always remember that I have been cast out of the Pack."

"And that thou mayest be cast out of another pack. Men are only men, Little Brother, and their talk is like the talk of frogs in a pond. When I come down here again, I will wait for thee in the bamboos at the edge of the grazing-ground."

For three months after that night Mowgli hardly ever left the village gate, he was so busy learning the ways and customs of men. First he had to wear a cloth round him, which annoyed him horribly; and then he had to learn about money, which he did not in the least understand, and about ploughing, of which he did not see the use. Then the little children in the village made him very angry. Luckily, the Law of the Jungle had taught him to keep his temper, for in the Jungle life and food depend on keeping your temper; but when they made fun of him because he would not play games or fly kites, or because he mispronounced some word, only the knowledge that it was unsportsmanlike to kill little naked cubs kept him from picking them up and breaking them in two.

He did not know his own strength in the least. In the Jungle he knew he was weak compared with the beasts, but in the village people said that he was as strong as a bull.

And Mowgli had not the faintest idea of the difference that caste makes between man and man. When the potter's donkey slipped in the clay-pit, Mowgli hauled it out by the tail, and helped to stack the pots for their journey to the market at Khanhiwara. That was very shocking, too, for the potter is a low-caste man, and his donkey is worse. When the priest scolded him, Mowgli threatened to put him on the donkey, too, and the priest told Messua's husband that Mowgli had better be set to work as soon as possible; and the village headman told Mowgli that he would have to go out with the buffaloes next day, and herd them while they grazed. No one was more pleased than Mowgli; and that night, because he had been appointed, as it were, a servant of the village, he went off to a circle that met every evening on a masonry platform under a great fig tree. It was the village club, and the headman and the watchman and the barber (who knew all the gossip of the village), and old Buldeo, the village hunter, who owned a Tower musket, met and smoked. The monkeys sat and talked in the upper branches, and there was a hole under the platform where a cobra lived, and he had his little platter of milk every night because he was sacred; and the old men sat around the tree and talked, and pulled at the big hookahs (water pipes) till far into the night. They told wonderful tales of gods and men and ghosts; and Buldeo told even more wonderful ones of the ways of beasts in the Jungle, till the eyes of the children sitting outside the circle bulged out of their heads. Most of the tales were about animals, for the Jungle was always at their door. The deer and the wild pig grubbed up their crops, and now and again the tiger carried off a man at twilight, within sight of the village gates.

Mowgli, who naturally, knew something about what they were talking of, had to cover his face not to show that he was laughing, while Buldeo, the Tower musket across his knees, climbed on from one wonderful story to another, and Mowgli's shoulders shook.

Buldeo was explaining how the tiger that had carried away Messua's son was a ghost-tiger, and his body was inhabited by the ghost of a wicked old money-lender, who had died some years ago. "And I know that this is true," he said, "because Purun Dass always limped from the blow that he got in a riot when his account-books were burned, and the tiger that I speak of, *he* limps, too, for the tracks of his pads are unequal."

"True, true; that must be the truth," said the grey beards, nodding together.

"Are all these tales such cobwebs and moon-talk?" said Mowgli. "That tiger limps because he was born lame, as everyone knows. To talk of the soul of a money-lender in a beast that never had the courage of a jackal is child's talk."

Buldeo was speechless with surprise for a moment, and the headman stared.

"Oho! It is the Jungle brat, is it?" said Buldeo. "If thou art so wise, better bring his hide to Khanhiwara, for the Government has set a hundred rupees on his life. Better still, do not talk when thy elders speak."

Mowgli rose to go. "All the evening I have lain here listening," he called back over his shoulder, "and, except once or twice, Buldeo has not said one word of truth concerning the Jungle, which is at his very doors. How, then, shall I believe the tales of ghosts and gods and goblins which he says he has seen?"

"It is full time that boy went to herding," said the headman, while Buldeo puffed and snorted at Mowgli's impertinence.

The custom of most Indian villages is for a few boys to take the cattle and buffaloes out to graze in the early morning, and bring them back at night; the very cattle that would trample a white man to death allow themselves to be banged and bullied and shouted at by children that hardly come up to their noses. So long as the boys keep with the herds they are safe, for not even the tiger will charge a mob of cattle. But if they straggle to pick flowers or hunt lizards, they are sometimes carried off. Mowgli went through the village street in the dawn, sitting on the back of Rama, the great herd bull; the slaty-blue buffaloes, with their long, backwards-sweeping horns and savage eyes, rose out their byres, one by one, and followed him, and Mowgli made it very clear to the children with him that he was the master. He beat the buffaloes with a long, polished bamboo, and told Kamya, one of the boys, to graze the cattle by themselves, while he went on with the buffaloes, and to be very careful not to stray away from the herd.

An Indian grazing-ground is all rocks and scrub and tussocks and little ravines, among which the herds scatter and disappear. The buffaloes generally keep to the pools and muddy places, where they lie wallowing or basking in the warm mud for hours. Mowgli drove them on to the edge of the plain where the Waingunga, came out of the Jungle; then he dropped from Rama's neck, trotted off to a bamboo clump, and found Grey Brother. "Ah!" said Grey Brother. "I have waited here very many days. What is the meaning of this cattle-herding work?"

"It is an order," said Mowgli. "I am a village herd for a while. What news of Shere Khan?"

"He has come back to this country, and has waited here a

long time for thee. Now he has gone off again, for the game is scarce. But he means to kill thee."

"Very good," said Mowgli. "So long as he is away do thou or one of the four brothers sit on that rock, so that I can see thee as I come out of the village. When he comes back wait for me in the ravine by the *dhak* tree in the centre of the plain. We need not walk into Shere Khan's mouth."

Then Mowgli picked out a shady place, and lay down and slept while the buffaloes grazed round him. Herding in India is one of the laziest things in the world. The cattle move and crunch, and lie down, and move on again, and they do not even low. They only grunt, and the buffaloes very seldom say anything, but get down into the muddy pools one after another, and work their way into the mud till only their noses and staring china-blue eyes show above the surface, and there they lie like logs. The sun makes the rocks dance in the heat, and the herd-children hear one kite (never any more) whistling almost out of sight overhead, and they know that if they died, or a cow died, that kite would sweep down, and the next kite miles away would see him drop and would follow, and the next, and the next, and almost before they were dead there would be a score of hungry kites come out of nowhere. Then they sleep and wake and sleep again, and weave little baskets of dried grass and put grasshoppers in them; or catch two praying mantises and make them fight; or string a necklace of red and black Jungle-nuts; or watch a lizard basking on a rock, or a snake hunting a frog near the wallows. Then they sing long, long songs with odd native quavers at the end of them, and the day seems longer than most people's whole lives, and perhaps they make a mud castle with mud figures of men and horses and buffaloes, and put reeds into the men's hands, and pretend that they are kings and the figures are their armies, or that they are gods to be worshiped. Then evening comes, and the children call, and the buffaloes lumber up out of the sticky mud with noises like gunshots going off one after the other, and they all string across the grey plain back to the twinkling village lights.

Day after day Mowgli would lead the buffaloes out to their wallows, and day after day he would see Grey Brother's back a mile and a half away across the plain (so he knew that Shere Khan had not come back), and day after day he would lie on the grass listening to the noises round him, and dreaming of old days in the Jungle. If Shere Khan had made a false step with his lame paw up in the Jungles by the Waingunga, Mowgli would have heard him in those long, still mornings.

At last a day came when he did not see Grey Brother at the signal-place, and he laughed and headed the buffaloes for the ravine by the *dhak* tree, which was all covered with golden-red flowers. There sat Grey Brother, every bristle on his back lifted.

"He has hidden for a month to throw thee off thy guard. He crossed the ranges last night with Tabaqui, hot-foot on thy trail," said the Wolf, panting.

Mowgli frowned. "I am not afraid of Shere Khan, but Tabaqui is very cunning."

"Have no fear," said Grey Brother, licking his lips a little. "I met Tabaqui in the dawn. Now he is telling all his wisdom to the kites, but he told *me* everything before I broke his back. Shere Khan's plan is to wait for thee at the village gate this evening – for thee and for no one else. He is lying up now in the big dry ravine of the Waingunga."

"Has he eaten today, or does he hunt empty?" said Mowgli, for the answer meant life and death to him.

"He killed at dawn – a pig – and he has drunk too. Remember, Shere Khan could never fast, even for the sake of revenge."

"Oh! Fool, fool! What a cub's cub it is! Eaten and drunk too, and he thinks that I shall wait till he has slept! Now, where does he lie up? If there were but ten of us we might pull him down as he lies. These buffaloes will not charge unless they wind him, and I cannot speak their language. Can we get behind his track so that they may smell it?"

"He swam far down the Waingunga to cut that off," said Grey Brother.

"Tabaqui told him that, I know. He would never have thought of it alone." Mowgli stood with his finger in his mouth, thinking. "The big ravine of the Waingunga. That opens out on the plain not half a mile from here. I can take the herd round through the Jungle to the head of the ravine and then sweep down – but he would slink out at the foot. We must block that end. Grey Brother, canst thou cut the herd in two for me?"

"Not I, perhaps – but I have brought a wise helper." Grey Brother trotted off and dropped into a hole. Then there lifted up a huge grey head that Mowgli knew well, and the hot air was filled with the most desolate cry of all the Jungle – the hunting-howl of a wolf at midday.

"Akela! Akela!" said Mowgli, clapping his hands. "I might have known that thou wouldst not forget me. We have a big work in hand. Cut the herd in two, Akela. Keep the cows and calves together, and the bulls and the plough-buffaloes by themselves."

The two wolves ran, ladies'-chain fashion, in and out of the herd, which snorted and threw up its head, and separated into two clumps. In one the cow-buffaloes stood, with their calves in the centre, and glared and pawed, ready, if a wolf would only stay still, to charge down and trample the life out of him. In the other the bulls and the young bulls snorted and stamped; but, though they looked more imposing, they were much less dangerous, for they had no calves to protect. No six men could have divided the herd so neatly.

"What orders!" panted Akela. "They are trying to join again."

Mowgli slipped on to Rama's back. "Drive the bulls away to

the left, Akela. Grey Brother, when we are gone, hold the cows together, and drive them into the foot of the ravine."

"How far?" said Grey Brother, panting and snapping.

"Till the sides are higher than Shere Khan can jump," shouted Mowgli. "Keep them there till we come down." The bulls swept off as Akela bayed, and Grey Brother stopped in front of the cows. They charged down on him, and he ran just before them to the foot of the ravine, as Akela drove the bulls far to the left.

"Well done! Another charge and they are fairly started. Careful, now – careful, Akela. A snap too much, and the bulls will charge. *Huyah!* This is wilder work than driving black-buck. Didst thou think these creatures could move so swiftly?" Mowgli called.

"I have – have hunted these too in my time," gasped Akela in the dust. "Shall I turn them into the Jungle?"

"Ay, turn! Swiftly turn them! Rama is mad with rage. Oh, if I could only tell him what I need of him today."

The bulls were turned to the right this time, and crashed into the standing thicket. The other herd-children, watching with the cattle half a mile away, hurried to the village as fast as their legs could carry them, crying that the buffaloes had gone mad and run away.

But Mowgli's plan was simple enough. All he wanted to do was to make a big circle uphill and get at the head of the ravine, and then take the bulls down it and catch Shere Khan between the bulls and the cows; for he knew that after a meal and a full drink Shere Khan would not be in any condition to fight or to clamber up the sides of the ravine. He was soothing the buffaloes now by voice, and Akela had dropped far to the rear, only whimpering once or twice to hurry the rearguard. It was a long, long circle, for they did not wish to get too near the ravine and give Shere Khan warning. At last Mowgli rounded up the bewildered herd at the head of the ravine on a grassy patch that sloped steeply down to the ravine itself. From that height you could see across the tops of the trees down to the plain below; but what Mowgli looked at was the sides of the ravine, and he saw with a great deal of satisfaction that they ran nearly straight up and down, while the vines and creepers that hung over them would give no foothold to a tiger who wanted to get out.

"Let them breathe, Akela," he said, holding up his hand. "They have not winded him yet. Let them breathe. I must tell Shere Khan who comes. We have him in the trap."

He put his hands to his mouth and shouted down the ravine – it was almost like shouting down a tunnel – and the echoes jumped from rock to rock.

After a long time there came back the drawling, sleepy snarl of a full-fed tiger just wakened.

"Who calls?" said Shere Khan, and a splendid peacock fluttered up out of the ravine screeching.

"I, Mowgli. Cattle thief, it is time to come to the Council Rock! Down – hurry them down, Akela! Down, Rama, down!"

The herd paused for an instant at the edge of the slope, but Akela gave tongue in the full hunting-yell, and they pitched over one after the other, just as steamers shoot rapids, the sand and stones spurting up round them. Once started, there was no chance of stopping, and before they were fairly in the bed of the ravine Rama winded Shere Khan and bellowed.

"Ha! Ha!" said Mowgli, on his back. "Now thou knowest!" and the torrent of black horns, foaming muzzles, and staring eyes whirled down the ravine, just as boulders go down in flood-time; the weaker buffaloes being shouldered out to the sides of the ravine where they tore through the creepers. They knew what the business was before them – the terrible charge of the buffalo-herd, against which no tiger can hope to stand. Shere Khan heard the thunder of their hoofs, picked himself up, and lumbered down the ravine, looking from side to side for some way of escape; but the walls of the ravine were straight and he had to keep on, heavy with his dinner and his drink, willing to do anything rather than fight. The herd splashed through the pool he had just left, bellowing till the narrow cut rang. Mowgli heard an answering bellow from the foot of the ravine, saw Shere Khan turn (the tiger knew if the worst came to the worst it was better to meet the bulls than the cows with their calves), and then Rama tripped, stumbled, and went on again over something soft, and, with the bulls at his heels, crashed full into the other herd, while the weaker buffaloes were lifted clean off their feet by the shock of the meeting. That charge carried both herds out into the plain, goring and stamping and snorting. Mowgli watched his time, and slipped off Rama's neck, laying about him right and left with his stick.

"Quick, Akela! Break them up. Scatter them, or they will be fighting one another. Drive them away, Akela. *Hai,* Rama! *Hai! hai! hai!* my children. Softly now, softly! It is all over."

Akela and Grey Brother ran to and fro nipping the buffaloes' legs, and though the herd wheeled once to charge up the ravine again, Mowgli managed to turn Rama, and the others followed him to the wallows.

Shere Khan needed no more trampling. He was dead, and the kites were coming for him already.

"Brothers, that was a dog's death," said Mowgli, feeling for the knife he always carried in a sheath round his neck now that he lived with men. "But he would never have shown fight. His hide will look well on the Council Rock. We must get to work swiftly."

A boy trained among men would never have dreamed of skinning a ten-foot tiger alone, but Mowgli knew better than anyone else how an animal's skin is fitted on, and how it can be taken off. But it was hard work, and Mowgli slashed and tore and grunted for an hour, while the wolves lolled out their tongues, or came forward and tugged as he ordered them.

Presently a hand fell on his shoulder, and looking up he saw

Buldeo with the Tower musket. The children had told the village about the buffalo stampede, and Buldeo went out angrily, only too anxious to correct Mowgli for not taking better care of the herd. The wolves dropped out of sight as soon as they saw the man coming.

"What is this folly?" said Buldeo angrily. "To think that thou canst skin a tiger! Where did the buffaloes kill him? It is the Lame Tiger, too, and there is a hundred rupees on his head. Well, well, we will overlook thy letting the herd run off, and perhaps I will give thee one of the rupees of the reward when I have taken the skin to Khanhiwara." He fumbled in his waist-cloth for flint and steel, and stooped down to singe Shere Khan's whiskers. Most native hunters always singe a tiger's whiskers to prevent his ghost from haunting them.

"Hum!" said Mowgli, half to himself as he ripped back the skin of a fore-paw. "So thou wilt take the hide to Khanhiwara for the reward, and perhaps give me one rupee? Now it is in my mind that I need the skin for my own use. Heh! old man, take away that fire!"

"What talk is this to the chief hunter of the village? Thy luck and the stupidity of thy buffaloes have helped thee to this kill. The tiger has just fed, or he would have gone twenty miles by this time. Thou canst not even skin him properly, little beggar-brat, and forsooth I, Buldeo, must be told not to singe his whiskers. Mowgli, I will not give thee one anna of the reward, but only a very big beating. Leave the carcass!"

"By the Bull that bought me," said Mowgli, who was trying to get at the shoulder, "must I stay babbling to an old ape all noon? Here, Akela, this man plagues me."

Buldeo, who was still stooping over Shere Khan's head, found himself sprawling on the grass, with a grey wolf standing over him, while Mowgli went on skinning as though he were alone in all India.

"Ye-es," he said, between his teeth. "Thou art altogether right, Buldeo. Thou wilt never give me one anna of the reward. There is an old war between this lame tiger and myself – a very old war, and – I have won."

To do Buldeo justice, if he had been ten years younger he would have taken his chance with Akela had he met the wolf in the woods; but a wolf who obeyed the orders of this boy who had private wars with man-eating tigers was not a common animal. It was sorcery, magic of the worst kind, thought Buldeo, and he wondered whether the amulet round his neck would protect him. He lay as still as still, expecting every minute to see Mowgli turn into a tiger too.

"Maharaj! Great King!" he said at last, in a husky whisper.

"Yes," said Mowgli, without turning his head, chuckling a little.

"I am an old man. I did not know that thou wast anything more than a herd-boy. May I rise up and go away, or will thy servant tear me to pieces?"

"Go, and peace go with thee. Only, another time do not meddle with my game. Let him go, Akela."

Buldeo hobbled away to the village as fast as he could, looking back over his shoulder in case Mowgli should change into something terrible. When he got to the village he told a tale of magic and enchantment and sorcery that made the priest look very grave.

Mowgli went on with his work, but it was nearly twilight before he and the wolves had drawn the great gay skin clear of the body.

"Now we must hide this and take the buffaloes home! Help me to herd them, Akela."

The herd rounded up in the misty twilight, and when they got near the village Mowgli saw lights, and heard the conches and bells in the temple blowing and banging. Half the village seemed to be waiting for him by the gate. "That is because I have killed Shere Khan," he said to himself; but a shower of stones whistled about his ears, and the villagers shouted: "Sorcerer! Wolf's brat! Jungle-demon! Go away! Get hence quickly, or the priest will turn thee into a wolf again. Shoot, Buldeo, shoot!"

The old Tower musket went off with a bang, and a young buffalo bellowed in pain.

"More sorcery!" shouted the villagers. "He can turn bullets. Buldeo, that was *thy* buffalo."

"Now what is this?" said Mowgli, bewildered, as the stones flew thicker.

"They are not unlike the Pack, these brothers of thine," said Akela, sitting down composedly. "It is in my head that, if bullets mean anything, they would cast thee out."

"Wolf! Wolf's cub! Go away!" shouted the priest, waving a sprig of the sacred *tulsi* plant.

"Again? Last time it was because I was a man. This time it is because I am a wolf. Let us go, Akela."

A woman – it was Messua – ran across to the herd, and cried: "Oh, my son, my son! They say thou art a sorcerer who can turn himself into a beast at will. I do not believe, but go away or they will kill thee. Buldeo says thou art a wizard, but I know thou hast avenged Nathoo's death."

"Come back, Messua!" shouted the crowd. "Come back, or we will stone thee."

Mowgli laughed a little short ugly laugh, for a stone had hit him in the mouth. "Run back, Messua. This is one of the foolish tales they tell under the big tree at dusk. I have at least paid for thy son's life. Farewell; and run quickly, for I shall send the herd in more swiftly than their brickbats. I am no wizard, Messua. Farewell!"

"Now, once more, Akela," he cried. "Bring the herd in."

The buffaloes were anxious enough to get to the village. They hardly needed Akela's yell, but charged through the gate like a whirlwind, scattering the crowd right and left.

"Keep count!" shouted Mowgli scornfully. "It may be that I have stolen one of them. Keep count, for I will do your herding no more. Fare you well, children of men, and thank Messua that I do not come in with my wolves and hunt you up and down your street."

He turned on his heel and walked away with the Lone Wolf; and as he looked up at the stars he felt happy. "No more sleeping in traps for me, Akela. Let us get Shere Khan's skin and go away. No; we will not hurt the village, for Messua was kind to me."

When the moon rose over the plain, making it look all milky, the horrified villagers saw Mowgli, with two wolves at his heels and a bundle on his head, trotting across at the steady wolf's trot that eats up the long miles like fire. Then they banged the temple bells and blew the conches louder than ever; and Messua cried, and Buldeo embroidered the story of his adventures in the Jungle, till he ended by saying that Akela stood up on his hind legs and talked like a man.

The moon was just going down when Mowgli and the two wolves came to the hill of the Council Rock, and they stopped at Mother Wolf's cave.

"They have cast me out from the Man Pack, Mother," shouted Mowgli, "but I come with the hide of Shere Khan to keep my word." Mother Wolf walked stiffly from the cave with the cubs behind her, and her eyes glowed as she saw the skin.

"I told him on that day, when he crammed his head and shoulders into this cave, hunting for thy life, Little Frog – I told him that the hunter would be the hunted. It is well done."

"Little Brother, it is well done," said a deep voice in the thicket.

"We were lonely in the Jungle without thee, and Bagheera came running to Mowgli's bare feet. They clambered up the Council Rock together, and Mowgli spread the skin out on the flat stone where Akela used to sit, and pegged it down with four slivers of bamboo, and Akela lay down upon it, and called the old call to the Council, "Look – look well, O Wolves!" exactly as he had called when Mowgli was first brought there.

Ever since Akela had been deposed, the Pack had been without a leader, hunting and fighting at their own pleasure. But they answered the call from habit, and some of them were lame from the traps they had fallen into, and some limped from shot- wounds, and some were mangy from eating bad food, and many were missing; but they came to the Council Rock, all that were left of them, and saw Shere Khan's striped hide on the rock, and the huge claws dangling at the end of the empty, dangling feet. It was then that Mowgli made up a song without any rhymes, a song that came up into his throat all by itself, and he shouted it aloud, leaping up and down on the rattling skin, and beating time with his heels till he had no more breath left, while Grey Brother and Akela howled between the verses.

"Look well, O Wolves! Have I kept my word?" said Mowgli when he had finished; and the wolves bayed, "Yes," and one tattered wolf howled –

"Lead us again, O Akela. Lead us again, O Man-cub, for we be sick of this lawlessness, and we would be the Free People once more."

"Nay," purred Bagheera, "that may not be. When ye are full-fed, the madness may come upon ye again. Not for nothing are ye called the Free People. Ye fought for freedom, and it is yours. Eat it, O Wolves."

"Man Pack and Wolf Pack have cast me out," said Mowgli. "Now I will hunt alone in the Jungle."

"And we will hunt with thee," said the four cubs.

So Mowgli went away and hunted with the four cubs in the Jungle from that day on. But he was not always alone, because, years afterward he became a man and married.

But that is a story for grown-ups.

6

Mowgli's Song

THAT HE SANG AT THE COUNCIL ROCK WHEN HE DANCED ON SHERE KHAN'S HIDE

THE SONG of Mowgli – I, Mowgli, am singing. Let the Jungle listen to the things I have done.

Shere Khan said he would kill – would kill! At the gates in the twilight he would kill Mowgli, the Frog!

He ate and he drank. Drink deep, Shere Khan, for when wilt thou drink again? Sleep and dream of the kill.

I am alone on the grazing-grounds. Grey Brother, come to me! Come to me, Lone Wolf, for there is big game afoot.

Bring up the great bull-buffaloes, the blue-skinned herd-bulls with the angry eyes. Drive them to and fro as I order.

Sleepest thou still, Shere Khan? Wake, oh, wake! Here come I, and the bulls are behind.

Rama, the King of the Buffaloes, stamped with his foot. Waters of the Waingunga, whither went Shere Khan?

He is not Ikki to dig holes, nor Mao, the Peacock, that he should fly. He is not Mang, the Bat, to hang in the branches. Little bamboos that creak together, tell me where he ran.

Ow! He is there. *Ahoo!* He is there. Under the feet of Rama lies the Lame One! Up, Shere Khan! Up and kill! Here is meat; break the necks of the bulls!

Hsh! He is asleep. We will not wake him, for his strength is very great. The kites have come down to see it. The black ants have come up to know it. There is a great assembly in his honour.

Alala! I havc no cloth to wrap me. The kites will see that I am naked. I am ashamed to meet all these people. Lend me thy coat, Shere Khan. Lend me thy gay striped coat that I may go to the Council Rock.

By the Bull that bought me, I have made a promise – a little promise. Only thy coat is lacking before I keep my word.

With the knife – with the knife that men use – with the knife of the hunter, the man, I will stoop down for my gift.

Waters of the Waingunga, bear witness that Shere Khangives me his coat for the love that he bears me. Pull, Grey Brother! Pull, Akela! Heavy is the hide of Shere Khan.

The Man Pack are angry. They throw stones and talk child's talk. My mouth is bleeding. Let us run away.

Through the night, through the hot night, run swiftly with me, my brothers. We will leave the lights of the village and go to the low moon.

Waters of the Waingunga, the Man Pack have cast me out. I did them no harm, but they were afraid of me. Why?

Wolf Pack, ye have cast me out too. The Jungle is shut to me, And the village gates are shut. Why?

As Mang flies between the beasts and birds, so fly I between the village and the jungle. Why?

I dance on the hide of Shere Khan, but my heart is very heavy. My mouth is cut and wounded with the stones from the village, but my heart is very light because I have come back to the Jungle. Why?

These two things fight together in me as the snakes fight in the spring.

The water comes out of my eyes; yet I laugh while it falls. Why?

I am two Mowglis, but the hide of Shere Khan is under my feet.

All the Jungle knows that I have killed Shere Khan. Look – look well, O Wolves!

Ahae! My heart is heavy with the things that I do not understand.

7

'Rikki-Tikki-Tavi'

AT THE hole where he went in
Red-Eye called to Wrinkle-Skin.
Hear what little Red-Eye saith:
"Nag, come up and dance with death!"

Eye to eye and head to head,
(Keep the measure, Nag.)
This shall end when one is dead;
(At thy pleasure, Nag.)

Turn for turn and twist for twist –
(Run and hide thee, Nag.)
Hah! The hooded Death has missed!
(Woe betide thee, Nag!)

This is the story of the great war that Rikki-tikki-tavi fought single-handed, through the bathrooms of the big bungalow in Segowlee cantonment. Darzee, the tailorbird, helped him, and Chuchundra, the musk-rat, who never comes out into the middle of the floor, but always creeps round by the wall, gave him advice; but Rikki-tikki did the real fighting.

He was a mongoose, rather like a little cat in his fur and his tail, but quite like a weasel in his head and his habits. His eyes and the end of his restless nose were pink; he could scratch himself anywhere he pleased, with any leg, front or back, that he chose to use; he could fluff up his tail till it looked like a bottle-brush, and his war-cry, as he scuttled through the long grass, was: *"Rikk-tikk-tikki-tikki-tchk!"*

One day, a high summer flood washed him out of the burrow where he lived with his father and mother, and carried him, kicking and clucking, down a road-side ditch. He found a little wisp of grass floating there, and clung to it till he lost his senses. When he revived, he was lying in the hot sun on the middle of a garden path, very draggled indeed, and a small boy was saying: "Here's a dead mongoose. Let's have a funeral."

"No," said his mother; "let's take him in and dry him. Perhaps he isn't really dead."

They took him into the house, and a big man picked him up between his finger and thumb, and said he was not dead but half choked; so they wrapped him in cotton-wool, and warmed him, over a little fire, and he opened his eyes and sneezed.

"Now," said the big man (he was an Englishman who had

just moved into the bungalow); "don't frighten him, and we'll see what he'll do."

It is the hardest thing in the world to frighten a mongoose, because he is eaten up from nose to tail with curiosity. The motto of all the mongoose family is, "Run and find out;" and Rikki-tikki was a true mongoose. He looked at the cottonwool, decided that it was not good to eat, ran all round the table, sat up and put his fur in order, scratched himself, and jumped on the small boy's shoulder.

"Don't be frightened, Teddy," said his father. "That's his way of making friends."

"Ouch! He's tickling under my chin," said Teddy.

Rikki-tikki looked down between the boy's collar and neck, snuffed at his ear, and climbed down to the floor, where he sat rubbing his nose.

"Good gracious," said Teddy's mother, "and that's a wild creature! I suppose he's so tame because we've been kind to him."

"All mongooses are like that," said her husband. "If Teddy doesn't pick him up by the tail, or try to put him in a cage, he'll run in and out of the house all day long. Let's give him something to eat."

They gave him a little piece of raw meat. Rikki-tikki liked it immensely, and when it was finished he went out into the veranda and sat in the sunshine and fluffed up his fur to make it dry to the roots. Then he felt better.

"There are more things to find out about in this house," he said to himself, "than all my family could find out in all their lives. I shall certainly stay and find out."

He spent all that day roaming over the house. He nearly drowned himself in the bath-tubs, put his nose into the ink on a writing-table, and burnt it on the end of the big man's cigar, for he climbed up in the big man's lap to see how writing was done. At nightfall he ran into Teddy's nursery to watch how kerosene-lamps were lighted, and when Teddy went to bed Rikki-tikki climbed up too; but he was a restless companion, because he had to get up and attend to every noise all through the night, and find out what made it. Teddy's mother and father came in, the last thing, to look at their boy, and Rikki-tikki was awake on the pillow. "I don't like that," said Teddy's mother; "he may bite the child." "He'll do no such thing," said the father. "Teddy's safer with that little beast than if he had a bloodhound to watch him. If a snake came into the nursery now –

But Teddy's mother wouldn't think of anything so awful.

Early in the morning Rikki-tikki came to early breakfast in the veranda riding on Teddy's shoulder, and they gave him banana and some boiled egg; and he sat on all their laps one after the other, because every well-brought-up mongoose always hopes tobe a house-mongoose someday and have rooms to run about in, and Rikki - tikki's mother (she used to live in the General's house at Segowlee) had carefully told Rikki what to do if ever he came across white men.

Then Rikki-tikki went out into the garden to see what was to be seen. It was a large garden, only half cultivated, with bushes, as big as summerhouses of Marshal Niel roses, lime and orange trees, clumps of bamboos, and thickets of high grass. Rikki-tikki licked his lips. "This is a splendid hunting-ground," he said, and his tail grew bottle-brushy at the thought of it, and he scuttled up and down the garden, snuffing here and there till he heard very sorrowful voices in a thorn bush.

It was Darzee, the tailor-bird, and his wife. They had made a beautiful nest by pulling two big leaves together and stitching them up the edges with fibres, and had filled the hollow with cotton and downy fluff. The nest swayed to and fro, as they sat on the rim and cried.

"What is the matter?" asked Rikki-tikki.

"We are very miserable," said Darzee. "One of our babies fell out of the nest yesterday, and Nag ate him."

"H'm!" said Rikki-tikki, "that is very sad – but I am a stranger here. Who is Nag?"

Darzee and his wife only cowered down in the nest without answering, for from the thick grass at the foot of the bush there came a low hiss – a horrid cold sound that made Rikki-tikki jump back two clear feet. Then inch by inch out of the grass rose up the head and spread hood of Nag, the big black cobra, and he was five feet long from tongue to tail. When he had lifted one-third of himself clear of the ground, he stayed balancing to and fro exactly as a dandelion-tuft balances in the wind, and he looked at Rikki-tikki with the wicked snake's eyes that never change their expression, whatever the snake may be thinking of.

"Who is Nag?" said he. "*I* am Nag. The great god Brahm put his mark upon all our people when the first cobra spread his hood to keep the sun off Brahm as he slept. Look, and be afraid!"

He spread out his hood more than ever, and Rikki-tikki saw the spectacle-mark on the back of it that looks exactly like the eye part of a hook-and-eye fastening. He was afraid for the minute; but it is impossible for a mongoose to stay frightened for any length of time, and though Rikki-tikki had never met a live cobra before, his mother had fed him on dead ones, and he knew that all a grown mongoose's business in life was to fight and eat snakes. Nag knew that too, and at the bottom of his cold heart he was afraid.

"Well," said Rikki-tikki, and his tail began to fluff up again, "marks or no marks, do you think it is right for you to eat fledglings out of a nest?"

Nag was thinking to himself, and watching the least little movement in the grass behind Rikki-tikki. He knew that mongooses in the garden meant death sooner or later for him and his family, but he wanted to get Rikki-tikki off his guard. So he dropped his head a little, and put it on one side.

"Let us talk," he said. "You eat eggs. Why should not I eat birds?"

"Behind you! Look behind you!" sang Darzee.

Rikki-tikki knew better than to waste time in staring. He jumped up in the air as high as he could go, and just under him whizzed by the head of Nagaina, Nag's wicked wife. She had crept up behind him as he was talking, to make an end of him; he heard her savage hiss as the stroke missed. He came down almost across her back, and if he had been an old mongoose he would have known that then was the time to break her back with one bite; but he was afraid of the terrible lashing return-stroke of the cobra. He bit, indeed, but did not bite long enough, and he jumped clear of the whisking tail, leaving Nagaina torn and angry.

"Wicked, wicked Darzee!" said Nag, lashing up as high as he could reach toward the nest in the thornbush; but Darzee had built it out of reach of snakes, and it only swayed to and fro.

Rikki-tikki felt his eyes growing red and hot (when a mongoose's eyes grow red, he is angry), and he sat back on his tail and hind legs like a little kangaroo, and looked all round him, and chattered with rage. But Nag and Nagaina had disappeared into the grass. When a snake misses its stroke, it never says anything or gives any sign of what it means to do next. Rikki-tikki did not care to follow them, for he did not feel sure that he could manage two snakes at once. So he trotted off to the gravel path near the house, and sat down to think. It was a serious matter for him.

If you read the old books of natural history, you will find they say that when the mongoose fights the snake and happens to get bitten, he runs off and eats some herb that cures him. That is not true. The victory is only a matter of quickness of eye and quickness of foot – snake's blow against mongoose's jump –

and as no eye can follow the motion of a snake's head when it strikes, that makes things much more wonderful than any magic herb. Rikki-tikki knew he was a young mongoose, and it made him all the more pleased to think that he had managed to escape a blow from behind. It gave him confidence in himself, and when Teddy came running down the path, Rikki-tikki was ready to be petted.

But just as Teddy was stooping, something wriggled a little in the dust, and a tiny voice said: "Be careful. I am death!" It was Karait, the dusty brown snakeling that lies for choice on the dusty earth; and his bite is as dangerous as the cobra's. But he is so small that nobody thinks of him, and so he does the more harm to people.

Rikki-tikki's eyes grew red again, and he danced up to Karait with the peculiar rocking, swaying motion that he had inherited from his family. It looks very funny, but it is so perfectly balanced a gait that you can fly off from it at any angle you please; and in dealing with snakes this is an advantage. If Rikki-tikki had only known, he was doing a much more dangerous thing than fighting Nag, for Karait is so small, and can turn so quickly, that unless Rikki bit him close to the back of the head, he would get the return-stroke in his eye or lip. But Rikki did not know: his eyes were all red, and he rocked back and forth, looking for a good place to hold. Karait struck out. Rikki jumped sideways and tried to run in, but the wicked little dusty grey head lashed within a fraction of his shoulder, and he had to jump over the body, and the head followed his heels close.

Teddy shouted to the house: "Oh, look here! Our mongoose is killing a snake;" and Rikki-tikki heard a scream from Teddy's mother. His father ran out with a stick, but by the time he came up, Karait had lunged out once too far, and Rikki-tikki had sprung, jumped on the snake's back, dropped his head far between his fore-legs, bitten as high up the back as he could get hold, and rolled away. That bite paralysed Karait, and Rikki-tikki was just going to eat him up from the tail, after the custom of his family at dinner, when he remembered that a full meal makes a slow mongoose, and if he wanted all his strength and quickness ready, he must keep himself thin.

He went away for a dust-bath under the castor-oil bushes, while Teddy's father beat the dead Karait. "What is the use of that?" thought Rikki-tikki. "I have settled it all;" and then Teddy's mother picked him up from the dust and hugged him, crying that he had saved Teddy from death, and Teddy's father said that he was a providence, and Teddy looked on with big scared eyes. Rikki-tikki was rather amused at all the fuss, which, of course, he did not understand. Teddy's mother might just as well have petted Teddy for playing in the dust. Rikki was thoroughly enjoying himself.

That night, at dinner, walking to and fro among the wine-glasses on the table, he couldhave stuffed himself three times over with nice things; but he remembered Nag and Nagaina, and though it was very pleasant to be patted and petted by Teddy's mother, and to sit on Teddy's shoulder, his eyes would get red from time to time, and he would go off into his long war-cry of *"Rikk-tikk tikki-tikki-tchk!"*

Teddy carried him off to bed, and insisted on Rikki-tikki sleeping under his chin. Rikki-tikki was too well-bred to bite or scratch, but as soon as Teddy was asleep he went off for his nightly walk round the house, and in the dark he ran up against Chuchundra, the musk-rat, creeping round by the wall. Chuchundra is a broken-hearted little beast. He whimpers and cheeps all the night, trying to make up his mind to run into the middle of the room; but he never gets there.

"Don't kill me," said Chuchundra, almost weeping. "Rikki-tikki, don't kill me."

"Do you think a snake-killer kills musk-rats?" said Rikki-tikki scornfully.

"Those who kill snakes get killed by snakes," said Chuchundra, more sorrowfully than ever. "And how am I to be sure that Nag won't mistake me for you some dark night?"

"There's not the least danger," said Rikki-tikki; but Nag is in the garden, and I know you don't go there."

"My cousin Chua, the rat, told me –" said Chuchundra, and then he stopped.

"Told you what?"

"H'sh! Nag is everywhere, Rikki-tikki. You should have talked to Chua in the garden."

"I didn't – so you must tell me. Quick, Chuchundra, or I'll bite you!"

Chuchundra sat down and cried till the tears rolled off his whiskers. "I am a very poor man," he sobbed. "I never had spirit enough to run out into the middle of the room. H'sh! I mustn't tell you anything. Can't you *hear*, Rikki-tikki?"

Rikki-tikki listened. The house was as still as still, but he thought he could just catch the faintest *scratch-scratch* in the world – a noise as faint as that of a wasp walking on a window-pane – the dry scratch of a snake's scales on brick work.

"That's Nag or Nagaina," he said to himself; "and he is crawling into the bathroom sluice. You're right, Chuchundra; I should have talked to Chua."

He stole off to Teddy's bathroom, but there was nothing there, and then to Teddy's mother's bathroom. At the bottom of the smooth plaster wall there was a brick pulled out to make a sluice for the bath-water, and as Rikki-tikki stole in by the masonry curb where the bath is put, he heard Nag and Nagaina whispering together outside in the moonlight.

"When the house is emptied of people," said Nagaina to her husband, "*he* will have to go away, and then the garden will be our own again. Go in quietly, and remember that the big man who killed Karait is the first one to bite. Then come out and tell me, and we will hunt for Rikki-tikki together."

"But are you sure that there is anything to be gained by killing the people?" said Nag.

"Everything. When there were no people in the bungalow, did we have any mongoose in the garden? So long as the bungalow is empty, we are king and queen of the garden; and remember that as soon as our eggs in the melon-bed hatch (as they may tomorrow), our children will need room and quiet."

"I had not thought of that," said Nag. "I will go, but there is no need that we should hunt for Rikki-tikki afterward. I will kill the big man and his wife, and the child if I can, and come away quietly. Then the bungalow will be empty, and Rikki-tikki will go."

Rikki-tikki tingled all over with rage and hatred at this, and then Nag's head came through the sluice, and his five feet of cold body followed it. Angry as he was, Rikki-tikki was very frightened as he saw the size of the big cobra. Nag coiled himself up, raised his head, and looked into the bathroom in the dark, and Rikki could see his eyes glitter.

"Now, if I kill him here, Nagaina will know; and if I fight him on the open floor, the odds are in his favour. What am I to do?" said Rikki-tikki-tavi.

Nag waved to and fro, and then Rikki-tikki heard him drinking from the biggest waterjar that was used to fill the bath. "That is good," said the snake. "Now, when Karait was killed, the big man had a stick. He may have that stick still, but when he comes in to bathe in the morning he will not have a stick. I shall wait here till he comes. Nagaina – do you hear me? – I shall wait here in the cool till daytime."

There was no answer from outside, so Rikki-tikki knew Nagaina had gone away. Nag coiled himself down, coil by coil, round the bulge at the bottom of the waterjar, and Rikki-tikki stayed still as death. After an hour he began to move, muscle by muscle, toward the jar. Nag was asleep, and Rikki-tikki looked at his big back, wondering which would be the best place for a good hold. "If I don't break his back at the first jump," said Rikki, "he can still fight; and if he fights – oh Rikki!" He looked at the thickness of the neck below the hood, but that was too much for him; and a bite near the tail would only make Nag savage.

"It must be the head," he said at last; "the head above the hood; and when I am once there, I must not let go."

Then he jumped. The head was lying a little clear of the waterjar, under the curve of it; and, as his teeth met, Rikki braced his back against the bulge of the red earthenware to hold down the head. This gave him just one second's purchase, and he made the most of it. Then he was battered to and fro as a rat is shaken by a dog – to and fro on the floor, up and down, and round in great circles but his eyes were red, and he held on as the body cart-whipped over the floor, upsetting the tin dipper and the soap-dish and the flesh-brush, and banged against the tin side of the bath. As he held he closed his jaws tighter and tighter, for he made sure he would be banged to death, and, for the honour of his family, he preferred to be found with his teeth locked. He was dizzy, aching, and felt shaken to pieces when something went off like a thunderclap just behind him; a hot wind knocked him senseless, and red fire singed his fur. The big man had been wakened by the noise, and had fired both barrels of a shotgun into Nag just behind the hood.

Rikki-tikki held on with his eyes shut, for now he was quite sure he was dead; but the head did not move, and the big man picked him up and said: "It's the mongoose again, Alice; the little chap has saved *our* lives now."

Then Teddy's mother came in with a very white face, and saw what was left of Nag, and Rikki-tikki dragged himself to

Teddy's bedroom and spent half the rest of the night shaking himself tenderly to find out whether he really was broken into forty pieces, as he fancied.

When morning came he was very stiff, but well pleased with his doings. "Now I have Nagaina to settle with, and she will be worse than five Nags, and there's no knowing when the eggs she spoke of will hatch. Goodness! I must go and see Darzee," he said.

Without waiting for breakfast, Rikki-tikki ran to the thornbush where Darzee was singing a song of triumph at the top of his voice. The news of Nag's death was all over the garden, for the sweeper had thrown the body on the rubbish-heap.

"Oh, you stupid tuft of feathers!" said Rikki-tikki angrily. "Is this the time to sing?"

"Nag is dead – is dead – is dead!" sang Darzee. "The valiant Rikki-tikki caught him by the head and held fast. The big man brought the bang-stick, and Nag fell in two pieces! He will never eat my babies again."

"All that's true enough; but where's Nagaina?" said Rikki-tikki, looking carefully round him.

"Nagaina came to the bathroom sluice and called for Nag," Darzee went on; "and Nag came out on the end of a stick – the sweeper picked him up on the end of a stick and threw him upon the rubbish-heap. Let us sing about the great, the red-eyed Rikki-tikki!" And Darzee filled his throat and sang.

"If I could get up to your nest, I'd roll your babies out!" said Rikki-tikki. "You don't know when to do the right thing at the right time. You're safe enough in your nest there, but it's war for me down here. Stop singing a minute, Darzee."

"For the great, the beautiful Rikki-tikki's sake I will stop," said Darzee. "What is it, O Killer of the terrible Nag?"

"Where is Nagaina, for the third time?"

"On the rubbish-heap by the stables, mourning for Nag. Great is Rikki-tikki with the white teeth."

"Bother my white teeth! Have you ever heard where she keeps her eggs?"

"In the melon-bed, on the end nearest the wall, where the sun strikes nearly all day. She hid them there weeks ago."

"And you never thought it worth while to tell me? The end nearest the wall, you said?"

"Rikki-tikki, you are not going to eat her eggs?"

"Not eat exactly; no. Darzee, if you have a grain of sense you will fly off to the stables and pretend that your wing is broken, and let Nagaina chase you away to this bush. I must get to the melon-bed, and if I went there now she'd see me."

Darzee was a feather-brained little fellow who could never hold more than one idea at a time in his head; and just because he knew that Nagaina's children were born in eggs like his own, he didn't think at first that it was fair to kill them. But his wife was a sensible bird, and she knew that cobra's eggs meant young cobras later on; so she flew off from the nest, and left Darzee to keep the babies warm, and continue his song about the death of Nag. Darzee was very like a man in some ways.

She fluttered in front of Nagaina by the rubbish-heap, and cried out: "Oh, my wing is broken! The boy in the house threw a stone at me and broke it." Then she fluttered more desperately than ever.

Nagaina lifted up her head and hissed: "You warned Rikki-tikki when I would have killed him. Indeed and truly, you've chosen a bad place to be lame in." And she moved toward Darzee's wife, slipping along over the dust.

"The boy broke it with a stone!" shrieked Darzee's wife.

"Well, it may be some consolation to you when you're dead to know that I shall settle accounts with the boy. My husband lies on the rubbish-heap this morning, but before night the boy in the house will lie very still. What is the use of running away? I am sure to catch you. Little fool, look at me!"

Darzee's wife knew better than to do *that,* for a bird who looks at a snake's eyes gets so frightened that she cannot move. Darzee's wife fluttered on, piping sorrowfully, and never leaving the ground, and Nagaina quickened her pace.

Rikki-tikki heard them going up the path from the stables, and he raced for the end of the melon-patch near the wall. There, in the warm litter above the melons, very cunningly hidden, he found twenty-five eggs, about the size of a bantam's eggs, but with whitish skin instead of shell.

"I was not a day too soon," he said; for he could see the baby cobras curled up inside the skin, and he knew that the minute they were hatched they could each kill a man or a mongoose. He bit off the tops of the eggs as fast as he could, taking care to crush the young cobras, and turned over the litter from time to time to see whether he had missed any. At last there were only three eggs left, and Rikki-tikki began to chuckle to himself, when he heard Darzee's wife screaming:

"Rikki-tikki, I led Nagaina toward the house, and she has gone into the veranda, and – oh, come quickly – she means killing!"

Rikki-tikki smashed two eggs, and tumbled backward down the melon-bed with the third egg in his mouth, and scuttled to the veranda as hard as he could put foot to the ground. Teddy and his mother and father were there at early breakfast; but Rikki-tikki saw that they were not eating anything. They sat stone-still, and their faces were white. Nagaina was coiled up on the matting by Teddy's chair, within easy striking-distance of Teddy's bare leg, and she was swaying to and fro singing a song of triumph.

"Son of the big man that killed Nag," she hissed, "stay still. I am not ready yet. Wait a little. Keep very still, all you three. If you move I strike, and if you do not move I strike. Oh, foolish people, who killed my Nag!"

Teddy's eyes were fixed on his father, and all his father could do was to whisper: "Sit still, Teddy. You mustn't move. Teddy, keep still."

Then Rikki-tikki came up and cried: "Turn round, Nagaina; turn and fight!"

"All in good time," said she, without moving her eyes. "I will settle my account with *you* presently. Look at your friends, Rikki-tikki. They are still and white; they are afraid. They dare not move, and if you come a step nearer I strike."

"Look at your eggs," said Rikki-tikki, "in the melon-bed near the wall. Go and look, Nagaina."

The big snake turned half round, and saw the egg on the veranda. "Ah-h! Give it to me," she said.

Rikki-tikki put his paws one on each side of the egg, and his eyes were blood-red. "What price for a snake's egg? For a young cobra? For a young king-cobra? For the last – the very last of the brood? The ants are eating all the others down by the melon-bed."

Nagaina spun clear round, forgetting everything for the sake of the one egg; and Rikki-tikki saw Teddy's father shoot out a big hand, catch Teddy by the shoulder, and drag him across the little table with the tea-cups, safe and out of reach of Nagaina.

"Tricked! Tricked! Tricked! *Rikk-tck-tck*!" chuckled Rikki tikki. "The boy is safe, and it was I – I – I that caught Nag by the hood last night in the bathroom." Then he began to jump up and down, all four feet together, his head close to the floor. "He threw me to and fro, but he could not shake me off. He was dead before the big man blew him in two. I did it. *Rikki-tikki-tck-tck!* Come then, Nagaina. Come and fight with me. You shall not be a widow long."

Nagaina saw that she had lost her chance of killing Teddy, and the egg lay between Rikki-tikki's paws. "Give me the egg, Rikki tikki. Give me the last of my eggs, and I will go away and never come back," she said, lowering her hood.

"Yes, you will go away, and you will never come back; for you will go to the rubbish-heap with Nag. Fight, widow! The big man has gone for his gun! Fight!"

Rikki-tikki was bounding all round Nagaina, keeping just out of reach of her stroke, his little eyes like hot coals. Nagaina gathered herself together, and flung out at him. Rikki-tikki jumped up and backward. Again and again and again she struck, and each time her head came with a whack on the matting of the veranda, and she gathered herself together like a watch-spring. Then Rikki-tikki danced in a circle to get behind her, and Nagaina spun round to keep her head to his head, so that the rustle of her tail on the matting sounded like dry leaves blown along by the wind.

He had forgotten the egg. It still lay on the veranda, and Nagaina came nearer and nearer to it, till at last, while Rikki-tikki was drawing breath, she caught it in her mouth, turned to the veranda steps, and flew like an arrow down the path, with Rikki-tikki behind her. When the cobra runs for her life, she goes like a whiplash flicked across a horse's neck.

Rikki-tikki knew that he must catch her, or all the trouble would begin again. She headed straight for the long grass by the thornbush, and as he was running Rikki-tikki heard Darzee still singing his foolish little song of triumph. But Darzee's wife was wiser. She flew off her nest as Nagaina came along, and flapped her wings about Nagaina's head. If Darzee had helped they might have turned her; but Nagaina only lowered her hood and went on. Still, the instant's delay brought Rikki-tikki up to her, and as she plunged into the rat-hole where she and Nag used to live, his little white teeth were clenched on her tail, and he went down with her – and very few mongooses, however wise and old they may be, care to follow a cobra into its hole. It was dark in the hole; and Rikki-tikki never knew when it might open out and give Nagaina room to turn and strike at him. He held on savagely, and struck out his feet to act as brakes on the dark slope of the hot, moist earth.

Then the grass by the mouth of the hole stopped waving, and Darzee said: "It is all over with Rikki-tikki! We must sing his death-song. Valiant Rikki-tikki is dead! For Nagaina will surely kill him underground."

So he sang a very mournful song that he made up on the spur of the minute, and just as he got to the most touching part the grass quivered again, and Rikki-tikki, covered with dirt, dragged himself out of the hole leg by leg, licking his whiskers. Darzee stopped with a little shout. Rikki-tikki shook some of the dust out of his fur and sneezed. "It is all over," he said. "The widow will never come out again." And the red ants that live between the grass-stems heard him, and began to troop down one after another to see if he had spoken the truth.

Rikki-tikki curled himself up in the grass and slept where he was – slept and slept till it was late in the afternoon, for he had done a hard day's work.

"Now," he said, when he awoke, "I will go back to the house. Tell the Coppersmith, Darzee, and he will tell the garden that Nagaina is dead."

The Coppersmith is a bird who makes a noise exactly like the beating of a little hammer on a copper pot; and the reason he is always making it is because he is the town-crier to every Indian garden, and tells all the news to everybody who cares to listen. As Rikki-tikki went up the path, he heard his "attention" notes like a tiny dinner-gong; and then the steady *"Ding-dong-tock!* Nag is dead – *dong!* Nagaina is dead! *Ding-dong-tock!"* That set all the birds in the garden singing, and the frogs croaking; for Nag and Nagaina used to eat frogs as well as little birds.

When Rikki got to the house, Teddy and Teddy's mother (she still looked very white, for she had been fainting) and Teddy's father came out and almost cried over him; and that night he ate all that was given him till he could eat no more, and went to bed on Teddy's shoulder, where Teddy's mother saw him when she came to look late at night.

"He saved our lives and Teddy's life," she said to her husband. "Just think, he saved all our lives."

Rikki-tikki woke up with a jump, for all the mongooses are light sleepers.

"Oh, it's you," said he. "What are you bothering for? All the cobras are dead; and if they weren't, I'm here."

Rikki-tikki had a right to be proud of himself; but he did not grow too proud, and he kept that garden as a mongoose should keep it, with tooth and jump and spring and bite, till never a cobra dared show its head inside the walls.

8

Darzee's Chant

(SUNG IN HONOUR OF RIKKI-TIKKI-TAVI)

SINGER AND tailor am I –
Doubled the joys that I know –
Proud of my lilt through the sky,
Proud of the house that I sew –

Over and under, so weave I my music – so weave I the
house that I sew.

Sing to your fledglings again,
Mother, oh, lift up your head!
Evil that plagued us is slain,
Death in the garden lies dead.
Terror that hid in the roses is impotent – flung on the
dung-hill and dead!

Who hath delivered us, who?
Tell me his nest and his name.
Rikki, the valiant, the true,
Tikki, with eyeballs of flame,
Rik-tikki-tikki, the ivory-fanged, the hunter with eyeballs
of flame.

Give him the Thanks of the Birds,
Blowing with tail-feathers spread!
Praise him with nightingale-words –
Nay, I will praise him instead.
Hear! I will sing you the praise of the bottle-tailed Rikki,
with eyeballs of red!

(Here Rikki-tikki interrupted, and the rest of the song is lost.)

9

The White Seal

OH! HUSH thee, my baby, the night is behind us,
And black are the waters that sparkled so green.
The moon, o'er the combers, looks downward to find us
At rest in the hollows that rustle between.
Where billow meets billow, there soft be thy pillow,
Ah, weary wee flipperling, curl at thy ease!
The storm shall not wake thee, nor shark overtake thee,
Asleep in the arms of the slow-swinging seas.

- *Seal Lullaby*

All these things happened several years ago at a place called Novastoshnah, or North-East Point, on the Island of St. Paul, away and away in the Bering Sea. Limmershin, the Winter Wren, told me the tale when he was blown on to the rigging of a steamer going to Japan, and I took him down into my cabin and warmed and fed him for a couple of days till he was fit to fly back to St. Paul's again. Limmershin is a very quaint little bird, but he knows how to tell the truth.

Nobody comes to Novastoshnah except on business, and the only people who have regular business there are the seals. They come in the summer months by hundreds and hundreds of thousands out of the cold grey sea; for Novastoshnah Beach has the finest accommodation for seals of any place in all the world.

Sea Catch knew that, and every spring would swim from whatever place he happened to be in – would swim like a torpedo-boat straight for Novastoshnah, and spend a month fighting with his companions for a good place on the rocks as close to the sea as possible. Sea Catch was fifteen years old, a huge gray fur-seal with almost a mane on his shoulders, and long, wicked dog-teeth. When he heaved himself up on his front flippers he stood more than four feet clear of the ground, and his weight, if anyone had been bold enough to weigh him, was nearly seven hundred pounds. He was scarred all over with the marks of savage fights, but he was always ready for just one fight more. He would put his head on one side, as though he were afraid to look his enemy in the face; then he would shoot it out like lightning, and when the big teeth were firmly fixed on the other seal's neck, the other seal might get away if he could, but Sea Catch would not help him.

Yet Sea Catch never chased a beaten seal, for that was against the Rules of the Beach. He only wanted room by the sea for his nursery; but as there were forty or fifty thousand other seals hunting for the same thing each spring, the whistling, bellowing, roaring, and blowing on the beach was something frightful.

From a little hill called Hutchinson's Hill you could look over three and a half miles of ground covered with fighting seals; and the surf was dotted all over with the heads of seals hurrying to land and begin their share of the fighting. They fought in the breakers, they fought in the sand, and they fought on the smooth-worn basalt rocks of the nurseries; for they were just as stupid and unaccommodating as men. Their wives never came to the island until late in May or early in June, for they did not care to be torn to pieces; and the young two -, three -, and four-year-old seals who had not begun housekeeping went inland about half a mile through the ranks of the fighters and played about on the sand-dunes in droves and legions, and rubbed off every single green thing that grew. They were called the holluschickie – the bachelors – and there were perhaps two or three hundred thousand of them at Novastoshnah alone.

Sea Catch had just finished his forty-fifth fight one spring when Matkah, his soft, sleek, gentle-eyed wife, came up out of the sea, and he caught her by the scruff of the neck and dumped her down on his reservation, saying gruffly: "Late, as usual. Where *have* you been?"

It was not the fashion for Sea Catch to eat anything during the four months he stayed on the beaches, and so his temper was generally bad. Matkah knew better than to answer back. She looked round and cooed: "How thoughtful of you! You've taken the old place again."

"I should think I had," said Sea Catch. "Look at me!"

He was scratched and bleeding in twenty places; one eye was almost blind, and his sides were torn to ribbons.

"Oh, you men, you men!" Matkah said, fanning herself with her hind flipper. "Why can't you be sensible and settle your places quietly? You look as though you had been fighting with the Killer Whale."

"I haven't been doing anything *but* fight since the middle of May. The beach is disgracefully crowded this season. I've met at least a hundred seals from Lukannon Beach, house-hunting. Why can't people stay where they belong?"

"I've often thought we should be much happier if we hauled out at Otter Island instead of this crowded place," said Matkah.

"Bah! Only the holluschickie go to Otter Island. If we went there they would say we were afraid. We must preserve appearances, my dear."

Sea Catch sunk his head proudly between his fat shoulders and pretended to go to sleep for a few minutes, but all the time he was keeping a sharp look-out for a fight. Now that all the seals and their wives were on the land, you could hear their clamour miles out to sea above the loudest gales. At the lowest counting there were over a million seals on the beach – old seals, mother seals, tiny babies, and holluschickie, fighting, scuffling, bleating, crawling, and playing together – going down to the sea and coming up from it in gangs and regiments, lying over every foot of ground as far as the eye could reach, and skirmishing about in brigades through the fog. It is nearly always foggy at Novastoshnah, except when the sun comes out and makes everything look all pearly and rainbow-coloured for a little while.

Kotick, Matkah's baby, was born in the middle of that confusion, and he was all head and shoulders, with pale, watery-blue eyes, as tiny seals must be; but there was something about his coat that made his mother look at him very closely.

"Sea Catch," she said at last, "our baby's going to be white!"

"Empty clam-shells and dry seaweed!" snorted Sea Catch. "There never has been such a thing in the world as a white seal."

"I can't help that," said Matkah; "there's going to be now." And she sang the low, crooning seal-song that all the mother seals sing to their babies –

You mustn't swim till you're six weeks old,
Or your head will be sunk by your heels;
And summer gales and Killer Whales
Are bad for baby seals.

Are bad for baby seals, dear rat,
As bad as bad can be;
But splash and grow strong,
And you can't be wrong.
Child of the Open Sea!

Of course the little fellow did not understand the words at

first. He paddled and scrambled about by his mother's side, and learned to scuffle out of the way when his father was fighting with another seal, and the two rolled and roared up and down the slippery rocks. Matkah used to go to sea to get things to eat, and the baby was fed only once in two days; but then he ate all he could, and throve upon it.

The first thing he did was to crawl inland, and there he met tens of thousands of babies of his own age, and they played together like puppies, went to sleep on the clean sand, and played again. The old people in the nurseries took no notice of them, and the holluschickie kept to their own grounds, so the babies had a beautiful playtime.

When Matkah came back from her deep-sea fishing she would go straight to their playground and call as a sheep calls for a lamb, and wait until she heard Kotick bleat. Then she would take the straightest of straight lines in his direction, striking out with her fore flippers and knocking the youngsters head over heels right and left. There were always a few hundred mothers hunting for their children through the playgrounds, and the babies were kept lively; but, as Matkah told Kotick, "So long as you don't lie in muddy water and get mange, or rub the hard sand into a cut or scratch, and so long as you never go swimming when there is a heavy sea, nothing will hurt you here."

Little seals can no more swim than little children, but they are unhappy till they learn. The first time that Kotick went down to the sea a wave carried him out beyond his depth, and his big head sank and his little hind flippers flew up exactly as his mother had told him in the song, and if the next wave had not thrown him back again he would have drowned.

After that he learned to lie in a beach-pool and let the wash of the waves just cover him and lift him up while he paddled, but he always kept his eye open for big waves that might hurt. He was two weeks learning to use his flippers; and all that while he floundered in and out of the water, and coughed and grunted and crawled up the beach and took cat-naps on the sand, and went back again, until at last he found that he truly belonged to the water.

Then you can imagine the times that he had with his companions, ducking under the rollers; or coming in on top of a comber and landing with a swash and a splutter as the big wave went whirling far up the beach; or standing up on his tail and scratching his head as the old people did; or playing "I'm the King of the Castle" on slippery, weedy rocks that just stuck out of the wash. Now and then he would see a thin fin, like a big shark's fin, drifting along close to shore, and he knew that that was the Killer Whale, the Grampus, who eats young seals when he can get them; and Kotick would head for the beach like an arrow, and the fin would jig off slowly, as if it were looking for nothing at all.

Late in October the seals began to leave St. Paul's for the deep sea, by families and tribes, and there was no more fighting over the nurseries, and the holluschickie played anywhere they liked. "Next year," said Matkah to Kotick, "you will be a holluschickie; but this year you must learn how to catch fish."

They set out together across the Pacific, and Matkah showed Kotick how to sleep on his back with his flippers tucked down by his side and his little nose just out of the water. No cradle is so comfortable as the long, rocking swell of the Pacific. When Kotick felt his skin tingle all over, Matkah told him he was learning the "feel of the water," and that tingly, prickly feelings meant bad weather coming, and he must swim hard and get away.

"In a little time," she said, "you'll know where to swim to, but just now we'll follow Sea Pig, the Porpoise, for he is very wise." A school of porpoises were ducking and tearing through the water, and little Kotick followed them as fast as he could. "How do you know where to go to?" he panted. The leader of the school rolled his white eyes and ducked under. "My tail tingles, youngster," he said. "That means there's a gale behind me. Come along! When you're south of the Sticky Water [he meant the Equator], and your tail tingles, that means there's a gale in front of you and you must head north. Come along! The water feels bad here."

This was one of very many things that Kotick learned, and he was always learning. Matkah taught him to follow the cod and the halibut along the under-sea banks, and wrench the rockling out of his hole among the weeds; how to skirt the wrecks lying a hundred fathoms below water, and dart like a rifle-bullet in at one port-hole and out at another as the fishes ran; how to dance on the top of the waves when the lightning was racing all over the sky, and wave his flipper politely to the stumpy-tailed Albatross and the Man-of-war Hawk as they went down the wind; how to jump three or four feet clear of the water, like a dolphin, flippers close to the side and tail curved; to leave the flying-fish alone because they are all bony; to take the shoulder-piece out of a cod at full speed ten fathoms deep; and never to stop and look at a boat or a ship, but particularly a row-boat. At the end of six months what Kotick did not know about deep-sea fishing was not worth the knowing; and all that time he never set flipper on dry ground.

One day, however, as he was lying half asleep in the warm water somewhere off the Island of Juan Fernandez, he felt faint and lazy all over, just as human people do when the spring is in their legs, and he remembered the good firm beaches of Novastoshnah seven thousand miles away, the games his companions played, the smell of the seaweed, the seal roar, and the fighting. That very minute he turned north, swimming steadily, and as he went on he met scores of his mates, all bound for the same place, and they said: "Greeting, Kotick! This year we are all holluschickie, and we can dance the Fire dance in the breakers off Lukannon and play on the new grass. But where did you get that coat?"

Kotick's fur was almost pure white now, and though he felt very proud of it, he only said: "Swim quickly! My bones are aching for the land." And so they all came to the beaches where they had been born, and heard the old seals, their fathers, fighting in the rolling mist.

That night Kotick danced the Fire dance with the yearling seals. The sea is full of fire on summer nights all the way down from Novastoshnah to Lukannon, and each seal leaves a wake like burning oil behind him, and a flaming flash when he jumps, and the waves break in great phosphorescent streaks and swirls. Then they went inland to the holluschickie grounds, and rolled up and down in the new wild wheat, and told stories of what they had done while they had been at sea. They talked about the Pacific as boys would talk about a wood that they had been nutting in, and if anyone had understood them, he could have gone away and made such a chart of that ocean as never was. The three- and four-year-old holluschickie romped down from Hutchinson's Hill, crying: "Out of the way, youngsters! The sea is deep, and you don't know all that's in it yet. Wait till you've rounded the Horn. Hi, you yearling, where did you get that white coat?"

"I didn't get it," said Kotick; "it grew." And just as he was going to roll the speaker over, a couple of black-haired men with flat red faces came from behind a sand-dune, and Kotick, who had never seen a man before, coughed and lowered his head. The holluschickie just bundled off a few yards and sat staring stupidly. The men were no less than Kerick Booterin, the chief of the seal -hunters on the island, and Patalamon, his son. They came from the little village not half a mile from the seal-nurseries, and they were deciding what seals they would drive up to the killing-pens (for the seals were driven just like sheep), to be turned into sealskin jackets later on.

"Ho!" said Patalamon. "Look! There's a white seal!"

Kerick Booterin turned nearly white under his oil and smoke, for he was an Aleut, and Aleuts are not clean people. Then he began to mutter a prayer. "Don't touch him, Patalamon. There has never been a white seal since – since I was born. Perhaps it is old Zaharrof's ghost. He was lost last year in the big gale."

"I'm not going near him," said Patalamon. "He's unlucky. Do you really think he is old Zaharrof come back? I owe him for some gulls' eggs."

"Don't look at him," said Kerick. "Head off that drove of four-year-olds. The men ought to skin two hundred today, but it's the beginning of the season, and they are new to the work. A hundred will do. Quick!"

Patalamon rattled a pair of seal's shoulder-bones in front of a herd of holluschickie, and they stopped dead, puffing and blowing. Then he stepped near, and the seals began to move, and Kerick headed them inland, and they never tried to get back to their companions. Hundreds and hundreds of thousands of seals watched them being driven, but they went on playing just the same. Kotick was the only one who asked questions, and none of his companions could tell him anything, except that the men always drove seals in that way for six weeks or two months of every year.

"I am going to follow," he said, and his eyes nearly popped out of his head as he shuffled along in the wake of the herd.

"The white seal is coming after us," cried Patalamon. "That's the first time a seal has ever come to the killing grounds alone."

"Hsh! Don't look behind you," said Kerick. "It is Zaharrof's ghost! I must speak to the priest about this."

The distance to the killing-grounds was only half a mile, but it took an hour to cover, because if the seals went too fast Kerick knew that they would get heated and then their fur would come off in patches when they were skinned. So they went on very slowly, past Sea-Lion's Neck, past Webster House, till they came to the Salt House just beyond the sight of the seals on the beach. Kotick followed, panting and wondering. He thought that he was at the world's end, but the roar of the seal-nurseries behind him sounded as loud as the roar of a train in a tunnel. Then Kerick sat down on the moss and pulled out a heavy pewter watch and let the drove cool off for thirty minutes, and Kotick could hear the fog-dew dripping from the brim of his cap. Then ten or twelve men, each with an iron-bound club three or four feet long, came up, and Kerick pointed out one or two of the drove that were bitten by their companions or were too hot, and the men kicked those aside with their heavy boots made of the skin of a walrus's throat, and then Kerick said "Let go!" and then the men clubbed the seals on the head as fast as they could.

Ten minutes later little Kotick did not recognize his friends any more, for their skins were ripped off from the nose to the hind flippers – whipped off and thrown down on the ground in a pile. That was enough for Kotick. He turned and galloped (a seal can gallop very swiftly for a short time) back to the sea, his little new mustache bristling with horror. At Sea-Lion's Neck, where the great sea-lions sit on the edge of the surf, he flung himself flipper over head into the cool water, and rocked there, gasping miserably. "What's here?" said a sea-lion gruffly; for as a rule the sea-lions keep themselves to themselves.

"*Scoochnie! Ochen scoochnie!* [I'm lonesome, very lonesome!]" said Kotick. "They're killing all the holluschickie on *all* the beaches!"

The sea-lion turned his head inshore. "Nonsense!" he said; "your friends are making as much noise as ever. You must have seen old Kerick polishing off a drove. He's done that for thirty years."

"It's horrible," said Kotick, backing water as a wave went over him, and steadying himself with a screw-stroke of his flippers that brought him all standing within three inches of a jagged edge of rock.

"Well done for a yearling!" said the sea-lion, who could appreciate good swimming. "I suppose it *is* rather awful from your way of looking at it; but if you seals will come here year after year, of course the men get to know of it, and unless you can find an island where no men ever come, you will always be driven."

"Isn't there any such island?" began Kotick.

"I've followed the *poltoos* [the halibut] for twenty years, and I can't say I've found it yet. But look here – you seem to have a fondness for talking to your betters; suppose you go to Walrus Islet and talk to Sea Vitch. He may know something. Don't flounce off like that. It's a six-mile swim, and if I were you I should haul out and take a nap first, little one."

Kotick thought that that was good advice, so he swam round to his own beach, hauled out, and slept for half an hour, twitching all over, as seals will. Then he headed straight for Walrus Islet, a little low sheet of rocky island almost due north-east from Novastoshnah, all ledges and rock and gulls' nests, where the walrus herded by themselves.

He landed close to old Sea Vitch – the big, ugly, bloated, pimpled, fat necked, long-tusked walrus of the North Pacific, who has no manners except when he is asleep – as he was then, with his hind flippers half in and half out of the surf.

"Wake up!" barked Kotick, for the gulls were making a great noise.

"Hah! Ho! Hmph! What's that?" said Sea Vitch, and he struck the next walrus a blow with his tusks and waked him up, and the next struck the next, and so on till they were all awake and staring in every direction but the right one.

"Hi! It's me," said Kotick, bobbing in the surf and looking like a little white slug.

"Well! May I be – skinned!" said Sea Vitch, and they all looked at Kotick as you can fancy a club full of drowsy old gentlemen would look at a little boy. Kotick did not care to hear any more about skinning just then; he had seen enough of it; so he called out: "Isn't there any place for seals to go where men don't ever come?"

"Go and find out," said Sea Vitch, shutting his eyes. "Run away. We're busy here."

Kotick made his dolphin-jump in the air and shouted as loud as he could: "Clam-eater! Clam-eater!" He knew that Sea Vitch never caught a fish in his life, but always rooted for clams and seaweeds; though he pretended to be a very terrible person. Naturally the Chickies and the Gooverooskies and the Epatkas, the Burgomaster Gulls and the Kittiwakes and the Puffins, who are always looking for a chance to be rude, took up the cry, and – so Limmershin told me – for nearly five minutes you could not have heard a gun fired on Walrus Islet. All the population was yelling and screaming: "Clam-eater! *Stareek* [old man!]" while Sea Vitch rolled from side to side grunting and coughing.

"*Now* will you tell?" said Kotick, all out of breath.

"Go and ask Sea Cow," said Sea Vitch. "If he is living still, he'll be able to tell you."

"How shall I know Sea Cow when I meet him?" said Kotick, sheering off.

"He's the only thing in the sea uglier than Sea Vitch," screamed a Burgomaster Gull, wheeling under Sea Vitch's nose. "Uglier, and with worse manners! *Stareek!*"

Kotick swam back to Novastoshnah, leaving the gulls to scream. There he found that no one sympathised with him in his little attempt to discover a quiet place for the seals. They told him that men had always driven the holluschickie – it was part of the day's work – and that if he did not like to see ugly things he should not have gone to the killing-grounds. But none of the other seals had seen the killing, and that made the difference between him and his friends. Besides, Kotick was a white seal.

"What you must do," said old Sea Catch, after he had heard his son's adventures, "is to grow up and be a big seal like your father, and have a nursery on the beach, and then they will leave you alone. In another five years you ought to be able to fight for yourself." Even gentle Matkah, his mother, said: "You will never be able to stop the killing. Go and play in the sea, Kotick." And Kotick went off and danced the Fire dance with a very heavy little heart.

That autumn he left the beach as soon as he could, and set off alone because of a notion in his bullet-head. He was going to find Sea Cow, if there was such a person in the sea, and he was going to find a quiet island with good firm beaches for seals to live on, where men could not get at them. So he explored and explored by himself from the North to the South Pacific, swimming as much as three hundred miles in a day and a night. He met with more adventures than can be told, and narrowly escaped being caught by the Basking Shark, and the Spotted Shark, and the Hammerhead, and he met all the untrustworthy ruffians that loaf up and down the seas, and the heavy polite fish, and the scarlet-spotted scallops that are moored in one place for hundreds of years, and grow very proud of it; but he never met Sea Cow, and he never found an island that he could fancy.

If the beach was good and hard, with a slope behind it for seals to play on, there was always the smoke of a whaler on the horizon, boiling down blubber, and Kotick knew what *that* meant. Or else he could see that seals had once visited the island and been killed off, and Kotick knew that where men had come once they would come again.

He picked up with an old stumpy-tailed albatross, who told him that Kerguelen Island was the very place for peace and quiet, and when Kotick went down there he was all but smashed to pieces against some wicked black cliffs in a heavy sleet-storm with lightning and thunder. Yet as he pulled out against the gale he could see that even there had once been a seal-nursery. And so it was in all the other islands that he visited.

Limmershin gave a long list of them, for he said that Kotick spent five seasons exploring, with a four months' rest each year at Novastoshnah, when the holluschickie used to make fun of him and his imaginary islands. He went to the Gallapagos, a horrid dry place on the Equator, where he was nearly baked to death; he went to the Georgia Islands, the South Orkneys, Emerald Island, Little Nightingale Island, Gough's Island, Bouvet's Island, the Crossets, and even to a little speck of an island south of the Cape of Good Hope. But everywhere the People of the Sea told him the same things. Seals had come to those islands once upon a time, but men had killed them all off. Even when he swam thousands of miles out of the Pacific, and got to a place called Cape Corrientes (that was when he was coming back from Gough's Island), he found a few hundred mangy seals on a rock, and they told him that men came there too.

That nearly broke his heart, and he headed round the Horn back to his own beaches; and on his way north he hauled out on an island full of green trees, where he found an old, old seal who was dying, and Kotick caught fish for him, and told him all his sorrows. "Now," said Kotick, "I am going back to Novastoshnah, and if I am driven to the killing-pens with the holluschickie I shall not care."

The old seal said: "Try once more. I am the last of the Lost Rookery of Masafuera, and in the days when men killed us by the hundred thousand there was a story on the beaches that some day a white seal would come out of the north and lead the seal people to a quiet place. I am old and I shall never live to see that day, but others will. Try once more."

And Kotick curled up his moustache (it was a beauty), and

said: "I am the only white seal that has ever been born on the beaches, and I am the only seal, black or white, who ever thought of looking for new islands."

That cheered him immensely; and when he came back to Novastoshnah that summer, Matkah, his mother, begged him to marry and settle down, for he was no longer a holluschick but a full-grown sea-catch, with a curly white mane on his shoulders, as heavy, as big, and as fierce as his father. "Give me another season," he said. "Remember, mother, it is always the seventh wave that goes farthest up the beach."

Curiously enough, there was another seal who thought that she would put off marrying till the next year, and Kotick danced the Fire dance with her all down Lukannon Beach the night before he set off on his last exploration. This time he went westward, because he had fallen on the trail of a great shoal of halibut, and he needed at least one hundred pounds of fish a day to keep him in good condition. He chased them till he was tired, and then he curled himself up and went to sleep on the hollows of the groundswell that sets in to Copper Island. He knew the coast perfectly well, so about midnight, when he felt himself gently bumped on a weed-bed, he said, "Hm, tide's running strong tonight," and turning over under water opened his eyes slowly and stretched. Then he jumped like a cat, for he saw huge things nosing about in the shoal water and browsing on the heavy fringes of the weeds.

"By the Great Combers of Magellan!" he said, beneath his moustache. "Who in the Deep Sea are these people?"

They were like no walrus, sea-lion, seal, bear, whale, shark, fish, squid, or scallop that Kotick had ever seen before. They were between twenty and thirty feet long, and they had no hind flippers, but a shovel-like tail that looked as if it had been whittled out of wet leather. Their heads were the most foolish-looking things you ever saw, and they balanced on the ends of their tails in deep water when they weren't grazing, bowing solemnly to one another and waving their front flippers as a fat man waves his arm.

"Ahem!" said Kotick. "Good sport, gentlemen?" The big things answered by bowing and waving their flippers like the Frog-Footman. When they began feeding again Kotick saw that their upper lip was split into two pieces that they could twitch apart about a foot and bring together again with a whole bushel of seaweed between the splits. They tucked the stuff into their mouths and chumped solemnly.

"Messy style of feeding, that," said Kotick. They bowed again, and Kotick began to lose his temper. "Very good," he said. "If you do happen to have an extra joint in your front flipper you needn't show off so. I see you bow gracefully, but I should like to know your names." The split lips moved and twitched, and the glassy green eyes stared; but they did not speak.

"Well!" said Kotick. "You're the only people I've ever met uglier than Sea Vitch – and with worse manners."

Then he remembered in a flash what the Burgomaster Gull had screamed to him when he was a little yearling at Walrus Islet, and he tumbled backward in the water, for he knew that he had found Sea Cow at last.

The sea cows went on schlooping and grazing and chumping in the weed, and Kotick asked them questions in every language that he had picked up in his travels: and the Sea People talk nearly as many languages as human beings. But the Sea Cows did not answer, because Sea Cow cannot talk. He has only six bones in his neck where he ought to have seven, and they say under the sea that that prevents him from speaking even to his companions; but, as you know, he has an extra joint in his fore flipper, and by waving it up and down and about he makes a sort of clumsy telegraphic code.

By daylight Kotick's mane was standing on end and his temper was gone where the dead crabs go. Then the Sea Cow began to travel northward very slowly, stopping to hold absurd bowing councils from time to time, and Kotick followed them, saying to himself; "People who are such idiots as these are would have been killed long ago if they hadn't found out some safe island; and what is good enough for the Sea Cow is good enough for the Sea Catch. All the same, I wish they'd hurry."

It was weary work for Kotick. The herd never went more than forty or fifty miles a day, and stopped to feed at night, and kept close to the shore all the time; while Kotick swam round them, and over them, and under them, but he could not hurry them up one half-mile. As they went farther north they held a bowing council every few hours, and Kotick nearly bit off his moustache with impatience till he saw that they were following up a warm current of water, and then he respected them more.

One night they sank through the shiny water – sank like stones – and, for the first time since he had known them, began to swim quickly. Kotick followed, and the pace astonished him, for he never dreamed that Sea Cow was anything of a swimmer. They headed for a cliff by the shore – a cliff that ran down into deep water, and plunged into a dark hole at the foot of it, twenty fathoms under the sea. It was a long, long swim, and Kotick badly wanted fresh air before he was out of the dark tunnel that they led him through.

"My wig!" he said, when he rose, gasping and puffing, into open water at the farther end. "It was a long dive, but it was worth it."

The sea cows had separated, and were browsing lazily along the edges of the finest beaches that Kotick had ever seen. There were long stretches of smooth-worn rock running for miles, exactly fitted to make seal-nurseries, and there were play grounds of hard sand sloping inland behind them, and there were rollers for seals to dance in, and long grass to roll in, and sand-dunes to climb up and down; and, best of all, Kotick knew by the feel of the water, which never deceives a true Sea Catch, that no men had ever come there.

The first thing he did was to assure himself that the fishing was good, and then he swam along the beaches and counted up the delightful low sandy islands half hidden in the beautiful rolling fog. Away to the northward out to sea ran a line of bars and shoals and rocks that would never let a ship come within six miles of the beach; and between the islands and the mainland was a stretch of deep water that ran up to the perpendicular cliffs, and somewhere below the cliffs was the mouth of the tunnel.

"It's Novastoshnah over again, but ten times better," said 0 Kotick. "Sea Cow must be wiser than I thought. Men can't come down the cliffs, even if there were any men; and the shoals to seaward would knock a ship to splinters. If any place in the sea is safe, this is it."

He began to think of the seal he had left behind him, but though he was in a hurry to go back to Novastoshnah, he thoroughly explored the new country, so that he would be able to answer all questions.

Then he dived and made sure of the mouth of the tunnel, and raced through to the southward. No one but a sea cow or a seal would have dreamed of there being such a place, and when he looked back at the cliffs even Kotick could hardly believe that he had been under them.

He was six days going home, though he was not swimming slowly; and when he hauled out just above Sea-Lion's Neck the first person he met was the seal who had been waiting for him, and she saw by the look in his eyes that he had found his island at last.

But the holluschickie and Sea Catch, his father, and all the other seals, laughed at him when he told them what he had discovered, and a young seal about his own age said: "This is all very well, Kotick, but you can't come from no one knows where and order us off like this. Remember we've been fighting for our nurseries, and that's a thing you never did. You preferred prowling about in the sea."

The other seals laughed at this, and the young seal began twisting his head from side to side. He had just married that year, and was making a great fuss about it.

"I've no nursery to fight for," said Kotick. "I only want to show you all a place where you will be safe. What's the use of fighting?"

"Oh, if you're trying to back out, of course I've no more to say," said the young seal, with an ugly chuckle.

"Will you come with me if I win?" said Kotick; and a green light came into his eye, for he was very angry at having to fight at all.

"Very good," said the young seal carelessly. "*If* you win, I'll come."

He had no time to change his mind, for Kotick's head darted out and his teeth sank in the blubber of the young seal's neck. Then he threw himself back on his haunches and hauled his enemy down the beach, shook him, and knocked him over. Then Kotick roared to the seals: "I've done my best for you these five seasons past. I've found you the island where you'll be safe, but unless your heads are dragged off your silly necks you won't believe. I'm going to teach you now. Look out for yourselves!"

Limmershin told me that never in his life – and Limmershin sees ten thousand big seals fighting every year – never in all his little life did he see anything like Kotick's charge into the nurseries. He flung himself at the biggest sea-catch he could find, caught him by the throat, choked him and bumped him and banged him till he grunted for mercy, and then threw him aside and attacked the next. You see, Kotick had never fasted for four months as the big seals did every year, and his deep-sea swimming-trips kept him in perfect condition, and, best of all, he had never fought before. His curly white mane stood up with rage, and his eyes flamed, and his big dogteeth glistened, and he was splendid to look at. Old Sea Catch, his father, saw him tearing past, hauling the grizzled old seals about as though they had been halibut, and upsetting the young bachelors in all directions; and Sea Catch gave one roar and shouted: "He may be a fool, but he is the best fighter on the Beaches. Don't tackle your father, my son! He's with you!"

Kotick roared in answer, and old Sea Catch waddled in his moustache on end, blowing like a locomotive, while Matkah and the seal that was going to marry Kotick cowered down and admired their menfolk. It was a gorgeous fight, for the two fought as long as there was a seal that dared lift up his head, and when there were none they paraded grandly up and down the beach side by side, bellowing.

At night, just as the Northern Lights were winking and flashing through the fog, Kotick climbed a bare rock and looked down on the scattered nurseries and the torn and bleeding seals. "Now," he said, "I've taught you your lesson."

"My wig!" said old Sea Catch, boosting himself up stiffly, for he was fearfully mauled. "The Killer Whale himself could not have cut them up worse. Son, I'm proud of you, and what's more, *I*'ll come with you to your island – if there is such a place."

"Hear you fat pigs of the sea! Who comes with me to the Sea Cow's tunnel? Answer, or I shall teach you again," roared Kotick.

There was a murmur like the ripple of the tide all up and down the beaches. "We will come," said thousands of tired voices. "We will follow Kotick, the White Seal."

Then Kotick dropped his head between his shoulders and shut his eyes proudly. He was not a white seal any more, but red from head to tail. All the same, he would have scorned to look at or touch one of his wounds.

A week later he and his army (nearly ten thousand holluschickie and old seals) went away north to the Sea Cow's tunnel, Kotick leading them, and the seals that stayed at Novastoshnah called them idiots. But next spring, when they all met off the fishing-banks of the Pacific, Kotick's seals told such tales of the new beaches beyond Sea Cow's tunnel that more and more seals left Novastoshnah.

Of course it was not all done at once, for the seals are not very clever, and they need a long time to turn things over in their minds, but year after year more seals went away from Novastoshnah, and Lukannon, and the other nurseries, to the quiet, sheltered beaches where Kotick sits all the summer through, getting bigger and fatter and stronger each year, while the holluschickie play round him, in that sea where no man comes.

10

Lukannon

[This is the great deep-sea song that all the St. Paul seals sing when they are heading back to their beaches in the summer. It is a sort of very sad seal National Anthem.]

I met my mates in the morning (and oh, but I am old!)
Where roaring on the ledges the summer ground-swell rolled;
I heard them lift the chorus that drowned the breakers' song –

The Beaches of Lukannon – two million voices strong!

The song of pleasant stations beside the salt lagoons,
The song of blowing squadrons that shuffled down the dunes,
The song of midnight dances that churned the sea to flame –
The Beaches of Lukannon – before the sealers came!

I met my mates in the morning (I'll never meet them more!);
They came and went in legions that darkened all the shore.
And through the foam-flecked offing as far as voice could reach
We hailed the landing-parties and we sang them up the beach.

The Beaches of Lukannon – the winter-wheat so tall –
The dripping, crinkled lichens, and the sea-fog drenching all!
The platforms of our playground, all shining smooth and worn!
The Beaches of Lukannon – thee home where we were born!

I meet my mates in the morning, a broken, scattered band.
Men shoot us in the water and club us on the land;
Men drive us to the Salt House like silly sheep and tame,
And still we sing Lukannon – before the sealers came.
Wheel down, wheel down to southward! oh, Gooverooska, go!

And tell the Deep-Sea Viceroys the story of our woe;
Ere, empty as the shark's egg the tempest flings ashore,
The Beaches of Lukannon shall know their sons no more!

11

Toomai of the Elephants

I WILL remember what I was. I am sick of rope and chain
  I will remember my old strength and all my forest affairs.
I will not sell my back to man for a bundle of sugar-cane,
  I will go out to my own kind, and the wood-folk in their lairs.

I will go out until the day, until the morning break,
  Out to the winds' untainted kiss, the waters' clean caress!
I will forget my ankle-ring and snap my picket-stake. .
  I will revisit my lost loves, and playmates masterless!

Kala Nag which means Black Snake, had served the Indian Government in every way that an elephant could serve it for forty-seven years, and as he was fully twenty years old when he was caught, that makes him nearly seventy – a ripe age for an elephant. He remembered pushing, with a big leather pad on his forehead, at a gun stuck in deep mud, and that was before the Aghan War of 1842, and he had not then come to his full strength.

His mother Radha Pyari – Radha the darling – who had been caught in the same drive with Kala Nag, told him, before his little milk-tusks had dropped out, that elephants who were afraid always got hurt; and Kala Nag knew that that advice was good, for the first time that he saw a shell burst he backed, screaming, into a stand of piled rifles, and the bayonets pricked him in all his softest places. So before he was twenty-five he gave up being afraid, and so he was the best-loved and the best-looked-after elephant in the service of the Government of India. He had carried tents, twelve hundred pounds' weight of tents, on the march in Upper India; he had been hoisted into a ship at the end of a steam-crane and taken for days across the water, and made to carry a mortar on his back in a strange and rocky country very far from India, and had seen the Emperor Theodore lying dead in Magdala, and had come back again in the steamer, entitled, so the soldiers said, to the Abyssinian War medal. He had seen his fellow-elephants die of cold and epilepsy and starvation and sunstroke up at a place called Ali Musjid, ten years later; and afterward he had been sent down thousands of miles south to haul and pile big balks of teak in the timber-yards at Moulmein. There he had half killed an insubordinate young elephant who was shirking his fair share of work.

After that he was taken off timber-hauling, and employed, with a few score other elephants who were trained to the business, in helping to catch wild elephants among the Garo hills. Elephants are very strictly preserved by the Indian Government. There is one whole department which does nothing else but hunt them, and catch them, and break them in, and send them up and down the country as they are needed for work.

Kala Nag stood ten fair feet at the shoulders, and his tusks had been cut off short at five feet, and bound round the ends, to prevent them splitting, with bands of copper; but he could do more with those stumps than any untrained elephant could do with the real sharpened ones.

When, after weeks and weeks of cautious driving of scattered elephants across the hills, the forty or fifty wild monsters were driven into the last stockade, and the big drop-gate, made of tree trunks lashed together, jarred down behind them, Kala Nag, at the word of command, would go into that flaring, trumpeting pandemonium (generally at night, when the flicker of the torches made it difficult to judge distances), and, picking out the biggest and wildest tusker of the mob, would hammer him and hustle him into quiet while the men on the backs of the other elephants roped and tied the smaller ones.

There was nothing in the way of fighting that Kala Nag, the old wise Black Snake, did not know, for he had stood up more than once in his time to the charge of the wounded tiger, and, curling up his soft trunk to be out of harm's way, had knocked the springing brute sideways in mid-air with a quick sickle-cut of his head, that he had invented all by himself; had knocked him over, and kneeled upon him with his huge knees till the life went out with a gasp and a howl, and there was only a fluffy striped thing on the ground for Kala Nag to pull by the tail.

"Yes," said Big Toomai, his driver, the son of Black Toomai who had taken him to Abyssinia, and grandson of Toomai of the Elephants who had seen him caught, "there is nothing that the Black Snake fears except me. He has seen three generations of us feed him and groom him, and he will live to see four."

"He is afraid of *me* also," said Little Toomai, standing up to his full height of four feet, with only one rag upon him. He was ten years old, the eldest son of Big Toomai, and, according to custom, he would take his father's place on Kala Nag's neck when he grew up, and would handle the heavy iron ankus, the elephant-goad that had been worn smooth by his father, and his grandfather, and his great-grandfather.

He knew what he was talking of; for he had been born under Kala Nag's shadow, had played with the end of his trunk before he could walk, had taken him down to water as soon as he could walk, and Kala Nag would no more have dreamed of disobeying his shrill little orders than he would have dreamed of killing him on that day when Big Toomai carried the little brown baby under Kala Nag's tusks, and told him to salute his master that was to be.

"Yes," said Little Toomai, "he is afraid of me," and he took long strides up to Kala Nag, called him a fat old pig, and made him lift up his feet one after the other.

"Wah!" said Little Toomai, "thou art a big elephant," and he wagged his fluffy head, quoting his father. "The Government may pay for elephants, but they belong to us mahouts. When thou art old, Kala Nag, there will come some rich Rajah, and he will buy thee from the Government, on account of thy size and thy manners, and then thou wilt have nothing to do but to carry gold earrings in thy ears, and a gold howdah on thy back, and a red cloth covered with gold on thy sides, and walk at the head of the processions of the King. Then I shall sit on thy neck, O Kala Nag, with a silver ankus, and men will run before us with golden sticks, crying, 'Room for the King's elephant!' That will be good, Kala Nag, but not so good as this hunting in the jungles."

"Umph!" said Big Toomai. "Thou art a boy, and as wild as a buffalo-calf. This running up and down among the hills is not the best Government service. I am getting old, and I do not love wild elephants. Give me brick elephant-lines, one stall to each elephant, and big stumps to tie them to safely, and flat, broad roads to exercise upon, instead of this come-and-go camping. Aha, the Cawnpore barracks were good. There was a bazaar close by, and only three hours' work a day."

Little Toomai remembered the Cawnpore elephant-lines and said nothing. He very much preferred the camp life, and hated those broad, flat roads, with the daily grubbing for grass in the forage-reserve, and the long hours when there was nothing to do except to watch Kala Nag fidgeting in his pickets.

What Little Toomai liked was to scramble up bridle-paths that only an elephant could take; the dip into the valley below; the glimpses of the wild elephants browsing miles away; the rush of the frightened pig and peacock under Kala Nag's feet; the blinding warm rains, when all the hills and valleys smoked; the beautiful misty mornings when nobody knew where they would camp that night; the steady, cautious drive of the wild elephants, and the mad rush and blaze and hullabaloo of the last night's drive, when the elephants poured into the stockade like boulders in a landslide, found that they could not get out, and flung themselves at the heavy posts only to be driven back by yells and flaring torches and volleys of blank cartridge.

Even a little boy could be of use there, and Toomai was as useful as three boys. He would get his torch and wave it, and yell with the best. But the really good time came when the driving out began, and the Keddah – that is, the stockade – looked like a picture of the end of the world, and men had to make signs to one another, because they could not hear themselves speak. Then Little Toomai would climb up to the top of one of the quivering stockade-posts, his sun-bleached brown hair flying loose all over his shoulders, and he looking like a goblin in the torch-light; and as soon as there was a lull you could hear his high-pitched yells of encouragement to Kala Nag, above the trumpeting and crashing, and snapping of ropes, and groans of the tethered elephants. "*Mail, mail*, Kala Nag! [Go on, go on, Black Snake!] *Dant do*! [Give him the tusk!] *Somalo! Somalo*! [Careful, careful!] *Maro! Mar*! [Hit him, hit him!] Mind the post! *Arre! Arre! Hai! Yai! Kya-a-ah*!" he would shout, and the big fight between Kala Nag and the wild elephant would sway to and fro across the Keddah, and the old elephant-catchers would wipe the sweat out of their eyes, and find time to nod to Little Toomai wriggling with joy on the top of the posts.

He did more than wriggle. One night he slid down from the post and slipped in between the elephants, and threw up the loose end of a rope, which had dropped, to a driver who was trying to get a purchase on the leg of a kicking young calf (calves always give more trouble than full-grown animals). Kala Nag saw him, caught him in his trunk, and handed him up to Big Toomai, who slapped him then and there, and put him back on the post.

Next morning he gave him a scolding, and said: "Are not good brick elephant-lines and a little tent-carrying enough, that thou must needs go elephant-catching on thy own account, little worthless? Now those foolish hunters, whose pay is less than my pay, have spoken to Petersen Sahib of the matter." Little Toomai was frightened. He did not know much of white men, but Petersen Sahib was the greatest white man in the world to him. He was the head of all the Keddah operations – the man who caught all the elephants for the Government of India, and who knew more about the ways of elephants than any living man.

"What – what will happen?" said Little Toomai.

"Happen! The worst that can happen. Petersen Sahib is a madman. Else why should he go hunting these wild devils? He may even require thee to be an elephant-catcher, to sleep anywhere in these fever-filled jungles, and at last to be trampled to death in the Keddah. It is well that this nonsense ends safely. Next week the catching is over, and we of the plains are sent back to our stations. Then we will march on smooth roads, and forget all this hunting. But, son, I am angry that thou shouldst meddle in the business that belongs to these dirty Assamese jungle folk. Kala Nag will obey none but me, so I must go with him into the Keddah; but he is only a fighting elephant, and he does not help to rope them. So I sit at my ease, as befits a mahout – not a mere hunter – a mahout, I say, and a man who gets a pension at the end of his service. Is the family of Toomai of the Elephants to be trodden underfoot in the dirt of a Keddah? Bad one! Wicked one! Worthless son! Go and wash Kala Nag and attend to his ears, and see that there are no thorns in his feet; or else Petersen Sahib will surely catch thee and make thee a wild hunter – a follower of elephants' foot-tracks, a jungle-bear. Bah Shame! Go!"

Little Toomai went off without saying a word, but he told Kala Nag all his grievances while he was examining his feet. "No matter," said Little Toomai, turning up the fringe of Kala Nag's huge right ear. "They have said my name to Petersen Sahib, and perhaps – and perhaps – and perhaps – who knows? Hai! That is a big thorn that I have pulled out!"

The next few days were spent in getting the elephants together, in walking the newly caught wild elephants up and down between a couple of tame ones, to prevent them giving too much trouble on the downward march to the plains, and in taking stock of the blankets and ropes and things that had been worn out or lost in the forest.

Petersen Sahib came in on his clever she-elephant Pudmini. He had been paying off other camps among the hills, for the season was coming to an end, and there was a native clerk sitting at a table under a tree, to pay the drivers their wages. As each man was paid he went back to his elephant, and joined the line that stood ready to start. The catchers, and hunters, and beaters, the men of the regular Keddah, who stayed in the jungle year in and year out, sat on the backs of the elephants that belonged to Petersen Sahib's permanent force, or leaned against the trees with their guns across their arms, and made fun of the drivers who were going away, and laughed when the newly caught elephants broke the line and ran about.

Big Toomai went up to the clerk with Little Toomai behind him, and Machua Appa, the head-tracker, said in an undertone to a friend of his, "There goes one piece of good elephant-stuff at least. 'Tis a pity to send that young jungle-cock to moult in the plains."

Now Petersen Sahib had ears all over him, as a man must have who listens to the most silent of all living things – the wild elephant. He turned where he was lying all along on Pudmini's back, and said, "What is that? I did not know of a man among the plains-drivers who had wit enough to rope even a dead elephant."

"This is not a man, but a boy. He went into the Keddah at the last drive, and threw Barmao there the rope when we were trying to get that young calf with the blotch on his shoulder away from his mother."

Machua Appa pointed at Little Toomai, and Petersen Sahib looked, and Little Toomai bowed to the earth.

"He throw a rope? He is smaller than a picket-pin. Little one, what is thy name?" said Petersen Sahib.

Little Toomai was too frightened to speak, but Kala Nag was behind him, and Toomai made a sign with his hand, and the elephant caught him up in his trunk and held him level with Pudmini's forehead, in front of the great Petersen Sahib. Then Little Toomai covered his face with his hands, for he was only a child, and except where elephants were concerned, he was just as bashful as a child could be.

"Oho!" said Petersen Sahib, smiling underneath his moustache, "and why didst thou teach thy elephant *that* trick? Was it to help thee steal green corn from the roofs of the houses when the ears are put out to dry?"

"Not green corn, Protector of the Poor – melons," said Little Toomai, and all the men sitting about broke into a roar of laughter. Most of them had taught their elephants that trick when they were boys. Little Toomai was hanging eight feet up in the air, and he wished very much that he were eight feet under ground.

"He is Toomai, my son, Sahib," said Big Toomai, scowling. "He is a very bad boy, and he will end in a jail, Sahib."

"Of that I have my doubts," said Petersen Sahib. "A boy who can face a full Keddah at his age does not end in jails. See, little one, here are four annas to spend in sweetmeats because thou hast a little head under that great thatch of hair. In time thou mayest become a hunter too." Big Toomai scowled more than ever. "Remember, though, that Keddahs are not good for children to play in," Petersen Sahib went on.

"Must I never go there, Sahib?" asked Little Toomai, with a big gasp.

"Yes." Petersen Sahib smiled again. "When thou hast seen the elephants dance. That is the proper time. Come to me when thou hast seen the elephants dance, and then I will let thee go into all the Keddahs."

There was another roar of laughter, for that is an old joke among elephant-catchers, and it means just never. There are great cleared flat places hidden away in the forests that are called elephants' ball-rooms, but even these are only found by accident, and no man has ever seen the elephants dance. When a driver boasts of his skill and bravery the other drivers say, "And when didst *thou* see the elephants dance?"

Kala Nag put Little Toomai down, and he bowed to the earth again and went away with his father, and gave the silver four-anna piece to his mother, who was nursing his baby brother, and they all were put up on Kala Nag's back, and the line of grunting, squealing elephants rolled down the hill-path to the plains. It was a very lively march on account of the new elephants, who gave trouble at every ford, and needed coaxing or beating every other minute.

Big Toomai prodded Kala Nag spitefully, for he was very angry, but Little Toomai was too happy to speak. Petersen Sahib had noticed him, and given him money, so he felt as a private soldier would feel if he had been called out of the ranks and praised by his commander-in-chief.

"What did Petersen Sahib mean by the elephant-dance?" he said, at last, softly to his mother.

Big Toomai heard him and grunted. "That thou shouldst never be one of these hill-buffaloes of trackers. *That* was what he meant. Oh, you in front, what is blocking the way?"

An Assamese driver, two or three elephants ahead, turned round angrily, crying: "Bring up Kala Nag, and knock this youngster of mine into good behaviour. Why should Petersen Sahib have chosen *me* to go down with you donkeys of the rice-fields? Lay your beast alongside, Toomai, and let him prod with his tusks. By all the gods of the Hills, these new elephants are possessed, or else they can smell their companions in the jungle." Kala Nag hit the new elephant in the ribs and knocked the wind out of him, as Big Toomai said, "We have swept the hills of wild elephants at the last catch. It is only your carelessness in driving. Must I keep order along the whole line?"

"Hear him!" said the other driver. "*We* have swept the hills! Ho! ho! You are very wise, you plains-people. Anyone but a mud-head who never saw the jungle would know that *they* know that the drives are ended for the season. Therefore all the wild elephants tonight will – but why should I waste wisdom on a river-turtle?"

"What will they do?" Little Toomai called out.

"*Ohe,* little one. Art thou there? Well, I will tell thee, for thou hast a cool head. They will dance, and it behoves thy father, who has swept *all* the hills of *all* the elephants, to double-chain his pickets tonight."

"What talk is this?" said Big Toomai. "For forty years, father and son, we have tended elephants, and we have never heard such moonshine about dances."

"Yes; but a plains-man who lives in a hut knows only the four walls of his hut. Well, leave thy elephants unshackled tonight and see what comes; as for their dancing, I have seen the place where – *Bapree-bap!* how many windings has the Dihang River?

Here is another ford, and we must swim the calves. Stop still, you behind there."

And in this way, talking and wrangling and splashing through the rivers, they made their first march to a sort of receiving-camp for the new elephants; but they lost their tempers long before they got there.

Then the elephants were chained by their hind legs to their big stumps of pickets, and extra ropes were fitted to the new elephants, and the fodder was piled before them, and the hill-drivers went back to Petersen Sahib through the afternoon light, telling the plains-drivers to be extra careful that night, and laughing when the plains-drivers asked the reason.

Little Toomai attended to Kala Nag's supper, and as evening fell wandered through the camp, unspeakably happy, in search of a tom-tom. When an Indian child's heart is full, he does not run about and make a noise in an irregular fashion. He sits down to a sort of revel all by himself. And Little Toomai had been spoken to by Petersen Sahib! If he had not found what he wanted, I believe he would have bursted. But the sweetmeat-seller in the camp lent him a little tom-tom – a drum beaten with the flat of the hand – and he sat down, cross-legged, before Kala Nag as the stars began to come out, the tom-tom in his lap, and he thumped and he thumped and he thumped, and the more he thought of the great honour that had been done to him, the more he thumped, all alone among the elephant-fodder. There was no tune and no words, but the thumping made him happy.

The new elephants strained at their ropes, and squealed and trumpeted from time to time, and he could hear his mother in the camp hut putting his small brother to sleep with an old, old song about the great God Shiv, who once told all the animals what they should eat. It is a very soothing lullaby, and the first verse says –

Shiv, who poured the harvest and made the winds to blow,
Sitting at the doorways of a day of long ago,
Gave to each his portion, food and toil and fate,
From the King upon the *guddee* to the Beggar at the gate.
All things made he – Shiva the Preserver.
Mahadeo! Mahadeo! He made all –
Thorn for the camel, fodder for the kine,
And mother's heart for sleepy head, O little son of mine!

Little Toomai came in with a joyous *tunk-a-tunk* at the end of each verse, till he felt sleepy and stretched himself on the fodder at Kala Nag's side.

At last the elephants began to lie down one after another, as is their custom, till only Kala Nag at the right of the line was left standing up; and he rocked slowly from side to side, his ears put forward to listen to the night wind as it blew very slowly across the hills. The air was full of all the night noises that, taken together, make one big silence – the click of one bamboo-stem against the other, the rustle of something alive in the undergrowth, the scratch and squawk of a half-waked bird (birds are awake in the night much more often than we imagine), and the fall of water ever so far away. Little Toomai slept for some time, and when he waked it was brilliant moonlight, and Kala Nag was still standing up with his ears cocked. Little Toomai turned, rustling in the fodder, and watched the curve of his big back against half the stars in heaven; and while he watched he heard, so far away that it sounded no more than a pinhole of noise pricked through the stillness, the "hoot-toot" of a wild elephant.

All the elephants in the lines jumped up as if they had been shot, and their grunts at last waked the sleeping mahouts, and they came out and drove in the picket-pegs with big mallets, and tightened this rope and knotted that till all was quiet. One new elephant had nearly grubbed up his picket, and Big Toomai took off Kala Nag's leg-chain and shackled that elephant fore-foot to hind-foot, but slipped a loop of grass-string round Kala Nag's leg, and told him to remember that he was tied fast. He knew that he and his father and his grandfather had done the very same thing hundreds of times before. Kala Nag did not answer to the order by gurgling, as he usually did. He stood still, looking out across the moonlight, his head a little raised, and his ears spread like fans, up to the great folds of the Garo hills.

"Tend to him if he grows restless in the night," said Big Toomai to Little Toomai, and he went into the hut and slept. Little Toomai was just going to sleep, too, when he heard the coir string snap with a little "tang", and Kala Nag rolled out of his pickets as slowly and as silently as a cloud rolls out of the mouth of a valley. Little Toomai pattered after him, barefooted, down the road in the moonlight, calling under his breath, "Kala Nag! Kala Nag! Take me with you, O Kala Nag!" The elephant turned without a sound, took three strides back to the boy in the moonlight, put down his trunk, swung him up to his neck, and almost before Little Toomai had settled his knees slipped into the forest.

There was one blast of furious trumpeting from the lines, and then the silence shut down on everything, and Kala Nag began to move. Sometimes a tuft of high grass washed along his sides as a wave washes along the sides of a ship, and sometimes a cluster of wild-pepper vines would scrape along his back, or a bamboo would creak where his shoulder touched it; but between those times he moved absolutely without any sound, drifting through the thick Garo forest as though it had been smoke. He was going uphill, but though Little Toomai watched the stars in the rifts of the trees, he could not tell in what direction.

Then Kala Nag reached the crest of the ascent and stopped for a minute, and Little Toomai could see the tops of the trees lying all speckled and furry under the moonlight for miles and miles, and the blue-white mist over the river in the hollow. Toomai leaned forward and looked, and he felt that the forest was awake below him – awake and alive and crowded. A big brown fruit-eating bat brushed past his ear; a porcupine's quills rattled in the thicket; and in the darkness between the tree-stems he heard a hog-bear digging hard in the moist, warm earth, and snuffing as it digged.

Then the branches closed over his head again, and Kala Nag began to go slowly down into the valley – not quietly this time, but as a runaway gun goes down a steep bank – in one rush. The huge limbs moved as steadily as pistons, eight feet to each stride, and the wrinkled skin of the elbow-points rustled. The undergrowth on either side of him ripped with a noise like torn canvas, and the saplings that he heaved away right and left with his shoulders sprang back again, and banged him on the flank, and great trails of creepers, all matted together, hung from his tusks as he threw his head from side to side and ploughed out his pathway. Then Little Toomai laid himself down close to the great neck, lest a swinging bough should sweep him to the ground, and he wished that he were back in the lines again.

The grass began to get squashy, and Kala Nag's feet sucked and squelched as he put them down, and the night mist at the bottom of the valley chilled Little Toomai. There was a splash and a trample, and the rush of running water, and Kala Nag strode through the bed of a river, feeling his way at each step. Above the noise of the water, as it swirled round the elephant's legs, Little Toomai could hear more splashing and some trumpeting both upstream and down – great grunts and angry snortings, and all the mist about him seemed to be full of rolling, wavy shadows.

"*Ai!*" he said, half aloud, his teeth chattering. "The elephant-folk are out tonight. It *is* the dance, then."

Kala Nag swashed out of the water, blew his trunk clear, and began another climb; but this time he was not alone, and he had not to make his path. That was made already, six feet wide, in front of him, where the bent jungle-grass was trying to recover itself and stand up. Many elephants must have gone that way only a few minutes before. Little Toomai looked back, and behind him a great wild tusker, with his little pig's eyes glowing like hot coals, was just lifting himself out of the misty river. Then the trees closed up again, and they went on and up, with trumpetings and crashings, and the sound of breaking branches on every side of them.

At last Kala Nag stood still between two tree-trunks at the very top of the hill. They were part of a circle of trees that grew round an irregular space of some three or four acres, and in all that space, as Little Toomai could see, the ground had been trampled down as hard as a brick floor. Some trees grew in the centre of the clearing, but their bark was rubbed away, and the white wood beneath showed all shiny and polished in the patches of moonlight. There were creepers hanging from the upper branches, and the bells of the flowers of the creepers, great waxy white things like convolvuluses, hung down fast asleep; but within the limits of the clearing there was not a single blade of green – nothing but the trampled earth.

The moonlight showed it all iron-grey, except where some elephants stood upon it, and their shadows were inky black. Little Toomai looked, holding his breath, with his eyes starting out of his head, and as he looked, more and more and more elephants swung out into the open from between the tree-trunks. Little Toomai could only count up to ten, and he counted again and again on his fingers till he lost count of the tens, and his head began to swim. Outside the clearing he could hear them crashing in the undergrowth as they worked their way up the hillside; but as soon as they were within the circle of the tree-trunks they moved like ghosts.

There were white-tusked wild males, with fallen leaves and nuts and twigs lying in the wrinkles of their necks and the folds of their ears; fat, slow-footed she-elephants, with restless little pinky-black calves only three or four feet high running under their stomachs; young elephants with their tusks just beginning to show, and very proud of them; lanky, scraggy old-maid elephants, with their hollow, anxious faces, and trunks like rough bark; savage old bull-elephants, scarred from shoulder to flank with great weals and cuts of bygone fights, and the caked dirt of their solitary mud-baths dropping from their shoulders; and there was one with a broken tusk and the marks of the full-stroke, the terrible drawing scrape, of a tiger's claws on his side.

They were standing head to head, or walking to and fro across the ground in couples, or rocking and swaying all by themselves – scores and scores of elephants.

Toomai knew that, so long as he lay still on Kala Nag's neck, nothing would happen to him; for even in the rush and scramble of a Keddah-drive a wild elephant does not reach up with his trunk and drag a man off the neck of a tame elephant; and these elephants were not thinking of men that night. Once they started and put their ears forward when they heard the chinking of a leg-iron in the forest, but it was Pudmini, Petersen Sahib's pet elephant, her chain snapped short off, grunting, snuffling up the hillside. She must have broken her pickets, and come straight from Petersen Sahib's camp; and Little Toomai saw another elephant, one that he did not know, with deep rope-galls on his back and breast. He, too, must have run away from some camp in the hills about.

At last there was no sound of any more elephants moving in the forest, and Kala Nag rolled out from his station between the trees and went into the middle of the crowd, clucking and gurgling, and all the elephants began to talk in their own tongue, and to move about.

Still lying down, Little Toomai looked down upon scores and scores of broad backs, and wagging ears, and tossing trunks, and little rolling eyes. He heard the click of tusks as they crossed other tusks by accident, and the dry rustle of trunks twined together, and the chafing of enormous sides and shoulders in the crowd, and the incessant flick and *hissh* of the great tails. Then a cloud came over the moon, and he sat in black darkness; but the quiet, steady hustling and pushing and gurgling went on just the same. He knew that there were elephants all round Kala Nag, and that there was no chance of backing him out of the assembly; so he set his teeth and shivered. In a Keddah at least there was torch light and shouting, but here he was all alone in the dark, and once a trunk came up and touched him on the knee.

Then an elephant trumpeted, and they all took it up for five or ten terrible seconds. The dew from the trees above spattered down like rain on the unseen backs, and a dull booming noise began, not very loud at first, and Little Toomai could not tell what it was; but it grew and grew, and Kala Nag lifted up one fore-foot and then the other, and brought them down on the ground – one-two, one-two, as steadily as trip-hammers. The elephants were stamping all together now, and it sounded like a war-drum beaten at the mouth of a cave. The dew fell from the trees till there was no more left to fall, and the booming went on, and the ground rocked and shivered, and Little Toomai put his hands up to his ears to shut out the sound. But it was all one gigantic jar that ran through him – this stamp of hundreds of heavy feet on the raw earth. Once or twice he could feel Kala Nag and all the others surge forward a few strides, and the thumping would change to the crushing sound of juicy green things being bruised, but in a minute or two the boom of feet on hard earth began again. A tree was creaking and groaning somewhere near him. He put out his arm and felt the bark, but Kala Nag moved forward, still tramping, and he could not tell where he was in the clearing. There was no sound from the elephants, except once when two or three little calves squeaked together. Then he heard a thump and a shuffle, and the booming went on. It must have lasted fully two hours, and Little Toomai ached in every nerve; but he knew by the smell of the night air that the dawn was coming.

The morning broke in one sheet of pale yellow behind the green hills, and the booming stopped with the first ray, as though the light had been an order. Before Little Toomai had got the ringing out of his head, before even he had shifted his position, there was not an elephant in sight except Kala Nag, Pudmini, and the elephant with the rope-galls, and there was neither sign nor rustle nor whisper down the hillsides to show where the others had gone.

Little Toomai stared again and again. The clearing, as he remembered it, had grown in the night. More trees stood in the middle of it, but the undergrowth and the jungle-grass at the sides had been rolled back. Little Toomai stared once more. Now he understood the trampling. The elephants had stamped out more room – had stamped the thick grass and juicy cane to trash, the trash into slivers, the slivers into tiny fibres, and the fibres into hard earth.

"Wah!" said Little Toomai, and his eyes were very heavy. "Kala Nag, my lord, let us keep by Pudmini and go to Petersen Sahib's camp, or I shall drop from thy neck."

The third elephant watched the two go away, snorted, wheeled round, and took his own path. He may have belonged to some little native king's establishment, fifty or sixty or a hundred miles away.

Two hours later, as Petersen Sahib was eating early breakfast, his elephants, who had been double-chained that night, began to trumpet, and Pudmini, mired to the shoulders, with Kala Nag, very foot-sore, shambled into the camp. Little Toomai's face was grey and pinched, and his hair was full of leaves and drenched with dew; but he tried to salute Petersen Sahib, and cried faintly: "The dance – the elephant-dance! I have seen it, and – I die!" As Kala Nag sat down, he slid off his neck in a dead faint.

But, since native children have no nerves worth speaking of, in two hours he was lying very contentedly in Petersen Sahib's hammock with Petersen Sahib's shooting-coat under his head, and a glass of warm milk, a little brandy, with a dash of quinine; inside of him; and while the old hairy, scarred hunters of the jungles sat three-deep before him, looking at him as though he were a spirit, he told his tale in short words, as a child will, and wound up with –

"Now, if I lie in one word, send men to see, and they will find that the elephant-folk have trampled down more room in their dance-room, and they will find ten and ten, and many times ten, tracks leading to that dance-room. They made more room with their feet. I have seen it. Kala Nag took me, and I saw. Also Kala Nag is very leg-weary!"

Little Toomai lay back and slept all through the long afternoon and into the twilight, and while he slept Petersen Sahib and Machua Appa followed the track of the two elephants for fifteen miles across the hills. Petersen Sahib had spent eighteen years in catching elephants, and he had only once before found such a dance-place. Machua Appa had no need to look twice at the clearing to see what had been done there, or to scratch with his toe in the packed, rammed earth.

"The child speaks truth," said he. "All this was done last night, and I have counted seventy tracks crossing the river. See, Sahib, where Pudmini's leg-iron cut the bark off that tree! Yes; she was there too."

They looked at one another, and up and down, and they wondered; for the ways of elephants are beyond the wit of any man, black or white, to fathom.

"Forty years and five," said Machua Appa, "have I followed my lord the elephant, but never have I heard that any child of man had seen what this child has seen. By all the Gods of the Hills, it is – what can we say?" and he shook his head.

When they got back to camp it was time for the evening meal. Petersen Sahib ate alone in his tent, but he gave orders that the camp should have two sheep and some fowls, as well as a double ration of flour and rice and salt, for he knew that there would be a feast.

Big Toomai had come up hot-foot from the camp in the plains to search for his son and his elephant, and now that he had found them he looked at them as though he were afraid of them both. And there was a feast by the blazing campfires in front of the lines of picketed elephants, and Little Toomai was the hero of it all; and the big brown elephant-catchers, the trackers and drivers and ropers, and the men who know all the secrets of breaking the wildest elephants, passed him from one to the other, and they marked his forehead with blood from the breast of a newly killed jungle-cock, to show that he was a forester, initiated and free of all the jungles.

And at last, when the flames died down, and the red light of the logs made the elephants look as though they had been dipped in blood too, Machua Appa, the head of all the drivers of all the Keddahs – Machua Appa, Petersen Sahib's other self, who had never seen a made road in forty years: Machua Appa, who was so great that he had no other name than Machua Appa – leaped to his feet, with Little Toomai held high in the air above his head, and shouted: "Listen, my brothers. Listen, too, you my lords in the lines there, for I, Machua Appa, am speaking! This little one shall no more be called Little Toomai, but Toomai of the Elephants, as his great-grandfather was called before him. What never man has seen he has seen through the long night, and the favour of the elephant-folk and of the Gods of the Jungles is with him. He shall become a great tracker; he shall become greater than I, even I – Machua Appa! He shall follow the new trail, and the stale trail, and the mixed trail, with a clear eye! He shall take no harm in the Keddah when he runs under their bellies to rope the wild tuskers; and if he slips before the feet of the charging bull-elephant, that bull-elephant shall know who he is and shall not crush him. *Aihai!* my lords in the chains' –" he whirled up the line of pickets – "here is the little one that has seen your dances in your hidden places – the sight that never man saw! Give him honour, my lords! *Salaam karo*, my children! Make your salute to Toomai of the Elephants! Gunga Pershad, ahaa! Hira Guj, Birchi Guj, Kuttar Guj, ahaa! Pudmini – thou hast seen him at the dance, and thou too, Kala Nag, my pearl among elephants! – ahaa! Together! To Toomai of the Elephants. *Barrao*!"

And at that last wild yell the whole line flung up their trunks till the tips touched their foreheads, and broke out into the full salute, the crashing trumpet-peal that only the Viceroy of India hears – the Salaam-ut of the Keddah.

But it was all for the sake of Little Toomai, who had seen what never man had seen before – the dance of the elephants at night and alone in the heart of the Garo hills!

12

Shiv and the Grasshopper

(THE SONG THAT TOOMAI'S MOTHER SANG TO THE BABY)

SHIV, WHO poured the harvest and made the winds to blow,
Sitting at the doorways of a day of long ago,
Gave to each his portion, food and toil and fate,
From the King upon the *guddee* to the Beggar at the gate.

All things made he – Shiva the Preserver.
Mahadeo! Mahadeo! He made all –
Thorn for the camel, fodder for the kine,
And mother's heart for sleepy head, O little son of mine!

Wheat he gave to rich folk, millet to the poor,
Broken scraps for holy men that beg from door to door;
Cattle to the tiger, carrion to the kite,
And rags and bones to wicked wolves without the wall at night.

Naught he found too lofty, none he saw too low –
Parbati beside him watched them come and go;
Thought to cheat her husband, turning Shiv to jest –
Stole the little grasshopper and hid it in her breast.

So she tricked him, Shiva the Preserver.
Mahadeo! Mahadeo! turn and see.
Tall are the camels, heavy are the kine,
But this was least of little things, O little son of mine!

When the dole was ended, laughingly she said,
Master, of a million mouths, is not one unfed?"
Laughing, Shiv made answer, "All have had their part,
Even he, the little one, hidden 'neath thy heart."
From her breast she plucked it, Parbati the thief,
Saw the Least of Little Things gnawed a new-grown leaf!
Saw and feared and wondered, making prayer to Shiv,
Who hath surely given meat to all that live.

All things made he – Shiva the Preserver.
Mahadeo! Mahadeo! He made all, -
Thorn for the camel, fodder for the kine,
And mother's heart for sleepy head, O little son of mine!

13

Her Majesty's Servants

You can work it out by Fractions or by simple Rule of Three,
But the way of Tweedle-dum is not the way of Tweedle-dee.
You can twist it, you can turn it, you can plait it till you drop,
But the way of Pilly-Winky's not the way of Winkie-Pop!

It had been raining heavily for one whole month – raining on a camp of thirty thousand men, and thousands of camels, elephants, horses, bullocks, and mules all gathered together at a place called awalpindi, to be reviewed by the Viceroy of India. He was receiving a visit from the Amir of Afghanistan – a wild king of a very wild country; the Amir had brought with him for a bodyguard eight hundred men and horses who had never seen a camp or a locomotive before in their lives – savage men and savage horses from somewhere at the back of Central Asia. Every night a mob of these horses would be sure to break their heel-ropes and stampede up and down the camp through the mud in the dark, or the camels would break loose and run about and fall over the ropes of the tents, and you can imagine how pleasant that was for men trying to go to sleep. My tent lay far away from the camel-lines, and I thought it was safe; but one night a man popped his head in and shouted, "Get out, quick! They're coming! My tent's gone!"

I knew who "they" were; so I put on my boots and waterproof and scuttled out into the slush. Little Vixen, my fox-terrier, went out through the other side; and then there was a roaring and a grunting and bubbling, and I saw the tent cave in, as the pole snapped, and begin to dance about like a mad ghost. A camel had blundered into it, and wet and angry as I was, I could not help laughing. Then I ran on, because I did not know how many camels might have got loose, and before long I was out of sight of the camp, ploughing my way through the mud.

At last I fell over the tail-end of a gun, and by that knew I was somewhere near the Artillery lines where the cannon were stacked at night. As I did not want to plowter about any more in the drizzle and the dark, I put my waterproof over the muzzle of one gun, and made a sort of wigwam with two or three rammers that I found, and lay along the tail of another gun, wondering where Vixen had got to, and where I might be.

Just as I was getting ready to sleep I heard a jingle of harness and a grunt, and a mule passed me shaking his wet ears. He belonged to a screwgun battery, for I could hear the rattle of the straps and rings and chains and things on his saddle-pad. The screw-guns are tiny little cannon made in two pieces that are screwed together when the time comes to use them. They are taken up mountains, anywhere that a mule can find a road, and they are very useful for fighting in rocky country.

Behind the mule there was a camel, with his big soft feet squelching and slipping in the mud, and his neck bobbing to and fro like a strayed hen's. Luckily, I knew enough of beast language – not wild-beast language, but camp-beast language, of course – from the natives to know what he was saying.

He must have been the one that flopped into my tent, for he called to the mule, "What shall I do? Where shall I go? I have fought with a white thing that waved, and it took a stick and hit me on the neck." (That was my broken tentpole, and I was very glad to know it.) "Shall we run on?"

"Oh, it was you," said the mule, "you and your friends, that have been disturbing the camp? All right. You'll be beaten for this in the morning; but I may as well give you something on account now."

I heard the harness jingle as the mule backed and caught the camel two kicks in the ribs that rang like a drum. "Another time," he said, "you'll know better than to run through a mule-battery at night, shouting `Thieves and fire!' Sit down, and keep your silly neck quiet."

The camel doubled up camel-fashion, like a two-foot rule, and sat down whimpering. There was a regular beat of hoofs in the darkness, and a big troop-horse cantered up as steadily as though he were on parade, jumped a gun-tail, and landed close to the mule.

"It's disgraceful," he said, blowing out his nostrils. "Those camels have racketed through our lines again – the third time this week. How's a horse to keep his condition if he isn't allowed to sleep. Who's here?"

"I'm the breech-piece mule of Number Two gun of the First Screw Battery," said the mule, "and the other's one of your friends. He's waked me up too. Who are you?"

"Number Fifteen, E troop, Ninth Lancers – Dick Cunliffe's horse. Stand over a little, there."

"Oh, beg your pardon," said the mule. "It's too dark to see much. Aren't these camels too sickening for anything? I walked out of my lines to get a little peace and quiet here."

"My lords," said the camel humbly, "we dreamed bad dreams in the night, and we were very much afraid. I am only a baggage-camel of the 39th Native Infantry, and I am not as brave so you are, my lords."

"Then why the pickets didn't you stay and carry baggage for the 39th Native Infantry, instead of running all round the camp?" said the mule.

"They were such very bad dreams," said the camel. "I am sorry. Listen! What is that? Shall we run on again?"

"Sit down," said the mule, "or you'll snap your long legs between the guns." He cocked one ear and listened. "Bullocks!" he said. "Gun-bullocks. On my word, you and your friends have waked the camp very thoroughly. It takes a good deal of prodding to put up a gun-bullock."

I heard a chain dragging along the ground, and a yoke of the great sulky white bullocks that drag the heavy siege-guns when the elephants won't go any nearer to the firing, came shouldering along together; and almost stepping on the chain was another battery-mule, calling wildly for "Billy."

"That's one of our recruits," said the old mule to the troop-horse. "He's calling for me. Here, youngster, stop squealing. The dark never hurt anybody yet."

The gun-bullocks lay down together and began chewing the cud, but the young mule huddled close to Billy.

"Things!" he said. "Fearful and horrible things Billy! They came into our lines while we were asleep. D'you think they'll kill us?"

"I've a very great mind to give you a number-one kicking," said Billy. "The idea of a fourteen-hand mule with your training disgracing the battery before this gentleman!"

"Gently, gently!" said the troop-horse. "Remember they are always like this to begin with. The first time I ever saw a man (it was in Australia when I was a three-year-old) I ran for half a day, and if I'd seen a camel I should have been running still."

Nearly all our horses for the English cavalry are brought to India from Australia, and are broken in by the troopers themselves.

"True enough," said Billy. "Stop shaking, youngster. The first time they put the full harness with all its chains on my back I stood on my forelegs and kicked every bit of it off. I hadn't learned the real science of kicking then, but the battery said they had never seen anything like it."

"But this wasn't harness or anything that jingled," said the young mule. "You know I don't mind that now, Billy. It was Things like trees, and they fell up and down the lines and bubbled; and my head-rope broke, and I couldn't find my driver, and I couldn't find you, Billy, so I ran off with – with these gentlemen."

"H'm!" said Billy. "As soon as I heard the camels were loose I came away on my own account, quietly. When a battery – a screw-gun mule calls gun-bullocks gentlemen, he must be very badly shaken up. Who are you fellows on the ground there?"

The gun-bullocks rolled their cuds, and answered both together: "The seventh yoke of the first gun of the Big Gun Battery. We were asleep when the camels came, but when we were trampled on we got up and walked away. It is better to lie quiet in the mud than to be disturbed on good bedding. We told your friend here that there was nothing to be afraid of, but he knew so much that he thought otherwise. Wah!"

They went on chewing.

"That comes of being afraid," said Billy. "You get laughed at by gun-bullocks. I hope you like it, young un."

The young mule's teeth snapped, and I heard him say something about not being afraid of any beefy old bullock in the world; but the bullocks only clicked their horns together and went on chewing.

"Now, don't be angry *after* you've been afraid. That's the worst kind of cowardice," said the troop-horse. "Anybody can be forgiven for being scared in the night, I think, if they see things they don't understand. We've broken out of our pickets, again and again, four hundred and fifty of us, just because a new recruit got to telling tales of whip-snakes at home in Australia till we were scared to death of the loose ends of our head-ropes."

"That's all very well in camp," said Billy; "I'm not above stampeding myself, for the fun of the thing, when I haven't been out for a day or two; but what do you do on active service?"

"Oh, that's quite another set of new shoes," said the troop-horse. "Dick Cunliffe's on my back then, and drives his knees into me, and all I have to do is to watch where I am putting my feet and to keep my hind legs well under me, and be bridle wise."

"What's bridle-wise?" said the young mule.

"By the Blue Gums of the Back Blocks," snorted the troop-horse, "do you mean to say that you aren't taught to be bridle-wise in your business? How can you do anything, unless you can spin round at once when the rein is pressed on your neck? It means life or death to your man, and of course that's life or death to you. Get round with your hind legs under you the instant you feel the rein on your neck. If you haven't room to swing round, rear up a little and come round on your hind legs. That's being bridle-wise."

"We aren't taught that way," said Billy the mule stiffly. "We're taught to obey the man at our head: step off when he says so, and step in when he says so. I suppose it comes to the same thing. Now, with all this fine fancy business and rearing, which must be very bad for your hocks, what do you *do*?"

"That depends," said the troop-horse. "Generally I have to go in among a lot of yelling, hairy men with knives – long shiny knives, worse than the farrier's knives – and I have to take care that Dick's boot is just touching the next man's boot without crushing it. I can see Dick's lance to the right of my right eye, and I know I'm safe. I shouldn't care to be the man or horse that stood up to Dick and me when we're in a hurry."

"Don't the knives hurt?" said the young mule.

"Well, I got one cut across the chest once, but that wasn't Dick's fault – "

"A lot I should have cared whose fault it was, if it hurt!" said the young mule.

"You must," said the troop-horse. "If you don't trust your man, you may as well run away at once. That's what some of our horses do, and I don't blame them. As I was saying, it wasn't Dick's fault. The man was lying on the ground, and I stretched myself not to tread on him, and he slashed up at me. Next time I have to go over a man lying down I shall step on him – hard."

"H'm!" said Billy; "it sounds very foolish. Knives are dirty things at any time. The proper thing to do is to climb up a mountain with a well-balanced saddle, hang on by all four feet and your ears too, and creep and crawl and wriggle along, till you come out hundreds of feet above anyone else, on a ledge where there's just room enough for your hoofs. Then you stand still and keep quiet – never ask a man to hold your head, young un – keep quiet while the guns are being put together, and then you watch the little poppy shells drop down into the tree-tops ever so far below."

"Don't you ever trip?" said the troop-horse.

"They say that when a mule trips you can split a hen's ear," said Billy. "Now and again *per-haps* a badly packed saddle will upset a mule, but it's very seldom. I wish I could show you our business. It's beautiful. Why, it took me three years to find out what the men were driving at. The science of the thing is never to show up against the skyline, because, if you do, you may get fired at. Remember that, young un. Always keep hidden as much as possible, even if you have to go a mile out of your way. I lead the battery when it comes to that sort of climbing."

"Fired at without the chance of running into the people who are firing!" said the troop-horse, thinking hard. "I couldn't stand that. I should want to charge, with Dick."

"Oh no, you wouldn't; you know that as soon as the guns are in position *they*'ll do all the charging. That's scientific and neat; but knives – pah!"

The baggage-camel had been bobbing his head to and fro for some time past, anxious to get a word in edgeways. Then I heard him say, as he cleared his throat, nervously –

"I – I – I have fought a little, but not in that climbing way or that running way."

"No. Now you mention it," said Billy, "you don't look as though you were made for climbing or running – much. Well, how was it, old Haybales?"

"The proper way," said the camel. "We all sat down – "

"Oh, my cropper and breastplate!" said the troop-horse under his breath. "Sat down!"

"We sat down – a hundred of us," the camel went on, "in a big square, and the men piled our packs and saddles outside the square, and they fired over our backs, the men did, on all sides of the square."

"What sort of men? Any men that came along?" said the troop-horse. "They teach us in riding-school to lie down and let our masters fire across us, but Dick Cunliffe is the only man I'd trust to do that. It tickles my girths, and, besides, I can't see with my head on the ground."

"What does it matter who fires across you?" said the camel. "There are plenty of men and plenty of other camels close by, and a great many clouds of smoke. I am not frightened then. I sit still and wait."

"And yet," said Billy, "you dream bad dreams and upset the camp at night. Well well! Before I'd lie down, not to speak of sitting down, and let a man fire across me, my heels and his head would have something to say to each other. Did you ever hear anything so awful as that?"

There was a long silence, and then one of the gun-bullocks lifted up his big head and said, "This is very foolish indeed. There is only one way of fighting."

"Oh, go on," said Billy. "*Please* don't mind me. I suppose you fellows fight standing on your tails?"

"Only one way," said the two together. (They must have been twins.) "This is that way. To put all twenty yoke of us to the big gun as soon as Two Tails trumpets." ("Two Tails" is camp slang for the elephant.)

"What does Two Tails trumpet for?" said the young mule.

"To show that he is not going any nearer to the smoke on the other side. Two Tails is a great coward. Then we tug the big gun all together – *Heya – Hullah! Heeyah! Hullah*! *We* do not climb like cats nor run like calves. We go across the level plain, twenty yoke of us, till we are unyoked again, and we graze while the big guns talk across the plain to some town with mud walls, and pieces of the wall fall out, and the dust goes up as though many cattle were coming home."

"Oh! And you choose that time for grazing?" said the young mule.

"That time or any other. Eating is always good. We eat till we are yoked up again and tug the gun back to where Two Tails is waiting for it. Sometimes there are big guns in the city that speak back, and some of us are killed, and then there is all the more grazing for those that are left. This is Fate – nothing but Fate. None the less, Two Tails is a great coward. That is the proper way to fight. We are brothers from Hapur. Our father was a sacred bull of Shiva. We have spoken."

"Well, I've certainly learned something tonight," said the troop-horse. "Do you gentlemen of the screw-gun battery feel inclined to eat when you are being fired at with big guns, and Two Tails is behind you?"

"About as much as we feel inclined to sit down and let men sprawl all over us, or run into people with knives. I never heard such stuff. A mountain ledge, a well-balanced load, a driver you can trust to let you pick your own way, and I'm your mule; but the other things – no!" said Billy, with a stamp of his foot.

"Of course," said the troop-horse, "everyone is not made in the same way, and I can quite see that your family, on your father's side, would fail to understand a great many things."

"Never you mind my family on my father's side," said Billy angrily, for every mule hates to be reminded that his father was a donkey. "My father was a Southern gentleman, and he could pull down and bite and kick into rags every horse he came across. Remember that, you big brown Brumby!"

Brumby means wild horse without any breeding. Imagine the feelings of Sunol if a car-horse called her a "skate," and you can imagine how the Australian horse felt. I saw the white of his eye glitter in the dark.

"See here, you son of an imported Malaga jackass," he said between his teeth. "I'd have you know that I'm related on my mother's side to Carbine, winner of the Melbourne Cup; and where *I* come from we aren't accustomed to being ridden over roughshod by any parrot-mouthed, pig-headed mule in a pop-gun pea-shooter battery. Are you ready?"

"On your hind legs!" squealed Billy. They both reared up facing each other, and I was expecting a furious fight, when a gurgly, rumbly voice called out of the darkness to the right: "Children, what are you fighting about there? Be quiet."

Both beasts dropped down with a snort of disgust, for neither horse nor mule can bear to listen to an elephant's voice.

"It's Two Tails!" said the troop-horse. "I can't stand him. A tail at each end isn't fair!"

"My feelings exactly," said Billy, crowding into the troop-horse for company. "We're very alike in some things."

"I suppose we've inherited them from our mothers," said the troop-horse. "It's not worth quarreling about. Hi! Two Tails, are you tied up?"

"Yes," said Two Tails, with a laugh all up his trunk. "I'm picketed for the night. I've heard what you fellows have been saying. But don't be afraid. I'm not coming over."

The bullocks and the camel said, half aloud: "Afraid of Two Tails – what nonsense!" And the bullocks went on: "We are sorry that you heard, but it is true. Two Tails, why are you afraid of the guns when they fire?"

"Well," said Two Tails, rubbing one hind leg against the other, exactly like a little boy saying poetry, "I don't quite know whether you'd understand."

"We don't, but we have to pull the guns," said the bullocks.

"I know it, and I know you are a good deal braver than you think you are. But it's different with me. My battery captain called me a Pachydermatous Anachronism the other day."

"That's another way of fighting, I suppose?" said Billy, who was recovering his spirits.

"*You* don't know what that means, of course, but I do. It means betwixt and between, and that is just where I am. I can see inside my head what will happen when a shell bursts; and you bullocks can't."

"I can," said the troop-horse. "At least a little bit. I try not to think about it."

"I can see more than you, and I *do* think about it. I know there's a great deal of me to take care of, and I know that nobody knows how to cure me when I'm sick. All they can do is to stop my driver's pay till I get well, and I can't trust my driver."

"Ah!" said the troop-horse. "That explains it. I can trust Dick."

"You could put a whole regiment of Dicks on my back without making me feel any better. I know just enough to be uncomfortable, and not enough to go on in spite of it."

"We do not understand," said the bullocks.

"I know you don't. I'm not talking to you. You don't know what blood is."

"We do," said the bullocks. "It is red stuff that soaks into the ground and smells."

The troop-horse gave a kick and a bound and a snort.

"Don't talk of it," he said. "I can smell it now, just thinking of it. It makes me want to run – when I haven't Dick on my back."

"But it is not here," said the camel and the bullocks. "Why are you so stupid?"

"It's vile stuff," said Billy. "I don't want to run, but I don't want to talk about it."

"There you are!" said Two Tails, waving his tail to explain.

"Surely. Yes, we have been here all night," said the bullocks.

Two Tails stamped his foot till the iron ring on it jingled. "Oh,

I'm not talking to *you.* You can't see inside your heads."

"No. We see out of our four eyes," said the bullocks. "We see straight in front of us."

"If I could do that and nothing else you wouldn't be needed to pull the big guns at all. If I was like my captain – he can see things inside his head before the firing begins, and he shakes all over, but he knows too much to run away – if I was like him I could pull the guns. But if I were as wise as all that I should never be here. I should be a king in the forest, as I used to be, sleeping half the day and bathing when I liked. I haven't had a good bath for a month."

"That's all very fine," said Billy; "but giving a thing a long name doesn't make it any better."

"H'sh!" said the troop-horse. "I think I understand what Two Tails means."

"You'll understand better in a minute," said Two Tails angrily. "Now you just explain to me why you don't like *this*!"

He began trumpeting furiously at the top of his trumpet.

"Stop that!" said Billy and the troop-horse together, and I could hear them stamp and shiver. An elephant's trumpeting is always nasty, especially on a dark night.

"I shan't stop," said Two Tails. "Won't you explain that, please? *Hhrrmph! Rrrt! Rrrmph! Rrrhha!*" Then he stopped suddenly, and I heard a little whimper in the dark, and knew that Vixen had found me at last. She knew as well as I did that if there is one thing in the world the elephant is more afraid of than another, it is a little barking dog; so she stopped to bully Two Tails in his pickets, and yapped round his big feet. Two Tails shuffled and squeaked. "Go away, little dog!" he said. "Don't snuff at my ankles, or I'll kick at you. Good little dog – nice little doggie, then! Go home, you yelping little beast! Oh, why doesn't someone take her away? She'll bite me in a minute."

"Seems to me," said Billy to the troop-horse, "that our friend Two Tails is afraid of most things. Now, if I had a full meal for every dog I've kicked across the parade-ground, I should be nearly as fat as Two Tails."

I whistled, and Vixen ran up to me, muddy all over, and licked my nose, and told me a long tale about hunting for me all through the camp. I never let her know that I understood beast talk, or she would have taken all sorts of liberties. So I buttoned her into the breast of my overcoat, and Two Tails shuffled and stamped and growled to himself.

"Extraordinary! Most extraordinary!" he said. "It runs in our family. Now, where has that nasty little beast gone to?"

I heard him feeling about with his trunk.

"We all seem to be affected in various ways," he went on, blowing his nose. "Now, you gentlemen were alarmed, I believe, when I trumpeted."

"Not alarmed, exactly," said the troop-horse, "but it made me feel as though I had hornets where my saddle ought to be. Don't begin again."

"I'm frightened of a little dog, and the camel here is frightened by bad dreams in the night."

"It is very lucky for us that we haven't all got to fight in the same way," said the troop-horse.

"What I want to know," said the young mule, who had been quiet for a long time – "what I want to know is, why we have to fight at all."

"Because we're told to," said the troop-horse, with a snort of contempt.

"Orders," said Billy the mule, and his teeth snapped.

"*Hukm hai*! (It is an order)", said the camel with a gurgle and Two Tails and the bullocks repeated, "*Hukm hai!*"

"Yes, but who gives the orders?" said the recruit-mule.

"The man who walks at your head – Or sits on your back – Or holds the nose-rope – Or twists your tail," said Billy and the troop-horse and the camel and the bullocks one after the other.

"But who gives them the orders?"

"Now you want to know too much, young un," said Billy, "and that is one way of getting kicked. All you have to do is to obey the man at your head and ask no questions."

"He's quite right," said Two Tails. "I can't always obey, because I'm betwixt and between; but Billy's right. Obey the man next to you who gives the order, or you'll stop all the battery, besides getting a thrashing."

The gun-bullocks got up to go. "Morning is coming," they said. "We will go back to our lines. It is true that we only see out of our eyes, and we are not very clever; but still, we are the only people to night who have not been afraid. Good-night, you brave people."

Nobody answered, and the troop-horse said, to change the conversation, "Where's that little dog? A dog means a man somewhere about."

"Here I am," yapped Vixen, "under the guntail with my man. You big, blundering beast of a camel, you, you upset our tent. My man's very angry."

"Phew!" said the bullocks. "He must be white!"

"Of course he is," said Vixen. "Do you suppose I'm looked after by a black bullock-driver?"

"*Huah! Ouach! Ugh*!" said the bullocks. "Let us get away quickly."

They plunged forward in the mud, and managed somehow to run their yoke on the pole of an ammunition-wagon, where it jammed.

"Now you *have* done it," said Billy calmly. "Don't struggle. You're hung up till daylight. What on earth's the matter?"

The bullocks went off into the long, hissing snorts that Indian cattle give, and pushed and crowded and slued and stamped and slipped and nearly fell down in the mud, grunting savagely.

"You'll break your necks in a minute," said the troop-horse. "What's the matter with white men? I live with 'em."

"They – eat – us! Pull!" said the near bullock: the yoke snapped with a twang, and they lumbered off together.

I never knew before what made Indian cattle so scared of Englishmen. We eat beef – a thing that no cattle-driver touches – and of course the cattle do not like it.

"May I be flogged with my own pad-chains! Who'd have thought of two big lumps like those losing their heads?" said Billy.

"Never mind. I'm going to look at this man. Most of the white men, I know, have things in their pockets," said the troop-horse.

"I'll leave you, then. I can't say I'm overfond of 'em myself. Besides, white men who haven't a place to sleep in are more than likely to be thieves, and I've a good deal of Government property on my back. Come along, young un, and we'll go back to our lines. Good-night, Australia! See you on parade tomorrow, I suppose. Good-night old Hay-bales! – try to control your feelings, won't you? Good-night, Two Tails! If you pass us on the ground tomorrow, don't trumpet. It spoils our formation."

Billy the mule stumped off with the swaggering limp of an old campaigner, as the troop-horse's head came nuzzling into my breast, and I gave him biscuits; while Vixen, who is a most conceited little dog, told him fibs about the scores of horses that she and I kept.

"I'm coming to the parade tomorrow in my dog-cart," she

said. "Where will you be?"

"On the left hand of the second squadron. I set the time for all my troop, little lady," he said politely. "Now I must go back to Dick. My tail's all muddy, and he'll have two hours' hard work dressing me for parade."

The big parade of all the thirty thousand men was held that afternoon, and Vixen and I had a good place close to the Viceroy and the Amir of Afghanistan, with his high, big black hat of astrakhan wool and the great diamond star in the centre. The first part of the review was all sunshine, and the regiments went by in wave upon wave of legs all moving together, and guns all in a line, till our eyes grew dizzy. Then the cavalry came up, to the beautiful cavalry canter of "Bonnie Dundee," and Vixen cocked her ear where she sat on the dog-cart. The second squadron of the Lancers shot by, and there was the troop-horse, with his tail like spun silk, his head pulled into his breast, one ear forward and one back, setting the time for all his squadron, his legs going as smoothly as waltz-music. Then the big guns came by, and I saw Two Tails and two other elephants harnessed in line to a forty-pounder siege-gun, while twenty yoke of oxen walked behind. The seventh pair had a new yoke, and they looked rather stiff and tired. Last came the screw-guns, and Billy the mule carried himself as though he commanded all the troops, and his harness was oiled and polished till it winked. I gave a cheer all by myself for Billy the mule, but he never looked right or left.

The rain began to fall again, and for a while it was too misty to see what the troops were doing. They had made a big half-circle across the plain, and were spreading out into a line. That line grew and grew and grew till it was three-quarters of a mile long from wing to wing – one solid wall of men, horses, and guns. Then it came on straight toward the Viceroy and the Amir, and as it got nearer the ground began to shake, like the deck of a steamer when the engines are going fast.

Unless you have been there you cannot imagine what a frightening effect this steady come-down of troops has on the spectators, even when they know it is only a review. I looked at the Amir. Up till then he had not shown the shadow of a sign of astonishment or anything else; but now his eyes began to get bigger and bigger, and he picked up the reins on his horse's neck and looked behind him. For a minute it seemed as though he were going to draw his sword and slash his way out through the English men and women in the carriages at the back. Then the advance stopped dead, the ground stood still, the whole line saluted, and thirty bands began to play all together. That was the end of the review, and the regiments went off to their camps in the rain; and an infantry band struck up –

> The animals went in two by two,
> Hurrah!
> The animals went in two by two,
> The elephant and the battery mul',
> and they all got into the Ark
> For to get out of the rain!

Then I heard an old grizzled, long-haired Central Asian chief, who had come down with the Amir, asking questions of a native officer.

"Now," said he, "in what manner was this wonderful thing done?"

And the officer answered, "An order was given, and they obeyed."

"But are the beasts as wise as the men?" said the chief.

"They obey, as the men do. Mule, horse, elephant, or bullock, he obeys his driver, and the driver his sergeant, and the sergeant his lieutenant, and the lieutenant his captain, and the captain his major, and the major his colonel, and the colonel his brigadier commanding three regiments, and the brigadier his general, who obeys the Viceroy, who is the servant of the Empress. Thus it is done."

"Would it were so in Afghanistan!" said the chief; "for there we obey only our own wills."

"And for that reason," said the native officer, twirling his moustache, "your Amir whom you do not obey must come here and take orders from our Viceroy."

14

Parade Song of the Camp Animals

ELEPHANTS OF THE GUN-TEAMS

WE LENT to Alexander the strength of Hercules,
The wisdom of our foreheads, the cunning of our knees;
We bowed our necks to service; they ne'er were loosed again –
Make way there, way for the ten-foot teams
Of the Forty-Pounder train!

Gun-Bullocks

Those heroes in their harnesses avoid a cannon-ball,
And what they know of powder upsets them one and all;
Then we come into action and tug the guns again –
Make way there way for the twenty yoke
Of the Forty-Pounder train!

Cavalry Horses

By the brand on my withers, the finest of tunes
Is played by the Lancers, Hussars, and Dragoons,
And it's sweeter than "Stables" or "Water" to me,
The Cavalry Canter of "Bonnie Dundee"!

Then feed us and break us and handle and groom,
And give us good riders and plenty of room,
And launch us in column of squadron and see
The way of the war-horse to "Bonnie Dundee"!

Screw-Gun Mules

As me and my companions were scrambling up a hill,
The path was lost in rolling stones, but we went forward still;
For we can wriggle and climb, my lads, and turn up everywhere,
And it's our delight on a mountain height, with a leg or two to spare!

Good luck to every sergeant, then, that lets us pick our road!
Bad luck to all the driver-men that cannot pack a load!
For we can wriggle and climb, my lads, and turn up everywhere,
And it's our delight on a mountain height, with a leg or two to spare!

COMMISSARIAT CAMELS

We haven't a camelty tune of our own
To help us trollop along,
But every neck is a hair-trombone
(Rtt-ta-ta-ta! is a hair-trombone!)
And this our marching-song:
Can't! Don't! Shan't! Won't!
Pass it along the line!
Somebody's pack has slid from his back,
'Wish it were only mine!
Somebody's load has tipped off in the road –
Cheer for a halt and a row!
Urrr! Yarrh! Grr! Arrh!
Somebody's catching it now.

All the Beasts Together

Children of the Camp are we,
Serving each in his degree;
Children of the yoke and goad,
Pack and harness, pad and load.
See our line across the plain,
Like a heel-rope bent again,
Reaching, writhing, rolling far,
Sweeping all away to war!
While the men that walk beside,
Dusty, silent, heavy-eyed,
Cannot tell why we or they
March and suffer day by day.

Children of the Camp are we,
Serving each in his degree;
Children of the yoke and goad,
Pack and harness, pad and load!

THE END

KIM

CHAPTER 1

Oh ye who tread the Narrow Way
By Tophet-flare to Judgment Day,
Be gentle when the heathen pray
To Buddha at *Kamakura*!

HE SAT, In Defiance of municipal orders, astride the gun Zam-Zammah on her brick platform opposite the old Ajaib-Gher – the Wonder House, as the natives call the Lahore Museum. Who hold Zam-Zammah, that 'fire-breathing dragon,' hold the Punjab; for the great green-bronze piece is always first of the conqueror's loot.

There was some justification for Kim, – he had kicked Lala Dinanath's boy off the trunnions – since the English held the Punjab and Kim was English. Though he was burned black as any native; though he spoke the vernacular by preference, and his mother-tongue in a clipped uncertain sing-song; though he consorted on terms of perfect equality with the small boys of the bazar; Kim was white – a poor white of the very poorest. The half-caste woman who looked after him (she smoked opium, and pretended to keep a second-hand furniture shop by the square where the cheap cabs wait) told the missionaries that she was Kim's mother's sister; but his mother had been nursemaid in a colonel's family and had married Kimball O'Hara, a young colour-sergeant of the Mavericks, an Irish regiment. He afterwards took a post on the Sind, Punjab, and Delhi railway, and his regiment went home without him. The wife died of cholera in Ferozepore, and O'Hara fell to drink and loafing up and down the line with the keen-eyed three-year-old baby. Societies and chaplains anxious for the child, tried to catch him, but O'Hara drifted away, till he came across the woman who took opium and learned the taste from her, and died as poor whites die in India. His estate at death consisted of three papers – one he called his '*ne varietur*'* because those words were written below his signature thereon, and another his 'clearance-certificate.' The third was Kim's birth-certificate. Those things, he was used to say, in his glorious opium hours, would yet make little Kimball a man. On no account was Kim to part with them, for they belonged to a great piece of magic – such magic as men practised over yonder behind the Museum, in the big blue and white Jadoo-Gher – the Magic House, as we name the Masonic Lodge. It would, he said, all come right some day, and Kim's horn would be exalted between pillars – monstrous pillars – of beauty and strength. The Colonel himself, riding on a horse, at the head of the finest regiment in the world, would attend to Kim, – little Kim that should have been better off than his father. Nine hundred first-class devils, whose god was a Red Bull on a green field, would attend to Kim, if they had not forgotten O'Hara – poor O'Hara that was gang-foreman on the Ferozepore line. Then he would weep bitterly in the broken rush chair on the verandah. So it came about after his death that the woman sewed parchment, paper, and birth-certificate into a leather amulet-case which she strung round Kim's neck.

'And some day,' she said, confusedly remembering O'Hara's prophecies, 'there will come for you a great Red Bull on a green field, and the Colonel riding on his tall horse, yes, and' – dropping into English – 'nine hundred devils.'

'Ah,' said Kim, 'I shall remember. A Red Bull and a Colonel on a horse will come, but first, my father said, will come the two men making ready the ground for these matters. That is how, my father said, they always did; and it is always so when men work magic.'

* Not true.

If the woman had sent Kim up to the local Jadoo-Gher with those papers, he would, of course, have been taken over by the Provincial Lodge and sent to the Masonic Orphanage in the Hills; but what she had heard of magic she distrusted. Kim, too, held views of his own. As he reached the years of indiscretion, he learned to avoid missionaries and white men of serious aspect who asked who he was, and what he did. For Kim did nothing with an immense success. True, he knew the wonderful walled city of Lahore from the Delhi Gate to the outer Fort Ditch; was hand in glove with men who led lives stranger than anything Haroun al Raschid dreamed of; and he lived in a life wild as that of the Arabian Nights, but missionaries and secretaries of charitable societies could not see the beauty of it. His nickname through the wards was 'Little Friend of all the World'; and very often, being lithe and inconspicuous, he executed commissions by night on the crowded housetops for sleek and shiny young men of fashion. It was intrigue, of course, – he knew that much, as he had known all evil since he could speak, – but what he loved was the game for its own sake – the stealthy prowl through the dark gullies and lanes, the crawl up a water-pipe, the sights and sounds of the women's world on the flat roofs, and the headlong flight from housetop to housetop under cover of the hot dark. Then there were holy men, ash-smeared *faquirs* by their brick shrines under the trees at the riverside, with whom he was quite familiar – greeting them as they returned from begging-tours, and, when no one was by, eating from the same dish. The woman who looked after him insisted with tears that he should wear European clothes – trousers, a shirt, and a battered hat. Kim found it easier to slip into Hindu or Mohammedan garb when engaged on certain businesses. One of the young men of fashion – he who was found dead at the bottom of a well on the night of the earthquake – had once given him a complete suit of Hindu kit, the costume of a low-caste street boy, and Kim stored it in a secret place under some baulks in Nila Ram's timber-yard, beyond the Punjab High Court, where the fragrant deodar logs lie seasoning after they have driven down the Ravee. When there was business or frolic afoot, Kim would use his properties, returning at dawn to the verandah, all tired out from shouting at the heels of a marriage procession, or yelling at a Hindu festival. Sometimes there was food in the house, more often there was not, and then Kim went out again to eat with his native friends.

As he drummed his heels against Zam-Zammah he turned now and again from his king-of-the-castle game with little Chota Lal, and Abdullah the sweetmeat-seller's son, to make a rude remark to the native policeman on guard over rows of shoes at the Museum door. The big Punjabi grinned tolerantly: he knew Kim of old. So did the water-carrier, sluicing water on the dry road from his goat-skin bag. So did Jawahir Singh, the Museum carpenter, bent over new packing-cases. So did everybody in sight except the peasants from the country, hurrying up to the Wonder House to view the things that men made in their own Province and elsewhere. The Museum was given up to Indian arts and manufactures, and anybody who sought wisdom could ask the curator to explain.

'Off! Off! Let me up!' cried Abdullah, climbing up Zam-Zammah's wheel.

'Thy father was a pastry-cook, Thy mother stole the *ghi,*' sang Kim. 'All Mussalmans fell off Zam-Zammah long ago!'

'Let *me* up!' shrilled little Chota Lal in his gilt-embroidered cap. His father was worth perhaps half a million sterling, but India is the only democratic land in the world.

'The Hindus fell off Zam-Zammah too. The Mussalmans pushed them off. Thy father was a pastry-cook – '

He stopped; for there shuffled round the corner, from the roaring Motee Bazar, such a man as Kim, who thought he knew all castes, had never seen. He was nearly six feet high, dressed in fold upon fold of dingy stuff like horse-blanketing, and not one fold of it could Kim refer to any known trade or profession. At his belt hung a long open-work iron pen-case and a wooden rosary such as holy men wear. On his head was a gigantic sort of tam-o'-shanter.* His face was yellow and wrinkled, like that of Fook Shing, the Chinese bootmaker in the bazar. His eyes turned up at the corners and looked like little slits of onyx.

'Who is that?' said Kim to his companions.

'Perhaps it is a man,' said Abdullah, finger in mouth, staring.

'Without doubt,' returned Kim; 'but he is no man of India that *I* have ever seen.'

'A priest, perhaps,' said Chota Lal, spying the rosary. 'See! He goes into the Wonder House!'

'Nay, nay,' said the policeman, shaking his head. 'I do not understand your talk.' The constable spoke Punjabi. 'Oh, The Friend of all the World, what does he say?'

Send him hither," said Kim, dropping from Zam-Zammah, flourishing his bare heels. 'He is a foreigner, and thou art a buffalo.'

The man turned helplessly and drifted towards the boys. He was old, and his woollen gaberdine still reeked of the stinking artemisia of the mountain passes.

'O Children, what is that big house?' he said in very fair Urdu.

"The Ajaib-Gher, the Wonder House!' Kim gave him no title – such as Lala or Mian. He could not divine the man's creed.

* A woollen cap of Scottish origin with a tight headband, wide flat circular crown, and usually a pompon in the centre.

'Ah! The Wonder House! Can any enter?'

'It is written above the door – all can enter.'

'Without payment?'

'I go in and out. I am no banker,' laughed Kim.

'Alas! I am an old man. I did not know.' Then, fingering his rosary, he half turned to the Museum.

'What is your caste? Where is your house? Have you come far?' Kim asked.

'I came by Kulu – from beyond the Kailas – but what know you? From the hills where' he sighed – 'the air and water are fresh and cool.'

'Aha! Khitai (Chinaman),' said Abdullah proudly. Fook Shing had once chased him out of his shop for spitting at the joss above the boots.

Pahari? (a hillman),' said little Chota Lal.

'Ay, child – a hillman from hills thou'lt never see. Didst hear of Bhotiyal (Tibet)? I am no Khitai, but a Bhotiya (Tibetan), since you must know – a lama – or, say a *guru* in your tongue.'

'A *guru* from Tibet,' said Kim. 'I have not seen such a man. They be Hindus in Tibet, then?'

'We be followers of the Middle Way, living in peace in our lamasseries, and I go to see the Four Holy Places before I die. Now do you, who are children, know as much as I do who am old?' He smiled benignantly on the boys.

'Hast thou eaten?'

He fumbled in his bosom and drew forth a worn wooden begging-bowl. The boys suddenly nodded. All priests of their acquaintance begged.

'I do not wish to eat yet.' He turned his head like an old tortoise in the sunlight. 'Is it true that there are many images in the Wonder House of Lahore?' He repeated the last words as one making sure of an address.

'That is true.' said Abdullah. 'It is full of heathen *bûts*. Thou also art an idolater.'

'Never mind him,' said Kim. 'That is the Government's house and there is no idolatry in it, but only a Sahib with a white beard. Come with me and I will show.'

'Strange priests eat boys,' whispered Chota Lal.

'And he is a stranger and a *bût-parast*' (idolater)' said Abdullah, the Mohammedan.

Kim laughed. 'He is new. Run to your mothers' laps, and be safe. Come!'

Kim clicked round the self-registering turnstile; the old man followed and halted amazed. In the entrance-hall stood the larger figures of the Greco-Buddhist sculptures done, savants know how long since, by forgotten workmen whose hands were feeling, and not unskilfully, for the mysteriously transmitted Grecian touch. There were hundreds of pieces, friezes of figures in relief, fragments of statues and slabs crowded with figures that had encrusted the brick walls of the Buddhist *stupas* and *viharas* of the North Country and now, dug up and labelled, made the pride of the Museum. In open-mouthed wonder the lama turned to this and that, and finally checked in rapt attention before a large alto-relief representing a coronation or apotheosis of the Lord Buddha. The Master was represented seated on a lotus the petals of which were so deeply undercut as to show almost detached. Round Him was an adoring hierarchy of kings, elders, and old-time Buddhas. Below were lotus-covered waters with fishes and water-birds. Two butterfly-winged dewas held a wreath over His head; above them another pair supported an umbrella surmounted by the jewelled headdress of the Bodhisat.

'The Lord! The Lord! It is Sakya Muni himself,' the lama half sobbed; and under his breath began the wonderful Buddhist invocation:

'To Him the Way – the Law – Apart –
Whom Maya held beneath her heart
Ananda's Lord – the Bodhisat.'

'And He is here! The Most Excellent Law is here also! My pilgrimage is well begun. And what work! What work!'

'Yonder is the Sahib," said Kim, and dodged sideways among the cases of the arts and manufacture wing. A white-bearded Englishman was looking at the lama, who gravely turned and saluted him and after some fumbling drew forth a note-book and a scrap of paper.

'Yes, that is my name,' smiling at the clumsy, childish print.

'One of us who had made pilgrimage to the Holy Places – he is now Abbot of the Lung-Cho Monastery – gave it me,' stammered the lama. 'He spoke of these.' His lean hand moved tremulously round.

'Welcome, then, O lama from Tibet. Here be the images, and I am here' – he glanced at the lama's face – 'to gather knowledge. Come to my office awhile.' The old man was trembling with excitement.

The office was but a little wooden cubicle partitioned off from the sculpture-lined gallery. Kim laid himself down, his ear against a crack in the heat-split cedar door, and, following his instinct, stretched out to listen and watch.

Most of the talk was altogether above his head. The lama, haltingly at first, spoke to the curator of his own lamassery, the Such-zen, opposite the Painted Rocks, four months' march away. The curator brought out a huge book of photos and showed him that very place, perched on its crag, overlooking the gigantic valley of many-hued strata.

'Ay, ay!' The lama mounted a pair of horn-rimmed spectacles of Chinese work. 'Here is the little door through which we bring wood before winter. And thou – the English know of these things? He who is now Abbot of Lung-Cho told me, but I did not believe. The Lord – the Excellent One – He has honour here too? And His life is known?'

'It is all carven upon the stones. Come and see, if thou art rested.'

Out shuffled the lama to the main hall, and, the curator beside him, went through the collection with the reverence of a devotee and the appreciative instinct of a craftsman.

Incident by incident in the beautiful story he identified on the blurred stone, puzzled here and there by the unfamiliar Greek convention, but delighted as a child at each new trove. Where the sequence failed, as in the Annunciation, the curator supplied it from his mound of books – French and German, with photographs and reproductions.

Here was the devout Asita, the pendant of Simeon in the Christian story, holding the Holy Child on his knee while mother and father listened; and here were incidents in the legend of the cousin Devadatta. Here was the wicked woman who accused the Master of impurity, all confounded; here was the teaching in the Deer-park; the miracle that stunned the fire-worshippers; here was the Bodhisat in royal state as a prince; the miraculous birth; the death at Kusinagara, where the weak disciple fainted; while there were almost countless repetitions of the meditation under the Bodhi tree; and the adoration of the alms-bowl was everywhere. In a few minutes the curator saw that his guest was no mere bead-telling mendicant, but a scholar of parts. And they went at it all over again, the lama taking snuff, wiping his spectacles, and talking at railway speed in a bewildering mixture of Urdu and Tibetan. He had heard of the travels of the Chinese pilgrims, Fo-Hian and Hwen-Thiang, and was anxious to know if there was any translation of their record. He drew in his breath as he turned helplessly over the pages of Beal and Stanislas Julien. ''Tis all here. A treasure locked.' Then he composed himself reverently to listen to fragments, hastily rendered into Urdu. For the first time he heard of the labours of European scholars, who by the help of these and a hundred other documents have identified the Holy Places of Buddhism. Then he was shown a mighty map, spotted and traced with yellow. The brown finger followed the curator's pencil from point to point. Here was Kapilavastu, here the Middle Kingdom, and here Mahabodi, the Mecca of Buddhism; and here was Kusinagara, sad place of the Holy One's death. The old man bowed his head over the sheets in silence for a while, and the curator lit another pipe. Kim had fallen asleep. When he waked, the talk, still in spate, was more within his comprehension.

'And thus it was, O Fountain of Wisdom, that I decided to go to the Holy Places which His foot had trod – to the Birthplace, even to Kapila; then to Maha Bodhi, which is Buddh Gaya – to the Monastery – to the Deer-park – to the place of His death.'

The lama lowered his voice. 'And I come here alone. For five – seven – eighteen – forty years it was in my mind that the Old Law was not well followed; being overlaid, as thou knowest, with devildom, charms, and idolatry. Even as the child outside said but now. Ay, even as the child said, with *bût-parasti.*'

'So it comes with all faiths.'

'Thinkest thou? The books of my lamassery I read, and they were dried pith; and the later ritual with which we of the Reformed Law have cumbered ourselves – that, too, had no worth to these old eyes. Even the followers of the Excellent One are at feud on feud with one another. It is all illusion. Ay, *maya,* illusion. But I have another desire' – the seamed yellow face drew within three inches of the curator, and the long forefinger nail tapped on the table. 'Your scholars, by these books, have followed the Blessed Feet in all their wanderings; but there are things which they have not sought out. I know nothing – nothing do I know, – but I go to free myself from the Wheel of Things by a broad and open road.' He smiled with most simple triumph. 'As a pilgrim to the Holy Places I acquire merit. But there is more. Listen to a true thing. When our gracious Lord, being as yet a youth, sought a mate, men said, in His father's court, that He was too tender for marriage. Thou knowest?'

The curator nodded; wondering what would come next.

'So they made the triple trial of strength against all comers. And at the test of the Bow, our Lord first breaking that which they gave Him, called for such a bow as none might bend. Thou knowest?'

'It is written. I have read.'

'And, overshooting all other marks, the arrow passed far and far beyond sight. At the last it fell; and, where it touched earth, there broke out a stream which presently became a River, whose nature, by our Lord's beneficence, and that merit He acquired ere He freed himself, is that whoso bathes in it washes away all taint and speckle of sin.'

So it is written,' said the curator sadly. The lama drew a long breath. 'Where is that River? Fountain of Wisdom, where fell the arrow?'

'Alas, my brother, I do not know,' said the curator.

'Nay, if it please thee to forget – the one thing only that thou hast not told me. Surely thou must know? See, I am an old man! I ask with my head between thy feet, O Fountain of Wisdom. We *know* He drew the bow! We *know* the arrow fell! We *know* the stream gushed! Where, then, is the River? My dream told me to find it. So I came. I am here. But where is the River?'

'If I knew, think you I would not cry it aloud?'

'By it one attains freedom from the Wheel of Things,' the lama went on, unheeding. 'The River of the Arrow! Think again! Some little stream, may be – dried in the heats? But the Holy One would never so cheat an old man.'

'I do not know. I do not know.'

The lama brought his thousand-wrinkled face once more a handsbreadth from the Englishman's. 'I see thou dost not know. Not being of the Law, the matter is hid from thee.'

'Ay – hidden – hidden.'

'We are both bound, thou and I, my brother. But I' – he rose with a sweep of the soft thick drapery –'I go to cut myself free. Come also!'

'I am bound,' said the curator. 'cut whither goest thou?'

'First to Kashi (Benares): where else? There I shall meet one of the pure faith in a Jain temple of that city. He also is a Seeker in secret, and from him haply I may learn. May be he will go with me to Buddh Gaya. Thence north and west to Kapilavastu, and there will I seek for the River. Nay, I will seek everywhere as I go – for the place is not known where the arrow fell.'

'And how wilt thou go? It is a far cry to Delhi, and farther to Benares.'

'By road and the trains. From Pathânkot, having left the Hills, I came hither in a *te-rain*. It goes swiftly. At first I was amazed to see those tall poles by the side of the road snatching up and snatching up their threads' – he illustrated the stoop and whirl of a telegraph-pole flashing past the train. 'But later, I was cramped and desired to walk, as I am used.'

'And thou art sure of thy road?' said the curator.

'Oh, for that one but asks a question and pays money, and the appointed persons despatch all to the appointed place. That much I knew in my lamassery from sure report,' said the lama proudly.

'And when dost thou go?' The curator smiled at the mixture of old-world piety and modern progress that is the note of India to-day.

'As soon as may be. I follow the places of His life till I come to the River of the Arrow. There is, moreover, a written paper of the hours of the trains that go south.'

'And for food?' Lamas, as a rule, have good store of money somewhere about them, but the curator wished to make sure.

'For the journey, I take up the Master's begging-bowl. Yes. Even as He went so go I, forsaking the ease of my monastery. There was with me when I left the hills a *chela* (disciple) who begged for me as the Rule demands, but halting in Kulu awhile a fever took him and he died. I have now no *chela*, but I will take the alms-bowl and thus enable the charitable to acquire merit.' He nodded his head valiantly.

Learned doctors of a lamassery do not beg, but the lama was an enthusiast in this quest.

'Be it so,' said the curator, smiling. 'Suffer me now to acquire merit. We be craftsmen together, thou and I. Here is a new book of white English paper: here be sharpened pencils two and three – thick and thin, all good for a scribe. Now lend me thy spectacles.'

The curator looked through them. They were heavily scratched, but the power was almost exactly that of his own pair, which he slid into the lama's hand, saying: 'Try these.'

'A feather! A very feather upon the face!' The old man turned his head delightedly and wrinkled up his nose. 'How scarcely do I feel them! How clearly do I see!'

'They be *bilaur* – crystal and will never scratch. May they help thee to thy River, for they are thine.'

'I will take them and the pencils and the white note-book,' said the lama, 'as a sign of friendship between priest and priest – and now' – he fumbled at his belt, detached the open iron-work pen-case, and laid it on the curator's table. 'That is for a memory between thee and me – my pen-case. It is something old – even as I am.'

It was a piece of ancient design, Chinese, of an iron that is not smelted these days; and the collector's heart in the curator's bosom had gone out to it from the first. For no persuasion would the lama resume his gift.

'When I return, having found the River, I will bring thee a written picture of the Padma Samthora – such as I used to make on silk at the lamassery. Yes – and of the Wheel of Life,' he chuckled, 'for we be craftsmen together, thou and I.'

The curator would have detained him: they are few in the world who still have the secret of the conventional brush-pen Buddhist pictures which are, as it were, half written and half drawn. But the lama strode out, head high in air, and pausing an instant before the great statue of a Bodhisat in meditation, brushed through the turnstiles.

Kim followed like a shadow. What he had overheard excited him wildly. This man was entirely new to all his experience, and he meant to investigate further: precisely as he would have investigated a new building or a strange festival in Lahore city. The lama was his trove, and he purposed to take possession. Kim's mother had been Irish too.

The old man halted by Zam-Zammah and looked round till his eye fell on Kim. The inspiration of his pilgrimage had left him for awhile, and he felt old, forlorn, and very empty.

'Do not sit under that gun,' said the policeman loftily.

'Huh! Owl!' was Kim's retort on the lama's behalf. 'Sit under that gun if it please thee. When didst thou steal the milk-woman's slippers, Dunnoo?'

That was an utterly unfounded charge sprung on the spur of the moment, but it silenced Dunnoo, who knew that Kim's clear yell could call up legions of bad bazar boys if need arose.

'And whom didst thou worship within?' said Kim affably, squatting in the shade beside the lama.

'I worshipped none, child. I bowed before the Excellent Law.'

Kim accepted this new god without emotion. He knew already a few score.

'And what dost thou do?'

'I beg. I remember now it is long since I have eaten or drunk. What is the custom of charity in this town? In silence, as we do of Tibet, or speaking aloud?'

'Those who beg in silence starve in silence,' said Kim, quoting a native proverb. The lama tried to rise, but sank back again, sighing for his disciple, dead in faraway Kulu. Kim watched – head to one side, considering and interested.

'Give me the bowl. I know the people of this city – all who are charitable. Give, and I will bring it back filled.' Simply as a child the old man handed him the bowl.

'Rest thou. *I* know the people.'

He trotted off to the open shop of a *kunjri*, a low-caste vegetable-seller, which lay opposite the belt-tramway line down the Motee Bazar. She knew Kim of old.

'Oho, hast thou turned yogi with thy begging-bowl?' she cried.

'Nay,' said Kim proudly. 'There is a new priest in the city – a man such as I have never seen.'

'Old priest – young tiger,' said the woman angrily. 'I am tired of new priests! They settle on our wares like flies. Is the father of my son a well of charity to give to all who ask?'

'No,' said Kim. 'Thy man is rather *yagi* (bad-tempered) than *yogi* (a holy man). But this priest is new. The Sahib in the Wonder House has talked to him like a brother. O my mother, fill me this bowl. He waits.'

'That bowl indeed! That cow-bellied basket! Thou hast as much grace as the holy bull of Shiv. He has taken the best of a basket of onions already, this morn; and forsooth, I must fill thy bowl. He comes here again.'

The huge, mouse-coloured Brahminee bull of the ward was shouldering his way through the many-coloured crowd, a stolen plantain hanging out of his mouth. He headed straight for the shop, well knowing his privileges as a sacred beast, lowered his head, and puffed heavily along the line of baskets ere making his choice. Up flew Kim's hard little heel and caught him on his moist blue nose. He snorted indignantly, and walked away across the tram rails, his hump quivering with rage.

'See! I have saved more than the bowl will cost thrice over. Now, mother, a little rice and some dried fish atop – yes, and some vegetable curry.'

A growl came out of the back of the shop, where a man lay.

'He drove away the bull,' said the woman in an undertone. 'It is good to give to the poor.' She took the bowl and returned it full of hot rice.

'But my yogi is not a cow,' said Kim gravely, making a hole with his fingers in the top of the mound. 'A little curry is good, and a fried cake, and a morsel of conserve would please him, I think.'

'It is a hole as big as thy head,' said the woman fretfully. But she filled it, none the less, with good, steaming vegetable curry, clapped a dried cake atop, and a morsel of clarified butter on the cake, dabbed a lump of sour tamarind conserve at the side; and Kim looked at the load lovingly.

'That is good. When I am in the bazar the bull shall not come to this house. He is a bold beggarman.'

'And thou?' laughed the woman. 'But speak well of bulls. Hast thou not told me that some day a Red Bull will come out of a field to help thee? Now hold all straight and ask for the holy man's blessing upon me. Perhaps, too, he knows a cure for my daughter's sore eyes. Ask him that also, O thou Little Friend of all the World.'

But Kim had danced off ere the end of the sentence, dodging pariah dogs and hungry acquaintances.

'Thus do we beg who know the way of it,' said he proudly to the lama, who opened his eyes at the contents of the bowl. 'Eat now and – I will eat with thee. Ohé *bhistie*!' he called to the water-carrier, sluicing the crotons by the Museum. 'Give water here. We men are thirsty.'

'We men!' said the *bhistie*, laughing. 'Is one skinful enough for such a pair? Drink then, in the name of the Compassionate.'

He loosed a thin stream into Kim's hands, who drank native fashion; but the lama must needs pull out a cup from his inexhaustible upper draperies and drink ceremonially.

'*Pardesi* (a foreigner),' Kim explained, as the old man delivered in an unknown tongue what was evidently a blessing.

They ate together in great content, clearing the beggar's bowl. Then the lama took snuff from a portentous wooden snuff-gourd, fingered his rosary awhile, and so dropped into the easy sleep of age, as the shadow of Zam-Zammah grew long.

Kim loafed over to the nearest tobacco-seller, a rather lively young Mohammedan woman, and begged a rank cigar of the brand that they sell to students of the Punjab University who copy English customs. Then he smoked and thought, knees to chin, under the belly of the gun, and the outcome of his thoughts was a sudden and stealthy departure in the direction of Nila Ram's timber-yard.

The lama did not wake till the evening life of the city had begun with lamp-lighting and the return of white-robed clerks and subordinates from the Government offices. He stared dizzily in all directions, but none looked at him save a Hindu urchin in a dirty turban and Isabella-coloured clothes. Suddenly he bowed his head on his knees and wailed.

'What is this?' said the boy, standing before him. 'Hast thou been robbed?'

'It is my new *chela* (my disciple) that is gone away from me, and I know not where he is.'

'And what like of man was thy disciple?'

'It was a boy who came to me in place of him who died, on account of the merit which I had gained when I bowed before the Law within there.' He pointed towards the Museum. 'He came upon me to show me a road which I had lost. He led me into the Wonder House, and by his talk emboldened to speak to the Keeper of the Images, so that I was cheered and made strong. And when I was faint with hunger he begged for me, as would a *chela* for his teacher. Suddenly was he sent. Suddenly has he gone away. It was in my mind to have taught him the Law upon the road to Benares.'

Kim stood amazed at this, because he had overheard the talk in the Museum, and knew that the old man was speaking the truth, which is a thing a native seldom presents to a stranger.

'But I see now that he was but sent upon a purpose. By this I know that I shall find a certain River for which I seek.'

'The River of the Arrow?' said Kim, with a superior smile.

'Is this yet another Sending?' cried the lama. 'To none have I spoken of my search, save to the Priest of the Images. Who art thou?'

'Thy chela,' said Kim simply, sitting on his heels. 'I have never seen any one like to thee in all this my life. I go with thee to Benares. And, too, I think that so old a man as thou, speaking the truth to chance-met people at dusk, is in great need of a disciple.'

'But the River – the River of the Arrow?'

'Oh, that I heard when thou wast speaking to the Englishman. I lay against the door.'

The lama sighed. 'I thought thou hadst been a guide permitted. Such things fall sometimes – but I am not worthy. Thou dost not, then, know of the River?'

'Not I.' Kim laughed uneasily. 'I go to look for – for a bull – a Red Bull on a green field who shall help me.' Boy-like, if an acquaintance had a scheme, Kim was quite ready with one of his own; and, boy-like, he had really thought for as much as twenty minutes at a time of his father's prophecy.

'To what, child?' said the lama.

'God knows, but so my father told me. I heard thy talk in the Wonder House of all those new strange places in the Hills, and if one so old and so little – so used to truth-telling – may go out for the small matter of a river, it seemed to me that I too must go a-travelling. If it is our fate to find those things we shall find them – thou, thy River; and I, my Bull, and the strong Pillars and some other matters that I forget.'

'It is not pillars but a Wheel from which I would be free,' said the lama.

'That is all one. Perhaps they will make me a king,' said Kim, serenely prepared for anything.

'I will teach thee other and better desires upon the road,' the lama replied in the voice of authority. 'Let us go to Benares.'

'Not by night. Thieves are abroad. Wait till the day.'

'But there is no place to sleep.' The old man was used to the order of his monastery, and though he slept on the ground, as the Rule decrees, preferred a decency in these things.

'We shall get good lodging at the Kashmir Serai,' said Kim, laughing at his perplexity. 'I have a friend there. Come!'

The hot and crowded bazars blazed with light as they made their way through the press of all the races in Upper India, and the lama mooned through it like a man in a dream. It was his first experience of a large manufacturing city, and the crowded tram-car with its continually squealing brakes frightened him. Half pushed, half towed, he arrived at the high gate of the Kashmir Serai: that huge open square over against the railway station, surrounded with arched cloisters where the camel and horse-caravans put up on their return from Central Asia. Here were all manner of Northern folk, tending tethered ponies and kneeling camels; loading and unloading bales and bundles; drawing water for the evening meal at the creaking well-windlasses; piling grass before the shrieking, wild-eyed stallions; cuffing the surly caravan dogs; paying off camel-drivers; taking on new grooms; swearing, shouting, arguing, and chaffering in the packed square. The cloisters, reached by three or four masonry steps, made a haven of refuge around this turbulent sea. Most of them were rented to traders, as we rent the arches of a viaduct; the space between pillar and pillar being bricked or boarded off into rooms, which were guarded by heavy wooden doors and cumbrous native padlocks. Locked doors showed that the owner was away, and a few rude – sometimes very rude – chalk or paint scratches told where he had gone. Thus: 'Lutuf Ullah is gone to Kurdistan.' Below, in coarse verse: 'O Allah, who sufferest lice to live on the coat of a Kabuli, why hast thou allowed this louse Lutuf to live so long?'

Kim, fending the lama between excited men and excited beasts, sidled along the cloisters to the far end, nearest the railway station, where Mahbub Ali, the horse-trader, lived when he came in from that mysterious land beyond the Passes of the North.

Kim had had many dealings with Mahbub in his little life, – especially between his tenth and his thirteenth year, – and the big burly Afghan, his beard dyed scarlet with lime (for he was elderly and did not wish his gray hairs to show) knew the boy's value as a gossip. Sometimes he would tell Kim to watch a man who had nothing whatever to do with horses: to follow him for one whole day and report every soul with whom he talked. Kim would deliver himself of his tale at evening, and Mahbub would listen without a word or gesture. It was intrigue of some kind, Kim knew; but its worth lay in saying nothing whatever to any one except Mahbub, who gave him beautiful meals all hot from the cook-shop at the head of the serai, and once as much as eight annas in money.

'He is here,' said Kim, hitting a bad-tempered camel on the nose. 'Ohé, Mahbub Ali!' He halted at a dark arch and slipped behind the bewildered lama.

The horse-trader, his deep, embroidered Bokhariot belt unloosed, was lying on a pair of silk carpet saddle-bags, pulling lazily at an immense silver hookah. He turned his head very slightly at the cry; and seeing only the tall silent figure, chuckled in his deep chest.

'Allah! A lama! A Red Lama! It is far from Lahore to the Passes. What dost thou do here?'

The lama held out the begging-bowl mechanically.

'God's curse on all unbelievers!' said Mahbub. 'I do not give to a lousy Tibetan; but ask my Baltis over yonder behind the camels. They may value your blessings. Oh, horse-boys, here is a countryman of yours. See if he be hungry.'

A shaven, crouching Balti, who had come down with the horses, and who was nominally some sort of degraded Buddhist, fawned upon the priest, and in thick gutturals besought the Holy One to sit at the horse-boys' fire.

'Go!' said Kim, pushing him lightly, and the lama strode away, leaving Kim at the edge of the cloister.

'Go!' said Mahbub Ali, returning to his hookah. 'Little Hindu, run away. God's curse on all unbelievers! Beg from those of my tail who are of thy faith.'

'Maharaj,' whined Kim, using the Hindu form of address, and thoroughly enjoying the situation; 'my father is dead – my mother is dead – my stomach is empty.'

'Beg from my men among the horses, I say. There must be some Hindus in my tail.'

'Oh, Mahbub Ali, but am *I* a Hindu?' said Kim in English.

The trader gave no sign of astonishment, but looked under shaggy eyebrows.

'Little Friend of all the World,' said he, 'what is this?'

'Nothing. I am now that holy man's disciple; and we go a pilgrimage together – to Benares, he says. He is quite mad, and I am tired of Lahore city. I wish new air and water.'

'But for whom dost thou work? Why come to me?' The voice was harsh with suspicion.

'To whom else should I come? I have no money. It is not good to go about without money. Thou wilt sell many horses to the officers. They are very fine horses, these new ones: I have seen them. Give me a rupee, Mahbub Ali, and when I come to my wealth I will give thee a bond and pay.'

'Um,' said Mahbub Ali, thinking swiftly. 'Thou hast never before lied to me. Call that lama – stand back in the dark.'

'Oh, our tales will agree,' said Kim laughing.

'We go to Benares,' said the lama, as soon as he understood the drift of Mahbub Ali's questions. 'The boy and I. I go to seek for a certain River.'

'Maybe – but the boy?'

'He is my disciple. He was sent, I think, to guide me to that River. Sitting under a gun was I when he came suddenly. Such things have befallen the fortunate to whom guidance was allowed. But I remember now, he said he was of this world – a Hindu.'

'And his name?'

'That I did not ask. Is he not my disciple?'

'His country – his face – his village? Mussalman – Sikh – Hindu – Jain – low caste or high?'

'Why should I ask? There is neither high nor low in the Middle Way. If he is my *chela* – does – will – can any one take him from me? For, look you, without him I shall not find my River.' He wagged his head solemnly.

'None shall take him from thee. Go, sit among my Baltis,' said Mahbub Ali, and the lama drifted off, soothed by the promise.

'Is he not quite mad?' said Kim, coming forward to the light again. 'Why should I lie to thee, Hajji?'

Mahbub puffed his hookah in silence. Then he began, almost whispering: 'Umballa is on the road to Benares – if indeed ye two go there.'

'Tck! Tck! I tell thee he does not know how to lie – as we two know.'

'And if thou wilt carry a message for me as far as Umballa, I will give thee money. It concerns a horse – a white stallion which I have sold to an officer upon the last time I returned from the Passes. But then – stand nearer and hold up hands as begging – the pedigree of the white stallion was not fully established, and that officer, who is now at Umballa, bade me make it clear.' (Mahbub here described the horse and the appearance of the officer.) 'So the message to that officer will be: "The pedigree of the white stallion is fully established." By this will he know that thou comest from me. He will then say "What proof has thou?" and thou wilt answer: "Mahbub Ali has given me the proof." '

'And all for the sake of a white stallion,' said Kim, with a giggle, his eyes aflame.

'That pedigree I will give thee now – in my own fashion – and some hard words as well.' A shadow passed behind Kim, and a feeding camel. Mahbub Ali raised his voice.

'Allah! Art thou the only beggar in the city? Thy mother is dead. Thy father is dead. So is it with all of them. Well, well – 'he turned as feeling on the floor beside him and tossed a flap of soft, greasy Mussalman bread to the boy. 'Go and lie among my horse-boys for to-night – thou and the lama. Tomorrow I may give thee service.'

Kim slunk away, his teeth in the bread, and, as he expected, he found a small wad of folded tissue-paper wrapped in oilskin, with three silver rupees – enormous largesse. He smiled and thrust money and paper into his leather amulet-case. The lama, sumptuously fed by Mahbub's Baltis, was already asleep in a corner of one of the stalls. Kim lay down beside him and laughed. He knew he had rendered a service to Mahbub Ali, and not for one little minute did he believe the tale of the stallion's pedigree.

But Kim did not suspect that Mahbub Ali, known as one of the best horse-dealers in the Punjab, a wealthy and enterprising trader, whose caravans penetrated far and far into the Back of Beyond, was registered in one of the locked books of the Indian Survey Department as C.25. I B. Twice or thrice yearly C.25 would send in a little story, baldly told but most interesting, and generally – it was checked by the statements of R.17 and M. 4 – quite true. It concerned all manner of out-of-the-way mountain principalities, explorers of nationalities other than English, and the gun-trade – was, in brief, a small portion of that vast mass of 'information received' on which the Indian Government acts. But, recently, five confederated Kings, who had no business to confederate, had been informed by a kindly Northern Power that there was a leakage of news from their territories into British India. So those Kings' prime ministers were seriously annoyed and took steps, after the Oriental fashion. They suspected, among many others, the bullying, red-bearded horse-dealer whose caravans ploughed through their fastnesses belly deep in snow. At least, his caravan that season had been ambushed and shot at twice on the way down, when Mahbub's men accounted for three strange ruffians who might, or might not, have been hired for the job. Therefore Mahbub had avoided halting at the insalubrious city of Peshawur, and had come through without stop to Lahore, where, knowing his country-people, he anticipated curious developments.

And there was that on Mahbub Ali which he did not wish to keep an hour longer than was necessary – a wad of closely folded tissue-paper, wrapped in oil-skin – an impersonal, unaddressed statement, with five microscopic pin-holes in one corner, that most scandalously betrayed the five confederated Kings, the sympathetic Northern Power, a Hindu banker in Peshawur, a firm of gun-makers in Belgium, and an important, semi-independent Mohammedan ruler to the south. This last was R.17's work, which Mahbub had picked up beyond the Dora Pass and was carrying in for R.17, who, owing to circumstances over which he had no control, could not leave his post of observation. Dynamite was milky and innocuous beside that report of C.25; and even an Oriental, with an Oriental's views of the value of time, could see that the sooner it was in the proper hands the better. Mahbub had no particular desire to die by violence, because two or three family blood-feuds across the border hung unfinished on his hands, and when these scores were cleared he intended to settle down as a more or less virtuous citizen. He had never passed the serai gate since his arrival two days ago, but had been ostentatious in sending telegrams to Bombay, where be banked some of his money; to Delhi, where a sub-partner of his own clan was selling horses to the agent of a Rajputana state; and to Umballa, where an Englishman was excitedly demanding the pedigree of a white stallion. The public letter-writer, who knew English, composed excellent telegrams, such as: –

CREIGHTON, LAUREL BANK, UMBALLA – HORSE IS ARABIAN AS ALREADY ADVISED. SORROWFUL DELAYED-PEDIGREE WHICH AM TRANSLATING.

And later to the same address:

MUCH SORROWFUL DELAY. WILL FORWARD PEDIGREE.

To this sub-partner at Delhi he wired:

LUTUF ULLAH – HAVE WIRED TWO THOUSAND RUPEES YOUR CREDIT LUCHMAN NARAIN'S BANK.

This was entirely in the way of trade, but every one of those telegrams was discussed and re-discussed, by parties who conceived themselves to be interested, before they went over to the railway station in charge of a foolish Balti, who allowed all sorts of people to read them on the road.

When, in Mahbub's own picturesque language, he had muddied the wells of inquiry with the stick of precaution, Kim had dropped on him, sent from heaven; and, being as prompt as he was unscrupulous, Mahbub Ali, used to taking all sorts of gusty chances, pressed him into service on the spot.

A wandering lama with a low-caste boy-servant might attract a moment's interest as they wandered about India, the land of pilgrims; but no one would suspect them or, what was more to the point, rob.

He called for a new light-ball to his hookah, and considered the case. If the worst came to the worst, and the boy came to harm, the paper would incriminate nobody. And he would go up to Umballa leisurely and – at a certain risk of exciting fresh suspicion – repeat his tale by word of mouth to the people concerned.

But R.17's report was the kernel of the whole affair, and it would be distinctly inconvenient if that failed to come to hand. However, God was great, and Mahbub Ali felt he had done all he could for the time being. Kim was the one soul in the world who had never told him a lie. That would have been a fatal blot on Kim's character if Mahbub had not known that to others, for his own ends or Mahbub's business, Kim could lie like an Oriental.

Then Mahbub Ali rolled across the serai to the Gate of the Harpies who paint their eyes and trap the stranger, and was at some pains to call on the one girl who, he had reason to believe, was a particular friend of a smooth-faced Kashmiri pundit who had waylaid his simple Balti in the matter of the telegrams. It was an utterly foolish thing to do; because they fell to drinking perfumed brandy against the Law of the Prophet, and Mahbub grew wonderfully drunk, and the gates of his mouth were loosened, and he pursued the Flower of Delight with the feet of intoxication till he fell flat among the cushions, where the Flower of Delight, aided by a smooth-faced Kashmiri pundit, searched him from head to foot most thoroughly.

About the same hour Kim heard soft feet in Mahbub's deserted stall. The horse-trader, curiously enough, had left his door unlocked, and his men were busy celebrating their return to India with a whole sheep of Mahbub's bounty. A sleek young gentleman from Delhi, armed with a bunch of keys which the Flower had unshackled from the senseless one's belt, went through every single box, bundle, mat, and saddlebag in Mahbub's possession even more systematically than the Flower and the pundit were searching the owner.

'And I think,' said the Flower scornfully an hour later, one rounded elbow on the snoring carcase, 'that he is no more than a pig of an Afghan horse-dealer, with no thought except women and horses. Moreover, he may have sent it away by now – if ever there were such a thing.'

'Nay – in a matter touching Five Kings it would be next his black heart,' said the pundit. 'Was there nothing?'

The Delhi man laughed and resettled his turban as he entered. 'I searched between the soles of his slippers as the Flower searched his clothes. This is not the man but another. I leave little unseen.'

'They did not say he was the very man,' said the pundit thoughtfully. 'They said, "Look if he be the man, since our councils are troubled." '

'That North country is full of horse-dealers as an old coat of lice. There is Sikandar Khan, Nur Ali Beg, and Farrukh Shah – all heads of Kafilas – who deal there,' said the Flower.

'They have not yet come in,' said the pundit. 'Thou must ensnare them later.'

'Phew!' said the Flower with deep disgust, rolling Mahbub's head from her lap. 'I earn my money. Farrukh Shah is a bear, Ali Beg a swashbuckler, and old Sikandar Khan – yaie! Go! I sleep now. This swine will not stir till dawn.'

When Mahbub woke, the Flower talked to him severely on the sin of drunkenness. Asiatics do not wink when they have out-manoeuvred an enemy, but as Mahbub Ali cleared his throat, tightened his belt, and staggered forth under the early morning stars, he came very near to it.

'What a colt's trick,' said he to himself. 'As if every girl in Peshawur did not use it! But 'twas prettily done. Now God He knows how many more there be upon the road who have orders to test me – perhaps with the knife. So it stands that the boy must go to Umballa – and by rail – for the writing is something urgent. I abide here, following the Flower and drinking wine as an Afghan coper should.'

He halted at the stall next but one to his own. His men lay there heavy with sleep. There was no sign of Kim or the lama.

'Up!' He stirred a sleeper. 'Whither went those who lay here last even – the lama and the boy? Is aught missing?'

'Nay,' grunted the man, 'the old madman rose at second cockcrow saying he would go to Benares, and the young one led him away.'

'The curse of Allah on all unbelievers,' said Mahbub heartily, and climbed into his own stall, growling in his beard.

But it was Kim who had wakened the lama – Kim with one eye laid against a knot-hole in the planking, who had seen the Delhi man's search through the boxes. This was no common thief that turned over letters, bills, and saddles – no mere burglar who ran a little knife sideways into the soles of Mahbub's slippers, or picked the seams of the saddle-bags so deftly. At first Kim had been minded to give the alarm – the long-drawn *cho-or – cho-or!* (thief! thief!) that sets the serai ablaze of nights; but he looked more carefully, and, hand on amulet, drew his own conclusions.

'It must be the pedigree of that made-up horse-lie,' said he, 'the thing that I carry to Umballa. Better that we go now. Those who search bags with knives may presently search bellies with knives. Surely there is a woman behind this. Hai! Hai!' in a whisper to the light-sleeping old man. 'Come. It is time – time to go to Benares.'

The lama rose obediently, and they passed out of the serai like shadows.

CHAPTER 2

For whoso will, from Pride released,
Contemning neither man nor beast,
May hear the Soul of all the East
About him at *Kamakura*.

THEY ENTERED the fort-like railway station, black in the end of night; the electrics sizzling over the goods-yard where they handle the heavy Northern grain-traffic.

'This is the work of devils!' said the lama, recoiling from the hollow echoing darkness, the glimmer of rails between the masonry platforms, and the maze of girders above. He stood in a gigantic stone hall paved, it seemed, with the sheeted dead – third-class passengers who had taken their tickets overnight and were sleeping in the waiting-rooms. All hours of the twenty-four are alike to Orientals, and their passenger traffic is regulated accordingly.

'This is where the fire-carriages come. One stands behind that hole' – Kim pointed to the ticket-office – 'who will give thee a paper to take thee to Umballa.'

'But we go to Benares,' he replied petulantly.

'All one. Benares then. Quick: she comes!'

'Take thou the purse.'

The lama, not so well used to trains as he had pretended, started as the 3.25 A.M. south bound roared in. The sleepers sprang to life, and the station filled with clamour and shoutings, cries of water and sweetmeat vendors, shouts of native policemen, and shrill yells of women gathering up their baskets, their families, and their husbands.

'It is the train – only the *te-rain*. It will come here. Wait!' Amazed at the lama's immense simplicity (he had handed him a small bag full of rupees), Kim asked and paid for a ticket to Umballa. A sleepy clerk grunted and flung out a ticket to the next station, just six miles distant.

'Nay,' said Kim, scanning it with a grin. 'This may serve for farmers, but I live in the city of Lahore. It was cleverly done, babu. Now give the ticket to Umballa.'

The babu scowled and dealt the proper ticket.

'Now another to Amritzar,' said Kim, who had no notion of spending Mahbub Ali's money on anything so crude as a paid ride to Umballa. 'The price is so much. The small money in return is just so much. I know the ways of the te-rain. . . . Never did *yogi* need *chela* as thou dost,' he went on merrily to the bewildered lama. 'They would have flung thee out at Mian Mir but for me. This way! Come.' He returned the money, keeping only one anna in each rupee of the price of the Umballa ticket as his commission – the immemorial commission of Asia.

The lama jibbed at the open door of a crowded third-class carriage. 'Were it not better to walk?' said he weakly.

A burly Sikh artisan thrust forth his bearded head. 'Is he afraid? Do not be afraid. I remember the time when I was afraid of the train. Enter! This thing is the work of the Government.'

'I do not fear,' said the lama. 'Have ye room within for two?'

'There is no room even for a mouse,' shrilled the wife of a well-to-do cultivator – a Hindu Jat from the rich Jullundur district. 'Our night trains are not as well looked after as the day ones, where the sexes are very strictly kept to separate carriages.'

' Oh, mother of my son, we can make space,' said the blue-turbaned husband. 'Pick up the child. It is a holy man, see'st thou?'

'And my lap full of seventy times seven bundles! Why not bid him sit on my knee, Shameless? But men are ever thus!' She looked round for approval. An Amritzar courtesan near the window sniffed behind her head drapery.

'Enter! Enter!' cried a fat Hindu money-lender, his folded account-book in a cloth under his arm. With an oily smirk: 'It is well to be kind to the poor.'

'Ay, at seven per cent a month with a mortgage on the unborn calf,' said a young Dogra soldier going south on leave; and they all laughed.

'Will it travel to Benares?' said the lama.

'Assuredly. Else why should we come? Enter, or we are left,' cried Kim.

'See!' shrilled the Amritzar girl. 'He has never entered a train. Oh see!'

'Nay, help,' said the cultivator, putting out a large brown hand and hauling him in. 'Thus is it done, father.'

'But – but – I sit on the floor. It is against the Rule to sit on a bench,' said the lama. 'Moreover, it cramps me.'

'I say,' began the money-lender, pursing his lips, 'that there is not one rule of right living which these *te-rains* do not cause us to break. We sit, for example, side by side with all castes and peoples.'

'Yea, and with most outrageously shameless ones,' said the wife, scowling at the Amritzar girl making eyes at the young sepoy.

'I said we might have gone by cart along the road," said the husband, 'and thus have saved some money.'

'Yes – and spent twice over what we saved on food by the way. That was talked out ten thousand times.'

'Ay, by ten thousand tongues,' grunted he.

'The Gods help us poor women if we may not speak. Oho! He is of that sort which may not look at or reply to a woman.' For the lama, constrained by his Rule, took not the faintest notice of her. 'And his disciple is like him?'

'Nay, mother,' said Kim most promptly. 'Not when the woman is well-looking and above all charitable to the hungry.'

'A beggar's answer,' said the Sikh, laughing. 'Thou hast brought it on thyself, sister!' Kim's hands were crooked in supplication.

'And whither goest thou?' said the woman, handing him the half of a cake from a greasy package.

'Even to Benares.'

'Jugglers belike?' the young soldier suggested. 'Have ye any tricks to pass the time? Why does not that yellow man answer?'

'Because,' said Kim stoutly, 'he is holy, and thinks upon matters hidden from thee.'

'That may be well. We of the Loodhiana Sikhs,' he rolled it out sonorously, 'do not trouble our heads with doctrine. We fight.'

'My sister's brother's son is *naik* (corporal) in that regiment,' said the Sikh craftsman quietly. 'There are also some Dogra companies there.' The soldier glared, for a Dogra is of other caste than a Sikh, and the banker tittered.

'They are all one to me,' said the Amritzar girl.

'That we believe,' snorted the cultivator's wife malignantly.

'Nay, but all who serve the Sirkar with weapons in their hands are, as it were, one brotherhood. There is one brotherhood of the caste, but beyond that again' – she looked round timidly – 'the bond of the *Pulton* – the Regiment – eh?'

'My brother is in a Jat regiment,' said the cultivator. 'Dogras be good men.'

'Thy Sikhs at least were of that opinion,' said the soldier, with a scowl at the placid old man in the corner. '*Thy* Sikhs thought so when our two companies came to help them at the Pirzai Kotal in the face of eight Afreedee standards on the ridge not three months gone.'

He told the story of a border action in which the Dogra companies of the Loodhiana Sikhs had acquitted themselves well. The Amritzar girl smiled; for she knew the tale was to win her approval.

'Alas!' said the cultivator's wife at the end. 'So their villages were burnt and their little children made homeless?'

'They had marked our dead. They paid a great payment after we of the Sikhs had schooled them. So it was. Is this Amritzar?'

'Ay, and here they cut our tickets,' said the banker, fumbling at his belt.

The lamps were paling in the dawn when the half-caste guard came round. Ticket-collecting is a slow business in the East, where people secrete their tickets in all sorts of curious places. Kim produced his and was told to get out.

'But I go to Umballa,' he protested. 'I go with this holy man.'

'Thou canst go to Jehannum for aught I care. This ticket is only to Amritzar. Out!'

Kim burst into a flood of tears, protesting that the lama was his father and his mother, that he was the prop of the lama's declining years, and that the lama would die without his care. All the carriage bade the guard be merciful, – the banker was specially eloquent here, – but the guard hauled Kim on to the platform. The lama blinked, he could not overtake the situation, and Kim lifted up his voice and wept outside the carriage window.

'I am very poor. My father is dead – my mother is dead. Oh, charitable ones, if I am left here, who shall tend that old man?'

'What – what is this?' the lama repeated. 'He must go to Benares. He must come with me. He is my *chela.* If there is money to be paid – '

'Oh, be silent,' whispered Kim; 'are we Rajahs to throw away good silver when the world is so charitable?'

The Amritzar girl stepped out with her bundles, and it was on her that Kim kept his watchful eye. Ladies of that persuasion, he knew, were generous.

'A ticket – a little *tikkut* to Umballa – O Breaker of Hearts!' She laughed. 'Hast thou no charity?'

'Does the holy man come from the North?'

'From far and far in the North he comes,' cried Kim. "From among the hills.'

'There is snow among the pine trees in the North – in the hills there is snow. My mother was from Kulu. Get thee a ticket. Ask him for a blessing.'

'Ten thousand blessings,' shrilled Kim. 'O Holy One, a woman has given us in charity so that I can come with thee – a woman with a golden heart. I run for the *tikkut.*'

The girl looked up at the lama, who had mechanically followed Kim to the platform. He bowed his head that he might not see her, and muttered in Tibetan as she passed on with the crowd.

'Light come – light go,' said the cultivator's wife viciously.

'She has acquired merit,' returned the lama. 'Beyond doubt it was a nun.'

'There be ten thousand such nuns in Amritzar alone. Return, old man, or the train may depart without thee,' cried the banker.

'Not only was it sufficient for the ticket, but for a little food also,' said Kim, leaping to his place. 'Now eat, Holy One. Look. Day comes!'

Golden, rose, saffron, and pink, the morning mists smoked away across the flat green levels. All the rich Punjab lay out in the splendour of the keen sun. The lama flinched a little as the telegraph-posts swung by.

'Great is the speed of the train,' said the banker, with a patronising grin. 'We have gone farther since Lahore than thou couldst walk in two days: at even, we shall enter Umballa.'

'And that is still far from Benares,' said the lama wearily, mumbling over the cakes that Kim offered. They all unloosed their bundles and made their morning meal. Then the banker, the cultivator, and the soldier prepared their pipes and wrapped the compartment in choking, acrid smoke, spitting and coughing and enjoying themselves. The Sikh and the cultivator's wife chewed *pan;* the lama took snuff and told his beads, while Kim, cross-legged, smiled over the comfort of a full stomach.

'What rivers have ye by Benares?' said the lama of a sudden to the carriage at large.

'We have Gunga,' returned the banker, when the little titter had subsided.

'What others?'

'What other than Gunga?'

'Nay, but in my mind was the thought of a certain River of healing.'

'That is Gunga. Who bathes in her is made clean and goes to the Gods. Thrice have I made pilgrimage to Gunga.' He looked round proudly.

'There was need,' said the young sepoy drily, and the travellers' laugh turned against the banker.

'Clean – to return again to the Gods,' the lama muttered. 'And to go forth on the round of lives anew – still tied to the Wheel.' He shook his head testily. 'But maybe there is a mistake. Who, then, made Gunga in the beginning'

'The Gods. Of what known faith art thou?' the banker said appalled.

'I follow the Law – the Most Excellent Law. So it was the Gods that made Gunga. What like of Gods were they?'

The carriage looked at him in amazement. It was inconceivable that anyone should be ignorant of Gunga.

'What – what is thy God?' said the money-lender at last.

'Hear!' said the lama, shifting the rosary to his hand. 'Hear: for I speak of Him now! O people of Hind, listen!'

He began in Urdu the tale of the Lord Buddha, but, borne by his own thoughts, slid into Tibetan and long-droned texts from a Chinese book of the Buddha's life. The gentle, tolerant folk looked on reverently. All India is full of holy men stammering gospels in strange tongues; shaken and consumed in the fires of their own zeal; dreamers, babblers, and visionaries: as it has been from the beginning and will continue to the end.

'Um!' said the soldier of the Loodhiana Sikhs. 'There was a Mohammedan regiment lay next to us at the Pirzai Kotal, and a priest of theirs, – he was, as I remember, a *naik,* – when the fit was on him, spake prophecies. But the mad all are in God's keeping. His officers overlooked much in that man.'

The lama fell back on Urdu, remembering that he was in a strange land. 'Hear the tale of the Arrow which our Lord loosed from the bow,' he said.

This was much more to their taste, and they listened curiously while he told it. 'Now, O people of Hind, I go to seek that River. Know ye aught that may guide me, for we be all men and women in evil case.'

'There is Gunga – and Gunga alone – who washes away sin,' ran the murmur round the carriage.

'Though past question we have good Gods Jullundur-way,' said the cultivator's wife, looking out of window. 'See how they have blessed the crops.'

'To search every river in the Punjab is no small matter,' said her husband. 'For me, a stream that leaves good silt on my land suffices, and I thank Bhumia, the God of the Homestead.' He shrugged one knotted, bronzed shoulder.

'Think you our Lord came so far north?' said the lama, turning to Kim.

'It may be,' Kim replied soothingly, as he spat red *pan*-juice on the floor.

'The last of the Great Ones,' said the Sikh with authority, 'was Sikander Julkarn (Alexander the Great). He paved the streets of Jullundur and built a great tank near Umballa. That pavement holds to this day; and the tank is there also. I never heard of thy God.'

'Let thy hair grow long and talk Punjabi,' said the young soldier jestingly to Kim, quoting a Northern proverb. 'That is all that makes a Sikh.' But he did not say this very loud.

The lama sighed and shrank into himself, a dingy, shapeless mass. In the pauses of their talk they could hear the low droning – *'Om mane pudme hum! Om mane pudme hum!'* – and the thick click of the wooden rosary beads.

'It irks me," he said at last. 'The speed and the clatter irk me. Moreover, my *chela*, I think that may be we have overpassed that River."

'Peace, peace,' said Kim. 'Was not the River near Benares? We are yet far from the place.

'But – if our Lord came north, it may be any one of these little ones that we have run across.'

'I do not know.'

'But thou wast sent to me – wast thou sent to me? – for the merit I had acquired over yonder at Such-zen. From beside the cannon didst thou come – bearing two faces – and two garbs.'

'Peace. One must not speak of these things here,' whispered Kim. 'There was but one of me. Think again and thou wilt remember. A boy – a Hindu boy – by the great green cannon.'

'But was there not also an Englishman with a white beard – holy among images – who himself made more sure my assurance of the River of the Arrow?'

'He – we – went to the Ajaib-Gher in Lahore to pray before the gods there,' Kim explained to the openly listening company. 'And the Sahib of the Wonder House talked to him – yes, this is truth – as a brother. He is a very holy man, from far beyond the hills. Rest thou. In time we come to Umballa.'

'But my River – the River of my healing?'

'And then, if it please thee, we will go hunting for that River on foot. So that we miss nothing – not even a little rivulet in a field-side.'

'But thou hast a Search of thine own?' The lama – very pleased that he remembered so well – sat bolt upright.

'Ay,' said Kim, humouring him. The boy was entirely happy to be out chewing *pan* and seeing new people in the great good-tempered world.

'It was a Bull – a Red Bull that shall come and help thee – and carry thee – whither? I have forgotten. A Red Bull on a green field, was it not?'

'Nay, it will carry me nowhere,' said Kim. 'It is but a tale I told thee.'

'What is this?' the cultivator's wife leaned forward, her bracelets clinking on her arm. 'Do ye both dream dreams? A Red Bull on a green field, that shall carry thee to the Heavens – or what? Was it a vision? Did one make a prophecy? *We* have a Red Bull in our village behind Jullundur city, and he grazes by choice in the very greenest of our fields!'

'Give a woman an old wife's tale and a weaver-bird a leaf and a thread, they will weave wonderful things,' said the Sikh. 'All holy men dream dreams, and by following holy men their disciples attain that power.'

'A Red Bull on a green field, was it?' the lama repeated. 'In a former life it may be thou hast acquired merit, and the Bull will come to reward thee.'

'Nay – nay – it was but a tale one told to me – for a jest belike. But I will seek the Bull about Umballa, and thou canst look for thy River and rest from the clatter of the train.'

'It may be that the Bull knows – that he is sent to guide us both,' said the lama, hopefully as a child. Then to the company, indicating Kim: 'This one was sent to me but yesterday. He is not, I think, of this world.'

'Beggars a plenty have I met, and holy men to boot, but never such a *yogi* nor such a disciple,' said the woman.

Her husband touched his forehead lightly with one finger and smiled. But the next time the lama would eat they took care to give him their best.

And at last – tired, sleepy, and dusty – they reached Umballa City Station.

'We abide here upon a law-suit,' said the cultivator's wife to Kim. 'We lodge with my man's cousin's younger brother. There is room also in the courtyard for thy *yogi* and for thee. Will – will he give me a blessing?'

'O holy man! A woman with a heart of gold gives us lodging for the night. It is a kindly land, this land of the South. See how we have been helped since the dawn!'

The lama bowed his head in benediction.

'To fill my cousin's younger brother's house with wastrels – ' the husband began, as he shouldered his heavy bamboo staff.

'Thy cousin's younger brother owes my father's cousin something yet on his daughter's marriage-feast,' said the woman crisply. 'Let him put their food to that account. The *yogi* will beg, I doubt not.'

'Ay, I beg for him,' said Kim, anxious only to get the lama under shelter for the night, that he might seek Mahbub Ali's Englishman and deliver himself of the white stallion's pedigree.

'Now,' said he, when the lama had come to an anchor in the inner courtyard of a decent Hindu house behind the cantonments, 'I go away for a while – to – to buy us victual in the bazar. Do not stray abroad till I return.'

'Thou wilt return? Thou wilt surely return?' The old man caught at his wrist. 'And thou wilt return in this very same shape? Is it too late to look to-night for the River?'

'Too late and too dark. Be comforted. Think how far thou art on the road – an hundred *kôs* from Lahore already.'

'Yea – and farther from my monastery. Alas! It is a great and terrible world.'

Kim stole out and away, as unremarkable a figure as ever carried his own and a few score thousand other folk's fate slung round his neck. Mahbub Ali's directions left him little doubt of the house in which his Englishman lived; and a groom, bringing a dog-cart home from the Club, made him quite sure. It remained only to identify his man, and Kim slipped through the garden hedge and hid in a clump of plumed grass close to the verandah. The house blazed with lights, and servants moved about tables dressed with flowers, glass, and silver. Presently forth came an Englishman, dressed in black and white, humming a tune. It was too dark to see his face, so Kim, beggar-wise, tried an old experiment.

'Protector of the Poor!'

The man backed towards the voice.

'Mahbub Ali says – '

'Hah! What says Mahbub Ali?' He made no attempt to look for the speaker, and that showed Kim that he knew.

'The pedigree of the white stallion is fully established.'

'What proof is there?' The Englishman switched at the rose-hedge in the side of the drive.

'Mahbub Ali has given me this proof.' Kim flipped the wad of folded paper into the air, and it fell on the path beside the man, who put his foot on it as a gardener came round the corner. When the servant passed he picked it up, dropped a rupee, – Kim could hear the clink, – and strode into the house, never turning round. Swiftly Kim took up the money; but, for all his training, he was Irish enough by birth to reckon silver the least part of any game. What he desired was the visible effect of action; so, instead of slinking away, he lay close in the grass and wormed nearer to the house.

He saw – Indian bungalows are open through and through – the Englishman return to a small dressing-room, in a corner of the verandah, that was half-office, littered with papers and despatch-boxes, and sit down to study Mahbub Ali's message. His face, by the full ray of the kerosene lamp, changed and darkened, and Kim, used as every beggar must be to watching countenances, took good note.

'Will! Will, dear!' called a woman's voice. 'You ought to be in the drawing-room. They'll be here in a minute.'

The man still read intently.

'Will!' said the voice, five minutes later. '*He's* come. I can hear the troopers in the drive.'

The man dashed out bareheaded as a big landau with four native troopers behind it halted at the verandah, and a tall, black-haired man, erect as an arrow, swung out, preceded by a young officer who laughed pleasantly.

Flat on his belly lay Kim, almost touching the high wheels. His man and the black stranger exchanged two sentences.

'Certainly, sir,' said the young officer promptly. 'Everything waits while a horse is concerned.'

'We shan't be more than twenty minutes,' said Kim's man. 'You can do the honours – keep 'em amused, and all that.'

'Tell one of the troopers to wait,' said the tall man, and they both passed into the dressing-room together as the landau rolled away. Kim saw their heads bent over Mahbub Ali's message, and heard the voices – one low and deferential the other sharp and decisive.

'It isn't a question of weeks. It is a question of days – hours almost,' said the elder. 'I'd been expecting it for some time, but this' – he tapped Mahbub Ali's paper – 'clinches it. Grogan's dining here to-night, isn't he?'

'Yes, sir, and Macklin too.'

'Very good. I'll speak to them myself. That matter will be referred to the Council, of course, but this is a case where one is justified in assuming that we take action at once. Warn the Pindi and Peshawur brigades. It will disorganise all the summer reliefs, but we can't help that. This comes of not smashing them thoroughly the first time. Eight thousand should be enough.'

'What about artillery, sir?'

'I must consult Macklin.'

'Then it means war?'

'No. Punishment. When a man is bound by the action of his predecessor – '

'But C.25 may have lied.'

'He bears out the other's information. Practically, they showed their hand six months back. But Devenish would have it there was a chance of peace. Of course they used it to make themselves stronger. Send off those telegrams at once, – the new code, not the old, – mine and Wharton's. I don't think we need keep the ladies waiting any longer. We can settle the rest over the cigars. I thought it was coming. It's punishment – not war.'

As the trooper cantered off Kim crawled round to the back of the house, where, going on his Lahore experiences, he judged there would be food – and information. The kitchen was crowded with excited scullions, one of whom kicked him.

'Aie,' said Kim, feigning tears. 'I came only to wash dishes in return for a bellyful.'

'All Umballa is on the same errand. Get hence. They go in now with the soup. Think you that we who serve Creighton Sahib need strange scullions to help us through a big dinner?'

'It is a very big dinner,' said Kim, looking at the plates.

'Small wonder. The guest of honour is none other than the Jang-i-Lat Sahib (the Commander-in-Chief).'

'Ho!' said Kim, with the correct guttural note of wonder. He had learned what he wanted, and when the scullion turned he was gone.

'And all that trouble," said he to himself, thinking as usual in Hindustanee, 'for a horse's pedigree! Mahbub Ali should have come to me to learn a little lying. Every time before that I have borne a message it concerned a woman. Now it is men. Better. The tall man said that they will loose a great army to punish someone – somewhere – the news goes to Pindi and Peshawur. There are also guns. Would I had crept nearer. It is big news!'

He returned to find the cultivator's cousin's younger brother discussing the family lawsuit in all its bearings with the cultivator and his wife and a few friends, while the lama dozed. After the evening meal some one passed him a water-pipe; and Kim felt very much of a man as he pulled at the smooth cocoanut-shell, his legs spread abroad in the moonlight, his tongue clicking in remarks from time to time. His hosts were most polite; for the cultivator's wife had told them of his vision of the Red Bull, and of his probable descent from another world. Moreover, the lama was a great and venerable curiosity. The family priest, an old, tolerant Sarsut Brahmin, dropped in later, and naturally started a theological argument to impress the family. By creed, of course, they were all on their priest's side, but the lama was the guest and the novelty. His gentle kindliness, and his impressive Chinese quotations, that sounded like spells, delighted them hugely; and in this sympathetic, simple air he expanded like the Bodhisat's own lotus, speaking of his life in the great hills of Such-zen, before, as he said, 'I rose up to seek enlightenment.'

Then it came out that in those worldly days he had been a master-hand at casting horoscopes and nativities; and the family priest led him on to describe his methods; each giving the planets names that the other could not understand, and pointing upwards as the big stars sailed across the dark. The children of the house tugged un-rebuked at his rosary; and he clean forgot the Rule which forbids looking at women as he talked of enduring snows, landslips, blocked passes, the remote cliffs where men find sapphires and turquoise, and that wonderful upland road that leads at last into Great China itself.

'How thinkest thou of this one?' said the cultivator aside to the priest.

'A holy man – a holy man indeed. His Gods are not the Gods, but his feet are upon the Way,' was the answer. 'And his methods of nativities, though that is beyond thee, are wise and sure.'

'Tell me,' said Kim lazily, 'whether I find my Red Bull on a green field, as was promised me.'

'What knowledge hast thou of thy birth-hour?' the priest asked, swelling with importance.

'Between first and second cockcrow of the first night in May.'

'Of what year?'

'I do not know; but upon the hour that I cried first fell the great earthquake in Srinagur which is in Kashmir.' This Kim had from the woman who took care of him, and she again from Kimball O'Hara. The earthquake had been felt in India, and for long stood a leading date in the Punjab.

'Ai!' said a woman excitedly. This seemed to make Kim's supernatural origin more certain. 'Was not such an one's daughter born then – '

'And her mother bore her husband four sons in four years – all likely boys,' cried the cultivator's wife, sitting outside the circle in the shadow.

'None reared in the knowledge,' said the family priest, 'forget how the planets stood in their Houses upon that night.' He began to draw in the dust of the courtyard. 'At least thou hast good claim to a half of the House of the Bull. How runs thy prophecy?'

'Upon a day,' said Kim, delighted at the sensation he was creating, 'I shall be made great by means of a Red Bull on a green field, but first there will enter two men making all things ready.'

'Yes: thus ever at the opening of a vision. A thick darkness that clears slowly; anon one enters with a broom making ready the place. Then begins the Sight. Two men – thou sayest? Ay, ay. The Sun, leaving the House of the Bull, enters that of the Twins. Hence the two men of the prophecy. Let us now consider. Fetch me a twig, little one.'

He knitted his brows, scratched, smoothed out, and scratched again in the dust mysterious signs – to the wonder of all save the lama, who, with fine instinct, forbore to interfere.

At the end of half an hour he tossed the twig from him with a grunt.

'Hm. Thus say the stars. Within three days come the two men to make all things ready. After them follows the Bull; but the sign over against him is the sign of War and armed men.'

'There was indeed a man of the Ludhiana Sikhs in the carriage from Lahore," said the cultivator's wife hopefully.

'Tck! Armed men – many hundreds. What concern hast thou with war?' said the priest to Kim. 'Thine is a red and an angry sign of War to be loosed very soon.'

'None – none,' said the lama earnestly. 'We seek only peace and our River.'

Kim smiled, remembering what he had overheard in the dressing-room. Decidedly he was a favourite of the stars.

The priest brushed his foot over the rude horoscope. 'More than this I cannot see. In three days comes the Bull to thee, boy.'

'And my River, my River,' pleaded the lama. 'I had hoped his Bull would lead us both to the River.'

'Alas, for that wondrous River, my brother,' the priest replied. 'Such things are not common.'

Next morning, though they were pressed to stay, the lama insisted on departure. They gave Kim a large bundle of good food and nearly three annas in copper money for the needs of the road, and with many blessings watched the two go southward in the dawn.

'Pity it is that these and such as these could not be freed from the Wheel of Things,' said the lama.

'Nay, then would only evil people be left on the earth, and who would give us meat and shelter?' quoth Kim, stepping merrily under his burden.

'Yonder is a small stream. Let us look,' said the lama, and he led from the white road across the fields; walking into a very hornets'-nest of pariah dogs.

CHAPTER 3

Yea, voice of every Soul that clung
To Life that strove from rung to rung
When Devadatta's rule was young,
The warm wind brings *Kamakura*.

BEHIND THEM an angry farmer brandished a bamboo pole. He was a market-gardener, Arain by caste, growing vegetables and flowers for Umballa city, and well Kim knew the breed.

'Such an one,' said the lama, disregarding the dogs, 'is impolite to strangers, intemperate of speech and uncharitable. Be warned by his demeanour, my disciple.'

'Ho, shameless beggars!' shouted the farmer. 'Begone! Get hence!'

'We go,' the lama returned, with quiet dignity. 'We go from these unblessed fields.'

'Ah,' said Kim, sucking in his breath. 'If the next crop fails, thou canst only blame thy own tongue.'

The man shuffled uneasily in his slippers. 'The land is full of beggars,' he began, half apologetically.

And by what sign didst thou know that we would beg from thee, O Mali?' said Kim tartly, using the name that a market-gardener least likes. 'All we sought was to look at that river beyond the field there.'

'River, forsooth!' the man snorted. 'What city do ye hail from not to know a canal-cut? It runs as straight as an arrow, and I pay for the water as though it were molten silver. There is a branch of a river beyond. But if ye need water I can give that – and milk.'

'Nay, we will go to the river,' said the lama, striding out.

'Milk and a meal,' the man stammered, as he looked at the strange tall figure. 'I – I would not draw evil upon myself – or my crops; but beggars are so many in these hard days.'

'Take notice,' the lama turned to Kim. 'He was led to speak harshly by the Red Mist of anger. That clearing from his eyes, he becomes courteous and of an affable heart. May his fields be blessed. Beware not to judge men too hastily, O farmer.'

'I have met holy ones who would have cursed thee from hearthstone to byre,' said Kim to the abashed man. 'Is he not wise and holy? I am his disciple.'

He cocked his nose in the air loftily and stepped across the narrow field-borders with great dignity.

'There is no pride,' said the lama, after a pause, 'there is no pride among such as follow the Middle Way.'

'But thou hast said he was low caste and discourteous.'

'Low caste I did not say, for how can that be which is not? Afterwards he amended his discourtesy, and I forgot the offense. Moreover, he is as we are, bound upon the Wheel of Things; but he does not tread the way of deliverance.' He halted at a little runlet among the fields, and considered the hoof-pitted bank.

'Now, how wilt thou know thy River?' said Kim, squatting in the shade of some tall sugar-cane.

'When I find it, an enlightenment will surely be given. This, I feel, is not the place. O littlest among the waters, if only thou couldst tell me where runs my River! But be thou blessed to make the fields bear!'

'Look! Look!' Kim sprang to his side and dragged him back. A yellow and brown streak glided from the purple rustling stems to the bank, stretched its neck to the water, drank, and lay still – a big cobra with fixed, lidless eyes.

'I have no stick – I have no stick,' said Kim. 'I will get me one and break his back.'

'Why? He is upon the Wheel as we are – a life ascending or descending – very far from deliverance. Great evil must the soul have done that is cast into this shape.'

'I hate all snakes,' said Kim. No native training can quench the white man's horror of the Serpent.

'Let him live out his life.' The coiled thing hissed and half opened its hood. 'May thy release come soon, brother,' the lama continued placidly. 'Hast thou knowledge, by chance, of my River?'

'Never have I seen such a man as thou art,' Kim whispered, overwhelmed. 'Do the very snakes understand thy talk?'

'Who knows?' He passed within a foot of the cobra's poised head. It flattened itself among the dusty coils.

'Come thou!' he called over his shoulder.

'Not I,' said Kim. 'I go round.'

'Come. He does no hurt.'

Kim hesitated for a moment. The lama backed his order by some droned Chinese quotation which Kim took for a charm. He obeyed and bounded across the rivulet, and the snake, indeed, made no sign.

'Never have I seen such a man.' Kim wiped the sweat from his forehead. 'And now, whither go we?'

'That is for thee to say. I am old, and a stranger – far from my own place. But that the *rêl*-carriage fills my head with noises of devil-drums I would go in it to Benares now. . . . Yet by so going we may miss the River. Let us find another river.'

Where the hard-worked soil gives three and even four crops a year – through patches of sugar-cane, tobacco, long white radishes, and nol-kol, all that day they strolled on, turning aside to every glimpse of water; rousing village dogs and sleeping villages at noonday; the lama replying to the vollied questions with an unswerving simplicity. They sought a River – a River of miraculous healing. Had any one knowledge of such a stream? Sometimes men laughed, but more often heard the story out to the end and offered them a place in the shade, a drink of milk, and a meal. The women were always kind, and the little children as children are the world over, alternately shy and venturesome. Evening found them at rest under the village tree of a mud-walled, mud-roofed hamlet, talking to the headman as the cattle came in from the grazing-grounds and the women prepared the day's last meal. They had passed beyond the belt of market-gardens round hungry Umballa, and were among the mile-wide green of the staple crops.

He was a white-bearded and affable elder, used to entertaining strangers. He dragged out a string bedstead for the lama, set warm cooked food before him, prepared him a pipe, and, the evening ceremonies being finished in the village temple, sent for the village priest.

Kim told the older children tales of the size and beauty of Lahore, of railway travel, and such-like city things, while the men talked, slowly as their cattle chew the cud.

'I cannot fathom it,' said the headman at last to the priest. 'How readest thou this talk?' The lama, his tale told, was silently telling his beads.

'He is a Seeker,' the priest answered. 'The and is full of such. Remember him who came only last month – the *faquir* with the tortoise?'

'Ay, but that man had right and reason, for Krishna Himself appeared in a vision promising him Paradise without the burning-pyre if he journeyed to Prayag. This man seeks no god who is within my knowledge.'

'Peace, he is old: he comes from far off, and he is mad,' the smooth-shaven priest replied. 'Hear me.' He turned to the lama. 'Three *kôs* (six miles) to the westward runs the great road to Calcutta.'

'But I would go to Benares – to Benares.'

'And to Benares also. It crosses all streams on this side of Hind. Now my word to thee, Holy One, is rest here till tomorrow. Then take the road' (it was the Grand Trunk Road he meant) 'and test each stream that it overpasses; for, as I understand the virtue of thy River lies neither in one pool nor place, but throughout its length. Then, if thy Gods will, be assured that thou wilt come upon thy freedom.'

'That is well said.' The lama was much impressed by the plan. 'We will begin to-morrow, and a blessing on thee for showing old feet such a near road.' A deep, sing-song Chinese half-chant closed the sentence. Even the priest was impressed, and the headman feared an evil spell: but none could look at the lama's simple, eager face and doubt him long.

'Seest thou my *chela*?' he said, diving into his snuff-gourd with an important sniff. It was his duty to repay courtesy with courtesy.

'I see – and hear.' The headman rolled his eye where Kim was chatting to a girl in blue as she laid crackling thorns on a fire.

'He also has a Search of his own. No river, but a Bull. Yea, a Red Bull on a green field will some day raise him to honour. He is, I think, not altogether of this world. He was sent of a sudden to aid me in this search, and his name is Friend of all the World.'

The priest smiled. 'Ho there, Friend of all the World,' he cried across the sharp-smelling smoke, 'what art thou?'

'This Holy One's disciple,' said Kim.

'He says thou art a *bût'* (a spirit).

'Can *bûts* eat?' said Kim, with a twinkle. 'For I am hungry.'

'It is no jest,' cried the lama. 'A certain astrologer of that city whose name I have forgotten – '

'That is no more than the city of Umballa where we slept last night,' Kim whispered to the priest.

Ay, Umballa was it? He cast a horoscope and declared that my *chela* should find his desire within two days. But what said he of the meaning of the stars, Friend of all the World?'

Kim cleared his throat and looked around at the village graybeards.

'The meaning of my Star is War,' he replied pompously.

Somebody laughed at the little tattered figure strutting on the brickwork plinth under the great tree. Where a native would have lain down, Kim's white blood set him upon his feet.

'Ay, War,' he answered.

'That is a sure prophecy,' rumbled a deep voice. 'For there is always war along the Border – as I know.'

It was an old, withered man, who had served the Government in the days of the Mutiny as a native officer in a newly raised cavalry regiment.

The Government had given him a good holding in the village, and though the demands of his sons, now gray-bearded officers on their own account, had impoverished him, he was still a person of consequence. English officials – Deputy Commissioners even – turned aside from the main road to visit him, and on those occasions he dressed himself in the uniform of ancient days, and stood up like a ramrod.

'But this shall be a great war – a war of eight thousand,' Kim's voice shrilled across the quick-gathering crowd, astonishing himself.

'Redcoats or our own regiments?' the old man snapped, as though he were asking an equal. His tone made men respect Kim.

'Redcoats," said Kim at a venture. 'Redcoats and guns.'

'But – but the astrologer said no word of this,' cried the lama, snuffing prodigiously in his excitement.

'But *I* know. The word has come to me, who am this Holy One's disciple. There will rise a war – a war of eight thousand redcoats. From Pindi and Peshawur they will be drawn. This is sure.'

'The boy has heard bazar-talk,' said the priest.

'But he was always by my side,' said the lama. How should he know? I did not know.'

'He will make a clever juggler when the old man is dead,' muttered the priest to the headman. 'what new trick is this?'

'A sign. Give me a sign,' thundered the old soldier suddenly. 'If there were war my sons would have told me.'

'When all is ready, thy sons, doubt not, will be told. But it is a long road from thy sons to the man in whose hands these things lie.' Kim warmed to the game, for it reminded him of experiences in the letter-carrying line, when, for the sake of a few pice, he pretended to know more than he knew. But now he was playing for larger things – the sheer excitement and the sense of power. He drew a new breath and went on.

'Old man, give *me* a sign. Do underlings order the goings of eight thousand redcoats – with guns?'

'No.' Still the old man answered as though Kim were an equal.

'Dost thou know who He is then that gives the order?'

'I have seen Him.'

'To know again?'

'I have known Him since he was a lieutenant in the *top-khana* (the Artillery)'.

'A tall man. A tall man with black hair, walking thus?' Kim took a few paces in a stiff, wooden style.

'Ay. But that anyone may have seen.' The crowd were breathless – still through all this talk.

'That is true,' said Kim. 'But I will say more. Look now. First the great man walks thus. Then He thinks thus. (Kim drew a forefinger over his forehead and downwards till it came to rest by the angle of the jaw.) Anon He twitches his fingers thus. Anon He thrusts his hat under his left armpit.' Kim illustrated the motion and stood like a stork.

The old man groaned, inarticulate with amazement; and the crowd shivered.

'So – so – so. But what does He when He is about to give an order?'

'He rubs the skin at the back of his neck – thus. Then falls one finger on the table and he makes a small sniffing noise through his nose. Then He speaks, saying: 'Loose such and such a regiment. Call out such guns.'

The old man rose stiffly and saluted.

' "For" ' – Kim translated into the vernacular the clinching sentences he had heard in the dressing-room at Umballa – ' "For," says He, "we should have done this long ago. It is not war – it is a chastisement. Snff!" '

'Enough. I believe. I have seen Him thus in the smoke of battles. Seen and heard. It is He!'

'I saw no smoke' – Kim's voice shifted to the rapt sing-song of the wayside fortune-teller. 'I saw this in darkness. First came a man to make things clear. Then came horsemen. Then came He, standing in a ring of light. The rest followed as I have said. Old man, have I spoken truth?'

'It is He. Past all doubt it is He.'

The crowd drew a long, quavering breath, staring alternately at the old man, still at attention, and ragged Kim against the purple twilight.

'Said I not – said I not he was from the other world?' cried the lama proudly. 'He is the Friend of all the World. He is the Friend of the Stars!'

'At least it does not concern us,' a man cried. 'O thou young soothsayer, if the gift abides with thee at all seasons, I have a red-spotted cow. She may be sister to thy Bull for aught I know – '

'Or I care,' said Kim. 'My Stars do not concern themselves with thy cattle.'

Nay, but she is very sick,' a woman struck in. 'My man is a buffalo, or he would have chosen his words better. Tell me if she recover?'

Had Kim been at all an ordinary boy, he would have carried on the play; but one does not know Lahore city, and least of all the *faquirs* by the Taksali Gate, for thirteen years without also knowing human nature.

The priest looked at him sideways, something bitterly – a dry and blighting smile.

'Is there no priest then in the village? I thought I had seen a great one even now,' cried Kim.

'Ay – but – ' the woman began.

'But thou and thy husband hoped to get the cow cured for a handful of thanks.' The shot told: they were notoriously the closest-fisted couple in the village. 'It is not well to cheat the temples. Give a young calf to thy own priest, and, unless thy gods are angry past recall, she will give milk within a month.'

'A master-beggar art thou,' purred the priest approvingly. 'Not the cunning of forty years could have done better. Surely thou hast made the old man rich?'

'A little flour, a little butter and a mouthful of cardamoms,' Kim retorted, flushed with the praise, but still cautious – 'does one grow rich on that? And, as thou canst see, he is mad. But it serves me while I learn the road at least.'

He knew what the *faquirs* of the Taksali Gate were like when they talked among themselves, and copied the very inflection of their lewd disciples.

'Is his Search, then, truth or a cloak to other ends? It may be treasure.'

'He is mad – many times mad. There is nothing else.'

Here the old soldier hobbled up and asked if Kim would accept his hospitality for the night. The priest recommended him to do so, but insisted that the honour of entertaining the lama belonged to the temple – at which the lama smiled guilelessly. Kim glanced from one face to the other, and drew his own conclusions.

'Where is the money?' he whispered, beckoning the old man off into the darkness.

'In my bosom. Where else?'

'Give it me. Quietly and swiftly give it me.'

'But why? Here is no ticket to buy.'

'Am I thy *chela*, or am I not? Do I not safeguard thy old feet about the ways? Give me the money and at dawn I will return it.' He slipped his hand above the lama's girdle and brought away the purse.

'Be it so – be it so.' The old man nodded his head. 'This is a great and terrible world. I never knew there were so many men alive in it.'

Next morning the priest was in a very bad temper, but the lama was quite happy; and Kim had enjoyed a most interesting evening with the old man, who brought out his cavalry sabre and, balancing it on his dry knees, told tales of the Mutiny and young captains thirty years in their graves, till Kim dropped off to sleep.

'Certainly the air of this country is good,' said the lama. 'I sleep lightly, as do all old men; but last night I slept unwaking till broad day. Even now I am heavy.'

'Drink a draught of hot milk,' said Kim, who had carried not a few such remedies to opium-smokers of his acquaintance. 'It is time to take the road again.'

'The long road that overpasses all the rivers of Hind,' said the lama gaily. 'Let us go. But how thinkest thou, *chela,* to recompense these people, and especially the priest, for their great kindness? Truly they are *bût-parast*, but in other lives, may be, they will receive enlightenment. A rupee to the temple? The thing within is no more than stone and red paint, but the heart of man we must acknowledge when and where it is good.'

'Holy One, hast thou ever taken the road alone?' Kim looked up sharply, like the Indian crows so busy about the fields.

'Surely, child: from Kulu to Pathankot – from Kulu, where my first *chela* died. When men were kind to us we made offerings, and all men were well-disposed throughout all the Hills.'

'It is otherwise in Hind,' said Kim drily. 'Their Gods are many-armed and malignant. Let them alone.'

'I would set thee on thy road for a little, Friend of all the World – thou and thy yellow man.' The old soldier ambled up the village street, all shadowy in the dawn, on a gaunt, scissor-hocked pony. 'Last night broke up the fountains of remembrance in my so-dried heart, and it was as a blessing to me. Truly there is war abroad in the air. I smell it. See! I have brought my sword.'

He sat long-legged on the little beast, with his big sword at his side – hand dropped on the pommel – staring fiercely over the flat lands towards the north. 'Tell me again how He showed in thy vision. Come up and sit behind me. The beast will carry two.'

'I am this Holy One's disciple,' said Kim, as they cleared the village-gate. The villagers seemed almost sorry to be rid of them, but the priest's farewell was cold and distant. He had wasted some opium on a man who carried no money.

'That is well spoken. I am not much used to holy men, but respect is always good. There is no respect in these days – not even when a Commissioner Sahib comes to see me. But why should one whose Star leads him to war follow a holy man?'

'But he *is* a holy man,' said Kim earnestly. 'In truth, and in talk and in act, holy. He is not like the others. I have never seen such an one. We be not fortune-tellers, or jugglers, or beggars.'

'Thou art not, that I can see; but I do not know that other. He marches well, though.'

The first freshness of the day carried the lama forward with long, easy, camel-like strides. He was deep in meditation, mechanically clicking his rosary.

They followed the rutted and worn country road that wound across the flat between the great dark-green mangogroves, the line of the snow-capped Himalayas faint to the eastward. All India was at work in the fields, to the creaking of well-wheels, the shouting of ploughmen behind their cattle, and the clamour of the crows. Even the pony felt the good influence and almost broke into a trot as Kim laid a hand on the stirrup-leather.

'It repents me that I did not give a rupee to the shrine,' said the lama on the last bead of his eighty-one.

The old soldier growled in his beard, so that the lama for the first time was aware of him.

'Seekest thou the River also?' said he, turning.

'The day is new,' was the reply. 'What need of a river save to water at before sundown? I come to show thee a short lane to the Big Road.'

'That is a courtesy to be remembered, O man of good will; but why the sword?'

The old soldier looked as abashed as a child interrupted in his game of make-believe.

'The sword,' he said, fumbling it.' Oh, that was a fancy of mine – an old man's fancy. Truly the police orders are that no man must bear weapons throughout Hind, but' – he cheered up and slapped the hilt – 'all the constabeels hereabout know me.'

'It is not a good fancy,' said the lama. 'What profit to kill men?'

'Very little – as I know; but if evil men were not now and then slain it would not be a good world for weaponless dreamers. I do not speak without knowledge who have seen the land from Delhi south awash with blood.'

'What madness was that, then?'

'The Gods, who sent it for a plague, alone know. A madness ate into all the Army, and they turned against their officers. That was the first evil, but not past remedy if they had then held their hands. But they chose to kill the Sahibs' wives and children. Then came the Sahibs from over the sea and called them to most strict account.'

'Some such rumour, I believe, reached me once long ago. They called it the Black Year, as I remember.'

'What manner of life hast thou led, not to know The Year? A rumour indeed! All earth knew, and trembled.'

'Our earth never shook but once – upon the day that the Excellent One received Enlightenment.'

'Umph! I saw Delhi shake at least; and Delhi is the navel of the world.'

'So they turned against women and children? That was a bad deed, for which the punishment cannot be avoided.'

'Many strove to do so, but with very small profit. I was then in a regiment of cavalry. It broke. Of six hundred and eighty sabres stood fast to their salt – how many think you? Three. Of whom I was one.'

'The greater merit.'

'Merit! We did not consider it merit in those days. My people, my friends, my brothers fell from me. They said: "The time of the English is accomplished. Let each strike out a little holding for himself." But I had talked with the men of Sobraon, of Chillianwallah, of Moodkee and Ferozeshah. I said: "Abide a little and the wind turns. There is no blessing in this work." those days I rode seventy miles with an English mem-sahib and her babe on my saddle-bow. (Wow! That was a horse fit for a man!) I placed them in safety, and back came I to my officer – the one that was not killed of our five. "Give me work," said I, "for I am an outcast among my own kin, and my cousin's blood is wet on my sabre." "Be content," said he. "There is great work forward. When this madness is over there is a recompense." '

'Ay, there is a recompense when the madness is over, surely?' the lama muttered half to himself.

'They did not hang medals in those days on all who by accident had heard a gun fired. No! In nineteen pitched battles was I; in six-and-forty skirmishes of horse; and in small affairs without number. Nine wounds I bear; a medal and four clasps and the medal of an Order, for my captains who are now generals, remembered me when the Kaiser-i-Hind had accomplished fifty years of her reign, and all the land rejoiced. They said: "Give him the order of Berittish India." I carry it upon my neck now. I have also my *jaghir* (holding) from the hands of the State – a free gift to me and mine. The men of the old days – they are now Commissioners – come riding to me through the crops – high upon horses so that all the village sees, – and we talk out the old skirmishes, one dead man's name leading to another.'

'And after?' said the lama.

'Oh, afterwards they go away, but not before my village has seen.'

'And at the last what wilt thou do?'

'At the last I shall die.'

'And after?'

'Let the Gods order it. I have never pestered Them with prayers: I do not think they will pester me. Look you, I have noticed in my long life that those who eternally break in upon Those Above with complaints and reports and bellowings and weepings are presently sent for in haste, as our colonel used to send for slack-jawed down-country men who talked too much. No, I have never wearied the Gods. They will remember this, and give me a quiet place where I can drive my lance in the shade, and wait to welcome my sons: I have no less than three – ressaldar-majors all – in the regiments.'

'And they likewise, bound upon the Wheel, go forth from life to life – from despair to despair,' said the lama below his breath, 'hot, uneasy, snatching.'

'Ay,' the old soldier chuckled. 'Three ressaldar-majors in three regiments. Gamblers a little, but so am I. They must be well mounted; and one cannot take the horses as in the old days one took women. Well, well, my holding can pay for all. How thinkest thou? It is a well-watered strip, but my men cheat me. I do not know how to ask save at the lance's point. Ugh! I grow angry and I curse them, and they feign penitence, but behind my back I know they call me a toothless old ape.'

'Hast thou never desired any other thing?'

'Yes – yes – a thousand times! A straight back and a close-clinging knee once more; a quick wrist and a keen eye; and the marrow that makes a man. Oh, the old days – the good days of my strength!'

'That strength is weakness.'

'It has turned so; but fifty years since I could have proved it otherwise,' the old soldier retorted, driving his stirrup-edge into the pony's lean flank.

'But I know a River of great healing.'

'I have drunk Gunga-water to the edge of dropsy. All she gave me was a flux, and no sort of strength.'

'It is not Gunga. The River that I know washes from all taint of sin. Ascending the far bank one is assured of Freedom.

I do not know thy life, but thy face is the face of the honourable and courteous. Thou hast clung to thy Way, rendering fidelity when it was hard to give, in that Black Year of which I now remember other tales. Enter now upon the Middle Way, which is the path to Freedom. Hear the Most Excellent Law, and do not follow dreams.'

'Speak then, old man,' the soldier smiled, half saluting. 'We be all babblers at our age.'

The lama squatted under the shade of a mango tree, whose shadow played checkerwise over his face; the soldier sat stiffly on the pony; and Kim, making sure that there were no snakes, lay down in the crotch of the twisted roots.

There was a drowsy buzz of small life in hot sunshine, a cooing of doves, and a sleepy drone of well-wheels across the fields. Slowly and impressively the lama began. At the end of ten minutes the old soldier slid from his pony, to hear better as he said, and sat with the reins round his wrist. The lama's voice faltered – the periods lengthened. Kim was busy watching a gray squirrel. When the little scolding bunch of fur, close pressed to the branch, disappeared, preacher and audience were fast asleep, the old officer's strong-cut head pillowed on his arm, the lama's thrown back against the tree bole, where it showed like yellow ivory. A naked child toddled up, stared, and, moved by some quick impulse of reverence made a solemn little obeisance before the lama – only the child was so short and fat that it toppled over sideways, and Kim laughed at the sprawling, chubby legs. The child, seared and indignant, yelled aloud.

'Hai! Hai!' said the soldier leaping to his feet. 'What is it? What orders?. . . . It is. . . . a child! I dreamed it was an alarm. Little one – little one – do not cry. Have I slept? That was discourteous indeed!'

'I fear! I am afraid!' roared the child.

'What is it to fear? Two old men and a boy? How wilt thou ever make a soldier, Princeling?'

The lama had waked too, but, taking no direct notice of the child, clicked his rosary.

'What is that?' said the child, stopping a yell midway. 'I have never seen such things. Give them me.'

'Aha,' said the lama, smiling, and trailing a loop of it on the grass:

> 'This is a handful of cardamoms,
> This is a lump of *ghi*:
> This is millet and chillies and rice,
> A supper for thee and me!'

The child shrieked with joy, and snatched at the dark, glancing beads.

'Oho!' said the old soldier. 'Whence had thou that song, despiser of this world?'

'I learned it in Pathankot – sitting on a doorstep,' said the lama shyly. 'It is good to be kind to babes.'

'As I remember, before the sleep came on us, thou hadst told me that marriage and bearing were darkeners of the true light, stumbling-blocks upon the way. Do children drop from heaven in thy country? Is it the Way to sing them songs?'

'No man is all perfect,' said the lama gravely, re-coiling the rosary. 'Run now to thy mother, little one.'

'Hear him!' said the soldier to Kim. 'He is ashamed for that he has made a child happy. There was a very good householder lost in thee, my brother. Hai, child!' He threw it a pice. 'Sweetmeats are always sweet.' And as the little figure capered away into the sunshine: 'They grow up and become men. Holy One, I grieve that I slept in the midst of thy preaching. Forgive me.'

'We be two old men,' said the lama.' The fault is mine. I listened to thy talk of the world and its madness, and one fault led to the next.'

'Hear him! What harm do thy Gods suffer from play with a babe? And that song was very well sung. Let us go on and I will sing thee the song of Nikal Seyn before Delhi – the old song.'

And they fared out from the gloom of the mango tope, the old man's high, shrill voice ringing across the field, as wail by long-drawn wail he unfolded the story of Nikal Seyn (Nicholson) – the song that men sing in the Punjab to this day. Kim was delighted, and the lama listened with deep interest.

'Ahi! Nikal Seyn is dead –
he died before Delhi!
Lances of North take
vengeance for Nikal Seyn.'

He quavered it out to the end, marking the trills with the flat of his sword on the pony's rump.

'And now we come to the Big Road,' said he, after receiving the compliments of Kim; for the lama was markedly silent. 'It is long since I have ridden this way, but thy boy's talk stirred me. See, Holy One – the Great Road which is the backbone of all Hind. For the most part it is shaded, as here, with four lines of trees; the middle road – all hard – takes the quick traffic. In the days before rail-carriages the Sahibs travelled up and down here in hundreds. Now there are only country-carts and such like. Left and right is the rougher road for the heavy carts – grain and cotton and timber, bhoosa, lime and hides. A man goes in safety here – for at every few *kôs* is a police-station. The police are thieves and extortioners (I myself would patrol it with cavalry – young recruits under a strong captain), but at least they do not suffer any rivals. All castes and kinds of men move here. Look! Brahmins and chumars, bankers and tinkers, barbers and bunnias, pilgrims and potters – all the world going and coming. It is to me as a river from which I am withdrawn like a log after a flood.'

And truly the Grand Trunk Road is a wonderful spectacle. It runs straight, bearing without crowding India's traffic for fifteen hundred miles – such a river of life as nowhere else exists in the world. They looked at the green-arched, shade-flecked length of it, the white breadth speckled with slow-pacing folk; and the two-roomed police-station opposite.

'Who bears arms against the law?' a constable called out laughingly, as he caught sight of the soldier's sword. 'Are not the police enough to destroy evil-doers?'

'It was because of the police I bought it,' was the answer. 'Does all go well in Hind?'

'Ressaldar Sahib, all goes well.'

'I am like an old tortoise, look you, who puts his head out from the bank and draws it in again. Ay, this is the road of Hindustan. All men come by this way. . . . '

'Son of a swine, is the soft part of the road meant for thee to scratch thy back upon? Father of all the daughters of shame and husband of ten thousand virtueless ones, thy mother was devoted to a devil, being led thereto by her mother; thy aunts have never had a nose for seven generations! Thy sister – What owl's folly told thee to draw thy carts across the road? A broken wheel? Then take a broken head and put the two together at leisure!'

The voice and a venomous whip-cracking came out of a pillar of dust fifty yards away, where a cart had broken down. A thin, high Kattiawar mare, with eyes and nostrils aflame, rocketed out of the jam, snorting and wincing as her rider bent her across the road in chase of a shouting man. He was tall and gray-bearded, sitting the almost mad beast as a piece of her, and scientifically lashing his victim between plunges.

The old man's face lit with pride. 'My child!' said he briefly, and strove to rein the pony's neck to a fitting arch.

'Am I to be beaten before the police?' cried the carter. 'Justice! I will have Justice – '

'Am I to be blocked by a shouting ape who upsets ten thousand sacks under a young horse's nose? That is the way to ruin a mare.'

'He speaks truth. He speaks truth. But she follows her man close,' said the old man. The carter ran under the wheels of his cart and thence threatened all sorts of vengeance.

'They are strong men, thy sons,' said the policeman serenely, picking his teeth.

The horseman delivered one last vicious cut with his whip and came on at a canter.

'My father!' He reined back ten yards and dismounted.

The old man was off his pony in an instant, and they embraced as do father and son in the East.

CHAPTER 4

Good Luck, she is never a lady,
But the cursedest quean alive.
Tricksy, wincing, and jady –
Kittle to lead or drive.
Greet her – she hailing a stranger!
Meet her – she's busking to leave!
Let her alone for a shrew to the bone
And the hussy comes plucking your sleeve!
    Largesse! Largesse, O Fortune!
    Give or hold at your will
    If I've no care for Fortune,
    Fortune must follow me still!

– *The Wishing Caps.*

THEN, LOWERING their voices, they spoke together. Kim came to rest under a tree, but the lama tugged impatiently at his elbow.

'Let us go on. The River is not here.'

'Hai mai? Have we not walked enough for a little? Our River will not run away. Patience, and he will give us a dole.'

'That,' said the old soldier suddenly, 'is the Friend of the Stars. He brought me the news yesterday. Having seen the very man Himself, in a vision, giving orders for the war.'

'Hm!' said his son, all deep in his broad chest. 'He came by a bazar-rumour and made profit of it.'

His father laughed. 'At least he did not ride to me begging for a new charger and the Gods know how many rupees. Are thy brothers' regiments also under orders?'

'I do not know. I took leave and came swiftly to thee in case – '

'In case they ran before thee to beg. O gamblers and spendthrifts all! But thou hast never yet ridden in a charge. A good horse is needed there, truly. A good follower and a good pony also for the marching. Let us see – let us see.' He thrummed on the pommel.

'This is no place to cast thy accounts in, my father. Let us go to thy house.'

'At least pay the boy then: I have no pice with me, and he brought auspicious news. Ho! Friend of all the World, a war is toward as thou hast said.'

'Nay, as I know, *the* war,' returned Kim composedly.

'Eh?' said the lama, fingering his beads, all eager for the road.

'My master does not trouble the Stars for hire. We brought the news – bear witness, we brought the news, and now we go.' Kim half-crooked his hand at his side.

The son tossed a silver coin through the sunlight, grumbling something about beggars and jugglers. It was a four-anna piece, and would feed them well for some days. The lama, seeing the flash of the metal, droned a blessing.

'Go thy way, Friend of all the World,' piped the old soldier, wheeling his scrawny mount. 'For once in all my days I have met a true prophet – who was not in the Army.'

Father and son swung round together: the old man sitting as erect as the younger.

A Punjabi constable in yellow linen trousers slouched across the road. He had seen the money pass.

'Halt!' he cried in impressive English. 'Know ye not that there is a *takkus* of two annas a head, which is four annas, on those who enter the road from this side-road. It is the order of the Sirkar, and the money is spent for the planting of trees and the beautification of the ways.'

'And the bellies of the police,' said Kim, skipping out of arm's reach. 'Consider for a while, man with a mud head. Think you we came from the nearest pond like the frog, thy father-in-law. Hast thou ever heard the name of thy brother?'

'And who was he? Leave the boy alone,' cried a senior constable, immensely delighted, as he squatted down to smoke his pipe in the veranda.

'He took a label from a bottle of *belaitee-pani* (soda-water), and, affixing it to a bridge, collected taxes for a month from those who passed, saying that it was the Sirkar's order. Then came an Englishman and broke his head. 'Ah, brother, I am a town-crow, not a village-crow!'

The policeman drew back abashed, and Kim hooted at him all down the road.

'Was there ever such a disciple as I?' he cried merrily to the lama. 'All earth would have picked thy bones within ten mile of Lahore city if I had not guarded thee.'

'I consider in my own mind whether thou art a spirit, sometimes, or sometimes an evil imp,' said the lama, smiling slowly.

'I am thy *chela*.' Kim dropped into step at his side – that indescribable gait of the long-distance tramp all the world over.

'Now let us walk,' muttered the lama, and to the click of his rosary they walked in silence mile upon mile. The lama, as usual, was deep in meditation, but Kim's bright eyes were open wide. This broad, smiling river of life, he considered, was a vast improvement on the cramped and crowded Lahore streets. There were new people and new sights at every stride – castes he knew and castes that were altogether out of his experience.

They met a troop of long-haired, strong-scented Sansis with baskets of lizards and other unclean food on their backs, their lean dogs sniffing at their heels. These people kept their own side of the road, moving at a quick, furtive jog-trot, and all other castes gave them ample room; for the Sansi is deep pollution. Behind them, walking wide and stiffly across the strong shadows, the memory of his leg-irons still on him, strode one newly released from the jail; his full stomach and shiny skin to prove that the Government fed its prisoners better than most honest men could feed themselves. Kim knew that walk well, and made broad jest of it as they passed. Then an Akali, a wild-eyed, wild-haired Sikh devotee in the blue-checked clothes of his faith, with polished-steel quoits glistening on the cone of his tall blue turban, stalked past, returning from a visit to one of the independent Sikh States, where he had been singing the ancient glories of the Khalsa to College-trained princelings in top-boots and white-cord breeches. Kim was careful not to irritate that man; for the Akali's temper is short and his arm quick. Here and there they met or were overtaken by the gaily dressed crowds of whole villages turning out to some local fair; the women, with their babes on their hips, walking behind the men, the older boys prancing on sticks of sugar-cane, dragging rude brass models of locomotives such as they sell for a halfpenny, or flashing the sun into the eyes of their betters from cheap toy mirrors. One could see at a glance what each had bought; and if there were any doubt it needed only to watch the wives comparing, brown arm against brown arm, the newly purchased dull glass bracelets that come from the North-West. These merry-makers stepped slowly, calling one to the other and stopping to haggle with sweetmeat-sellers, or to make a prayer before one of the wayside shrines – sometimes Hindu, sometimes Mussalman – which the low caste of both creeds share with beautiful impartiality. A solid line of blue, rising and falling like the back of a caterpillar in haste, would swing up through the quivering dust and trot past to a chorus of quick cackling. That was a gang of *changars* – the women who have taken all the embankments of all the Northern railways under their charge – a flat-footed, big-bosomed, strong-limbed, blue-petticoated clan of earth-carriers, hurrying north on news of a job, and wasting no time by the road. They belong to the caste whose men do not count, and they walked with squared elbows, swinging hips, and heads on high, as suits women who carry heavy weights. A little later a marriage procession would strike into the Grand Trunk with music and shoutings, and a smell of marigold and jasmine stronger even than the reek of the dust. One could see the bride's litter, a blur of red and tinsel, staggering through the haze, while the bridegroom's bewreathed pony turned aside to snatch a mouthful from a passing fodder-cart. Then Kim would join the Kentish-fire of good wishes and bad jokes, wishing the couple a hundred sons and no daughters, as the saying is. Still more interesting and more to be shouted over it was when a strolling juggler with some half-trained monkeys, or a panting, feeble bear, or a woman who tied goats' horns to her feet, and with these danced on a slack-rope, set the horses to shying and the women to shrill, long-drawn quavers of amazement.

The lama never raised his eyes. He did not note the money-lender on his goose-rumped pony, hastening along to collect the cruel interest; or the long-shouting, deep-voiced little mob – still in military formation – of native soldiers on leave, rejoicing to be rid of their breeches and puttees, and saying the most outrageous things to the most respectable women in sight. Even the seller of Ganges-water he did not see, and Kim expected that he would at least buy a bottle of that precious stuff. He looked steadily at the ground, and strode as steadily hour after hour, his soul busied elsewhere. But Kim was in the seventh heaven of joy. The Grand Trunk at this point was built on an embankment to guard against winter floods from the foothills, so that one walked, as it were, a little above the country, along a stately corridor, seeing all India spread out to left and right. It was beautiful to behold the many-yoked grain and cotton waggons crawling over the country-roads: one could hear their axles, complaining a mile away, coming nearer, till with shouts and yells and bad words they climbed up the steep incline and plunged on to the hard main road, carter reviling carter. It was equally beautiful to watch the people, little clumps of red and blue and pink and white and saffron, turning aside to go to their own villages, dispersing and growing small by twos and threes across the level plain. Kim felt these things, though he could not give tongue to his feelings, and so contented himself with buying peeled sugar-cane and spitting the pith generously about his path. From time to time the lama took snuff, and at last Kim could endure the silence no longer.

'This is a good land – the land of the South!' said he. 'The air is good; the water is good. Eh?'

'And they are all bound upon the Wheel," said the lama. 'Bound from life after life. To none of these has the Way been shown.' He shook himself back to this world.

'And now we have walked a weary way," said Kim. 'Surely we shall soon come to a *parao* (a resting-place). Shall we stay there? Look, the sun is sloping.'

'Who will receive us this evening?'

'That is all one. This country is full of good folk. Besides' – he sunk his voice beneath a whisper, – 'we have money.'

The crowd thickened as they neared the resting-place which marked the end of their day's journey. A line of stalls selling very simple food and tobacco, a stack of firewood, a police-station, a well, a horse-trough, a few trees, and, under them, some trampled ground dotted with the black ashes of old fires, are all that mark a *parao* on the Grand Trunk; if you except the beggars and the crows – both hungry.

By this time the sun was driving broad golden spokes through the lower branches of the mango trees; the parakeets and doves were coming home in their hundreds; the chattering, gray-backed Seven Sisters, talking over the day's adventures, walked back and forth in twos and threes almost under the feet of the travellers; and shufflings and scufflings in the branches showed that the bats were ready to go out on the night-picket. Swiftly the light gathered itself together, painted for an instant the faces and the cart-wheels and the bullocks' horns as red as blood. Then the night fell, changing the touch of the air, drawing a low, even haze, like a gossamer veil of blue, across the face of the country, and bringing out, keen and distinct, the smell of wood-smoke and cattle and the good scent of wheaten cakes cooked on ashes. The evening patrol hurried out of the police-station with important coughings and reiterated orders; and a live charcoal ball in the cup of a wayside carter's hookah glowed red while Kim's eye mechanically watched the last flicker of the sun on the brass tweezers.

The life of the *parao* was very like that of the Kashmir Serai on a small scale. Kim dived into the happy Asiatic disorder which, if you only allow time, will bring you everything that a simple man needs.

His wants were few, because, since the lama had no caste scruples, cooked food from the nearest stall would serve; but, for luxury's sake, Kim bought a handful of dung-cakes to build a fire. All about, coming and going round the little flames, men cried for oil, or grain, or sweetmeats, or tobacco, jostling one another while they waited their turn at the well; and under the men's voices you heard from halted, shuttered carts the high squeals and giggles of women whose faces should not be seen in public.

Nowadays, well-educated natives are of opinion that when their womenfolk travel – and they visit a good deal – it is better to take them quickly by rail in a properly screened compartment; and that custom is spreading. But there are always those of the old rock who hold by the use of their forefathers; and, above all, there are always the old women, – more conservative than the men,– who toward the end of their days go a pilgrimage. They, being withered and undesirable, do not, under certain circumstances, object to unveiling. After their long seclusion, during which they have always been in business touch with a thousand outside interests, they love the bustle and stir of the open road, the gatherings at the shrines, and the infinite possibilities of gossip with like-minded dowagers. Very often it suits a long-suffering family that a strong-tongued, iron-willed old lady should disport herself about India in this fashion; for certainly pilgrimage is grateful to the Gods. So all about India, in the most remote places, as in the most public, you find some knot of grizzled servitors in nominal charge of an old lady who is more or less curtained and hid away in a bullock-cart. Such men are staid and discreet, and when a European or a high-caste native is near will net their charge with most elaborate precautions; but in the ordinary haphazard chances of pilgrimage the precautions are not taken. The old lady is, after all, intensely human, and lives to look upon life.

Kim marked down a gaily ornamented *ruth* or family bullock-cart, with a broidered canopy of two domes, like a double-humped camel, which had just been drawn into the *parao*. Eight men made its retinue, and two of the eight were armed with rusty sabres – sure signs that they followed a person of distinction, for the common folk do not bear arms. An increasing cackle of complaints, orders, and jests, and what to a European would have been bad language, came from behind the curtains. Here was evidently a woman used to command.

Kim looked over the retinue critically. Half of them were thin-legged, gray-bearded Ooryas from down country. The other half were duffle-clad, felt-hatted hillmen of the North; and that mixture told its own tale, even if he had not overheard the incessant sparring between the two divisions. The old lady was going south on a visit – probably to a rich relative, most probably to a son-in-law, who had sent up an escort as a mark of respect. The hillmen would be of her own people – Kulu or Kangra folk. It was quite clear that she was not taking her daughter down to be wedded, or the curtains would have been laced home and the guard would have allowed no one near the car. A merry and a high-spirited dame, thought Kim, balancing the dung-cake in one hand, the cooked food in the other, and piloting the lama with a nudging shoulder. Something might be made out of the meeting. The lama would give him no help, but, as a conscientious *chela*, Kim was delighted to beg for two.

He built his fire as close to the cart as he dared, waiting for one of the escort to order him away. The lama dropped wearily to the ground, much as a heavy fruit-eating bat cowers, and returned to his rosary.

'Stand farther off, beggar!' The order was shouted in broken Hindustanee by one of the hillmen.

'Huh! It is only a *pahari*' (a hillman), said Kim over his shoulder. 'Since when have the hill-asses owned all Hindustan?'

The retort was a swift and brilliant sketch of Kim's pedigree for three generations.

'Ah!' Kim's voice was sweeter than ever, as he broke the dung-cake into fit pieces. 'In *my* country we call that the beginning of love-talk.'

A harsh, thin cackle behind the curtains put the hillman on his mettle for a second shot.

'Not so bad – not so bad,' said Kim with calm. 'But have a care, my brother, lest we – *we*, I say – be minded to give a curse or so in return. And our curses have the knack of biting home.'

The Ooryas laughed; the hillman sprang forward threateningly; the lama suddenly raised his head, bringing his huge tam-o'-shanter cap into the full light of Kim's new-started fire.

'What is it?' said he.

The man halted as though struck to stone. 'I – I – am saved from a great sin,' he stammered.

'The foreigner has found him a priest at last,' whispered one of the Ooryas.

'Hai! Why is that beggar-brat not well beaten?' the old woman cried.

The hillman drew back to the cart and whispered something to the curtain. There was dead silence, then a muttering.

'This goes well,' thought Kim, pretending neither to see nor hear.

'When – when – he has eaten' – the hillman fawned on Kim – 'it – it is requested that the Holy One will do the honour to talk to one who would speak to him.'

'After he has eaten he will sleep,' Kim returned loftily. He could not quite see what new turn the game had taken, but stood resolute to profit by it. 'Now, I will get him his food.' The last sentence, spoken loudly, ended with a sigh as of faintness.

'I – I myself and the others of my people will look to that – if it is permitted.'

'It is permitted,' said Kim, more loftily than ever. 'Holy One, these people will bring us food.

'The land is good. All the country of the South is good – a great and a terrible world,' mumbled the lama drowsily.

'Let him sleep,' said Kim, 'but look to it that we are well fed when he wakes. He is a very holy man.'

Again one of the Ooryas said something contemptuously.

'He is not a *faquir*. He is not a down-country beggar," Kim went on severely, addressing the stars. 'He is the most holy of holy men. He is above all castes. I am his *chela*.'

'Come here!' said the flat thin voice behind the curtain; and Kim came, conscious that eyes he could not see were staring at him. One skinny brown finger heavy with rings lay on the edge of the cart, and the talk went this way:

'Who is that one?'

'An exceedingly holy one. He comes from far off. He comes from Tibet.'

'Where in Tibet?'

'From behind the snows – from a very far place. He knows the stars; he makes horoscopes; he reads nativities. But he does not do this for money. He does it for kindness and great charity. I am his disciple. I am called also the Friend of the Stars.'

'Thou art no hillman.'

'Ask him. He will tell thee I was sent to him from the stars to show him an end to his pilgrimage.'

'Humph! Consider, brat, that I am an old woman and not altogether a fool. Lamas I know, and to these I give reverence, but thou art no more a lawful *chela* than this my finger is the pole of this waggon. Thou art a casteless Hindu – a bold and unblushing beggar, attached, belike, to the Holy One for the sake of gain.'

'Do we not all work for gain?' Kim changed his tone promptly to match that altered voice. 'I have heard' – this was a bow drawn at a venture – 'I have heard – '

'What hast thou heard?' she snapped, rapping with the finger.

'Nothing that I well remember, but some talk in the bazars, which is doubtless a lie, that even Rajahs – small hill Rajahs – '

'But none the less of good Rajput blood.'

'Assuredly of good blood. That these even sell the more comely of their womenfolk for gain. Down south they sell them – to zemindars and such-all of Oudh.'

If there be one thing in the world that the small hill Rajahs deny it is just this charge; but it happens to be one thing that the bazars believe, when they discuss the mysterious slave-traffics of India. The old lady explained to Kim, in a tense, indignant whisper, precisely what manner and fashion of malignant liar he was. Had Kim hinted this when she was a girl, he would have been pommelled to death that same evening by an elephant. This was perfectly true.

'Ahai! I am only a beggar's brat, as the Eye of Beauty has said,' he wailed in extravagant terror.

'Eye of Beauty, forsooth! Who am I that thou shouldst fling beggar-endearments at me?' And yet she laughed at the long-forgotten word. 'Forty years ago that might have been said, and not without truth. Ay, thirty years ago. But it is the fault of this gadding up and down Hind that a king's widow must jostle all the scum of the land, and be made a mock by beggars.'

'Great Queen,' said Kim promptly, for he heard her shaking with indignation, 'I am even what the Great Queen says I am; but none the less is my master holy. He has not yet heard the Great Queen's order that – '

'Order? I order a Holy One – a Teacher of the Law – to come and speak to a woman? Never!'

'Pity my stupidity. I thought it was given as an order – '

'It was not. It was a petition. Does this make all clear?'

A silver coin clicked on the edge of the cart. Kim took it and salaamed profoundly. The old lady recognised that, as the eyes and the ears of the lama, he was to be propitiated.

'I am but the Holy One's disciple. When he has eaten perhaps he will come.'

'Oh, villain and shameless rogue!' The jewelled forefinger shook itself at him reprovingly; but he could hear the old lady's chuckle.

'Nay, what is it?' he said, dropping into his most caressing and confidential tone – the one, he well knew, that few could resist. 'Is – is there any need of a son in thy family? Speak freely, for we priests – 'That last was a direct plagiarism from a *faquir* by the Taksali Gate.

'We priests! Thou art not yet old enough to – ' She checked the joke with another laugh. 'Believe me, now and again, we women, O priest, think of other matters than sons. Moreover, my daughter has borne her man-child.'

'Two arrows in the quiver are better than one; and three are better still.' Kim quoted the proverb with a meditative cough, looking discreetly earthward.

'True – oh, true. But perhaps that will come. Certainly those down-country Brahmins are utterly useless. I sent gifts and monies and gifts again to them and they prophesied.'

'Ah,' drawled Kim, with infinite contempt, 'they prophesied!' A professional could have done no better.

'And it was not till I remembered my own Gods that my prayers were heard. I chose an auspicious hour, and – perhaps thy Holy One has heard of the Abbot of the Lung-Cho lamassery. It was to him I put the matter, and behold in the due time all came about as I desired. The Brahmin in the house of the father of my daughter's son has since said that it was through *his* prayers – which is a little error that I will explain to him when we reach our journey's end. And so afterwards I go to Buddh Gaya, to make *shraddha* for the father of my children.'

'Thither go we.'

'Doubly auspicious,' chirruped the old lady. 'A second son at least!'

'O Friend of all the World!' The lama had waked, and, simply as a child bewildered in a strange bed, called for Kim.

'I come! I come, Holy One!' He dashed to the fire, where he found the lama already surrounded by dishes of food, the hillmen visibly adoring him and the Southerners looking sourly.

'Go back! Withdraw!' Kim cried. 'Do we eat publicly like dogs?' They finished the meal in silence, each turned a little from the other, and Kim topped it with a native-made cigarette.

'Have I not said an hundred times that the South is a good land? Here is a virtuous and high-born widow of a Hill Rajah on pilgrimage, she says, to Buddh Gaya. She it is sends us those dishes; and when thou art well rested she would speak to thee.'

'Is this also thy work?' The lama dipped deep into his snuff-gourd.

'Who else watched over thee since our wonderful journey began?' Kim's eyes danced in his head as he blew the rank smoke through his nostrils and stretched himself on the dusty ground. 'Have I failed to oversee thy comforts, Holy One?'

'A blessing on thee.' The lama inclined his solemn head. 'I have known many men in my so long life, and disciples not a few. But to none among men, if so be thou art woman-born, has my heart gone out as it has to thee – thoughtful, wise, and courteous, but something of a small imp.'

'And I have never seen such a priest as thou.' Kim considered the benevolent yellow face wrinkle by wrinkle. 'It is less than three days since we took road together, and it is as though it were a hundred years.'

'Perhaps in a former life it was permitted that I should have rendered thee some service. May be' – he smiled – 'I freed thee from a trap; or, having caught thee on a hook in the days when I was not enlightened, cast thee back into the river.'

'May be,' said Kim quietly. He had heard this sort of speculation again and again, from the mouths of many whom the English would not consider imaginative. 'Now, as regards that woman in the bullock-cart, *I* think she needs a second son for her daughter.' 'That is not part of the Way,' sighed the lama. 'But at least she is from the Hills. Ah, the Hills, and the snow of the Hills!'

He rose and stalked to the cart. Kim would have given his ears to come too, but the lama did not invite him; and the few words he caught were in an unknown tongue, for they spoke some common speech of the mountains. The woman seemed to ask questions which the lama turned over in his mind before answering. Now and again he heard the sing-song cadence of a Chinese quotation. It was a strange picture that Kim watched between drooped eyelids. The lama, very straight and erect, the deep folds of his yellow clothing slashed with black in the light of the *parao* fires precisely as a knotted tree-trunk is slashed with the shadow of the long sun, addressed a tinsel and lacquered *ruth* which burned like a many-coloured jewel in the same uncertain light. The patterns on the gold-worked curtains ran up and down, melting and re-forming as the folds shook and quivered to the night wind; and when the talk grew more earnest the jewelled forefinger snapped out little sparks of light between the embroideries. Behind the cart was a wall of uncertain darkness speckled with little flames and alive with half-caught forms and faces and shadows. The voices of early evening had settled down to one soothing hum whose deepest note was the steady chumping of the bullocks above their chopped straw, and whose highest was the tinkle of a Bengali dancing-girl's *sitar*. Most men had eaten and pulled deep at their gurgling, grunting hookahs, which in full blast sound like bull-frogs.

At last the lama returned. A hillman walked behind him with a wadded cotton-quilt and spread it carefully by the fire.

'She deserves ten thousand grandchildren,' thought Kim. 'None the less, but for me, these gifts would not have come.'

'A virtuous woman – and a wise one.' The lama slackened off, joint by joint, like a slow camel. 'The world is full of charity to those who follow the Way.' He flung a fair half of the quilt over Kim.

'And what said she?' Kim rolled up in his share of it.

'She asked me many questions and propounded many problems – the most of which were idle tales which she had heard from devil-serving priests who pretend to follow the Way. Some I answered, and some I said were foolish. Many wear the Robe, but few keep the Way.'

'True. That is true.' Kim used the thoughtful, conciliatory tone of those who wish to draw confidences.

'But by her lights she is most right-minded. She desires greatly that we should go with her to Buddh Gaya; her road being ours, as I understand, for many days' journey to the southward.'

'And?'

'Patience a little. To this I said that my Search came before all things. She had heard many foolish legends, but this great truth of my River she had never heard. Such are the priests of the lower hills! She knew the Abbot of Lung-Cho, but she did not know of my River – nor the tale of the Arrow.'

'And?'

'I spoke therefore of the Search, and of the Way, and of matters that were profitable; she desiring only that I should accompany her and make prayer for a second son.'

'Aha! "We women" do *not* think of anything save children,' said Kim sleepily.

'Now, since our roads run together for a while, I do not see that we in any way depart from our Search if so be we accompany her – at least as far as – I have forgotten the name of the city.'

'Ohe!' said Kim, turning and speaking in a sharp whisper to one of the Ooryas a few yards away. 'Where is your master's house?'

'A little behind Saharunpore, among the fruit gardens.' He named the village.

'That was the place,' said the lama. 'So far, at least, we can go with her.'

'Flies go to carrion,' said the Oorya, in an abstracted voice.

'For the sick cow a crow; for the sick man a Brahmin.' Kim breathed the proverb impersonally to the shadow-tops of the trees overhead.

The Oorya grunted and held his peace.

'So then we go with her, Holy One?'

'Is there any reason against? I can still step aside and try all the rivers that the road overpasses. She desires that I should come. She very greatly desires it.'

Kim stifled a laugh in the quilt. When once that imperious old lady had recovered from her natural awe of a lama he thought it probable that she would be worth listening to.

He was nearly asleep when the lama suddenly quoted a proverb: 'The husbands of the talkative have a great reward hereafter.' Then Kim heard him snuff thrice, and dozed off, still laughing.

The diamond-bright dawn woke men and crows and bullocks together. Kim sat up and yawned, shook himself, and thrilled with delight. This was seeing the world in real truth; this was life as he would have it – bustling and shouting, the buckling of belts, and beating of bullocks and creaking of wheels, lighting of fires and cooking of food, and new sights at every turn of the approving eye. The morning mist swept off in a whorl of silver, the parrots shot away to some distant river in shrieking green hosts: all the well-wheels within earshot went to work. India was awake, and Kim was in the middle of it, more awake and more excited than any one, chewing on a twig that he would presently use as a toothbrush; for he borrowed right – and left-handedly from all the customs of the country he knew and loved. There was no need to worry about food – no need to spend a cowrie at the crowded stalls. He was the disciple of a holy man annexed by a strong-willed old lady. All things would be prepared for them, and when they were respectfully invited so to do they would sit and eat. For the rest, – Kim giggled here as he cleaned his teeth, – his hostess would rather heighten the enjoyment of the road. He inspected her bullocks critically, as they came up grunting and blowing under the yokes. If they went too fast – it was not likely – there would be a pleasant seat for himself along the pole; the lama would sit beside the driver. The escort, of course, would walk. The old lady, equally of course, would talk a great deal, and by what he had heard that conversation would not lack salt. She was already ordering, haranguing, rebuking, and, it must be said, cursing her servants for delays.

'Get her her pipe. In the name of the Gods, get her her pipe and stop her ill-omened mouth,' cried an Oorya, tying up his shapeless bundles of bedding. 'She and the parrots are alike. They screech in the dawn.'

'The lead-bullocks! Hai! Look to the lead-bullocks!' They were backing and wheeling as a grain-cart's axle caught them by the horns. 'Son of an owl, where dost thou go?' This to the grinning carter.

'Ai! Yai! Yai! That within there is the Queen of Delhi going to pray for a son,' the man called back over his high load. 'Room for the Queen of Delhi and her prime minister the gray monkey climbing up his own sword!' Another cart loaded with bark for a down-country tannery followed close behind, and its driver added a few compliments as the *ruth*-bullocks backed and backed again.

From behind the shaking curtains came one volley of invective. It did not last long, but in kind and quality, in blistering, biting appropriateness, it was beyond anything that even Kim had heard. He could see the carter's bare chest collapse with amazement, as the man salaamed reverently to the voice, leaped from the pole, and helped the escort haul their volcano on to the main road. Here the voice told him truthfully what sort of wife he had wedded, and what she was doing in his absence.

'Oh, *shabash*!' murmured Kim, unable to contain himself, as the man slunk away.

'Well done, indeed? It is a shame and a scandal that a poor woman may not go to make prayer to her Gods except she be jostled and insulted by all the refuse of Hindustan – that she must eat *gali* (abuse) as men eat *ghi*. But I have yet a wag left to my tongue – a word or two well spoken that serves the occasion. And *still* am I without my tobacco! Who is the one-eyed and luckless son of shame that has not yet prepared my pipe?'

It was hastily thrust in by a hillman, and a trickle of thick smoke from each corner of the curtains showed that peace was restored.

If Kim had walked proudly the day before, disciple of a holy man, to-day he paced with tenfold pride in the train of a semi-royal procession, with a recognised place under the patronage of an old lady of charming manners and infinite resource. The escort, their heads tied up native fashion, fell in on either side the cart, shuffling enormous clouds of dust.

The lama and Kim walked a little to one side; Kim chewing his stick of sugar-cane, and making way for no one under the status of a priest. They could hear the old lady's tongue clack as steadily as a rice-husker. She bade the escort tell her what was going on on the road; and so soon as they were clear of the *parao* she flung back the curtains and peered out, her veil a third across her face. Her men did not eye her directly when she addressed them, and thus the proprieties were more or less observed.

A dark, sallowish District Superintendent of Police, faultlessly uniformed, an Englishman, trotted by on a tired horse, and, seeing from her retinue what manner of person she was, chaffed her.

'O mother,' he cried, 'do they do this in the *zenanas?* Suppose an Englishman came by and saw that thou hadst no nose?'

'What?' she shrilled back. 'Thy own mother has no nose? Why say so, then, on the open road?'

It was a fair counter. The Englishman threw up his hand with the gesture of a man hit at sword-play. She laughed and nodded.

'Is this a face to tempt virtue aside?' She withdrew all her veil and stared at him.

It was by no means lovely, but as the man gathered up his reins he called it a Moon of Paradise, a Disturber of Integrity, and a few other fantastic epithets which doubled her up with mirth.

'That is a *nut-cut*' (rogue), she said. 'All police-constables are *nut-cuts*; but the police-wallahs are the worst. Hai, my son, thou hast never learned all that since thou camest from *Belait* (Europe). Who suckled thee?'

'A *pahareen* – a hillwoman of Dalhousie, my mother. Keep thy beauty under a shade – O Dispenser of Delights,' and he was gone.

'These be the sort' – she took a fine judicial tone, and stuffed her mouth with *pan*. 'These be the sort to oversee justice. They know the land and the customs of the land. The others, all new from Europe, suckled by white women and learning our tongues from books, are worse than the pestilence. They do harm to Kings.' Then she told a long, long tale to the world at large, of an ignorant young policeman who had disturbed some small Hill Rajah, a ninth cousin of her own, in the matter of a trivial land-case, winding up with a quotation from a work by no means devotional.

Then her mood changed, and she bade one of the escort ask whether the lama would walk alongside and discuss matters of religion. So Kim dropped back into the dust and returned to his sugar-cane. For an hour or more the lama's tam-o'-shanter showed like a moon through the haze; and, from all he heard, Kim gathered that the old woman wept. One of the Ooryas half apologised for his rudeness overnight, saying that he had never known his mistress of so bland a temper, and he ascribed it to the presence of the strange priest.

Personally, he believed in Brahmins, though, like all natives, he was acutely aware of their cunning and their greed. Still, when Brahmins but irritated with begging demands the mother of his master's wife, and when she sent them away so angry that they cursed the whole retinue (which was the real reason of the second off-side bullock going lame, and of the pole breaking the night before), he was prepared to accept any priest of any other denomination in or out of India. To this Kim assented with wise nods, and bade the Oorya observe that the lama took no money, and that the cost of his and Kim's food would be repaid a hundred times in the good luck that would attend the caravan henceforward. He also told stories of Lahore city, and sang a song or two which made the escort laugh. As a town-mouse well acquainted with the latest songs by the most fashionable composers,– they are women for the most part,– Kim had a distinct advantage over men from a little fruit-village behind Saharunpore, but he let that advantage be inferred.

At noon they turned aside to eat, and the meal was good, plentiful, and well served on plates of clean leaves, in decency, out of drift of the dust. They gave the scraps to certain beggars, that all requirements might be fulfilled, and sat down to a long, luxurious smoke. The old lady had retreated behind her curtains, but mixed most freely in the talk, her servants arguing with and contradicting her as servants do throughout the East. She compared the cool and the pines of the Kangra and Kulu hills with the dust and the mangoes of the South; she told a tale of some old local Gods at the edge of her husband's territory; she roundly abused the tobacco which she was then smoking, reviled all Brahmins, and speculated without reserve on the coming of many grandsons.

CHAPTER 5

Here come I to my own again –
Fed, forgiven, and known again –
Claimed by bone of my bone again,
  And sib to flesh of my flesh!
The fatted calf is dressed for me,
But the husks have greater zest for me. . .
I think my pigs will be best for me,
  So I'm off to the styes afresh.

– The Prodigal Son

ONCE MORE the lazy, string-tied, shuffling procession got under way, and she slept till they reached the next halting-stage. It was a very short march, and time lacked an hour to sundown, so Kim cast about for means of amusement.

'But why not sit and rest?' said one of the escort. 'Only the devils and the English walk to and fro without reason.'

'Never make friends with the Devil, a monkey, or a boy. No man knows what they will do next,' said his fellow.

Kim turned a scornful back – he did not want to hear the old story how the Devil played with the boys and repented of it – and walked idly across country.

The lama strode after him. All that day, whenever they passed a stream, he had turned aside to look at it, but in no case had he received any warning that he had found his River. Insensibly too the comfort of speaking to some one in a reasonable tongue, and of being properly considered and respected as her spiritual adviser by a well-born woman, had weaned his thoughts a little from the Search. And further, he was prepared to spend serene years in his quest; having nothing of the white man's impatience, but a great faith.

'Where goest thou?' he called after Kim.

'No whither – it was a small march, and all this' – Kim waved his hands abroad – 'is new to me.'

'She is beyond question a wise and a discerning woman. But it is hard to meditate when – '

'All women are thus.' Kim spoke as might have Solomon.

'Before the lamassery was a broad platform,' the lama muttered, looping up the well-worn rosary, 'of stone. On that I have left the marks of my feet – pacing to and fro with these.'

He clicked the beads, and began the '*Om mane pudme hum'* of his devotion; grateful for the cool, the quiet, and the absence of dust.

One thing after another drew Kim's idle eye across the plain. There was no purpose in his wanderings, except that the build of the huts near by seemed new, and he wished to investigate.

They came out on a broad tract of grazing-ground, brown and purple in the afternoon light, with a heavy clump of mangoes in the centre. It struck Kim as curious that no shrine stood in so eligible a spot: the boy was observing as any priest for these things. Far across the plain walked side-by-side four men, made small by the distance. He looked intently under his curved palms and caught the sheen of brass.

'Soldiers. White soldiers!' said he. 'Let us see.'

'It is always soldiers when thou and I go out alone together. But I have never seen the white soldiers.'

'They do no harm except when they are drunk. Keep behind this tree.'

They stepped behind the thick trunks in the cool dark of the mango-tope. Two little figures halted; the other two came forward uncertainly. They were the advance-party of a regiment on the march, sent out, as usual, to mark the camp. They bore five-foot sticks with fluttering flags, and called to each other as they spread over the flat earth.

At last they entered the mango-grove, walking heavily.

'It's here or hereabouts – officers' tents under the trees, I take it, an' the rest of us can stay outside. Have they marked out for the baggage-waggons behind?'

They cried again to their comrades in the distance, and the rough answer came back faint and mellowed.

'Shove the flag in here, then,' said one.

'What do they prepare?' said the lama, wonder-struck. 'This is a great and terrible world. What is the device on the flag?'

A soldier thrust a stave within a few feet of them, grunted discontentedly, pulled it up again, conferred with his companion, who looked up and down the shaded cave of greenery, and returned it.

Kim stared with all his eyes, his breath coming short and sharp between his teeth. The soldiers stamped off into the sunshine.

'O Holy One, 'he gasped, 'my horoscope! The drawing in the dust by the priest at Umballa! Remember what he said. First come two – *ferashes* – to make all things ready – in a dark place, as it is always at the beginning of a vision.'

'But this is not vision,' said the lama. 'It is the world's Illusion, and no more.'

'And after them comes the Bull – the Red Bull on the green field. Look! It is he!'

He pointed to the flag that was snap-snapping in the evening breeze not ten feet away. It was no more than an ordinary camp marking-flag; but the regiment, always punctilious in matters of millinery, had charged it with the regimental device, the Red Bull, which is the crest of the Mavericks – the great Red Bull on a background of Irish green.

'I see, and now I remember,' said the lama. 'Certainly it is thy Bull. Certainly, also, the two men came to make all ready.'

'They are soldiers – white soldiers. What said the priest? "The sign over against the Bull is the sign of War and armed men." Holy One, this thing touches my Search.

'True. It is true.' The lama stared fixedly at the device that flamed like a ruby in the dusk. 'The priest at Umballa said that thine was the sign of War.'

'What is to do now?'

'Wait. Let us wait '

'Even now the darkness clears,' said Kim. It was only natural that the descending sun should at last strike through the tree-trunks, across the grove, filling it with mealy gold light for a few minutes; but to Kim it was the crown of the Umballa Brahmin's prophecy.

'Hark!' said the lama. 'One beats a drum – far off!'

At first the sound, carrying diluted through the still air, resembled the beating of an artery in the head. Soon a sharpness was added.

'Ah! The music,' Kim explained. He knew the sound of a regimental band, but it amazed the lama.

At the far end of the plain a heavy, dusty column crawled in sight. Then the wind brought the tune: –

We crave your condescension
To tell you what we know
Of marching in the Mulligan Guards
To Sligo Port below.

Here broke in the shrill-tongued fifes: –

We shouldered arms,
We marched – we marched away
From Phœnix Park
We marched to Dublin Bay.
The drums and the fifes,
Oh, sweetly they did play,
As we marched – marched – marched –
with the Mulligan Guards!

It was the band of the Mavericks playing the regiment to camp; for the men were route-marching with their baggage. The rippling column swung into the level carts behind it – divided left and right, ran about like an ant-hill, and . . .

'But this is sorcery!' – said the lama.

The plain dotted itself with tents that seemed to rise, all spread, from the carts. Another rush of men invaded the grove, pitched a huge tent in silence, ran up yet eight or nine more by the side of it, unearthed cooking-pots, pans, and bundles, which were taken possession of by a crowd of native servants; and behold the mango-tope turned into an orderly town as they watched!

'Let us go,' said the lama, sinking back afraid, as the fires twinkled and white officers with jingling swords stalked into the mess-tent.

'Stand back in the shadow. No one can see beyond the light of a fire,' said Kim, his eyes still on the flag. He had never before watched the routine of a seasoned regiment pitching camp in thirty minutes.

'Look! look! look!' clucked the lama. 'Yonder comes a priest.'

It was Bennett, the Church of England chaplain of the regiment, limping in dusty black. One of his flock had made some rude remarks about the chaplain's mettle; and to abash him Bennett had marched step by step with the men that day. The black dress, gold cross on the watch-chain, the hairless face, and the soft, black wide awake hat would have marked him as a holy man anywhere in all India. He dropped into a camp-chair by the door of the mess-tent and slid off his boots. Three or four officers gathered round him, laughing and joking over his exploit.

'The talk of white men is wholly lacking in dignity,' said the lama, who judged only by tone. 'But I have considered the countenance of that priest, and I think he is learned. Is it likely that he will understand our talk? I would talk to him of my Search.'

'Never speak to a white man till he is fed,' said Kim, quoting a well-known proverb. 'They will eat now, and – and I do not think they are good to beg from. Let us go back to the resting-place. After we have eaten we will come again. It certainly was a Red Bull – *my* Red Bull.'

They were both noticeably absent-minded when the old lady's retinue set their meal before them; so none broke their reserve, for it is not lucky to annoy guests.

'Now,' said Kim, picking his teeth, 'we will return to that place; but thou, O Holy One, must wait a little way off, because thy feet are heavier than mine and I am anxious to see more of that Red Bull.'

'But how canst thou understand the talk? Walk slowly. The road is dark,' the lama replied uneasily.

Kim put the question aside. 'I marked a place near to the trees,' said he, 'where thou canst sit till I call. Nay,' as the lama made some sort of protest, 'remember this is *my* Search

– the Search for my Red Bull. The sign in the Stars was not for thee. I know a little of the customs of white soldiers, and I always desire to see some new things.'

'What dost thou not know of this world?' The lama squatted obediently in a little hollow of the ground not a hundred yards from the hump of the mango trees dark against the star-powdered sky.

'Stay till I call.' Kim flitted into the dusk. He knew that in all probability there would be sentries round the camp, and smiled to himself as he heard the thick boots of one. A boy who can dodge over the roofs of Lahore city on a moonlight night, using every little patch and corner of darkness to discomfit his pursuer, is not likely to be checked by a line of well-trained soldiers. He paid them the compliment of crawling between a couple, and, running and halting, crouching and dropping flat, worked his way toward the lighted mess-tent where, close pressed behind the mango tree, he waited till some chance word should give him a returnable lead.

The one thing in his mind now was further information as to the Red Bull. For aught he knew, and Kim's limitations were as curious and sudden as his expansions, the men, the nine hundred thorough devils of his father's prophecy, might pray to the beast after dark, as Hindus pray to the Holy Cow. That at least would be entirely right and logical, and the Padre with the gold cross would be therefore the man to consult in the matter. On the other hand, remembering sober-faced padres whom he had avoided in Lahore city, the priest might be an inquisitive nuisance who would bid him learn. But had it not been proven at Umballa that his sign in the high heavens portended war and armed men? Was he not the Friend of the Stars as well as of all the world, crammed to the teeth with dreadful secrets? Lastly,– and firstly as the undercurrent of all his quick thoughts, – this adventure, though he did not know the English word, was a stupendous lark – a delightful continuation of his old flights across the housetops, as well as the fulfilment of sublime prophecy. He lay belly-flat and wriggled towards the mess-tent door, a hand on the amulet round his neck.

It was as he suspected. The Sahibs prayed to their God; for in the centre of the mess-table – its sole ornament when they were on the line of march – stood a golden bull fashioned from old-time loot of the Summer Palace at Pekin – a red-gold bull with lowered head, ramping upon a field of Irish green. To him the Sahibs held out their glasses and cried aloud confusedly.

Now the Reverend Arthur Bennett always left mess after that toast, and being rather tired by his march his movements were more abrupt than usual. Kim, with slightly raised head, was still staring at his totem on the table, when the chaplain stepped on his right shoulder-blade. Kim flinched under the leather, and, rolling sideways, brought down the chaplain, who, ever a man of action, caught him by the throat and nearly choked the life out of him. Kim then kicked him desperately in the stomach. Mr. Bennett gasped and doubled up but without relaxing his grip, rolled over again, and silently hauled Kim to his own tent. The Mavericks were incurable practical jokers; and it occurred to the Englishman that silence was best till he had made complete inquiry.

'Why, it's a boy!' he said, as he drew his prize under the light of the tent-pole lantern, then shaking him severely cried: 'What were you doing? You're a thief. *Choor? Mallum?*' His Hindustanee was very limited, and the ruffled and disgusted Kim intended to keep to the character laid down for him. As he recovered his breath he was inventing a beautifully plausible tale of his relations to some mess-scullion, and at the same time keeping a keen eye on and a little under the chaplain's left armpit. The chance came; he ducked for the doorway, but a long arm shot out and clutched at his neck, snapping the amulet string and closing on the amulet.

'Give it me. O give it me. Is it lost? Give me the papers.'

The words were in English – the tinny, saw-cut English of the native-bred, and the chaplain jumped.

'A scapular,' said he, opening his hand. 'No, some sort of heathen charm. Why – why, do you speak English? Little boys who steal are beaten. You know that?'

'I do not – I did not steal.' Kim danced in agony like a terrier at a lifted stick. 'O give it me. It is my charm. Do not thieve it from me.'

The chaplain took no heed, but, going to the tent door, called aloud. A fattish, clean-shaven man appeared.

'I want your advice, Father Victor,' said Bennett. 'I found this boy in the dark outside the mess-tent. Ordinarily, I should have chastised him and let him go, because I believe him to be a thief. But it seems he talks English, and he attaches some sort of value to a charm round his neck. I thought perhaps you might help me.'

Between himself and the Roman Catholic chaplain of the Irish contingent lay, as Bennett believed, an unbridgeable gulf, but it was noticeable that whenever the Church of England dealt with a human problem she was likely to call in the Church of Rome. Bennett's official abhorrence of the Scarlet Woman and all her ways was only equalled by his private respect for Father Victor.

'A thief talking English is it? Let's look at his charm. No, it's not a scapular, Bennett.' He held out his hand.

'But have we any right to open it? A sound whipping – '

'I did *not* thieve,' protested Kim. 'You have hit me kicks all over my body. Now give me my charm and I will go away.'

'Not quite so fast; we'll look first,' said Father Victor, leisurely rolling out poor Kimball O'Hara's '*ne varietur*' parchment, his clearance-certificate, and Kim's baptismal certificate. On this last O'Hara – with some confused idea that he was doing wonders for his son – had scrawled scores of times: '*Look after the boy. Please look after the boy*,' – signing his name and regimental number in full.

'Powers of Darkness below!' said Father Victor, passing all over to Mr. Bennett. 'Do you know what these things are?'

'Yes," said Kim. 'They are mine, and I want to go away.'

'I do not quite understand,' said Mr. Bennett. 'He probably brought them on purpose. It may be a begging trick of some kind.'

'I never saw a beggar less anxious to stay with his company, then. There's the makings of a gay mystery here. Ye believe in Providence, Bennett?'

'I hope so.'

'Well, I believe in miracles, so it comes to the same thing. Powers of Darkness! Kimball O'Hara! And his son! But then he's a native, and I saw Kimball married myself to Annie Shott. How long have you had these things, boy?'

'Ever since I was a little baby.' Father Victor stepped forward quickly and opened the front of Kim's upper garment. 'You see, Bennett, he's not very black. What's your name?'

'Kim.'

'Or Kimball?'

'Perhaps. Will you let me go away?'

'What else?'

'They call me Kim Rishti ke. That is Kim of the Rishti.'

'What is that – "Rishti"?'

'*Eye*-rishti – that was the regiment – my father's.'

'Irish, oh I see.'

'Yess. That was how my father told me. My father, he has lived.'

'Has lived where?'

'Has lived. Of *course* he is dead – gone-out.'

'Oh. That's your abrupt way of putting it, is it?'

Bennett interrupted. 'It is possible I have done the boy an injustice. He is certainly white, though evidently neglected. I am sure I must have bruised him. I do not think spirits – '

'Get him a glass of sherry, then, and let him squat on the cot. Now, Kim,' continued Father Victor, 'no one is going to hurt you. Drink that down and tell us about yourself. The truth, if you've no objection.'

Kim coughed a little as he put down the empty glass, and considered. This seemed a time for caution and fancy. Small boys who prowl about camps are generally turned out after a whipping. But he had received no stripes; the amulet was evidently working in his favour, and it looked as though the Umballa horoscope and the few words that he could remember of his father's maunderings fitted in most miraculously. Else why did the fat padre seem so impressed, and why the glass of hot yellow wine from the lean one?

'My father, he is dead in Lahore city since I was very little. The woman, she kept *kabarri* shop near where the hire-carriages are.' Kim began with a plunge, not quite sure how far the truth would serve him.

'Your mother?'

'*No*' – with a gesture of disgust. 'She went out when I was born. My father, he got these papers from the Jadoo-Gher

– what do you call that?' (Bennett nodded) 'because he was in – good-standing. What do you call that?' (again Bennett nodded). 'My father told me that. He said too, and also the Brahmin who made the drawing in the dust at Umballa two days ago, *he* said, that I shall find a Red Bull on a green field and that the Bull shall help me.'

'A phenomenal little liar,' muttered Bennett.

'Powers of Darkness below, what a country!' murmured Father Victor. 'Go on, Kim.'

'I did *not* thieve. Besides, I am just now disciple of a very holy man. He is sitting outside. We saw two men come with flags, making the place ready. That is *always* so in a dream, or on account of a – a – prophecy. So I knew it was come true. I saw the Red Bull on the green field, and my father he said: "Nine hundred *pukka* devils and the Colonel riding on a horse will look after you when you find the Red Bull!" I did not know what to do when I saw the Bull, but I went away and I came again when it was dark. I wanted to see the Bull again, and I saw the Bull again with the – the Sahibs praying to it. I think the Bull shall help me. The holy man said so too. He is sitting outside. Will you hurt him, if I call him a shout now? He is very holy. He can witness to all the things I say, and he knows I am not a thief.'

' "Officers praying to a bull!" What in the world do you make of that?' said Bennett. ' "Disciple of a holy man!" Is the boy mad?'

'It's O'Hara's boy, sure enough. O'Hara's boy leagued with all the Powers of Darkness. It's very much what his father would have done – if he was drunk. We'd better invite the holy man. He may know something.'

'He does not know anything,' said Kim. 'I will show you him if you come. He is my master. Then afterwards we can go.'

'Powers of Darkness!' was all that Father Victor could say, as Bennett marched off, with a firm hand on Kim's shoulder.

They found the lama where he had dropped.

'The Search is at an end for me,' shouted Kim in the vernacular. 'I have found the Bull, but God knows what comes next. They will not hurt you. Come to the fat priest's tent with this thin man and see the end. It is all new, and they cannot talk Hindi. They are only uncurried donkeys.'

'Then it is not well to make a jest of their ignorance,' the lama returned. 'I am glad if thou art rejoiced, *chela*.'

Dignified and unsuspicious, he strode into the little tent, saluted the Churches as a Churchman, and sat down by the open charcoal brazier. The yellow lining of the tent reflected in the lamplight made his face red-gold.

Bennett looked at him with the triple-ringed un-interest of the creed that lumps nine-tenths of the world under the title of 'heathen.'

'And what was the end of the search? What gift has the Red Bull brought?' The lama addressed himself to Kim.

'He says, "What are you going to do?" ' Bennett was staring uneasily at Father Victor, and Kim, for his own ends, took upon himself the office of interpreter.

'I do not see what concern this *faquir* has with the boy, who is probably his dupe or his confederate,' Bennett began. 'We cannot allow an English boy – Assuming that he is the son of a Mason, the sooner he goes to the Masonic Orphanage the better.'

'Ah! That's your opinion as Secretary to the Regimental Lodge,' said Father Victor; 'but we might as well tell the old man what we are going to do. He doesn't look like a villain.'

'My experience is that one can never fathom the Oriental mind. Now, Kimball, I wish you to tell this man what I say – word for word.'

Kim gathered the import of the next few sentences and began thus:

'Holy One, the thin fool who looks like a camel says that I am the son of a Sahib.'

'But how?'

'Oh, it is true. I knew it since my birth, but *he* could only find it out by rending the amulet from my neck and reading all the papers. He thinks that once a Sahib is always a Sahib, and between the two of them they purpose to keep me in this regiment or to send me to a *madrissah* (a school). It has happened before. I have always avoided it. The fat fool is of one mind and the camel-like one of another. But that is no odds. I may spend one night here and perhaps the next. It has happened before. Then I will run away and return to thee.'

'But tell them that thou art my *chela*. Tell them how thou didst come to me when I was faint and bewildered. Tell them of our Search, and they will surely let thee go now.'

'I have already told them. They laugh, and they talk of the police.'

'What are you saying?' asked Mr. Bennett.

'Oah. He only says that if you do not let me go it will stop him in his business – his ur-gent private af-fairs.' This last was a reminiscence of some talk with a Eurasian clerk in the Canal Department, but it only drew a smile, which nettled him. 'And if you *did* know what his business was you would not be in such a beastly hurry to interfere.'

'What is it then?' said Father Victor, not without feeling, as he watched the lama's face.

'There is a River in this country which he wishes to find so verree much. It was put out by an Arrow which – ' Kim tapped his foot impatiently as he translated in his own mind from the vernacular to his clumsy English. 'Oah, it was made by our Lord God Buddha, you know, and if you wash there you are washed away from all your sins and made as white as cotton-wool.' (Kim had heard mission-talk in his time.) 'I am his disciple, and we *must* find that River. It is so verree valuable to us.'

'Say that again,' said Bennett. Kim obeyed, with amplifications.

'But this is gross blasphemy!' cried the Church of England.

'Tck! Tck!' said Father Victor sympathetically. 'I'd give a good deal to be able to talk the vernacular. A river that washes away sin! And how long have you two been looking for it?'

'Oh, many days. Now we wish to go away and look for it again. It is not here, you see.'

'I see,' said Father Victor gravely. 'But he can't go on in that old man's company. It would be different, Kim, if you were not a soldier's son. Tell him that the regiment will take care of you and make you as good a man as your – as good a man as can be. Tell him that if he believes in miracles he must believe that – '

'There is no need to play on his credulity,' Bennett interrupted.

'I'm doing no such thing. He must believe that the boy's coming here – to his own regiment – in search of his Red Bull is in the nature of a miracle. Consider the chances against it, Bennett. This one boy in all India, and our regiment of all others on the line o' march for him to meet with! It's predestined on the face of it. Yes, tell him it's *Kismet. Kismet, mallum?* (Fate! Do you understand?)'

He turned towards the lama, to whom he might as well have talked of Mesopotamia.

'They say' – the old man's eye lighted at Kim's speech, – 'they say that the meaning of my horoscope is now accomplished, and that being led back – though as thou knowest I went out of curiosity – to these people and their Red Bull I must needs go to a *madrissah* and be turned into a Sahib. Now I make pretence of agreement, for at the worst it will be but a few meals eaten away from thee. Then I will slip away and follow down the road to Saharunpore. Therefore, Holy One, keep with that Kulu woman – on no account stray far from her cart till I come again. Past question, my sign is of War and of armed men. See how they have given me wine to drink and set me upon a bed of honour! My father must have been some great person. So if they raise me to honour among them, good. If not, good again. However it goes, I will run back to thee when I am tired. But stay with the Rajputni, or I shall miss thy feet. . . . Oah yess,' said the boy, 'I have told him everything you tell me to say.'

'And I cannot see any need why he should wait,' said Bennett, feeling in his trouser-pocket. 'We can investigate the details later – and I will give him a ru – '

'Give him time. May be he's fond of the lad,' said Father Victor, half-arresting the clergyman's motion.

The lama dragged forth his rosary and pulled his huge hat-brim over his eyes.

'What can he want now?'

'He says' – Kim put up one hand. 'He says: Be quiett. He wants to speak to me by himself. You see you do not know one little word of what he says, and I think if you talk he will perhaps give you very bad curses. When he takes those beads like that, you see he always wants to be quiett.'

The two Englishmen sat overwhelmed, but there was a look in Bennett's eye that promised ill for Kim when he should be relaxed to the religious arm.

'A Sahib and the son of a Sahib – ' The lama's voice was harsh with pain. 'But no white man knows the land and the customs of the land as thou knowest. How comes it this is true?'

'What matter, Holy One: but remember it is only for a night or two. Remember, I can change swiftly. It will be as it was when I first spoke to thee under Zam-Zammah the great gun – '

'As a boy in the dress of white men – when I first went to the Wonder House. And a second time thou wast a Hindu. What shall the third incarnation be?' He chuckled drearily. 'Ah, *chela,* thou hast done a wrong to an old man because my heart went out to thee.'

'And mine to thee. But how could I know that the Red Bull would bring me to this business?'

The lama covered his face afresh, and nervously rattled the rosary. Kim squatted beside him and laid hold upon a fold of his clothing.

'Now it is understood that the boy is a Sahib?' he went on in a muffled tone. 'Such a Sahib as was he who kept the images in the Wonder House.' The lama's experience of white men was limited. He seemed to be repeating a lesson. 'So then it is not seemly that he should do other than as the Sahibs do. He must go back to his own people.'

'For a day and a night and a day,' Kim pleaded.

'No, ye don't!' Father Victor saw Kim edging towards the door, and interposed a strong leg.

'I do not understand the customs of white men. The Priest of the Images in the Wonder House in Lahore was more courteous than the thin one here. This boy will be taken from me. They will make a Sahib of my disciple? Woe to me, how shall I find my River? Have *they* no disciples? Ask.'

'He says he is very sorry that he cannot find the River now any more. He says, Why have you no disciples, and stop bothering him? He wants to be washed of his sins.'

Neither Bennett nor Father Victor found any answer ready.

Said Kim in English, distressed for the lama's agony: 'I think if you will let me go now we will walk away quietly and not steal. We will look for that River like before I was caught. I wish I did not come here to find the Red Bull and all that sort of thing. I do not want it.'

'It's the very best day's work you ever did for yourself, young man,' said Bennett.

'Good heavens, I don't know how to console him,' said Father Victor, watching the lama intently. 'He can't take the boy away with him, and yet he's a good man – I'm sure he's a good man. Bennett, if you give him that rupee he'll curse you root and branch!' They listened to each other's breathing – three – five full minutes. Then the lama raised his head, and looked forth across them into space and emptiness.

'And I am a follower of the Way,' he said bitterly. 'The sin is mine and the punishment is mine. I made believe to myself – for now I see it was but make-belief – that thou wast sent to me to aid in the Search. So my heart went out to thee for thy charity and thy courtesy and the wisdom of thy little years. But those who follow the Way must permit not the fire of any desire or attachment, for that is all illusion. As says. . . . He quoted an old, old Chinese text, backed it with another, and reinforced these with a third. 'I stepped aside from the Way, my *chela*. It was no fault of thine. I delighted in the sight of life, the new people upon the roads, and in thy joy at seeing these things. I was pleased with thee who should have considered my Search and my Search alone. Now I am sorrowful because thou art taken away and my River is far from me. It is the Law which I have broken!'

'Powers of Darkness below!' said Father Victor, who, wise in the confessional, heard the pain in every sentence.

'I see now that the sign of the Red Bull was a sign for me as well as for thee. All Desire is red – and evil. I will do penance and find my River alone.'

'At least go back to the Kulu woman,' said Kim, 'otherwise thou wilt be lost upon the roads. She will feed thee till I run back to thee.'

The lama waved a hand to show that the matter was finally settled in his mind.

'Now,' – his tone altered as he turned to Kim, – 'what will they do with thee? At least I may, acquiring merit, wipe out past ill.'

'Make me a Sahib – so they think. The day after tomorrow I return. Do not grieve.'

'Of what sort? Such an one as this or that man?' He pointed to Father Victor. Such an one as those I saw this evening – men wearing swords and stamping heavily?'

'May be.'

'That is not well. These men follow desire and come to emptiness. Thou must not be of their sort.'

'The Umballa priest said that my Star was War,' Kim interjected. 'I will ask these fools – but there is truly no need. I will run away this night, for all I wanted to see the new things.'

Kim put two or three questions in English to Father Victor, translating the replies to the lama.

Then: 'He says, "You take him from me and you cannot say what you will make him." He says, "Tell me before I go, for it is not a small thing to make a child.' "

'You will be sent to a school. Later on, we shall see. Kimball, I suppose you'd like to be a soldier?'

'*Gorah-log* (white-folk). No-ah! No-ah!' Kim shook his head violently. There was nothing in his composition to which drill and routine appealed. 'I will not be a soldier.'

'You will be what you're told to be,' said Bennett; 'and you should be grateful that we're going to help you.'

Kim smiled compassionately. If these men lay under the delusion that he would do anything that he did not fancy, so much the better.

Another long silence followed. Bennett fidgeted with impatience, and suggested calling a sentry to evict the *faquir*.

'Do they give or sell learning among the Sahibs? Ask them,' said the lama, and Kim interpreted.

'They say that money is paid to the teacher – but that money the regiment will give.... What need? It is only for a night.'

'And – the more money is paid the better learning is given?" The lama disregarded Kim's plans for an early flight. "It is no wrong to pay for learning; to help the ignorant to wisdom is always a merit." The rosary clicked furiously as an abacus. Then he faced his oppressors.

'Ask them for how much money do they give a wise and suitable teaching? and in what city is that teaching given?'

'Well,' said Father Victor in English, when Kim had translated, 'that depends. The regiment would pay for you all the time you are at the Military Orphanage; or you might go on the Punjab Masonic Orphanage's list (not that he or you 'ud understand what that means); but the best schooling a boy can get in India is, of course, at St. Xavier's in Partibus at Lucknow.' This took some time to interpret, for Bennett wished to cut it short.

'He wants to know how much?' said Kim placidly.

'Two or three hundred rupees a year.' Father Victor was long past any sense of amazement. Bennett, impatient, did not understand.

'He says: "Write that name and the money upon a paper and give it him." And he says you must write your name below, because he is going to write a letter in some days to you. He says you are a good man. He says the other man is a fool. He is going away.'

The lama rose suddenly. 'I follow my Search,' he cried, and was gone.

'He'll run slap into the sentries,' cried Father Victor, jumping up as the lama stalked out; 'but I can't leave the boy.' Kim made swift motion to follow, but checked himself. There was no sound of challenge outside. The lama had disappeared.

Kim settled himself composedly on the chaplain's cot. At least the lama had promised that he would stay with the Rajput woman from Kulu, and the rest was of the smallest importance. It pleased him that the two padres were so evidently excited. They talked long in undertones, Father Victor urging some scheme on Mr. Bennett, who seemed incredulous. All this was very new and fascinating, but Kim felt sleepy. They called men into the tent – one of them certainly was the Colonel, as his father had prophesied – and they asked him an infinity of questions, chiefly about the woman who looked after him, all of which Kim answered truthfully. They did not seem to think the woman a good guardian.

After all, this was the newest of his experiences. Sooner or later, if he chose, he could escape into great, gray, formless India, beyond tents and padres and colonels. Meantime, if the Sahibs were to be impressed, he would do his best to impress them. He too was a white man.

After much talk that he could not comprehend, they handed him over to a sergeant, who had strict instructions not to let him escape. The regiment would go on to Umballa, and Kim would be sent up, partly at the expense of the Lodge and in part by subscription, to a place called Sanawar.

'It's miraculous past all whooping, Colonel,' said Father Victor, when he had talked without a break for ten minutes. 'His Buddhist friend has levanted after taking my name and address. I can't quite make out whether he'll pay for the boy's education or whether he is preparing some sort of witchcraft on his own account.' Then to Kim: 'You'll live to be grateful to your friend the Red Bull yet. We'll make a man of you at Sanawar – even at the price o' making you a Protestant.'

'Certainly – most certainly,' said Bennett.

'But you will not go to Sanawar,' said Kim.

'But we will go to Sanawar, little man. That's the order of the Commander-in-Chief, who's a trifle more important than O'Hara's son.'

'You will not go to Sanawar. You will go to thee war.'

There was a shout of laughter from the full tent.

'When you know your own regiment a trifle better you won't confuse the line of march with line of battle, Kim. We hope to go to 'thee war' sometime.'

'Oah, I know all thatt.'Kim drew his bow again at a venture. If they were not going to the war, at least they did not know what he knew of the talk in the verandah at Umballa.

'I know you are not at thee war now; but I tell *you* that as soon as you get to Umballa you will be sent to the war – the new war. It is a war of eight thousand men, besides the guns.'

'That's explicit. D'you add prophecy to your other gifts? Take him along, Sergeant. Take up a suit for him from the Drums, an' take care he doesn't slip through your fingers. Who says the age of miracles is gone by? I think I'll go to bed. My poor mind's weakening.'

At the far end of the camp, silent as a wild animal, an hour later sat Kim, newly washed all over, in a horrible stuff suit that rasped his arms and legs.

'A most amazin' young bird,' said the Sergeant. He turns up in charge of a yellow-headed buck-Brahmin priest, with his father's Lodge certificates round his neck, talkin' God knows what all of a red bull. The buck-Brahmin evaporates without explanations, an' the bhoy sets cross-legged on the chaplain's bed prophesyin' bloody war to the men at large. Injia's a wild land for a God-fearin' man. I'll just tie his leg to the tent-pole in case he'll go through the roof. What did ye say about the war?'

'Eight thousand men, besides guns,' said Kim. 'Very soon you will see.'

'You're a consolin' little imp. Lie down between the Drums an' go to bye-bye. Those two boys beside ye will watch your slumbers.'

CHAPTER 6

Now I remember comrades –
   Old playmates on new seas –
Whenas we traded orpiment
   Among the savages.
Ten thousand leagues to southward,
   And thirty years removed –
They knew not noble Valdez,
   But me they knew and loved.

– *Song of Diego Valdez*

VERY EARLY in the morning the white tents came down and disappeared as the Mavericks took a side road to Umballa. It did not skirt the resting-place, and Kim, trudging beside a baggage-cart under fire of comments from soldiers' wives, was not so confident as overnight. He discovered that he was closely watched – Father Victor on the one side, and Mr. Bennett on the other.

In the forenoon the column checked. A camel-orderly handed the Colonel a letter. He read it, and spoke to a major. Half a mile in the rear, Kim heard a hoarse and joyful clamour rolling down on him through the thick dust. Then some one beat him on the back, crying: 'Tell us how ye knew, ye little limb of Satan? Father dear, see if ye can make him tell.'

A pony ranged alongside, and he was hauled on to the priest's saddle-bow.

'Now, my son, your prophecy of last night has come true. Our orders are to entrain at Umballa for the front to-morrow.'

'What is that?' said Kim, for '*front*' and '*entrain*' were newish words to him.

'We are going to "thee war," as you called it.'

'Of course you are going to thee war. I said last night.'

'Ye did; but, Powers o' Darkness, how did ye know?'

Kim's eyes sparkled. He shut his lips, nodded his head, and looked unspeakable things. The chaplain moved on through the dust, and privates, sergeants, and subalterns called one another's attention to the boy. The Colonel, at the head of the column, stared at him curiously. 'It was probably some bazar rumour,' he said; 'but even then – ' He referred to the paper in his hand. 'Hang it all, the thing was only decided within the last forty-eight hours.'

'Are there many more like you in India?' said Father Victor, 'or are you by way o' being *a lusus naturæ*?'*

'Now I have told you,' said the boy, 'will you let me go back to my old man? If he has not stayed with that woman from Kulu, I am afraid he will die.'

'By what I saw of him he's as well able to take care of himself as you. No. Ye've brought us luck, an' we're goin' to make a man of you. I'll take ye back to your baggage-cart and ye'll come to me this evening.'

For the rest of the day Kim found himself an object of distinguished consideration among a few hundred white men. The story of his appearance in camp, the discovery of his parentage, and his prophecy, had lost nothing in the telling. A big, shapeless white woman of a pile of bedding asked him mysteriously whether he thought her husband would come back from the war. Kim reflected gravely, and said that he would, and the woman gave him food. In many respects, this big procession that played music at intervals – this crowd that talked and laughed so easily – resembled a festival in Lahore city. So far, there was no sign of hard work, and he resolved to lend the spectacle his patronage. At evening there came out to

* A freak of nature.

meet them bands of music, and played the Mavericks into camp near Umballa railway station. That was an interesting night. Men of other regiments came to visit the Mavericks. The Mavericks went visiting on their own account. Their pickets hurried forth to bring them back, met pickets of strange regiments on the same duty; and, after a while, the bugles blew madly for more pickets with officers to control the tumult. The Mavericks had a reputation for liveliness to live up to. But they fell in on the platform next morning in perfect shape and condition; and Kim, left behind with the sick, women, and boys, found himself shouting farewells excitedly as the trains drew away. Life as a Sahib was amusing so far; but he touched it with a cautious hand. Then they marched him back in charge of a drummer-boy to empty, lime-washed barracks, whose floors were covered with rubbish and string and paper, and whose ceilings gave back his lonely footfall. Native fashion, he curled himself up on a stripped cot and went to sleep. An angry man stumped down the verandah, woke him up, and said he was a schoolmaster. This was enough for Kim, and he retired into his shell. He could just puzzle out the various English Police notices in Lahore city, because they affected his comfort; and among the many guests of the woman who looked after him had been a queer German who painted scenery for the Parsee travelling theatre. He told Kim that he had been 'on the barricades in Forty-eight,' and therefore – at least that was how it struck Kim – he would teach the boy to write in return for food. Kim had been kicked as far as single letters, but did not think well of them.

'I do not know anything. Go away!' said Kim, scenting evil. Hereupon the man caught him by the ear, dragged him to a room in a far-off wing where a dozen drummer-boys were sitting on forms, and told him to be still if he could do nothing else. This he managed very successfully. The man explained something or other with white lines on a black board for at least half an hour, and Kim continued his interrupted nap. He much disapproved of the present aspect of affairs, for this was the very school and discipline he had spent two-thirds of his young life in avoiding. Suddenly a beautiful idea occurred to him, and he wondered that he had not thought of it before.

The man dismissed them, and first to spring through the veranda into the open sunshine was Kim.

'Ere you! 'Alt! Stop!' said a high voice at his heels. 'I've got to look after you. My orders are not to let you out of my sight. Where are you goin'?'

It was the drummer-boy who had been hanging round him all the forenoon – a fat and freckled person of about fourteen, and Kim loathed him from the soles of his boots to his cap-ribbons.

'To the bazar – to get sweets – for you,' said Kim, after thought.

'Well, the bazar's out o' bounds. If we go there we'll get a dressing-down. You come back.'

'How near can we go?' Kim did not know what bounds meant, but he wished to be polite – for the present.

' 'Ow near? 'Ow far, you mean? We can go as far as that tree down the road.'

'Then I will go there.'

'All right. I ain't goin'. It's too 'ot. I can watch you from 'ere. It's no good runnin' away. If you did, they'd spot you by your clothes. That's regimental stuff you're wearin'. There ain't a picket in Umballa wouldn't 'ead you back quicker than you started out.'

This did not impress Kim as much as the knowledge that his raiment would tire him out if he tried to run. He slouched to the tree at the corner of a bare road leading towards the bazar, and eyed the natives passing. Most of them were barrack-servants of the lowest caste. Kim hailed a sweeper, who promptly retorted with a piece of unnecessary insolence, in the natural belief that the European boy could not follow. The low, quick answer undeceived him. Kim put his fettered soul into it, thankful for the late chance to abuse somebody in the tongue he knew best. 'And now, go to the nearest letter-writer in the bazar and tell him to come here. I would write a letter.'

'But – but what manner of white man's son art thou, to need a bazar letter-writer? Is there not a schoolmaster in the barracks?'

'Ay; and Hell is full of the same sort. Do my order, you – you Od! Thy mother was married under a basket! Servant of Lal Beg' (Kim knew the god of the sweepers), 'run on my business or we will talk again.'

The sweeper shuffled off in haste. 'There is a white boy by the barracks waiting under a tree who is not a white boy,' he stammered to the first bazar letter-writer he came across. 'He needs thee.'

'Will he pay?' said that spruce scribe, gathering up his desk and pens and sealing-wax all in order.

'I do not know. He is not like other boys. Go and see. It is well worth.'

Kim danced with impatience when the slim young Kayeth hove in sight. As soon as his voice could carry he cursed him volubly.

'First I will take my pay," the letter-writer said. "Bad words have made the price higher. But who art thou, dressed in that fashion, to speak in this fashion?'

'Aha! That is in the letter which thou shalt write. Never was such a tale. But I am in no haste. Another writer will serve me. Umballa city is as full of them as is Lahore.'

'Four annas,' said the writer, sitting down and spreading his cloth in the shade of a deserted barrack-wing.

Mechanically Kim squatted beside him – squatted as only the natives can, – in spite of the abominable clinging trousers.

The writer regarded him sideways.

'That is the price to ask of Sahibs,' said Kim. "Now fix me a true one.'

'An anna and a half. How do I know, having written the letter, that thou wilt not run away?'

'I must not go beyond this tree, and there is also the stamp to be considered.'

"I get no commission on the price of the stamp. Once more, what manner of white boy art thou?"

'That shall be said in the letter, which is to Mahbub Ali, the horse-dealer in the Kashmir Serai, at Lahore. He is my friend.'

'Wonder on wonder!' murmured the letter-writer, dipping a reed in the inkstand. 'To be written in Hindi?'

'Assuredly. To Mahbub Ali then. Begin! *I have come down with the old man as far as Umballa in the train. At Umballa I carried the news of the bay mare's pedigree*.' After what he had seen in the garden, he was not going to write of white stallions.

'Slower a little. What has a bay mare to do. . . . Is it Mahbub Ali the great dealer?'

'Who else? I have been in his service. Take more ink. Again. *As the order was, so I did it. We then went on foot towards Benares, but on the third day we found a certain regiment.* Is that down?'

'Ay, *pulton*,' murmured the writer, all ears.

'I went into their camp and was caught, and by means of the charm about my neck, which thou knowest, it was established that I was the son of some man in the regiment:

according to the prophecy of the Red Bull, which thou knowest was common talk of our bazar.' Kim waited for this shaft to sink into the letter-writer's heart, cleared his throat, and continued: *'A priest clothed me and gave me a new name. . . . One priest, however, was a fool. The clothes are very heavy, but I am a Sahib and my heart is heavy too. They send me to a school and beat me. I do not like the air and water here. Come then and help me, Mahbub Ali, or send me some money, for I have not sufficient to pay the writer who writes this.'*

' "Who writes this." It is my own fault that I was tricked. Thou art as clever as Husain Bux that forged the Treasury stamps at Nucklao. But what a tale! What a tale! Is it true by any chance?'

'It does not profit to tell lies to Mahbub Ali. It is better to help his friends by lending them a stamp. When the money comes I will repay.'

The writer grunted doubtfully, but took a stamp out of his desk, sealed the letter, handed it over to Kim, and departed. Mahbub Ali's was a name of power in Umballa.

'That is the way to win a good account with the Gods,' Kim shouted after him.

'Pay me twice over when the money comes,' the man cried over his shoulder.

'What was you bukkin' to that nigger about?' said the drummer-boy when Kim returned to the veranda. "I was watchin' you.'

'I was only talkin' to him.'

'You talk the same as a nigger, don't you?'

'No-ah! No-ah! I onlee speak a little. What shall we do now?'

'The bugles 'ill go for dinner in arf a minute. My Gawd! I wish I'd gone up to the front with the regiment. It's awful doin' nothin' but school down 'ere. Don't you 'ate it?'

'Oah yess!'

'I'd run away if I knew where to go to, but, as the men say, in this bloomin' Injia you're only a prisoner at large. You can't desert without bein' took back at once. I'm fair sick of it.'

'You have been in Be – England?'

'W'y, I only come out last troopin' season with my mother. I should think I 'ave been in England. What a ignorant little beggar you are. You was brought up in the gutter, wasn't you?'

'Oah yess. Tell me something about England. My father he came from there.'

Though he would not say so, Kim of course disbelieved every word the drummer-boy spoke about the Liverpool suburb which was his England. It passed the heavy time till dinner – a most unappetising meal served to the boys and a few invalids in a corner of a barrack-room. But that he had written to Mahbub Ali, Kim would have been almost depressed. The indifference of native crowds he was used to; but this strong loneliness among white men preyed on him. He was grateful when, in the course of the afternoon, a big soldier took him over to Father Victor, who lived in another wing across another dusty parade-ground. The priest was reading an English letter written in purple ink. He looked at Kim more curiously than ever.

'An' how do you like it, my son, as far as you've gone? Not much, eh? It must be hard – very hard on a wild animal. Listen now. I've an amazin' epistle from your friend.'

'Where is he? Is he well? Oah! If he knows to write me letters, it is all right.'

'You're fond of him then?'

'*Of* course I am fond of him. He was fond of me.'

'It seems so by the look of this. He can't write English, can he?'

'Oah no. Not that I know, but of course he found a letter-writer who can write English verree well, and so he wrote. I do hope you understand.'

'That accounts for it. D'you know anything about money affairs?" Kim's face showed that he did not.

'How can I tell?'

'That's what I'm askin'. Now listen if you can make head or tail o' this. We'll skip the first part. . . . It's written from Jagadhir Road. . . . "*Sitting on wayside in grave meditation, trusting to be favoured with your Honour's applause of present step, which recommend your Honour to execute for Almighty God's sake. Education is greatest blessing if of best sorts. Otherwise no earthly use.*" Faith, the old man's hit the bull's-eye that time! "*If your Honour condescending giving my boy best educations Xavier*" (I suppose that's St. Xavier's in Partibus) "*in terms of our conversation dated in your tent 15th instant*' (a business-like touch there!) "*then Almighty God blessing your Honour's succeedings to third an' fourth generation and*" – now listen! – '*your Honour's humble servant for adequate remuneration per hoondie per confide in annum three hundred rupees a year to one expensive education St. Xavier, Lucknow, and allow small time to forward same per hoondie sent to any part of India as your Honour shall address yourself. This servant of your Honour has presently no place to lay crown of his head, but going to Benares by train on account of persecution of old woman talking so much and unanxious residing Saharunpore in any domestic capacity.*" Now what in the world does that mean?'

'She has asked him to be *puro* – her clergyman – at Saharunpore, I think. He would not do that on account of his River. She *did* talk.'

'It's clear to you, is it? It beats me altogether. "*So going to Benares, where will find address and forward rupees for boy who is apple of eye, and for Almighty God's sake execute this education, and your petitioner as in duty bound shall ever awfully pray. Written by Sobrao Satai, Failed Entrance Allahabad University, for Venerable Teshoo Lama the priest of Such-zen looking for a River, address care of Tirthankers' Temple, Benares. P.M. – Please note boy is apple of eye, and rupees shall be sent per hoondie three hundred per annum. For God Almighty's sake.*" Now, is that ravin' lunacy or a business proposition? I ask you, because I'm fairly at my wits' end.'

'He says he will give me three hundred rupees a year, so he will give me them.'

'Oh, that's the way you look at it, is it?'

'*Of* course. If he says so!'

The priest whistled; then he addressed Kim as an equal.

'I don't believe it; but we'll see. You were goin' off to-day to the Military Orphanage at Sanawar, where the regiment would keep you till you were old enough to enlist. Ye'd be brought up to the Church of England. Bennett arranged for that. On the other hand, if ye go to St. Xavier's ye'll get a better education an' – an' can have the religion. D'ye see my dilemma?'

Kim saw nothing save a vision of the lama going south in a train with none to beg for him.

'Like most people, I'm going to temporise. If your friend sends the money from Benares – Powers of Darkness below, where's a street-beggar to raise three hundred rupees? – ye'll go down to Lucknow and I'll pay your fare, because I can't touch the subscription-money if I intend, as I do, to make ye a Catholic. If he doesn't, ye'll go to the Military Orphanage at the regiment's expense. I'll allow him three days' grace, though

I don't believe it at all. Even then, if he fails in his payments later on. . . . but it's beyond me. We can only walk one step at a time in this world, praise God! An' they sent Bennett to the front an' left me behind. Bennett can't expect anything.'

'Oah yess,' said Kim vaguely.

The priest leaned forward. 'I'd give a month's pay to find what's goin' on inside that little round head of yours.'

'There is nothing,' said Kim, and scratched it. He was wondering whether Mahbub Ali would send him as much as a whole rupee. Then he could pay the letter-writer and write letters to the lama at Benares. Perhaps Mahbub Ali would visit him next time he came south with horses. Surely he must know that Kim's delivery of the letter to the officer at Umballa had caused the great war which the men and boys had discussed so loudly over the barrack dinner-tables. But if Mahbub Ali did not know this, it would be very unsafe to tell him so. Mahbub Ali was hard upon boys who knew, or thought they knew, too much.

'Well, till I get further news' – Father Victor's voice interrupted the reverie – 'ye can run along and play with the other boys. They'll teach ye something – but I don't think ye'll like it.'

The day dragged to its weary end. When he wished to sleep he was instructed how to fold up his clothes and set out his boots; the other boys deriding. Bugles waked him in the dawn; the schoolmaster caught him after breakfast, thrust a page of meaningless characters under his nose, gave them senseless names, and whacked him without reason. Kim meditated poisoning him with opium borrowed from a barrack-sweeper, but reflected that, as they all ate at one table in public (this was peculiarly revolting to Kim, who preferred to turn his back on the world at his meals), the stroke might be dangerous. Then he attempted running off to the village where the priest had tried to drug the lama – the village where the old soldier lived. But far-seeing sentries at every exit headed back the little scarlet figure. Trousers and jacket crippled body and mind alike, so he abandoned the project and fell back, Oriental fashion, on time and chance. Three days of torment passed in the big, echoing white rooms. He walked out of afternoons under escort of the drummer-boy, and all he heard from his companion were the few useless words which seemed to make two-thirds of the white man's abuse. Kim knew and despised them all long ago. The boy resented his silence and lack of interest by beating him, as was only natural. He did not care for any of the bazars which were in bounds. He styled all natives 'niggers'; yet servants and sweepers called him abominable names to his face, and, misled by their deferential attitude, he never understood. This somewhat consoled Kim for the beatings.

On the morning of the fourth day a judgment overtook that drummer. They had gone out together towards Umballa race-course. He returned alone, weeping, with news that young O'Hara, to whom he had been doing nothing in particular, had hailed a scarlet-bearded nigger on horseback; that the nigger had then and there laid into him with a peculiarly adhesive quirt, picked up young O'Hara, and borne him off at full gallop. These tidings came to Father Victor, and he drew down his long upper lip. He was already sufficiently startled by a letter from the Temple of the Tirthankers at Benares, enclosing a native banker's note of hand for three hundred rupees, and an amazing prayer to 'Almighty God.' The lama would have been more annoyed than the priest had he known how the bazar letter-writer had translated his phrase 'to acquire merit.'

'Powers of Darkness below!' Father Victor fumbled with the note. 'An' now he's off with another of his peep-o'-day friends. I don't know whether it will be a greater relief to me to get him back or to have him lost. He's beyond my comprehension. How the Divil – yes, He's the man I mean – can a street-beggar raise money to educate white boys?'

Three miles off, on Umballa race-course, Mahbub Ali, reining a gray Cabuli stallion with Kim in front of him, was saying:

'But, Little Friend of all the World, there is *my* honour and reputation to be considered. All the officer-sahibs in all the regiments, and all Umballa, know Mahbub Ali. Men saw me pick thee up and chastise that boy. We are seen now from far across this plain. How can I take thee away, or account for thy disappearing if I set thee down and let thee run off into the crops? They would put me in jail. Be patient. Once a Sahib, always a Sahib. When thou art a man – who knows – thou wilt be grateful to Mahbub Ali.'

'Take me beyond their sentries where I can change this red. Give me money and I will go to Benares and be with my lama again. I do not want to be a Sahib, and remember I did deliver that message.'

The stallion bounded wildly. Mahbub Ali had incautiously driven home the sharp-edged stirrup. (He was not the new sort of fluent horse-dealer who wears English boots and spurs.) Kim drew his own conclusions from that betrayal.

'That was a small matter. It lay on the road to Benares. I and the Sahib have by this time forgotten it. I send so many letters and messages to men who ask questions about horses, I cannot well remember one from the other. Was it some matter of a bay mare that Peters Sahib wished the pedigree of?'

Kim saw the trap at once. If he had said "bay mare" Mahbub would have known by his very readiness to fall in with the amendment that the boy suspected something. Kim replied therefore:

'Bay mare? No. I do not forget my messages thus. It was a white stallion.'

'Ay, so it was. A white Arab stallion. But thou didst write bay mare to me.'

'Who cares to tell truth to a letter-writer?' Kim answered, feeling Mahbub's palm on his heart.

'Hi! Mahbub, you old villain, pull up!' cried a voice, and an Englishman raced alongside on a little polo-pony. 'I've been chasing you half over the country. That Cabuli of yours can go. For sale, I suppose?'

'I have some young stuff coming on made by Heaven for the delicate and difficult polo-game. He has no equal. He – '

'Plays polo and waits at table. Yes. We know all that. What the deuce have you got there?'

'A boy,' said Mahbub gravely. 'He was being beaten by another boy. His father was once a white soldier in the big war. The boy was a child in Lahore city. He played with my horses when he was a babe. Now I think they will make him a soldier. He has been newly caught by his father's regiment that went up to the war last week. But I do not think he wants to be a soldier. I take him for a ride. Tell me where thy barracks are and I will set thee there.'

'Let me go. I can find the barracks alone.'

'And if thou runnest away who will say it is not my fault?'

'He'll run back to his dinner. Where has he to run to?' the Englishman asked.

'He was born in the land. He has friends. He goes where he chooses. He is a *chabuk sawai* (a sharp chap). It needs only to change his clothing, and in a twinkling he would be a low-caste Hindi boy.'

'The deuce he would!' The Englishman looked critically at the boy as Mahbub headed towards the barracks. Kim ground his teeth. Mahbub was mocking him, as faithless Afghans will; for he went on:

'They will send him to a school and put heavy boots on his feet and swaddle him in these clothes. Then he will forget all he knows. Now which of the barracks is thine?'

Kim pointed – he could not speak – to Father Victor's wing, all staring white near by.

'Perhaps he will make a good soldier,' said Mahbub reflectively. 'He will make a good orderly at least. I sent him to deliver a message once from Lahore. A message concerning the pedigree of a white stallion.'

Here was deadly insult on deadlier injury – and the Sahib to whom he had so craftily given that war-making letter heard it all. Kim beheld Mahbub Ali frying in flame for his treachery, but for himself he saw one long gray vista of barracks, schools, and barracks again. He gazed imploringly at the clear-cut face in which there was no glimmer of recognition; but even at this extremity it never occurred to him to throw himself on the white man's mercy or to denounce the Afghan. And Mahbub stared deliberately at the Englishman, who stared as deliberately at Kim, quivering and tongue-tied.

'My horse is well trained,' said the dealer. 'Others would have kicked, Sahib.'

'Ah,' said the Englishman at last, rubbing his pony's damp withers with his whip-butt. 'Who makes the boy a soldier?'

'He says the regiment that found him, and especially the padre-sahib of that regiment.'

'There is the padre!' Kim choked as bare-headed Father Victor sailed down upon them from the verandah.

'Powers o' Darkness below, O'Hara! How many more mixed friends do you keep in Asia?' he cried, as Kim slid down and stood helplessly before him.

'Good morning, Padre,' the Colonel said cheerily. 'I know you by reputation well enough. Meant to have come over and called before this. I'm Creighton.'

'Of the Ethnological Survey?' said Father Victor. The Colonel nodded. 'Faith I'm glad to meet ye then; an' I owe you some thanks for bringing back the boy.'

'No thanks to me, Padre. Besides, the boy wasn't going away. You don't know old Mahbub Ali' – the horse-dealer sat impassive in the sunlight. 'You will when you have been in the station a month. He sells us all our crocks. That boy is rather a curiosity. Can you tell me anything about him?'

'Can I tell you?' puffed Father Victor. 'You'll be the one man that could help me in my quandaries. Tell you! Powers o' Darkness, I'm bursting to tell some one who knows something o' the native!'

A groom came round the corner. Colonel Creighton raised his voice, speaking in Urdu. 'Very good, Mahbub Ali, but what is the use of telling me all those stories about the pony. Not one pie more than three hundred and fifty rupees will I give.'

'The Sahib is a little hot and angry after riding,' the horse-dealer returned, with the leer of a privileged jester. 'Presently, he will see my horse's points more clearly. I will wait till he has finished his talk with the padre. I will wait under that tree.'

'Confound you!' The Colonel laughed. 'That comes of looking at one of Mahbub's horses. He's a regular old leech, Padre. Wait then, if thou hast so much time to spare, Mahbub. Now I'm at your service, Padre. Where is the boy? Oh, he's gone off to collogue with Mahbub. Queer sort of boy. Might I ask you to send my mare round under cover?'

He dropped into a chair which commanded a clear view of Kim and Mahbub Ali in conference beneath the tree. The padre went indoors for cheroots.

Creighton heard Kim say bitterly: 'Trust a Brahmin before a snake, and a snake before a harlot, and a harlot before an Afghan, Mahbub Ali.'

'That is all one,' the great red beard wagged solemnly. 'Children should not see a carpet on the loom till the pattern is made plain. Believe me, Friend of all the World, I do thee great service. They will not make a soldier of thee.'

'You crafty old sinner,' thought Creighton 'But you're not far wrong. That boy mustn't be wasted if he is as advertised.'

'Excuse me half a minute,' cried the padre from within, 'but I'm gettin' the documents of the case.'

'If through me the favour of this bold and wise Colonel Sahib comes to thee, and thou art raised to honour, what thanks will thou give Mahbub Ali when thou art a man?'

'Nay, nay; I begged thee to let me take the road again, where I should have been safe; and thou hast sold me back to the English. What will they give thee for blood-money?'

'A cheerful young demon!' The Colonel bit his cigar, and turned politely to Father Victor.

'What are the letters that the fat priest is waving before the Colonel? Stand behind the stallion as though looking at my bridle!' said Mahbub Ali.

'A letter from my lama which he wrote from Jagadhir Road, saying that he will pay three hundred rupees by the year for my schooling.'

'Oho! Is old Red Hat of that sort? At which school?'

'God knows. I think in Nucklao.'

'Yes. There is a big school there for the sons of Sahibs – and half-Sahibs. I have seen it when I sell horses there. So the lama also loved the Friend of all the World?'

'Ay; and *he* did not tell lies, or return me to captivity.'

'Small wonder the padre does not know how to unravel the thread. How fast he talks to the Colonel Sahib.' Mahbub Ali chuckled. 'By Allah!' – the keen eyes swept the verandah for an instant – 'thy lama has sent what to me looks like a note of hand. I have had some small dealing in *hoondies*. The Colonel Sahib is looking at it.'

'What good is all this to me?' said Kim wearily. 'Thou wilt go away, and they will return me to those empty rooms where there is no good place to sleep and where the boys beat me.'

'I do not think that. Have patience, child. All Pathans are not faithless – except in horseflesh.'

Five – ten – fifteen minutes passed, Father Victor talking energetically or asking questions which the Colonel answered.

'Now I've told you everything that I know about the boy from beginnin' to end; and it's a blessed relief to me. Did ye ever hear the like?'

'At any rate, the old man has sent the money. Gobind Sahai's notes of hand are good from here to China,' said the Colonel. 'The more one knows about natives the less can one say what they will or won't do.'

'That's consolin' – from the head of the Ethnological Survey. It's this mixture of Red Bulls and Rivers of Healing (poor heathen, God help him!) an' notes of hand and Masonic certificates. Are you a Mason, by any chance?'

'By Jove, I am, now I come to think of it. That's an additional reason,' said the Colonel absently.

'I'm glad ye see a reason in it. But as I said, it's the mixture o' things that's beyond me. An' his prophesying' to our Colonel sitting on my bed with his little shimmy torn open showing his white skin; an' the prophecy comin' true! They'll cure all that nonsense at St. Xavier's, eh?'

'Sprinkle him with holy water,' the Colonel laughed.

'On my word, I fancy I ought to sometimes. But I'm hoping he'll be brought up as a good Catholic. All that troubles me is what'll happen if the old beggar man – '

'Lama, lama, my dear sir; and some of them are gentlemen in their own country.'

'The lama, then, fails to pay next year. He's a fine business head to plan on the spur of the moment, but he's bound to die some day. An' takin' a heathen's money to give a child a Christian education – '

'But he said explicitly what he wanted. As soon as he knew the boy was white he seems to have made his arrangements accordingly. I'd give a month's pay to hear how he explained it all at the Tirthankers' Temple at Benares. Look here, Padre, I don't pretend to know much about natives, but if he says he'll pay, he'll pay – dead or alive. I mean his heirs will assume the debt. My advice to you is, send the boy down to Lucknow. If your Anglican chaplain thinks you've stolen a march on him – '

'Bad luck to Bennett! He was sent to the front instead o' me. Doughty certified me medically unfit. I'll excommunicate Doughty if he comes back alive! Surely Bennett ought to be content with – '

'Glory, leaving you the religion. Quite so! As a matter of fact I don't think Bennett will mind. Put the blame on me. I – er – strongly recommend sending the boy to St. Xavier's. He can go down on pass as a soldier's orphan, so the railway fare will be saved. You can buy him an outfit from the regimental subscription. The Lodge will be saved the expense of his education, and that will put the Lodge in a good temper. It's perfectly easy. I've got to go down to Lucknow next week. I'll look after the boy on the way – give him in charge of my servants, and so on.'

'You're a good man.'

'Not in the least. Don't make that mistake. The lama has sent us money for a definite end. We can't very well return it. We shall have to do as he says. Well, that's settled, isn't it? Shall we say that, Tuesday next, you'll hand him over to me at the night train south? That's only three days. He can't do much harm in three days.'

'It's a weight off my mind, but – this thing here?" – he waved the note of hand – "I don't know Gobind Sahai: or his bank, which may be a hole in a wall.'

'*You*'ve never been a subaltern in debt. I'll cash it if you like, and send you the vouchers in proper order.'

'But with all your own work too! It's askin' – '

'It's not the least trouble indeed. You see, as an ethnologist, the thing's very interesting to me. I'd like to make a note of it for some Government work that I'm doing. The transformation of a regimental badge like your Red Bull into a sort of fetish that the boy follows is very interesting.'

'But I can't thank you enough.'

'There's one thing you can do. All we Ethnological men are as jealous as jackdaws of one another's discoveries. They're of no interest to anyone but ourselves, of course, but you know what book-collectors are like. Well, don't say a word, directly or indirectly, about the Asiatic side of the boy's character – his adventures and his prophecy, and so on. I'll worm them out of the boy later on and – you see?'

'I do. Ye'll make a wonderful account of it. Never a word will I say to any one till I see it in print.'

'Thank you. That goes straight to an ethnologist's heart. Well, I must be getting back to my breakfast. Good heavens! Old Mahbub here still?' He raised his voice, and the horse-dealer came out from under the shadow of the tree. 'Well, what is it?'

'As regards that young horse,' said Mahbub, 'I say that when a colt is born to be a polo-pony, closely following the ball without teaching – when such a colt knows the game by divination – then I say it is a great wrong to break that colt to a heavy cart, Sahib!'

'So do I say also, Mahbub. The colt will be entered for polo only. (These fellows think of nothing in the world but horses, Padre.) I'll see you to-morrow, Mahbub, if you've anything likely for sale.'

The dealer saluted, horseman fashion, with a sweep of the off hand. 'Be patient a little, Friend of all the World,' he whispered to the agonised Kim. 'Thy fortune is made. In a little while thou goest to Nucklao, and – here is something to pay the letter-writer. I shall see thee again, I think, many times,' and he cantered off down the road.

'Listen to me,' said the Colonel from the veranda, speaking in the vernacular. 'In three days thou wilt go with me to Lucknow, seeing and hearing new things all the while. Therefore sit still for three days and do not run away. Thou wilt go to school at Lucknow.'

'Shall I meet my Holy One there?' Kim whimpered.

'At least Lucknow is nearer to Benares than Umballa. It may be thou wilt go under my protection. Mahbub Ali knows this, and he will be angry if thou returnest to the road now. Remember – much has been told to me which I do not forget.'

'I will wait,' said Kim, 'but the boys will beat me.'

Then the bugles blew for dinner.

CHAPTER 7

Unto whose use the pregnant suns are poised
    With idiot moons and stars retracting stars?
Creep thou betweene – thy coming's all unnoised.
    Heaven hath her high, as earth her baser wars.
Heir to these tumults, this affright, that fray
(By Adam's, fathers', own, sin bound alway);
Peer up, draw out thy horoscope and say
    Which planet mends thy threadbare fate or mars!

– SIR JOHN CHRISTIE

IN THE afternoon the red-faced schoolmaster told Kim that he had been 'struck off the strength,' which conveyed no meaning to him till he was ordered to go away and play. Then he ran to the bazar, and found the young letter-writer to whom he owed a stamp.

'Now I pay,' said Kim royally, 'and now I need another letter to be written.'

'Mahbub Ali is in Umballa,' said the writer jauntily. He was, by virtue of his office, a bureau of general misinformation.

'This is not to Mahbub, but to a priest. Take thy pen and write quickly. *To Teshoo Lama, the holy one from Bhotiyal seeking for a River, who is now in the Temple of the Tirthankers at Benares*. Take more ink! *In three days I am to go down to Nucklao to the school at Nucklao. The name of the school is Xavier. I do not know where that school is, but it is at Nucklao.* '

'But I know Nucklao,' the writer interrupted. 'I know the school.'

'Tell him where it is, and I give half an anna.'

The reed pen scratched busily. 'He cannot mistake.' The man lifted his head. 'Who watches us across the street?'

Kim looked up hurriedly and saw Colonel Creighton in tennis-flannels.

'Oh, that is some Sahib who knows the fat priest in the barracks. He is beckoning me.'

'What dost thou?' said the Colonel, when Kim trotted up.

'I – I am not running away. I send a letter to my Holy One at Benares.'

'I had not thought of that. Hast thou said that I take thee to Lucknow?'

'Nay, I have not. Read the letter, if there be a doubt.'

'Then why hast thou left out my name in writing to that Holy One?' The Colonel smiled a queer smile. Kim took his courage in both hands.

'It was said once to me that it is inexpedient to write the names of strangers concerned in any matter, because by the naming of names many good plans are brought to confusion.'

'Thou hast been well taught,' the Colonel replied, and Kim flushed. 'I have left my cheroot-case on the padre's veranda. Bring it to my house this even.'

'Where is the house?' said Kim. His quick wit told him that he was being tested in some fashion or another, and he stood on guard.

'Ask anyone in the big bazar.' The Colonel walked on.

'He has forgotten his cheroot-case,' said Kim, returning. 'I must bring it to him this evening. That is all my letter except, thrice over, *Come to me! Come to me! Come to me! Now I will pay for a stamp and put it in the post.*' He rose to go, and as an afterthought asked, 'Who is that angry-faced Sahib who lost the cheroot-case?'

'Oh, he is only Creighton Sahib – a very foolish Sahib, who is a Colonel Sahib without a regiment.'

'What is his business?'

'God knows. He is always buying horses which he cannot ride, and asking riddles about the works of God – such as plants and stones and the customs of people. The dealers call him the father of fools, because he is so easily cheated about a horse. Mahbub Ali says he is madder than all other Sahibs.'

'Oh!' said Kim, and departed. His training had given him some small knowledge of character, and he argued that fools are not given information which leads to calling out eight thousand men besides guns. The Commander-in-Chief of all India does not talk, as Kim had heard him talk, to fools. Nor would Mahbub Ali's tone have changed, as it did every time he mentioned the Colonel's name, if the Colonel had been a fool. Consequently – and this set Kim to skipping – there was a mystery somewhere, and Mahbub Ali probably spied for the Colonel much as Kim had spied for Mahbub. And, like the horse-dealer, the Colonel evidently respected people who did not show themselves to be too clever.

He rejoiced that he had not betrayed his knowledge of the Colonel's house; and when, on his return to barracks, he discovered that no cheroot-case had been left behind, he beamed with delight. Here was a man after his own heart – a tortuous and indirect person playing a hidden game. Well, if he could be a fool, so could Kim.

He showed nothing of his mind when Father Victor, for three long mornings, discoursed to him of an entirely new set of gods and godlings – notably of a goddess called Mary, who, he gathered, was one with Bibi Miriam of Mahbub Ali's theology. He betrayed no emotion when, after the lecture, Father Victor dragged him from shop to shop buying articles of outfit, nor when envious drummer-boys kicked him because he was going to a superior school did he complain, but awaited the play of circumstances with an interested soul. Father Victor, good man, took him to the station, put him into an empty second-class next to Colonel Creighton's first, and bade him farewell with genuine feeling.

'They'll make a man o' you, O'Hara, at St. Xavier's – a white man, an', I hope, a good man. They know all about your comin', an' the Colonel will see that ye're not lost or mislaid anywhere on the road. I've given you a notion of religious matters, – at least I hope so, – and you'll remember, when they ask you your religion, that you're a Cath'lic. Better say Roman Cath'lic, tho' I'm not fond of the word.'

Kim lit a rank cigarette – he had been careful to buy a stock in the bazar – and lay down to think. This solitary passage was very different from that joyful down-journey in the third-class with the lama. 'Sahibs get little pleasure of travel,' he reflected. '*Hai mai*! I go from one place to another as it might be a kick-ball. It is my *Kismet*. No man can escape his *Kismet*. But I am to pray to Bibi Miriam, and I am a Sahib" – he looked at his boots ruefully. 'No; I am Kim. This is the great world, and I am only Kim. Who is Kim?' He considered his own identity, a thing he had never done before, till his head swam. He was one insignificant person in all this roaring whirl of India, going southward to he knew not what fate.

Presently the Colonel sent for him, and talked for a long time. So far as Kim could gather, he was to be diligent and enter the Survey of India as a chain-man. If he were very good, and passed the proper examinations, he would be earning thirty rupees a month at seventeen years old, and Colonel Creighton would see that he found a suitable employment.

Kim pretended at first to understand perhaps one word in three of this talk. Then the Colonel, seeing his mistake, turned to fluent and picturesque Urdu and Kim was contented. No man could be a fool who knew the language so intimately, who moved so gently and silently, and whose eyes were so different from the dull fat eyes of other Sahibs.

'Yes, and thou must learn how to make pictures of roads and mountains and rivers – to carry these pictures in thy eye till a suitable time comes to set them upon paper. Perhaps some day, when thou art a chain-man, I may say to thee when we are working together: "Go across those hills and see what lies beyond." Then one will say: "There are bad people living in those hills who will slay the chain-man if he be seen to look like a Sahib." What then?'

Kim thought. Would it be safe to return the Colonel's lead?

'I would tell what that other man had said.'

'But if I answered: "I will give thee a hundred rupees for knowledge of what is behind those hills – for a picture of a river and a little news of what the people say in the villages there"?'

'How can I tell? I am only a boy. Wait till I am a man.' Then, seeing the Colonel's brow clouded, he went on: 'But I think I should in a few days earn the hundred rupees.'

'By what road?'

Kim shook his head resolutely. 'If I said how I would earn them, another man might hear and forestall me. It is no good to sell knowledge for nothing.'

'Tell now.' The Colonel held up a rupee. Kim's hand half reached towards it, and dropped.

'Nay, Sahib; nay. I know the price that will be paid for the answer, but I do not know why the question is asked.'

'Take it for a gift, then,' said Creighton, tossing it over. 'There is a good spirit in thee. Do not let it be blunted at St. Xavier's. There are many boys there who despise the black men.'

'Their mothers were bazar-women,' said Kim. He knew well there is no hatred like that of the half-caste for his brother-in-law.

'True; but thou art a Sahib and the son of a Sahib. Therefore, do not at any time be led to contemn the black men. I have known boys newly entered into the service of the Government who feigned not to understand the talk or the customs of black men. Their pay was cut for ignorance. There is no sin so great as ignorance. Remember this.'

Several times in the course of the long twenty-four hours' run south did the Colonel send for Kim, always developing this latter text.

'We be all on one lead-rope, then,' said Kim at last, 'the Colonel, Mahbub Ali, and I – when I become a chain-man. He will use me as Mahbub Ali employed me, I think. That is good, if it allows me to return to the road again. This clothing grows no easier by wear.'

When they came to the crowded Lucknow station there was no sign of the lama. He swallowed his disappointment, while the Colonel bundled him into a *ticca-garri* with his neat belongings and despatched him alone to St. Xavier's.

'I do not say farewell, because we shall meet again,' he cried. 'Again, and many times, if thou art one of good spirit. But thou art not yet tried.'

'Not when I brought thee' – Kim actually dared to use the *tum* of equals – 'a white stallion's pedigree that night?'

'Much is gained by forgetting, little brother,' said the Colonel, with a look that pierced through Kim's shoulder-blades as he scuttled into the carriage.

It took him nearly five minutes to recover. Then he sniffed the new air appreciatively. 'A rich city,' he said. 'Richer than Lahore. How good the bazars must be! Coachman, drive me a little through the bazars here.'

'My order is to take thee to the school." The driver used the 'thou,' which is rudeness when applied to a white man. In the clearest and most fluent vernacular Kim pointed out his error, climbed on to the box-seat, and, perfect understanding established, drove for a couple of hours up and down, estimating, comparing, and enjoying. There is no city – except Bombay, the queen of all – more beautiful in her garish style than Lucknow, whether you see her from the bridge over the river, or from the top of the Imambara looking down on the gilt umbrellas of the Chutter Munzil, and the trees in which the town is bedded. Kings have adorned her with fantastic buildings, endowed her with charities, crammed her with pensioners, and drenched her with blood. She is the centre of all idleness, intrigue, and luxury, and shares with Delhi the claim to talk the only pure Urdu.

'A fair city – a beautiful city.' The driver, as a Lucknow man, was pleased with the compliment, and told Kim many astounding things where an English guide would have talked of the Mutiny.

'Now we will go to the school,' said Kim at last. The great old school of St. Xavier's in Partibus, block on block of low white buildings, stands in vast grounds over against the Gumti River, at some distance from the city.

'What like of folk are they within?' said Kim.

'Young Sahibs – all devils; but to speak truth, and I drive many of them to and fro from the railway station, I have never seen one that had in him the making of a more perfect devil than thou – this young Sahib whom I am now driving.'

Naturally, for he was never trained to consider them in any way improper, Kim had passed the time of day with one or two frivolous ladies at upper windows in a certain street, and naturally, in the exchange of compliments, had acquitted himself well. He was about to acknowledge the driver's last insolence, when his eye – it was growing dusk – caught a figure sitting by one of the white plaster gate-pillars in the long sweep of wall.

'Stop!' he cried. 'Stay here! I do not go to the school at once.'

'But what is to pay me for this coming and re-coming?' said the driver petulantly. 'Is the boy mad? Last time it was a dancing-girl. This time it is a priest.'

Kim was in the road headlong, patting the dusty feet beneath the dirty yellow robe.

'I have waited here a day and a half,' the lama's level voice began. 'Nay, I had a disciple with me. He that was my friend at the Temple of the Tirthankers gave me a guide for this journey. I came from Benares in the train, when thy letter was given me. Yes, I am well fed. I need nothing.'

'But why didst thou not stay with the Kulu woman, O Holy One? In what way didst thou get to Benares? My heart has been heavy since we parted.'

'The woman wearied me by constant flux of talk and requiring charms for children. I separated myself from that company, permitting her to acquire merit by gifts. She is at least a woman of open hands, and I made a promise to return to her house if need arose. Then, perceiving myself alone in this great and terrible world, I bethought me of the *te-rain* to Benares, where I knew one abode in the Tirthankers' Temple who was a Seeker, even as I.'

'Ah! Thy River,' said Kim. 'I had forgotten the River.'

'So soon, my *chela*? I have never forgotten it; but when I had left thee it seemed better that I should go to the temple and take counsel, for, look you, India is very large, and it may be that wise men before us, some two or three, have left a record of the place of our River. There is debate in the Temple of the Tirthankers on this matter; some saying one thing, and some another. They are courteous folk.'

'So be it; but what dost thou do now?'

'I acquire merit in that I help thee, my *chela*, to wisdom. The priest of that body of men who serve the Red Bull wrote me that all should be as I desired for thee. I sent the money to suffice for one year, and then I came, as thou seest me, to watch for thee going up into the Gates of Learning. A day and a half have I waited – not because I was led by any affection towards thee – that is not part of the Way – but, as they said at the Tirthankers' Temple, because, money having been paid for learning, it was right that I should oversee the end of the matter. They resolved my doubts most clearly. I had a fear that, perhaps, I came because I wished to see thee – misguided by the red mist of affection. It is not so. . . . Moreover, I am troubled by a dream.'

'But surely, Holy One, thou hast not forgotten the Road and all that befell on it? Surely it was a little to see me that thou didst come?'

'The horses are cold, and it is past their feeding-time,' whined the driver.

'Go to Jehannum and abide there with thy reputationless aunt!" Kim snarled over his shoulder. 'I am all alone in this land; I know not where I go nor what shall befall me. My heart was in that letter I sent thee. Except for Mahbub Ali, and he is a Pathan, I have no friend save thee, Holy One. Do not altogether go away.'

'I have considered that also,' the lama replied, in a shaking voice. 'It is manifest that from time to time I shall acquire merit – if before that I have not found my River – by assuring myself that thy feet are set on wisdom. What they will teach thee I do not know, but the priest wrote me that no son of a Sahib in all India will be better taught than thou. So from time to time, therefore, I will come again. May be thou wilt be such a Sahib as he who gave me these spectacles' – the lama wiped them elaborately – 'in the Wonder House at Lahore. That is my hope, for he was a Fountain of Wisdom – wiser than many abbots.... Again, may be thou wilt forget me and our meetings.'

'If I eat thy bread,' cried Kim passionately, 'how shall I ever forget thee?'

'No – no.' He put the boy aside. ' I must go back to Benares. From time to time, now that I know the customs of letter-writers in this land, I will send thee a letter, and from time to time I will come and see thee.'

'But whither shall I send my letters?' wailed Kim, clutching at the robe, all forgetful that he was a Sahib.

'To the Temple of the Tirthankers at Benares. That is the place I have chosen till I find my River. Do not weep; for, look you, all Desire is illusion and a new binding upon the Wheel. Go up to the Gates of Learning. Let me see thee go. . . . Dost thou love me? Then go, or my heart cracks. . . . I will come again. Surely I will come again.'

The lama watched the *ticca-garri* rumble into the compound, and strode off, snuffing between each long stride.

'The Gates of Learning' shut with a clang.

* * * * *

The country-born and bred boy has his own manners and customs, which do not resemble those of any other land; and his teachers approach him by roads which an English master would not understand. Therefore, you would scarcely be interested in Kim's experiences as a St. Xavier's boy among two or three hundred precocious youths, most of whom had never seen the sea. He suffered the usual penalties for breaking out of bounds when there was cholera in the city. This was before he had learned to write fair English, and so was obliged to find a bazar letter-writer. He was, of course, indicted for smoking and for the use of abuse more full-flavoured than even St. Xavier's had ever heard. He learned to wash himself with the Levitical scrupulosity of the native-born, who in his heart considers the Englishman rather dirty. He played the usual tricks on the patient coolies pulling the punkahs in the sleeping-rooms where the boys thrashed through the hot nights telling tales till the dawn; and quietly he measured himself against his self-reliant mates.

They were sons of subordinate officials in the Railway, Telegraph, and Canal services; of warrant-officers, sometimes retired and sometimes acting as commanders-in-chief to a feudatory Rajah's army; of captains of the Indian Marine, Government pensioners, planters, Presidency shopkeepers, and missionaries. A few were cadets of the old Eurasian houses that have taken strong root in Dhurrumtollah – Pereiras, De

Souzas, and D'Silvas. Their parents could well have educated them in England, but they loved the school that had served their own youth, and generation followed sallow-hued generation at St. Xavier's. Their homes ranged from Howrah of the railway people to abandoned cantonments like Monghyr and Chunar; lost tea-gardens Shillong-way; villages where their fathers were large landholders in Oudh or the Deccan; Mission-stations a week from the nearest railway line; seaports a thousand miles south, facing the brazen Indian surf; and cinchona-plantations south of all. The mere story of their adventures, which to them were no adventures, on their road to and from school would have crisped a Western boy's hair. They were used to jogging off alone through a hundred miles of jungle, where there was always the delightful chance of being delayed by tigers; but they would no more have bathed in the English Channel in an English August, than their brothers across the world would have lain still while a leopard snuffed at their palanquin. There were boys of fifteen who had spent a day and a half on an islet in the middle of a flooded river, taking charge, as by right, of a camp of frantic pilgrims returning from a shrine; there were seniors who had requisitioned a chance-met Rajah's elephant, in the name of St. Francis Xavier, when the rains once blotted out the cart-track that led to their father's estate, and had all but lost the huge beast in a quicksand. There was a boy who, he said, and none doubted, had helped his father to beat off with rifles from the veranda a rush of Akas in the days when those head-hunters were bold against lonely plantations.

And every tale was told in the even, passionless voice of the native-born, mixed with quaint reflections, borrowed unconsciously from native foster-mothers, and turns of speech that showed they had been that instant translated from the vernacular. Kim watched, listened, and approved. This was not insipid, single-word talk of drummer-boys. It dealt with a life he knew and in part understood. The atmosphere suited him, and he throve by inches. They gave him a white drill suit as the weather warmed, and he rejoiced in the new-found bodily comforts as he rejoiced to use his sharpened mind over the tasks they set him. His quickness would have delighted an English master; but at St. Xavier's they know the first rush of minds developed by sun and surroundings, as they know the half-collapse that sets in at twenty-two or twenty-three.

Nonetheless he remembered to hold himself lowly. When tales were told of hot nights, Kim did not sweep the board with his reminiscences; for St. Xavier's looks down on boys who 'go native altogether.' One must never forget that one is a Sahib, and that some day, when examinations are passed, one will command natives. Kim made a note of this, for he began to understand where examinations led.

Then came the holidays from August to October – the long holidays imposed by the heat and the rains. Kim was informed that he would go north to some station in the hills behind Umballa, where Father Victor would arrange for him.

'A barrack-school?' said Kim, who had asked many questions and thought more.

'Yes, I suppose so,' said the master. 'It will not do you any harm to keep you out of mischief. You can go up with young De Castro as far as Delhi.'

Kim considered it in every possible light. He had been diligent, even as the Colonel advised. A boy's holiday was his own property, – of so much the talk of his companions had advised him, – and a barrack-school would be torment after St. Xavier's. Moreover – this was magic worth anything else – he could write. In three months he had discovered how men can speak to each other without a third party, at the cost of half an anna and a little knowledge. No word had come from the lama, but there remained the Road. Kim yearned for the caress of soft mud squishing up between the toes, as his mouth watered for mutton stewed with butter and cabbages, for rice speckled with strong-scented cardamoms, for the saffron-tinted rice, garlic and onions, and the forbidden greasy sweetmeats of the bazars. They would feed him raw beef on a platter at the barrack-school, and he must smoke by stealth. But again, he was a Sahib and was at St. Xavier's, and that pig Mahbub Ali. . . . No, he would not test Mahbub's hospitality – and yet. . . . He thought it out alone in the dormitory, and came to the conclusion he had been unjust to Mahbub.

The school was empty; nearly all the masters had gone away; Colonel Creighton's railway-pass lay in his hand, and Kim puffed himself that he had not spent Colonel Creighton's or Mahbub's money in riotous living. He was still lord of two rupees seven annas. His new bullock-trunk, marked 'K. O'H.,' and bedding-roll lay in the empty sleeping-room. 'Sahibs are always tied to their baggage,' said Kim, nodding at them. 'You will stay here.' He went out into the warm rain, smiling sinfully, and sought a certain house whose outside he had noted down some time before. . . .

'Arré! Dost thou know what manner of women we be in this quarter? O shame!'

'Was I born yesterday?' Kim squatted native fashion on the cushions of that upper room. 'A little dye-stuff and three yards of cloth to help out a jest. Is it much to ask?'

'Who is *she*? Thou art full young, as Sahibs go, for this devilry.'

'Oh, she? She is the daughter of a certain schoolmaster of a regiment in the cantonments. He has beaten me twice because I went over their wall in these clothes. Now I would go as a gardener's boy. Old men are very jealous.'

'That is true. Hold thy face still while I dab on the juice.'

'Not too black, *Naikan*. I would not appear to her as a *hubshi* (nigger).'

'Oh, love makes nought of these things. And how old is she?'

'Twelve years, I think,' said the shameless Kim. 'Spread it also on the breast. It may be her father will tear my clothes off me and if I am piebald – ' he laughed.

The girl worked busily, dabbing a twist of cloth into a little saucer of brown dye that holds longer than any walnut juice.

'Now send out and get me a cloth for the turban. Woe is me, my head is all unshaved! And he will surely knock off my turban.'

'I am not a barber, but I will make shift. Thou wast born to be a breaker of hearts! All this disguise for one evening? Remember, the stuff does not wash away.' She shook with laughter till her bracelets and anklets jingled. 'But who is it pay me for this? Huneefa herself could not have given thee better stuff.'

'Trust in the Gods, my sister,' said Kim gravely screwing his face round as the stain dried. 'Besides, hast thou ever helped to paint a Sahib thus before?'

'Never indeed. But a jest is not money.'

'It is worth much more.'

'Child, thou art beyond all dispute the most shameless son of Shaitan that I have ever known to take up a poor girl's time with this play, and then to say: "Is not the jest enough?" Thou wilt go very far in this world.' She gave the dancing-girls' salutation in mockery.

'All one. Make haste and rough-cut my head.' Kim shifted from foot to foot, his eyes ablaze with mirth as he thought of the fat days before him. He gave the girl four annas, and ran down the stairs in the likeness of a low-caste Hindu boy – perfect in every detail. A cookshop was his next point of call, where he feasted in extravagance and greasy luxury.

On Lucknow station platform he watched young De Castro, all covered with prickly-heat, get into a second-class compartment. Kim patronised a third, and was the life and soul of it. He explained to the company that he was assistant to a juggler who had left him behind sick with fever, and that he would pick up his master at Umballa. As the occupants of the carriage changed, he varied this tale, or adorned it with all the shoots of a budding fancy, the more rampant for being held off native speech so long. In all India that night was no human being so joyful as Kim. At Umballa he got out and headed eastward, plashing over the sodden fields to the village where the old soldier lived.

About this time Colonel Creighton at Simla was advised from Lucknow by wire that young O'Hara had disappeared. Mahbub Ali was in town selling horses, and to him the Colonel confided the affair one morning cantering round Annandale race-course.

'Oh, that is nothing,' said the horse-dealer. 'Men are like horses. At certain times they need salt, and if that salt is not in the mangers they will lick it up from the earth. He has gone back to the Road again for a while. The *madrissah* wearied him. I knew it would. Another time, I will take him upon the Road myself. Do not be troubled, Creighton Sahib. It is as though a polo-pony, breaking loose, ran out to learn the game alone.'

'Then he is not dead, think you?'

'Fever might kill him. I do not fear for the boy otherwise. A monkey does not fall among trees.'

Next morning, on the same course, Mahbub's stallion ranged alongside the Colonel.

'It is as I had thought,' said the horse-dealer. 'He has come through Umballa at least, and there he has written a letter to me, having learned in the bazar that I was here.'

'Read,' said the Colonel, with a sigh of relief. It was absurd that a man of his position should take an interest in a little country-bred vagabond; but the Colonel remembered the conversation in the train, and often in the past few months had caught himself thinking of the queer, silent, self-possessed boy. His evasion, of course, was the height of insolence, but it argued some resource and nerve.

Mahbub's eyes twinkled as he reined out into the centre of the cramped little plain, where none could come near unseen.

' "*The Friend of the Stars, who is the Friend of all the World –*" '

'What is this?'

'A name we give him in Lahore city. "*The Friend of all the World takes leave to go to his own places. He will come back upon the appointed day. Let the box and the bedding-roll be sent for; and if there has been a fault, let the Hand of Friendship turn aside the Whip of Calamity.*" There is yet a little more, but – '

'No matter, read.'

' "*Certain things are not known to those who eat with forks. It is better to eat with both hands for a while. Speak soft words to those who do not understand this that the return may be propitious.*" Now the manner in which that was cast is of course the work of the letter-writer, but see how wisely the boy has devised the matter of it so that no hint is given except to those who know!'

'Is this the Hand of Friendship to avert the Whip of Calamity?' laughed the Colonel.

'See how wise is the boy. He would go back to the Road again, as I said. Not knowing yet thy trade – '

'I am not quite sure of that,' the Colonel muttered.

'He turns to me to make a peace between you. Is he not wise? He says he will return. He is but perfecting his knowledge. Think, Sahib! He has been three months at the school. And he is not mouthed to that bit. For my part, I rejoice: the pony learns the game.'

'Ay, but another time he must not go alone.'

'Why? He went alone before he came under the Colonel Sahib's protection. When he comes to the Great Game he must go alone – alone, and at peril of his head. *Then*, if he spits, or sneezes, or sits down other than as the people do whom he watches, he may be slain. Why hinder him now? Remember how the Persians say: The jackal that lives in the wilds of Mazanderan can only be caught by the hounds of Mazanderan.'

'True. It is true, Mahbub Ali. And if he comes to no harm, I do not desire anything better. But it is great insolence on his part.'

'He does not tell me, even, whither he goes,' said Mahbub. 'He is no fool. When his time is accomplished he will come to me. It is time the healer of pearls took him in hand. He ripens too quickly – as Sahibs reckon.'

This prophecy was fulfilled to the letter a month later. Mahbub had gone down to Umballa to bring up a fresh consignment of horses, and Kim met him on the Kalka road at dusk riding alone, begged an alms of him, was sworn at, and replied in English. There was nobody within earshot to hear Mahbub's gasp of amazement.

'Oho! And where hast thou been?'

'Up and down – down and up.'

'Come under a tree, out of the wet, and tell.'

'I stayed for a while with an old man near Umballa; anon with a household of my acquaintance in Umballa. With one of these I went as far as Delhi to the southward. That is a wondrous city. Then I drove a bullock for a *teli* (an oilman) coming north; but I heard of a great feast forward in Puttiala, and thither went I in the company of a firework-maker. It was a great feast' (Kim rubbed his stomach). 'I saw Rajahs, and elephants with gold and silver trappings; and they lit all the fireworks at once, whereby eleven men were killed, my firework-maker among them, and I was blown across a tent but took no harm. Then I came back to the *rel* with a Sikh horseman, to whom I was groom for my bread; and so here.'

'*Shabash*!' said Mahbub Ali.

'But what does the Colonel Sahib say? I do not wish to be beaten.'

'The Hand of Friendship has averted the Whip of Calamity; but another time, when thou takest the Road it will be with me. This is too early.'

'Late enough for me. I have learned to read and to write English a little at the *madrissah*. I shall soon be altogether a Sahib.'

'Hear him!' laughed Mahbub, looking at the little drenched figure dancing in the wet. 'Salaam – Sahib,' and he saluted ironically. 'Well, art tired of the Road, or wilt thou come on to Umballa with me and work back with the horses?'

'I come with thee, Mahbub Ali.'

CHAPTER 8

Something I owe to the soil that grew –
More to the life that fed –
But most to Allah Who gave me two
Separate sides to my head.

I would go without shirts or shoes,
Friends, tobacco or bread
Sooner than for an instant lose
Either side of my head.

'THEN IN God's Name take blue for red,' said Mahbub, alluding to the Hindu colour of Kim's disreputable turban.

Kim countered with the old proverb, 'I will change my faith and my bedding, but *thou* must pay for it.'

The dealer laughed till he nearly fell from his horse. At a shop on the outskirts of the city the change was made, and Kim stood up, externally at least, a Mohammedan.

Mahbub hired a room over against the railway station, sent for a cooked meal of the finest with almond-curd sweetmeats (*balushai* we call it) and fine-chopped Lucknow tobacco.

'This is better than some other meat that I ate with the Sikh,' said Kim, grinning as he squatted, 'and assuredly they give no such victuals at my *madrissah*.'

'I have a desire to hear of that same *madrissah*.' Mahbub stuffed himself with great boluses of spiced mutton fried in fat with cabbage and golden-brown onions. 'But tell me first, altogether and truthfully, the manner of thy escape. For, O Friend of all the World,' – he loosed his cracking belt, – 'I do not think it is often that a Sahib and the son of a Sahib runs away from there.'

'How should they? They do not know the land. It was nothing,' said Kim, and began his tale. When he came to the disguisement and the interview with the girl in the bazar, Mahbub Ali's gravity went from him. He laughed aloud and beat his hand on his thigh.

'*Shabash*! *Shabash*! Oh, well done, little one! What will the healer of turquoises say to this? Now, slowly, let us hear what befell afterwards – step by step, omitting nothing.'

Step by step then, Kim told his adventures between coughs as the full-flavoured tobacco caught his lungs.

'I said,' growled Mahbub Ali to himself, 'I *said* it was the pony breaking out to play polo. The fruit is ripe already – except that he must learn his distances and his pacings, and his rods and his compasses. Listen now. I have turned aside the Colonel's whip from thy skin, and that is no small service.'

'True.' Kim puffed serenely. 'That is all true.'

'But it is not to be thought that this running out and in is any way good.'

'It was my holiday, Hajji. I was a slave for many weeks. Why should I not run away when the school was shut? Look, too, how I, living upon my friends or working for my bread, as I did with the Sikh, have saved the Colonel Sahib a great expense."

Mahbub's lips twitched under his well-pruned Mohammedan moustache.

'What are a few rupees' – the Pathan threw out his open hand carelessly – 'to the Colonel Sahib? He spends them for a purpose, not in any way for love of thee.'

'That,' said Kim slowly, 'I knew a very long time ago.'

'Who told?'

'The Colonel Sahib himself. Not in those many words, but plainly enough for one who is not altogether a mud-head. Yea, he told me in the *te-rain* when we went down to Lucknow.'

'Be it so. Then I will tell thee more, Friend of all the World, though in the telling I lend thee my head.'

'It was forfeit to me,' said Kim, with deep relish, 'in Umballa, when thou didst pick me up on the horse after the drummer-boy beat me.'

'Speak a little plainer. All the world may tell lies save thou and I. For equally is thy life forfeit to me if I chose to raise my finger here.'

'And this is known to me also,' said Kim, readjusting the live charcoal-ball on the weed. 'It is a very sure tie between us. Indeed thy hold is surer even than mine; for who would miss a boy beaten to death, or, it may be, thrown into a well by the roadside? Many people here and in Simla and across the passes behind the Hills would, on the other hand, say: "What has come to Mahbub Ali," if he were found dead among his horses. Surely too the Colonel Sahib would make inquiries. But again,' – Kim's face puckered with cunning, – 'he would not make overlong inquiry, lest people should ask: "What has this Colonel Sahib to do with that horse-dealer?" But I – if I lived – '

'As thou wouldst surely die – '

'It may be; but I say, *if* I lived, I, and I alone, would know that one had come by night, as a common thief perhaps, to Mahbub Ali's bulkhead in the serai, and there had slain him, either before or after that thief had made a full search into his saddle-bags and between the soles of his slippers. Is that news to tell to the Colonel, or would he say to me – (I have not forgotten when he sent me back for a cigar-case that he had *not* left behind him) – "What is Mahbub Ali to me?" '

Up went a gout of heavy smoke. There was a long pause: then Mahbub Ali spoke in admiration: 'And with these things on thy mind, dost thou lie down and rise again among all the

Sahibs' little sons at the *madrissah* and meekly take instruction from thy teachers?'

'It is an order,' said Kim blandly. 'Who am I to dispute an order?'

'A most finished son of Eblis,' said Mahbub Ali. 'But what is this tale of the thief and the search?'

'That which I saw,' said Kim, 'the night that my lama and I lay next thy place in the Kashmir Serai. The door was left unlocked, which I think is not thy custom, Mahbub. He came in as one assured that thou wouldst not soon return. My eye was against a knot-hole in the plank. He searched as it were for something – not a rug, not stirrups, nor a bridle, nor brass pots – something little and most carefully hid. Else why did he prick with an iron between the soles of thy slippers?'

'Ha!' Mahbub Ali smiled gently. 'And seeing these things, what tale didst thou fashion to thyself, Well of the Truth?'

'None. I put my hand upon my amulet, which lies always next to my skin, and, remembering the pedigree of a white stallion that I had bitten out of a piece of Mussalmani bread, I went away to Umballa perceiving that a heavy trust was laid upon me. At that hour, had I chosen, thy head was forfeit. It needed only to say to that man, "I have here a paper concerning a horse which I cannot read." And then?' Kim peered at Mahbub under his eyebrows.

'Then thou wouldst have drunk water twice – perhaps thrice, afterwards. I do not think more than thrice,' said Mahbub simply.

'It is true. I thought of that a little, but most I thought that I loved thee, Mahbub. Therefore I went to Umballa, as thou knowest, but (and this thou dost not know) I lay hid in the garden-grass to see what Colonel Creighton Sahib might do upon reading the white stallion's pedigree.'

'And what did he?' for Kim had bitten off the conversation.

'Dost *thou* give news for love, or dost thou sell it?' Kim asked.

'I sell and – I buy.' Mahbub took a four-anna piece out of his belt and held it up.

'Eight!' said Kim, mechanically following the huckster instinct of the East.

Mahbub laughed, and put away the coin. 'It is too easy to deal in that market, Friend of all the World. Tell me for love. Our lives lie in each other's hand.'

'Very good. I saw the Jang-i-Lat Sahib (the Commander-in-Chief) come to a big dinner. I saw him in Creighton Sahib's office. I saw the two read the white stallion's pedigree. I heard the very orders given for the opening of a great war.'

'Hah!' Mahbub nodded with deepest eyes afire. 'The game is well played. That war is done now, and the evil, we hope, nipped before the flower – thanks to me – and thee. What didst thou later?'

'I made the news as it were a hook to catch me victual and honour among the villagers in a village whose priest drugged my lama. But I bore away the old man's purse, and the Brahmin found nothing. So next morning he was angry. Ho! Ho! And I also used the news when I fell into the hands of that white regiment with their Bull!'

'That was foolishness.' Mahbub scowled. 'News is not meant to be thrown about like dung-cakes, but used sparingly – like *bhang*.'

'So I think now, and, moreover, it did me no sort of good. But that was very long ago,'– he made as to brush it all away with a thin brown hand, – 'and since then, and especially in the nights under the punkah at the *madrissah,* I have thought very greatly.'

'Is it permitted to ask whither the Heaven-born's thought might have led?' said Mahbub, with an elaborate sarcasm, smoothing his scarlet beard.

'It is permitted,' said Kim, and threw back the very tone. 'They say at Nucklao that no Sahib must tell a black man that he has made a fault.'

Mahbub's hand shot into his bosom, for to call a Pathan a 'black man' (*kala admi*) is a blood-insult. Then he remembered and laughed. 'Speak, Sahib: thy black man bears.'

'But,'said Kim, 'I am *not* a Sahib, and I say I made a fault when I cursed thee, Mahbub Ali, on the day at Umballa I thought I was betrayed by a Pathan. I was senseless; for I was but newly caught, and I wished to kill that low-caste drummer-boy. I say now, Hajji, that it was well done; and I see my road all clear before me to a good service. I will stay in the *madrissah* till I am ripe.'

'Well said. Especially are distances and numbers and the manner of using compasses to be learned in that game. One waits in the Hills above to show thee.'

'I will learn their teaching upon a condition – that my time is given to me without question when the *madrissah* is shut. Ask that for me of the Colonel.'

'But why not ask the Colonel in the Sahib's tongue?'

'The Colonel is the servant of the Government. He is sent hither and yon at a word, and must consider his own advancement. (See how much I have already learned at Nucklao!) Moreover, the Colonel I know since three months only. I have known one Mahbub Ali for six years. So! To the *madrissah* I will go. At the *madrissah* I will learn. In the *madrissah* I will be a Sahib. But when the *madrissah* is shut, then must I be free and go among my people. Otherwise I die!'

'And who are thy People, Friend of all the World?'

'This great and beautiful land,' said Kim, waving his paw round the little clay-walled room where the oil-lamp in its niche burned heavily through the tobacco-smoke. 'And, further, I would see my lama again. And further, I need money.'

'That is the need of every one,' said Mahbub ruefully. 'I will give thee eight annas, for much money is not picked out of horses' hooves, and it must suffice for many days. As to all the rest, I am well pleased, and no further talk is needed. Make haste to learn, and in three years, or it may be less, thou wilt be an aid – even to me.'

'Have I been such a hindrance till now?' said Kim, with a boy's giggle.

'Do not give answers,' Mahbub grunted. 'Thou art my new horse-boy. Go and bed among my men. They are near the north end of the station, with the horses.'

'They will beat me to the south end of the station if I come without authority.'

Mahbub felt in his belt, wetted his thumb on a cake of Chinese ink, and dabbed the impression on a piece of soft native paper. From Balkh to Bombay men know that rough-ridged print with the old scar running diagonally across it.

'That is enough to show my headman. I come in the morning.'

'By which road?' said Kim.

'By the road from the City. There is but one, and then we return to Creighton Sahib. I have saved thee a beating.'

'Allah! What is a beating when the very head is loose on the shoulders?'

Kim slid out quietly into the night, walked half round the house, keeping close to the walls, and headed away from the station for a mile or so. Then, fetching a wide compass, he worked back at leisure, for he needed time to invent a story if any of Mahbub's retainers asked questions.

They were camped on a piece of waste ground beside the railway, and, being natives, had not, of course, unloaded the two trucks in which Mahbub's animals stood among a consignment of country-breds bought by the Bombay tram-company. The headman, a broken-down, consumptive-looking Mohammedan, promptly challenged Kim, but was pacified at sight of Mahbub's sign-manual.

'The Hajji has of his favour given me service,' said Kim testily. 'If this be doubted, wait till he comes in the morning. Meantime, a place by the fire.'

Followed the usual aimless babble that every low-caste native must raise on every occasion. It died down, and Kim lay out behind the little knot of Mahbub's followers, almost under the wheels of a horse-truck, a borrowed blanket for covering. Now a bed among brickbats and ballast-refuse on a damp night, between overcrowded horses and unwashen Baltis, would not appeal to many white boys; but Kim was utterly happy. Change of scene, service, and surroundings were the breath of his little nostrils, and thinking of the neat white cots of St. Xavier's all arow under the punkah gave him joy as keen as the repetition of the multiplication-table in English.

'I am very old,' he thought sleepily. 'Every month I become a year more old. I was very young, and a fool to boot, when I took Mahbub's message to Umballa. Even when I was with that white regiment I was very young and small and had no wisdom. But now I learn every day, and in three years the Colonel will take me out of the *madrissah* and let me go upon the Road with Mahbub hunting for horses' pedigrees, or maybe I shall go by myself; or maybe I shall find the lama and go with him. Yes; that is best. To walk again as a *chela* with my lama when he comes back to Benares.' The thoughts came more slowly and disconnectedly. He was plunging into a beautiful dreamland when his ears caught a whisper, thin and sharp, above the monotonous babble round the fire. It came from behind the iron-skinned horse-truck.

'He is not here then?'

'Where should he be but roystering in the City. Who looks for a rat in a frog-pond? Come away. He is not our man.'

'He must not go back beyond the Passes a second time. It is the order.'

'Hire some woman to drug him. It is a few rupees only, and there is no evidence.'

'Except the woman. It must be more certain; and remember the price upon his head.'

'Ay, but the police have a long arm, and we are far from the Border. If it were in Peshawur now!'

'Yes – in Peshawur,' the second voice sneered. 'Peshawur, full of his blood-kin – full of bolt-holes and women behind whose clothes he will hide. Yes, Peshawur or Jehannum would suit us equally well.'

'Then what is the plan?'

'O fool, have I not told it a hundred times. Wait till he comes to lie down, and then one sure shot. The trucks are between us and pursuit. We have but to run back over the lines and go our way. They will not see whence the shot came. Wait here at least till the dawn. What manner of *faquir* art thou to shiver at a little watching?'

'Oho!' thought Kim, behind close-shut eyes. 'Once again it is Mahbub. Indeed a white stallion's pedigree is not a good thing to peddle to Sahibs! Or maybe Mahbub has been selling other news. Now what is to do, Kim? I know not where Mahbub houses, and if he comes here before the dawn they will shoot him. That would be no profit for thee, Kim. And this is not a matter for the police. That would be no profit for Mahbub; and,' he giggled almost aloud, 'I do not remember any lesson at Nucklao which will help me. Allah! Here is Kim and yonder are they. First then, Kim must wake and go away, so that they shall not suspect. A bad dream wakes a man – thus – '

He threw the blanket off his face, and raised himself suddenly with the terrible, bubbling, meaningless yell of the Asiatic roused by nightmare.

'Urr-urr-urr-urr! Ya-la-la-la-la! *Narain*! The *churel*! The *churel*!'

A *churel* is the peculiarly malignant ghost of a woman who has died in child-bed. She haunts lonely roads, her feet are turned backwards on the ankles, and she leads men to torment.

Louder rose Kim's quavering howl, till at last he leaped to his feet and staggered off sleepily, while the camp cursed him for waking them. Some twenty yards farther up the line he lay down again, taking care that the whisperers should hear his grunts and groans as he recomposed himself. After a few minutes he rolled towards the road and stole away into the thick darkness.

He paddled along swiftly till he came to a culvert, and dropped behind it, his chin on a level with the coping-stone. Here he could command all the night-traffic, himself unseen.

Two or three carts passed, jingling out to the suburbs; a coughing policeman and a hurrying foot-passenger or two who sang to keep off evil spirits. Then rapped the shod feet of a horse.

'Ah! This is more like Mahbub,' thought Kim, as the beast shied at the little head above the culvert.

'Ohe, Mahbub Ali,' he whispered, 'have a care!'

The horse was reined back almost on its haunches, and forced towards the culvert.

'Never again,' said Mahbub, 'will I take a shod horse for night-work. They pick up all the bones and nails in the city.' He stooped to lift its forefoot, and that brought his head within a foot of Kim's. 'Down – keep down,' he muttered. 'The night is full of eyes.'

'Two men wait thy coming behind the horse-trucks. They will shoot thee at thy lying down, because there is a price on thy head. I heard, sleeping near the horses.'

'Didst thou see them?. . . . Hold still, Sire of Devils!' This furiously to the horse.

'No.'

'Was one dressed belike as a *faquir*?'

'One said to the other, "What manner of a *faquir* art thou, to shiver at a little watching?"'

'Good. Go back to the camp and lie down. I do not die to-night.'

Mahbub wheeled his horse and vanished. Kim tore back down the ditch till he reached a point opposite his second resting-place, slipped across the road like a weasel, and recoiled himself in the blanket.

'At least Mahbub knows,' he thought contentedly. 'And certainly he spoke as one expecting it. I do not think those two men will profit by to-night's watch.

An hour passed, and, with the best will in the world to keep awake all night, he slept deeply. Now and again a night train roared along the metals within twenty feet of him; but he had all the Oriental's indifference to mere noise, and it did not even weave a dream through his slumber.

Mahbub was anything but asleep. It annoyed him vehemently that people outside his tribe and unaffected by his casual amours should pursue him for the life. His first and natural impulse was to cross the line lower down, work up again, and, catching his well-wishers from behind, summarily slay them. Here, he reflected with sorrow, another branch of the Government, totally unconnected with Colonel Creighton, might demand explanations which would be hard to supply; and he knew that south the Border a perfectly ridiculous fuss is made about a corpse or so. He had not been troubled in this way since he sent Kim to Umballa with the message, and hoped that suspicion had been finally diverted.

Then a most brilliant notion struck him.

'The English do eternally tell the truth,' he said, 'therefore we of this country are eternally made foolish. By Allah, I will tell the truth to an Englishman! Of what use is the Government police if a poor Kabuli be robbed of his horses in their very trucks. This is as bad as Peshawur! I should lay a complaint at the station. Better still, some young Sahib on the Railway! They are zealous, and if they catch thieves it is remembered to their honour.'

He tied up his horse outside the station, and strode on to the platform.

'Hullo, Mahbub Ali!' said a young Assistant District Traffic Superintendent who was waiting to go down the line – a tall, tow-haired, horsey youth in dingy white linen. 'What are you doing here? Selling weeds – eh?'

'No; I am not troubled for my horses. I come to look for Lutuf Ullah. I have a truck-load up the line. Could any one take them out without the Railway's knowledge?'

'Shouldn't think so, Mahbub. You can claim against us if they do.'

'I have seen two men crouching under the wheels of one of the trucks nearly all the night. *Faquirs* do not steal horses, so I gave them no more thought. I would find Lutuf Ullah, my partner.'

'The deuce you did? And you didn't bother your head about it? 'Pon my word, it's just almost as well that I met you. What were they like, eh?'

'They were only *faquirs*. They will no more than take a little grain perhaps from one of the trucks. There are many up the line. The State will never miss the dole. I came here seeking for my partner, Lutuf Ullah – '

'Never mind your partner. Where are your horse-trucks?'

'A little to this side of the farthest place where they make lamps for the trains.'

'The signal-box. Yes.'

'And upon the rail nearest to the road upon the right-hand side – looking up the line thus. But as regards Lutuf Ullah – a tall man with a broken nose, and a Persian greyhound – Aie!'

The boy had hurried off to wake up a young and enthusiastic policeman; for, as he said, the Railway had suffered much from depredations in the goods-yard. Mahbub Ali chuckled in his dyed beard.

'They will walk in their boots, making a noise, and then they will wonder why there are no *faquirs*. They are very clever boys – Barton Sahib and Young Sahib.'

He waited idly for a few minutes, expecting to see them hurry up the line girt for action. A light engine slid through the station, and he caught a glimpse of young Barton in the cab.

'I did that child an injustice. He is not altogether a fool,' said Mahbub Ali. 'To take a fire-carriage for a thief is a new game!'

When Mahbub Ali came to his camp in the dawn, no one thought it worth while to tell him any news of the night. No one, at least, but one small horse-boy, newly advanced to the great man's service, whom Mahbub called to his tiny tent to assist in some packing.

'It is all known to me,' whispered Kim, bending above saddlebags. 'Two Sahibs came up on a *te-rain*. I was running to and fro in the dark on this side of the trucks as the *te-rain* moved up and down slowly. They fell upon two men sitting under this truck – Hajji, what shall I do with this lump of tobacco? Wrap it in paper and put it under the salt-bag? Yes – and struck them down. But one man struck at a Sahib with a *faquir*'s buck's horn – (Kim meant the conjoined black-buck horns, which are a *faquir*'s sole temporal weapon) – 'the blood came. So the other Sahib, first smiting his own man senseless, smote the stabber with a short gun which had rolled from the first man's hand. They all raged as though mad together.'

Mahbub smiled with heavenly resignation. 'No! That is not so much *dewanee* (madness, or a case for the civil court – the word can be punned upon both ways) as *nizamut* (a criminal case). A gun sayest thou? Ten good years in jail.'

'Then they both lay still, but I think they were nearly dead when they were put on the *te-rain*. Their heads moved thus. And there is much blood on the line. Come and see?'

'I have seen blood before. Jail is the sure place – and assuredly they will give false names, and assuredly no man will find them for a long time. They were unfriends of mine. Thy Fate and mine seem on one string. What a tale for the healer of pearls! Now swiftly with the saddle-bags and the cooking-platter. We will take out the horses and away to Simla.'

Swiftly, – as Orientals understand speed, – with long explanations, with abuse and windy talk, carelessly, amid a hundred checks for little things forgotten, the untidy camp broke up and led the half-dozen stiff and fretful horses along the Kalka road in the fresh of the rain-swept dawn. Kim, regarded as Mahbub Ali's favourite by all who wished to stand well with the Pathan, was not called upon to work. They strolled on by the easiest of stages, halting every few hours at a wayside shelter. Very many Sahibs travel along the Kalka road; and, as Mahbub Ali says, every young Sahib must needs esteem himself a judge of a horse, and, though he be over head in debt to the money-lender, must make as if to buy. That was the reason that Sahib after Sahib, rolling along in a stage-carriage, would stop and open talk. Some would even descend from their vehicles and feel the horses' legs; asking inane questions, or, through sheer ignorance of the vernacular, grossly insulting the imperturbable trader.

'When first I dealt with Sahibs, and that was when Colonel Soady Sahib was Governor of Fort Abazai and flooded the Commissioner's camping-ground for spite,' Mahbub confided to Kim as the boy filled his pipe under a tree, 'I did not know how greatly they were fools, and this made me wroth. As thus – ' and he told Kim a tale of an expression, misused in all innocence, that doubled Kim up with mirth. Now I see, however' – he exhaled smoke slowly – 'that it is with them as with all men – in certain matters they are wise, and in others most foolish. Very foolish it is to use the wrong word to a stranger; for though the heart may be clean of offence, how is the stranger to know that? He is more like to search truth with a dagger.'

'True. True talk,' said Kim solemnly. 'Fools speak of a cat when a woman is brought to bed, for instance. I have heard them.'

'Therefore, in one situate as thou art, it particularly behoves thee to remember this with both kinds of faces. Among Sahibs, never forgetting thou art a Sahib; among the folk of Hind, always remembering thou art – ' he paused, with a puzzled smile.

'What am I? Mussalman, Hindu, Jain, or Buddhist? That is a hard nut.'

'Thou art beyond question an unbeliever, and therefore thou wilt be damned. So says my Law – or I think it does. But thou art also my Little Friend of all the World, and I love thee. So says my heart. This matter of creeds is like horseflesh. The wise man knows horses are good – that there is a profit to be made from all; and for myself – but that I am a good Sunni and bate the men of Tirah – I could believe the same of all the Faiths. Now manifestly a Kattiawar mare taken from the sands of her birthplace and removed to the west of Bengal founders – nor is even a Balkh stallion (and there are no better horses than those of Balkh, were they not so heavy in the shoulder) of any account in the great Northern deserts beside the snow-camels I have seen. Therefore I say in my heart the Faiths are like the horses. Each has merit in its own country.'

'But my lama said altogether a different thing.'

'Oh, he is an old dreamer of dreams from Bhotiyal. My heart is a little angry, Friend of all the World, that thou shouldst see such worth in a man so little known.'

'It is true, Hajji; but that worth do I see; and to him my heart is drawn.'

'And his to thine, I hear. Hearts are like horses. They come and they go against bit or spur. Shout Gul Sher Khan yonder to drive in that bay stallion's pickets more firmly. We do not want a horse-fight at every resting-stage, and the dun and the black will be locked in a little . . . . Now hear me. Is it necessary to the comfort of thy heart to see that lama?'

'It is one part of my bond,' said Kim. 'If I do not see him, and if he is taken from me, I will go out of that *madrissah* in Nucklao and, and – once gone, who is to find me again?'

'It is true. Never was colt held on a lighter heel-rope than thou.' Mahbub nodded his head.

'Do not be afraid.' Kim spoke as though he could have evanished on the moment. 'My lama has said that he will come to see me at the *madrissah* – '

'A beggar and his bowl in the presence of those young Sa – '

'Not all!' Kim cut in with a snort. 'Their eyes are blued and their nails are blackened with low-caste blood, many of them. Sons of *metheeranees* – brothers-in-law to the *bhungi* (sweeper).'

We need not follow the rest of the pedigree; but Kim made his little point clearly and without heat, chewing a piece of sugar-cane the while.

'Friend of all the World,' said Mahbub, pushing over the pipe for the boy to clean, 'I have met many men, women, and boys, and not a few Sahibs. I have never in all my days met such an imp as thou art.'

'And why? When I always tell thee the truth.'

'Perhaps the very reason, for this is a world of danger to honest men.' Mahbub Ali hauled himself off the ground, girt in his belt, and went over to the horses.

'Or sell it?'

There was that in the tone that made Mahbub halt and turn. 'What new devilry?'

'Eight annas, and I will tell,' said Kim, grinning. 'It touches thy peace.'

'O Shaitan!' Mahbub gave the money.

'Rememberest thou the little business of the thieves in the dark, down yonder at Umballa?'

'Seeing they sought my life, I have not altogether forgotten. 'Why?'

'Rememberest thou the Kashmir Serai?'

'I will twist thy ears in a moment – Sahib.'

'No need – Pathan. Only, the second *faquir*, whom the Sahibs beat senseless, was the man who came to search thy bulkhead at Lahore. I saw his face as they helped him on the engine. The very same man.'

'Why didst thou not tell before?'

'Oh, he will go to jail, and be safe for some years. There is no need to tell more than is necessary at any one time. Besides, I did not then need money for sweetmeats.'

'Allah Karim!' said Mahbub Ali. 'Wilt thou some day sell my head for a few sweetmeats if the fit takes thee?'

* * * * *

Kim will remember till he dies that long, lazy journey from Umballa, through Kalka and the Pinjore Gardens near by, up to Simla. A sudden spate in the Gugger River swept down one horse (the most valuable, be sure), and nearly drowned Kim among the dancing boulders. Farther up the road the horses were stampeded by a Government elephant, and being in high condition of grass food, it cost a day and a half to get them together again. Then they met Sikandar Khan coming down with a few unsaleable screws, – remnants of his string, – and

Mahbub, who has more of horse-coping in his little finger nail than Sikandar Khan in all his tents, must needs buy two of the worst, and that meant eight hours' laborious diplomacy and untold tobacco. But it was all pure delight – the wandering road, climbing, dipping, and sweeping about the growing spurs; the flush of the morning laid along the distant snows; the branched cacti, tier upon tier on the stony hillsides; the voices of a thousand water-channels; the chatter of the monkeys; the solemn deodars, climbing one after another with down-drooped branches; the vista of the Plains rolled out far beneath them; the incessant twanging of the tonga-horns and the wild rush of the led horses when a tonga swung round a curve; the halts for prayers (Mahbub was very religious in dry-washings and bellowings when time did not press); the evening conferences by the halting-places, when camels and bullocks chewed solemnly together and the stolid drivers told the news of the Road – all these things lifted Kim's heart to song within him.

'But, when the singing and dancing is done,' said Mahbub Ali, 'comes the Colonel Sahib's, and that is not so sweet.'

'A fair land – a most beautiful land is this of Hind – and the land of the Five Rivers is fairer than all,' Kim half chanted. 'Into it I will go again if Mahbub Ali or the Colonel lift hand or foot against me. Once gone, who shall find me? Look, Hajji, is yonder the city of Simla? Allah, what a city!'

'My father's brother, and he was an old man when Mackerson Sahib's well was new at Peshawur, could recall when there were but two houses in it.'

He led the horses below the main road into the lower Simla bazar – the crowded rabbit-warren that climbs up from the valley to the town-hall at an angle of forty-five. A man who knows his way there can defy all the police of India's summer capital; so cunningly does veranda communicate with verandah, alley-way with alley-way, and bolt-hole with bolt-hole. Here live those who minister to the wants of the glad city – jhampanis who pull the pretty ladies' rickshaws by night and gamble till the dawn; grocers, oil-sellers, curio-vendors, firewood dealers, priests, pickpockets, and native employees of the Government: here are discussed by courtesans the things which are supposed to be profoundest secrets of the India Council; and here gather all the sub-sub-agents of half the native States. Here, too, Mahbub Ali rented a room, much more securely locked than his bulkhead at Lahore, in the house of a Mohammedan cattle-dealer. It was a place of miracles, too, for there went in at twilight a Mohammedan horse-boy, and there came out an hour later a Eurasian lad – the Lucknow girl's dye was of the best – in badly fitting shop-clothes.

'I have spoken with Creighton Sahib,' quoth Mahbub Ali, 'and a second time has the Hand of Friendship averted the Whip of Calamity. He says that thou hast altogether wasted sixty days upon the Road, and it is too late, therefore, to send thee to any hill-school.

'I have said that my holidays are my own. I do not go to school twice over. That is one part of my bond.'

'The Colonel Sahib is not yet aware of the contract. Thou art to lodge in Lurgan Sahib's house till it is time to go again to Nucklao.'

'I had sooner lodge with thee, Mahbub.'

'Thou dost not know the honour. Lurgan Sahib himself asked for thee. Thou wilt go up the hill and along the road atop, and there thou must forget for a while that thou hast ever seen or spoken to me, Mahbub Ali, who sells horses to Creighton Sahib, whom thou dost not know. Remember this order.'

Kim nodded. 'Good,' said he, 'and who is Lurgan Sahib? Nay' – he caught Mahbub's sword-keen glance – 'indeed I have never heard his name. Is he by chance' – he his voice – 'one of us?'

'What talk is this of *us,* Sahib?' Mahbub Ali returned, in the tone he used towards Europeans. 'I am a Pathan; thou art a Sahib and the son of a Sahib. Lurgan Sahib has a shop among the European shops. All Simla knows it. Ask there. . . . and, Friend of all the World, he is one to be obeyed to the last wink of his eyelashes. Men say he does magic, but that should not touch thee. Go up the hill and ask. Here begins the Great Game.'

CHAPTER 9

S'doaks was son of Yelth the wise –
  Chief of the Raven clan.
Itswoot the Bear had him in care
  To make him a medicine-man.

He was quick and quicker to learn –
  Bold and bolder to dare:
He danced the dread Kloo-Kwallie Dance
  To tickle Itswoot the Bear!

– *Oregon Legend.*

KIM FLUNG himself whole-heartedly upon the next turn of the wheel. He would be a Sahib again for a while. In that idea, so soon as he had reached the broad road under Simla town-hall, he cast about for one to impress. A Hindu child, some ten years old, squatted under a lamp-post.

'Where is Mr. Lurgan's house?' demanded Kim.

'I do not understand English,' was the answer, and Kim shifted his speech accordingly.

'I will show.'

Together they set off through the mysterious dusk, full of the noises of a city below the hillside, and the breath of a cool wind in deodar-crowned Jakko, shouldering the stars. The house-lights, scattered on every level made, as it were, a double firmament. Some were fixed, others belonged to the rickshaws of the careless, open-spoken English folk, going out to dinner.

'It is here,' said Kim's guide, and halted in a veranda flush with the main road. No door stayed them, but a curtain of beaded reeds that split up the lamp-light beyond.

'He is come,' said the boy, in a voice little louder than a sigh, and vanished. Kim felt sure that the boy had been posted to guide him from the first, but putting a bold face on it, parted the curtain. A black-bearded man, with a green shade over his eyes, sat at a table, and, one by one, with short, white hands, picked up globules of light from a tray before him, threaded them on a glancing silken string, and hummed to himself the while. Kim was conscious that beyond the circle of light the room was full of things that smelt like all the temples of all the East. A whiff of musk, a puff of sandalwood, and a breath of sickly jessamine-oil caught his opened nostrils.

'I am here,' said Kim at last, speaking in the vernacular: the smells made him forget that he was to be a Sahib.

'Seventy-nine, eighty, eighty-one,' the man counted to himself, stringing pearl after pearl so quickly that Kim could scarcely follow his fingers. He slid off the green shade and looked fixedly at Kim for a full half-minute. The pupils of the eyes dilated and closed to pin-pricks, as if at will. There was a *faquir* by the Taksali Gate who had just this gift and made money by it, especially when cursing silly women. Kim stared with interest. His disreputable friend could further twitch his ears, almost like a goat, and Kim was disappointed that this new man could not imitate him.

'Do not be afraid,' said Mr. Lurgan suddenly.

'Why should I fear?'

'Thou wilt sleep here to-night, and stay with me till it is time to go again to Nucklao. It is an order.'

'It is an order,' Kim repeated. 'But where shall I sleep?'

'Here, in this room.' Lurgan Sahib waved his hand towards the darkness behind him.

'So be it,' said Kim composedly. 'Now?'

He nodded and held the lamp above his head. As the light swept them, there leaped out from the walls a collection of Tibetan devil-dance masks, hanging above the fiend-embroidered draperies of those ghastly functions – horned masks, scowling masks, and masks of idiotic terror. In a corner, a Japanese warrior, mailed and plumed, menaced him with a halberd, and a score of lances and *khandas* and *kuttars* gave back the unsteady gleam. But what interested Kim more than all these things – he had seen devil-dance masks at the Lahore Museum – was a glimpse of the soft-eyed Hindu child who had left him in the doorway, sitting cross-legged under the table of pearls with a little smile on his scarlet lips.

'I think that Lurgan Sahib wishes to make me afraid. And I am sure that the devil's brat below the table wishes to see me afraid. This place,' he said aloud, 'is like a Wonder House. Where is my bed?'

Lurgan Sahib pointed to a native quilt in a corner by the loathsome masks, picked up the lamp, and left the room black.

'Was that Lurgan Sahib?' Kim asked as he cuddled down. No answer. He could hear the Hindu boy breathing, however, and, guided by the sound, crawled across the floor, and cuffed into the darkness, crying: 'Give answer, devil! Is this the way to lie to a Sahib?'

'From the darkness he fancied he could hear the echo of a chuckle. It could not be his soft-fleshed companion, because he was weeping. So Kim lifted up his voice and called aloud: 'Lurgan Sahib! O Lurgan Sahib! Is it an order that thy servant does not speak to me?'

'It is an order.' The voice came from behind him and he started.

'Very good. But remember,' he muttered, as he resought the quilt, 'I will beat thee in the morning. I do not love Hindus.'

That was no cheerful night; the room being overfull of voices and music. Kim was waked twice by some one calling his name. The second time he set out in search, and ended by bruising his nose against a box that certainly spoke with a human tongue, but in no sort of human accent. It seemed to end in a tin trumpet and to be joined by wires to a smaller box on the floor – so far, at least, as he could judge by touch. And the voice, very hard and whirring, came out of the trumpet. Kim rubbed his nose and grew furious, thinking, as usual in Hindi.

'This with a beggar from the bazar might be good but – I am a Sahib and the son of a Sahib and, which is twice as much more beside, a student of Nucklao. Yess' (here he turned to English), 'a boy of St. Xavier's. Damn Mr. Lurgan's eyes! – It is some sort of machinery like a sewing-machine. Oh, it is a *great* cheek of him – we are not frightened that way at Lucknow – No!' Then in Hindi: 'But what does *he* gain? He is only a trader – I am in his shop. But Creighton Sahib is a Colonel – and I think Creighton Sahib gave orders that it should be done. *How* I will beat that Hindu in the morning! What is this?'

The trumpet-box was pouring out a string of the most elaborate abuse that even Kim had ever heard, in a high uninterested voice, that for a moment lifted the short hairs of his neck. When the vile thing drew breath, Kim was reassured by the soft, sewing-machine-like whirr.

'*Chûp!*' (be still) he cried, and again he heard a chuckle that decided him. '*Chûp* – or I break your head.'

The box took no heed. Kim wrenched at the tin trumpet and something lifted with a click. He had evidently raised a lid. If there were a devil inside, now was its time for – he sniffed – thus did the sewing-machines of the bazar smell. He would clean that *shaitan*, He slipped off his jacket, and plunged it into the box's mouth. Something long and round bent under the pressure, there was a whirr and the voice stopped – as voices must if you ram a thrice-doubled coat on to the wax cylinder and into the works of an expensive phonograph. Kim finished his slumbers with a serene mind.

In the morning he was aware of Lurgan Sahib looking down on him.

'Oah!' said Kim, firmly resolved to cling to his Sahib-dom. 'There was a box in the night that gave me bad talk. So I stopped it. Was it your box?'

The man held out his hand.

'Shake hands, O'Hara,' he said. 'Yes, it was my box. I keep such things because my friends the Rajahs like them. That one is broken, but it was cheap at the price. Yes, my friends' the Kings' are very fond of toys – and so am I sometimes.'

Kim looked him over out of the corners of his eyes. He was a Sahib in that he wore Sahib's clothes; the accent of his Urdu, the intonation of his English, showed that he was anything but a Sahib. He seemed to understand what moved in Kim's mind ere the boy opened his mouth, and he took no pains to explain himself as did Father Victor or the Lucknow masters. Sweetest of all – he treated Kim as an equal on the Asiatic side.

'I am sorry you cannot beat my boy this morning. He says he will kill you with a knife or poison. He is jealous, so I have put him in the corner and I shall not speak to him to-day. He has just tried to kill me. You must help me with the breakfast. He is almost too jealous to trust, just now.'

Now a genuine imported Sahib from England would have made a great to do over this tale. Lurgan Sahib stated it as simply as Mahbub Ali was used to record his little affairs in the North.

The back veranda of the shop was built out over the sheer hillside, and they looked down into their neighbors' chimney-pots, as is the custom of Simla. But even more than the purely Persian meal cooked by Lurgan Sahib with his own hands, the shop fascinated Kim. The Lahore Museum was larger, but here were more wonders – ghost-daggers and prayer-wheels from Tibet; turquoise and raw amber necklaces; green jade bangles; curiously packed incense-sticks in jars crusted over with raw garnets; the devil-masks of overnight and a wall of peacock-blue draperies; gilt figures of Buddha, and little portable lacquer altars; Russian samovars with turquoises on the lid; egg-shell china sets in quaint octagonal cane boxes; yellow ivory crucifixes – from Japan of all places in the world, so Lurgan Sahib said; carpets in dusty bales, smelling atrociously, pushed back behind torn and rotten screens of geometrical work; Persian water-jugs for the hands after meals; dull copper incense-burners neither Chinese nor Persian, with friezes of fantastic devils running round them; tarnished silver belts that knotted like raw hide; hairpins of jade, ivory, and plasma; arms of all sorts and kinds, and a thousand other oddments were cased, or piled, or merely thrown into the room, leaving a clear space only round the rickety deal table, where Lurgan Sahib worked.

'Those things are nothing,' said his host, following Kim's glance. 'I buy them because they are pretty, and sometimes I sell – if I like the buyer's look. My work is on the table – some of it.'

It blazed in the morning light – all red and blue and green flashes, picked out with the vicious blue-white spurt of a diamond here and there. Kim opened his eyes.

'Oh, they are quite well, those stones. It will not hurt them to take the sun. Besides, they are cheap. But with sick stones it is very different.' He piled Kim's plate anew. 'There is no one but *me* can doctor a sick pearl and re-blue turquoises. I grant you opals – any fool can cure an opal – but for a sick pearl there is only me. Suppose I were to die! Then there would be no one. . . . Oh no! *You* cannot do anything with jewels. It will be quite enough if you understand a little about the Turquoise – some day.'

He moved to the end of the veranda to refill the heavy, porous clay water-jug from the filter.

'Do you want drink?'

Kim nodded. Lurgan Sahib, fifteen feet off, laid one hand on the jar. Next instant, it stood at Kim's elbow, full to within half an inch of the brim – the white cloth only showing, by a small wrinkle, where it had slid into place.

'Wah!' said Kim in most utter amazement. 'That is magic.' Lurgan Sahib's smile showed that the compliment had gone home.

'Throw it back.'

'It will break.'

'I say, throw it back.'

Kim pitched it at random. It fell short and crashed into fifty pieces, while the water dropped through the rough veranda boarding.

'I said it would break.'

'All one. Look at it. Look at the largest piece.'

That lay with a sparkle of water in its curve, as it were a star on the floor. Kim looked intently; Lurgan Sahib laid one hand gently on the nape of the neck, stroked it twice or thrice, and whispered: 'Look! It shall come to life again, piece by piece. First the big piece shall join itself to two others on the right and left – on the right and the left. Look!'

To save his life, Kim could not have turned his head. The light touch held him as in a vise, and his blood tingled pleasantly through him. There was one large piece of the jar where there had been three, and above them the shadowy outline of the entire vessel. He could see the veranda through it, but it was thickening and darkening with each beat of his pulse. Yet the jar – how slowly the thoughts came! – the jar had been smashed before his eyes. Another wave of prickling fire raced down his neck, as Lurgan Sahib moved his hand.

'Look! It is coming into shape,' said Lurgan Sahib.

So far Kim had been thinking in Hindi, but a tremor came on him, and with an effort like that of a swimmer before sharks, who hurls himself half out of the water, his mind leaped up from a darkness that was swallowing it and took refuge in – the multiplication-table in English!

'Look! It is coming into shape,' whispered Lurgan Sahib.

The jar had been smashed – yess, smashed – not the native word, he would not think of that – but smashed – into fifty pieces, and twice three was six, and thrice three was nine, and four times three was twelve. He clung desperately to the repetition. The shadow-outline of the jar cleared like a mist after rubbing eyes. There were the broken shards; there was the spilt water drying in the sun, and through the cracks of the veranda showed, all ribbed, the white house-wall below – and thrice twelve was thirty-six!

'Look! Is it coming into shape?' asked Lurgan Sahib.

'But it *is* smashed – smashed,' he gasped – Lurgan Sahib had been muttering softly for the last half-minute. Kim wrenched his head aside. 'Look! *Dekho!* It is there as it was there.'

'It is there as it was there,' said Lurgan, watching Kim closely while the boy rubbed his neck. 'But you are the first of a many who have ever seen it so.' He wiped his broad forehead.

'Was that more magic?' Kim asked suspiciously. The tingle had gone from his veins; he felt unusually wide awake.

'No, that was not magic. It was only to see if there was – a flaw in a jewel. Sometimes very fine jewels will fly all to pieces if a man holds them in his hand, and knows the proper way. That is why one must be careful before one sets them. Tell me, did you see the shape of the pot?'

'For a little time. It began to grow like a flower from the ground.'

'And then what did you do? I mean, how did you think?'

'Oah! I knew it was broken, and so, I think, that was what I thought – and it *was* broken.'

'Hm! Has anyone ever done that same sort of magic to you before?'

'If it was,' said Kim, 'do you think I should let it again? I should run away.'

'And now you are not afraid – eh?'

'Not now.'

Lurgan Sahib looked at him more closely than ever. 'I shall ask Mahbub Ali – not now, but some day later,' he muttered. 'I am pleased with you – yes; and I am pleased with you – no. You are the first that ever saved himself. I wish I knew what it was that. . . . But you are right. You should not tell that – not even to me.'

'He turned into the dusky gloom of the shop, and sat down at the table, rubbing his hands softly. A small, husky sob came from behind a pile of carpets. It was the Hindu child obediently facing towards the wall: his thin shoulders worked with grief.

'Ah! He is jealous, so jealous. I wonder if he will try to poison me again in my breakfast, and make me cook it twice.'

'*Kubbee – kubbee nahin*," came the broken answer.

'And whether he will kill this other boy?'

'*Kubbee – kubbee nahin*' (never – never. No!).

'What do *you* think he will do?' He turned suddenly on Kim.

'Oah! I do not know. Let him go, perhaps. Why did he want to poison you?'

'Because he is so fond of me. Suppose you were fond of some one, and you saw some one come, and the man you were fond of was more pleased with him than he was with you, what would you do?'

Kim thought. Lurgan repeated the sentence slowly in the vernacular.

'I should not poison that man,' said Kim reflectively, "but I should beat that boy – *if* that boy was fond of my man. But first I would ask that boy if it were true.'

'Ah! He thinks every one must be fond of me.'

'Then I think he is a fool.'

'Hearest thou?' said Lurgan Sahib to the shaking shoulders. 'The Sahib's son thinks thou art a little fool. Come out, and next time thy heart is troubled, do not try white arsenic quite so openly. Surely the Devil Dasim was lord of our table-cloth that day! It might have made me ill, child, and then a stranger would have guarded the jewels. Come!'

The child, heavy-eyed with much weeping, crept out from behind the bale and flung himself passionately at Lurgan Sahib's feet, with an extravagance of remorse that impressed even Kim.

'I will look into the ink-pools – I will faithfully guard the jewels! Oh, my father and my mother, send *him* away!' He indicated Kim with a backward jerk of his bare heel.

'Not yet – not yet. In a little while he will go away again. But now he is at school-at a new *madrissah* – and thou shalt be his teacher. Play the Play of the Jewels against him. I will keep tally.'

The child dried his tears at once, and dashed to the back of the shop, whence he returned with a copper tray.

'Give me!' he said to Lurgan Sahib. 'Let them come from thy hand, for he may say that I knew them before.'

'Gently – gently,' the man replied, and from a drawer under the table dealt a half handful of clattering trifles into the tray.

'Now,' said the child, waving an old newspaper. 'Look on them as long as thou wilt, stranger. Count and, if need be, handle. One look is enough for *me*.' He turned his back proudly.

'But what is the game?'

'When thou hast counted and handled and art sure that thou canst remember them all, I cover them with this paper, and thou must tell over the tally to Lurgan Sahib. *I* will write mine.'

'Oah!' The instinct of competition waked in his breast. He bent over the tray. There were but fifteen stones on it 'That is easy,' he said after a minute. The child slipped the paper over the winking jewels and scribbled in a native account-book.

'There are under that paper five blue stones – one big, one smaller, and three small,' said Kim, all in haste. 'There are four green stones, and one with a hole in it; there is one yellow stone that I can see through, and one like a pipe-stem. There are two red stones, and – and – I made the count fifteen, but two I have forgotten. No! Give me time. One was of ivory, little and brownish; and – and – give me time. . . .'

'One – two' – Lurgan Sahib counted him out up to ten. Kim shook his head.

'Hear my count!' the child burst in, trilling with laughter. 'First, are two flawed sapphires – one of two ruttees and one of four as I should judge. The four-ruttee sapphire is chipped at the edge. There is one Turkestan turquoise, plain with black veins, and there are two inscribed – one with a Name of God in gilt, and the other being cracked across, for it came out of an old ring, I cannot read. We have now all five blue stones. Four flawed emeralds there are, but one is drilled in two places, and one is a little carven – '

'Their weights?' said Lurgan Sahib impassively.

'Three – five – five – and four ruttees as I judge it. There is one piece of old greenish pipe amber, and a cut topaz from Europe. There is one ruby of Burma, of two ruttees, without a flaw, and there is a balas-ruby, flawed, of two ruttees. There is a carved ivory from China representing a rat sucking an egg; and there is last – ah ha! – a ball of crystal as big as a bean set in a gold leaf.'

He clapped his hands at the close.

'He is thy master,' said Lurgan Sahib, smiling.

'Huh! He knew the names of the stones,' said Kim, flushing. 'Try again! With common things such as he and I both know.'

They heaped the tray again with odds and ends gathered from the shop, and even the kitchen, and every time the child won, till Kim marvelled.

'Bind my eyes – let me feel once with my fingers, and even *then* I will leave thee open-eyed behind,' he challenged.

Kim stamped with vexation when the lad made his boast good.

'If it were men – or horses,' he said, 'I could do better. This playing with tweezers and knives and scissors is too little.'

'Learn first – teach later,' said Lurgan Sahib. 'Is he thy master?'

'Truly. But how is it done?'

'By doing it many times over till it is done perfectly – for it is worth doing.'

The Hindu boy, in highest feather, actually patted Kim on the back.

'Do not despair,' he said. "I myself will teach thee.'

'And I will see that thou art well taught,' said Lurgan Sahib, still speaking in the vernacular, 'for except my boy here – it was foolish of him to buy so much white arsenic when, if he had asked, I could have given it – except my boy here I have not in a long time met with one better worth teaching. And there are ten days more ere thou canst return to Lucknow where they teach nothing – at the long price. We shall, I think, be friends.'

They were a most mad ten days, but Kim enjoyed himself too much to reflect on their craziness. In the morning they played the Jewel Game – sometimes with veritable stones, sometimes with piles of swords and daggers, sometimes with photographs of natives. Through the afternoons he and the Hindu boy would mount guard in the shop, sitting dumb behind a carpet-bale or a screen and watching Mr. Lurgan's many and very curious visitors. There were small Rajahs, escorts coughing in the verandah, who came to buy curiosities – such as phonographs and mechanical toys. There were ladies in search of necklaces, and men, it seemed to Kim – but his mind may have been vitiated by early training – in search of the ladies; natives from independent and feudatory courts whose ostensible business was the repair of broken necklaces – rivers of light poured out upon the table – but whose true end seemed to be to raise money for angry Maharanees or young Rajahs. There were Babus to whom Lurgan Sahib talked with austerity and authority, but at the end of each interview he gave them money in coined silver and currency notes. There were occasional gatherings of long-coated theatrical natives who discussed metaphysics in English and Bengali, to Mr. Lurgan's great edification. He was always interested in religions. At the end of the day, Kim and the Hindu boy – whose name varied at Lurgan's pleasure – were expected to give a detailed account of all that they had seen and heard – their view of each man's character, as shown in his face, talk, and manner, and their notions of his real errand. After dinner, Lurgan Sahib's fancy turned more to what might be called dressing-up, in which game he took a most informing interest. He could paint faces to a marvel; with a brush-dab here and a line there changing them past recognition. The shop was full of all manner of dresses and turbans, and Kim was apparelled variously as a young Mohammedan of good family, an oilman, and once – which was a joyous evening – as the son of an Oudh landholder in the fullest of full dress. Lurgan Sahib had a hawk's eye to detect the least flaw in the make-up; and lying on a worn teak-wood couch, would explain by the half-hour together how such and such a caste talked, or walked, or coughed, or spat, or sneezed, and, since 'hows' matter little in this world, the 'why' of everything. The Hindu child played this game clumsily. That little mind, keen as an icicle where tally of jewels was concerned, could not temper itself to enter another's soul; but a demon in Kim woke up and sang with joy as he put on the changing dresses, and changed speech and gesture therewith.

Carried away by enthusiasm, he volunteered to show Lurgan Sahib one evening how the disciples of a certain caste of *faquir,* old Lahore acquaintances, begged doles by the roadside; and what sort of language he would use to an Englishman, to a Punjabi farmer going to a fair, and to a woman without a veil. Lurgan Sahib laughed immensely, and begged Kim to stay as he was, immobile for half an hour – cross-legged, ash-smeared, and wild-eyed, in the back room. At the end of that time entered a hulking, obese Babu whose stockinged legs shook with fat, and Kim opened on him with a shower of wayside chaff. Lurgan Sahib – this annoyed Kim – watched the Babu and not the play.

'I think,' said the Babu heavily, lighting a cigarette, 'I am of opeenion that it is most extraordinary and effeecient performance. Except that you had told me I should have opined that – that – that you were pulling my legs. How soon can he become approximately effeecient chain-man? Because *then* I shall indent for him.'

'That is what he must learn at Lucknow.'

'Then order him to be jolly dam-quick. Good-night, Lurgan.' The Babu swung out with the gait of a bogged cow.

When they were telling over the day's list of visitors, Lurgan Sahib asked Kim who he thought the man might be.

'God knows!' said Kim cheerily. The tone might almost have deceived Mahbub Ali, but it failed entirely with the healer of sick pearls.

'That is true. God, He knows; but I wish to know what you think.'

Kim glanced sideways at his companion, whose eye had a way of compelling truth.

'I – I think he will want me when I come from the school, but' – confidentially, as Lurgan Sahib nodded approval – 'I do not understand how *he* can wear many dresses and talk many tongues.'

'Thou wilt understand many things later. He is a writer of tales for a certain Colonel. His honour is great only in Simla, and it is noticeable that he has no name, but only a number and a letter – that is a custom among us.'

'And is there a price upon his head too – as upon Mah – all the others?'

'Not yet; but if a boy rose up who is now sitting here and went – look, the door is open! – as far as a certain house with a red-painted verandah, behind that which was the old theatre in the Lower Bazar, and whispered through the shutters: "Hurree Chunder Mookerjee bore the bad news of last month," that boy might take away a belt full of rupees.'

'How many?' said Kim promptly.

'Five hundred – a thousand – as many as he might ask for.'

'Good. And how long might such a boy live after the news was told?' He smiled merrily at Lurgan Sahib's very beard.

'Ah! That is to be well thought of. Perhaps if he were very clever, he might live out the day – but not the night. By no means the night.'

'Then what is the Babu's pay if so much is put upon his head?'

'Eighty – perhaps a hundred – perhaps a hundred and fifty rupees; but the pay is the least part of the work. From time to time, God causes men to be born – and thou art one of them – who have a lust to go abroad at the risk of their lives and discover news – to-day it may be of far-off things, to-morrow of some hidden mountain, and the next day of some near-by men who have done a foolishness against the State. These souls are very few; and of these few, not more than ten are of the best. Among these ten I count the Babu, and that is curious. How great therefore and desirable must be a business that brazens the heart of a Bengali!'

'True. But the days go slowly for me. I am yet a boy, and it is only within two months I learned to write Angrezi. Even now I cannot read it well. And there are yet years and years and long years before I can be even a chain-man.'

'Have patience, Friend of all the World' – Kim started at the title. 'Would I had a few of the years that so irk thee. I have proved thee in several small ways. This will not be forgotten when I make my report to the Colonel Sahib.' Then, changing suddenly into English with a deep laugh: –

'By Jove! O'Hara, I think there is a great deal in you; but you must not become proud and you must not talk. You must go back to Lucknow and be a good little boy and mind your book, as the English say, and perhaps, next holidays if you care, you can come back to me!' Kim's face fell. 'Oh, I mean *if* you like. I know where you want to go.'

Four days later a seat was booked for Kim and his small trunk at the rear of a Kalka tonga. His companion was the whale-like Babu, who, with a fringed shawl wrapped round his head, and his fat open-work-stockinged left leg tucked under him, shivered and grunted in the morning chill.

'How comes it that this man is one of *us*?' thought Kim, considering the jelly-back as they jolted down the road; and the reflection threw him into most pleasant day-dreams. Lurgan Sahib had given him five rupees – a splendid sum – as well as the assurance of his protection if he worked. Unlike Mahbub, Lurgan Sahib had spoken most explicitly of the reward that would follow obedience, and Kim was content. If only, like the Babu, he could enjoy the dignity of a letter and a number – and a price upon his head! Some day he would be all that and more. Some day he might be almost as great as Mahbub Ali! The housetops of his search should be half India; he would follow Kings and ministers, as in the old days he had followed *vakils* and lawyers' touts across Lahore city for Mahbub Ali's sake. Meantime, there was the present, and not at all unpleasant, fact of St. Xavier's immediately before him. There would be new boys to condescend to, and there would be tales of holiday adventures to hear. Young Martin, son of the tea-planter at Manipur, had boasted that he would go to war, with a rifle, against the head-hunters. That might be, but it was certain young Martin had not been blown half across the forecourt of a Patiala palace by an explosion of fireworks; nor had he. . . . Kim fell to telling himself the story of his own adventures through the last three months. He could paralyse St. Xavier's – even the biggest boys who shaved – with the recital, were that permitted. But it was, of course, out of the question. There would be a price upon his head in good time, as Lurgan Sahib had assured him; and if he talked foolishly now, not only would that price never be set, but Colonel Creighton would cast him off – and he would be left to the wrath of Lurgan Sahib and Mahbub Ali – for the short space of life that would remain to him.

'So I should lose Delhi for the sake of fish,' was his proverbial philosophy. It behoved him to forget his holiday (there would always remain the fun of inventing imaginary adventures) and, as Lurgan Sahib had said, to work.

Of all the boys hurrying back to St. Xavier's, from Sukkur in the sands to Galle beneath the palms, none was so filled with virtue as Kimball O'Hara, jiggetting down to Umballa behind Hurree Chunder Mookerjee, whose name on the books of one section of the Ethnological Survey was R.17.

And if additional spur were needed, the Babu supplied it. After a huge meal at Kalka, he spoke uninterruptedly. Was Kim going to school? Then he, an M.A. of Calcutta University, would explain the advantages of education. There were marks to be gained by due attention to Latin and Wordsworth's *Excursion* (all this was Greek to Kim). French, too, was vital, and the best was to be picked up in Chandernagore, a few miles from Calcutta. Also a man might go far, as he himself had done, by strict attention to plays called *Lear* and *Julius Caesar*, both much in demand by examiners. *Lear* was not so full of historical allusions as *Julius Caesar*; the book cost four annas, but could be bought second-hand in Bow Bazar for two. Still more important than Wordsworth, or the eminent authors, Burke and Hare, was the art and science of mensuration. A boy who had passed his examination in these branches – for which, by the way, there were no cram-books – could, by merely marching over a country with a compass and a level and a straight eye, carry away a picture of that country which might be sold for large sums in coined silver. But as it was occasionally inexpedient to carry about measuring-chains, a boy would do well to know the precise length of his own foot-pace, so that when he was deprived of what Hurree Chunder called 'adventitious aids' he might still tread his distances. To keep count of thousands of paces, Hurree Chunder's experience had shown him nothing more valuable than a rosary of eighty-one or a hundred and eight beads, for 'it was divisible and sub-divisible into many multiples and sub-multiples.' Through the volleying drifts of

English, Kim caught the general trend of the talk, and it interested him very much. Here was a new craft that a man could tuck away in his head; and by the look of the large wide world unfolding itself before him, it seemed that the more a man knew the better for him.

Said the Babu when he had talked for an hour and a half, 'I hope some day to enjoy your offeecial acquaintance. *Ad interim*, if I may be pardoned that expression, I shall give you this betel-box which is highly valuable article and cost me two rupees only four years ago.' It was a cheap, heart-shaped brass thing with three compartments for carrying the eternal betel-nut, lime and *pan-leaf*; but it was filled with little tabloid-bottles. 'That is reward of merit for your performance in character of that holy man. You see, you are so young you think you will last for ever and not take care of your body. It is great nuisance to go sick in the middle of business. I am fond of drugs myself, and they are handy to cure poor people too. These are good departmental drugs – quinine and so on. I give it you for souvenir. Now good-bye. I have urgent private business here by the roadside.'

He slipped out noiselessly as a cat, on the Umballa road, hailed a passing ekka and jingled away, while Kim, tongue-tied, twiddled the brass betel-box in his hands.

* * * * *

The record of a boy's education interests few save his parents, and, as you know, Kim was an orphan. It is written in the books of St. Xavier in Partibus that a report of Kim's progress was forwarded at the end of each term to Colonel Creighton and to Father Victor, from whose hands duly came the money for his schooling. It is further recorded in the same books that he showed a great aptitude for mathematical studies as well as map-making, and carried away a prize (*The Life of Lord Lawrence*, tree-calf, two vols., nine rupees, eight annas) for proficiency therein; and the same term played in St. Xavier's eleven against the Allyghur Mohammedan College, his age being fourteen years and ten months. He was also re-vaccinated (from which we may assume that there had been another epidemic of small-pox at Lucknow) about the same time. Pencil notes on the edge of an old muster-roll record that he was punished several times for 'conversing with improper persons,' and it seems that he was once sentenced to heavy pains for 'absenting himself for a day in the company of a street beggar.' That was when he got over the gate and pleaded with the lama through a whole day down the banks of the Goomtee to accompany him on the Road next holidays – for one month – for a little week; and the lama set his face as a flint against it, averring that the time had not yet come. Kim's business, said the old man as they ate cakes together, was to get all the wisdom of the Sahibs and then he would see. The hand of friendship must in some way have averted the whip of calamity, for six weeks later Kim seems to have passed an examination in elementary surveying 'with great credit,' his age being fifteen years and eight months. From this date the record is silent. His name does not appear in the year's batch of those who entered for the subordinate Survey of India, but against it stand the words 'removed on appointment.'

Several times in those three years, cast up at the Temple of the Tirthankers in Benares the lama, a little thinner and a shade yellower, if that were possible, but gentle and untainted as ever. Sometimes it was from the South that he came – from south of Tuticorin, whence the wonderful fire-boats go to Ceylon where are priests who know Pali; sometimes it was from the wet green West and the thousand cotton-factory chimneys that ring Bombay; and once from the North, where he had doubled back eight hundred miles to talk a day with the Keeper of the Images in the Wonder House. He would stride to his cell in the cool, cut marble – the priests of the temple were good to the old man – wash off the dust of travel, make prayer, and depart for Lucknow, well accustomed now to the ways of the rail, in a third-class carriage. Returning, it was noticeable, as his friend the Seeker pointed out to the head-priest, that he ceased for a while to mourn the loss of his River, or to draw wondrous pictures of the Wheel of Life, but preferred to talk of the beauty and wisdom of a certain mysterious *chela* whom no man of the temple had ever seen. Yes, he had followed the traces of the Blessed Feet throughout all India. (The curator has still in his possession a most marvellous account of his wanderings and meditations.) There remained nothing more in life but to find the River of the Arrow. Yet it was shown to him in dreams that it was a matter not to be undertaken with any hope of success unless that seeker had with him the one *chela* appointed to bring the event to a happy issue, and versed in great wisdom – such wisdom as white-haired Keepers of Images possess. For example, (here came out the snuff-gourd, and the kindly Jain priests made haste to be silent): –

'Long and long ago, when Devadatta was King of Benares – let all listen to the *Jâtaka* – an elephant was captured for a time by the king's hunters and, ere he broke free, be ringed with a grievous leg-iron. This he strove to remove with hate and frenzy in his heart, and hurrying up and down the forests, besought his brother-elephants to wrench it asunder. One by one, with their strong trunks, they tried and failed. At the last they gave it as their opinion that the ring was not to be broken by any bestial power. And in a thicket, newborn, wet with the moisture of birth, lay a day-old calf of the herd whose mother had died. The fettered elephant, forgetting his own agony, said: "If I do not help this suckling it will perish under our feet." So he stood above the young thing, making his legs buttresses against the uneasily moving herd; and he begged milk of a virtuous cow, and the calf throve, and the ringed elephant was the calf's guide and defense. Now the days of an elephant – let all listen to the *Jâtaka*! – are thirty-five years to his full strength, and through thirty-five Rains the ringed elephant befriended the younger, and all the while the fetter ate into the flesh.

'Then one day the young elephant saw the half-buried iron, and turning to the elder said: "What is this?" "It is even my sorrow," said he who had befriended him. Then that other put out his trunk and in the twinkling of an eyelash abolished the ring, saying: "The appointed time has come." So the virtuous elephant who had waited temperately and done kind acts was relieved, at the appointed time, by the very calf whom he had turned aside to cherish – let all listen to the *Jâtaka!* – for the Elephant was Ananda, and the Calf that broke the ring was none other than The Lord Himself. . . .'

Then he would shake his head benignly, and over the ever-clicking rosary point out how free that elephant calf was from the sin of pride. He was as humble as a *chela* who, seeing his master sitting in the dust outside the Gates of Learning, overleapt the gates (though they were locked) and took his master to his heart in the presence of the proud-stomached city. Rich would be the reward of such a master and such a *chela* when the time came for them to seek freedom together!

So did the lama speak, coming and going across India as softly as a bat. A sharp-tongued old woman in a house among the fruit-trees behind Saharunpore honoured him as the woman honoured the prophet, but his chamber was by no means upon the wall. In an apartment of the forecourt overlooked by cooing doves he would sit, while she laid aside her useless veil and chattered of spirits and friends of Kulu, of grandchildren unborn, and of the free-tongued brat who had talked to her in the resting-place. Once, too, he strayed alone from the Grand Trunk Road below Umballa to the very village whose priest had tried to drug him; but the kind heaven that guards lamas sent him at twilight through the crops, absorbed and unsuspicious, to the ressaldar's door. Here was like to have been a grave misunderstanding, for the old soldier asked him why the Friend of the Stars had gone that way only six days before.

'That may not be,' said the lama. 'He has gone back to his own people.'

'He sat in that corner telling a hundred merry tales five nights ago,' his host insisted. 'True, he vanished somewhat suddenly in the dawn after foolish talk with my grand-daughter. He grows apace, but he is the same Friend of the Stars as brought me true word of the war. Have ye parted?'

'Yes – and no,' the lama replied. 'We – we have not altogether parted, but the time is not ripe that we should take the Road together. He acquires wisdom in another place. We must wait.'

'All one – but if it were not the boy how did he come to speak so continually of thee?'

'And what said he?' asked the lama eagerly.

'Sweet words – an hundred thousand – that thou art his father and mother and such all. Pity that he does not take the Queen's service. He is fearless.'

This news amazed the lama, who did not then know how religiously Kim kept to the contract made with Mahbub Ali, and perforce ratified by Colonel Creighton. . . .

'There is no holding the young pony from the game,' said the horse-dealer when the Colonel pointed out that vagabonding over India in holiday time was absurd. 'If permission be refused to go and come as he chooses, he will make light of the refusal. Then who is to catch him? Colonel Sahib, only once in a thousand years is a horse born so well fitted for the game as this our colt. And we need men.'

CHAPTER 10

Your tiercel's too long at hack, Sire. He's no eyass
But a passage-hawk that footed ere we caught him,
Dangerously free o' the air. Faith! were he mine
(As mine's the glove he binds to for his tirings)
I'd fly him with a make-hawk. He's in yarak
Plumed to the very point – so manned so weathered. . . .
Give him the firmament God made him for,
And what shall take the air of him?

– *Old Play.*

LURGAN SAHIB did not use as direct speech, but his advice tallied with Mahbub's; and the upshot was good for Kim. He knew better now than to leave Lucknow city in native garb, and if Mahbub were anywhere within reach of a letter, it was to Mahbub's camp he headed, and made his change under the Pathan's wary eye. Could the little Survey paint-box that he used for map-tinting in term-time have found a tongue to tell of holiday doings, he might have been expelled. Once Mahbub and he went together as far as the beautiful city of

Bombay, with three truck-loads of tram-horses, and Mahbub nearly melted when Kim proposed a sail in a dhow across the Indian Ocean to buy Gulf Arabs, which he understood from a hanger-on of the dealer Abdul Rahman, fetched better prices than mere Kabulis.

He dipped his hand into the dish with that great trader when Mahbub and a few co-religionists were invited to a big Haj dinner. They came back by way of Karachi by sea, when Kim took his first experience of sea-sickness sitting on the fore-hatch of a coasting-steamer, well persuaded he had been poisoned. The Babu's famous drug-box proved useless, though Kim had restocked it at Bombay. Mahbub had business at Quetta, and there Kim, as Mahbub admitted, earned his keep, and perhaps a little over, by spending four curious days as scullion in the house of a fat Commissariat sergeant, from whose office-box, in an auspicious moment, he removed a little vellum ledger which he copied out – it seemed to deal entirely with cattle and camel sales – by moonlight, lying behind an outhouse, all through one hot night. Then he returned the ledger to its place, and, at Mahbub's word, left that service unpaid, rejoining him six miles down the road, the clean copy in his bosom.

'That soldier is a small fish,' Mahbub Ali explained, 'but in time we shall catch the larger one. He only sells oxen at two prices – one for himself and one for the Government – which I do not think is a sin.'

'Why could not I take away the little book and be done with it?'

'Then he would have been frightened, and he would have told his master. Then we should miss, perhaps, a great number of new rifles which seek their way up from Quetta to the North. The Game is so large that one sees but a little at a time.'

'Oho!' said Kim, and held his tongue. That was in the monsoon holidays, after he had taken the prize for mathematics. The Christmas holidays he spent – deducting ten days for private amusements – with Lurgan Sahib, where he sat for the most part in front of a roaring wood-fire – Jakko-road was four feet deep in snow that year – and – the small Hindu had gone away to be married – helped Lurgan to thread pearls. He made Kim learn whole chapters of the Koran by heart, till he could deliver them with the very roll and cadence of a mullah. Moreover, he told Kim the names and properties of many native drugs, as well as the runes proper to recite when you administer them. And in the evenings he wrote charms on parchment – elaborate pentagrams crowned with the names of devils – Murra, and Awan the Companion of Kings – all fantastically written in the corners. More to the point, he advised Kim as to the care of his own body, the cure of fever-fits, and simple remedies of the Road. A week before it was time to go down, Colonel Creighton Sahib – this was unfair – sent Kim a written examination-paper that concerned itself solely with rods and chains and links and angles.

Next holidays he was out with Mahbub, and here, by the way, he nearly died of thirst, plodding through the sand on a camel to the mysterious city of Bikaneer, where the wells are four hundred feet deep, and lined throughout with camel-bone. It was not an amusing trip from Kim's point of view, because – in defiance of the contract – the Colonel ordered him to make a map of that wild, walled city; and since Mohammedan horse-boys and pipe-tenders are not expected to drag Survey-chains round the capital of an independent native state, Kim was forced to pace all his distances by means of a bead rosary. He used the compass for bearings as occasion served – after dark chiefly, when the camels had been fed – and by the help of his little Survey paint-box of six colour-cakes and three brushes, he achieved something not remotely unlike the city of Jeysalmir. Mahbub laughed a great deal and advised him to make up a written report as well; and in the back of the big account-book that lay under the flap of Mahbub's pet saddle Kim fell to work.

'It must hold everything that thou hast seen or touched or considered. Write as though the Jung-i-Lat Sahib himself had come by stealth with a vast army outsetting to war.'

'How great an army?'

'Oh, half a lakh of men.'

'Folly! Remember how few and bad were the wells in the sand. Not a thousand thirsty men could come near by here.'

'Then write that down – also all the old breaches in the walls – and whence the firewood is cut – and what is the temper and disposition of the King. I stay here till all my horses are sold. I will hire a room by the gateway, and thou shalt be my accountant. There is a good lock to the door.'

The report in its unmistakable St. Xavier's running script, and the brown, yellow, and lake-daubed map, was on hand a few years ago (a careless clerk filed it with the rough notes of E.23's second Seistan survey), but by now the pencil characters must be almost illegible. Kim translated it, sweating under the light of an oil-lamp, to Mahbub, the second day of their return-journey. The Pathan rose and stooped over his dappled saddle-bags.

'I knew it would be worthy a dress of honour, and so I made one ready,' he said smiling. 'Were I Amir of Afghanistan (and some day we may see him), I would fill thy mouth with gold.' He laid the garments formally at Kim's feet. There was a gold-embroidered Peshawur turban-cap, rising to a cone, and a big turban-cloth ending in a broad fringe of gold. There was a Delhi embroidered waistcoat to slip over a milky-white shirt, fastening to the right, ample and flowing; green pyjamas with twisted silk waist-string; and that nothing might be lacking, russia-leather slippers, smelling divinely, with arrogantly curled tips.

'Upon a Wednesday, and in the morning, to put on new clothes is auspicious,' said Mahbub solemnly 'But we must not forget the wicked folk in the world. So!'

He capped all the splendour, that was taking Kim's delighted breath away, with a mother-of-pearl, nickel-plated, self-extracting •450 revolver.

'I had thought of a smaller bore, but reflected that this takes Government bullets. A man can always come by those – especially across the Border. Stand up and let me look.' He clapped Kim on the shoulder. 'May you never be tired, Pathan! Oh, the hearts to be broken! Oh, the eyes under the eyelashes, looking sideways!'

Kim turned about, pointed his toes, stretched, and felt mechanically for the moustache that was just beginning. Then he stooped towards Mahbub's feet to make proper acknowledgement with fluttering, quick-patting hands; his heart too full for words. Mahbub forestalled and embraced him.

'My son,' said he, 'what need of words between us? But is not the little gun a delight? All six cartridges come out at one twist. It is borne in the bosom next the skin, which, as it were, keeps it oiled. Never put it elsewhere, and please God, thou shalt some day kill a man with it.'

'*Hai mai!*' said Kim ruefully. 'If a Sahib kills a man he is hung in the jail.'

'True: but one pace beyond the Border, men are wiser. Put it away; but fill it first. Of what use is a gun unfed?'

'When I go back to the *madrissah* I must return it. They do not allow little guns. Thou wilt keep it for me?'

'Son, I am wearied of that *madrissah*, where they take the best years of a man to teach him what he can only learn upon the Road. The folly of the Sahibs has neither top nor bottom. No matter. Maybe thy written report shall save thee further bondage; and God He knows we need men more and more in the Game.'

They marched, jaw-bound against blowing sand, across the salt desert to Jodhpore, where Mahbub and his handsome nephew Habib-Ullah did much trading; and then sorrowfully, in European clothes, which he was fast outgrowing, Kim went second-class to St. Xavier's. Three weeks later, Colonel Creighton, pricing Tibetan ghost-daggers at Lurgan's shop, faced Mahbub Ali openly mutinous. Lurgan Sahib operated as support in reserve.

'The pony is made – finished – mouthed and paced, Sahib! From now on, day-by-day, he will lose his manners if he is kept at tricks. Drop the rein on his back and let go,' said the horse-dealer. 'We need him.'

'But he is so young, Mahbub – not more than sixteen – is he?'

'When I was fifteen, I had shot my man and begot my man, Sahib.'

'You impenitent old heathen.' Creighton turned to Lurgan. The black beard nodded assent to the wisdom of the Afghan's dyed scarlet.

'*I* should have used him long ago,' said Lurgan. 'The younger the better. That is why I always have my really valuable jewels watched by a child. You sent him to me to try. I tried him in every way: he is the only boy I could not make to see things.'

'In the crystal – in the ink-pool?' demanded Mahbub.

'No. Under my hand, as I told you. That has never happened before. It means that he is strong enough – but you think it skittles, Colonel Creighton – to make anyone do anything he wants. And that is three years ago. I have taught him a good deal since, Colonel Creighton. I think you waste him now.'

'Hmm! Maybe you're right. But, as you know, there is no Survey work for him at present.'

'Let him out – let him go,' Mahbub interrupted. 'Who expects any colt to carry heavy weight at first? Let him run with the caravans like our white camel-colts – for luck. I would take him myself, but – '

'There is a little business where he would be most useful – in the South,' said Lurgan, with peculiar suavity, dropping his heavy nude eyelids.

'E.23 has that in hand,' said Creighton quickly. 'He must not go down there. Besides, he knows no Turki.'

'Only tell him the shape and the smell of the letters we want and he will bring them back,' Lurgan insisted.

'No. That is a man's job,' said Creighton.

It was a wry-necked matter of unauthorised and incendiary correspondence between a person who claimed to be the ultimate authority in all matters of the Mohammedan religion throughout the world, and a younger member of a royal house who had been brought to book for kidnapping women within British territory. The Moslem Archbishop had been emphatic and over-arrogant; the young prince was merely sulky at the curtailment of his privileges, but there was no need he should continue a correspondence which might some day compromise him. One letter indeed had been procured, but the finder was later found dead by the roadside in the habit of an Arab trader, as E.23, taking up the work, duly reported.

These facts, and a few others not to be published, made both Mahbub and Creighton shake their heads.

'Let him go out with his Red Lama,' said the horse-dealer with visible effort. 'He is fond of the old man. He can learn his paces by the rosary at least.'

'I have had some dealings with the old man – by letter,' said Colonel Creighton, smiling to himself. 'Whither goes he?'

'Up and down the land, as he has these three years. He seeks a River of Healing. God's curse upon all – ' Mahbub checked himself. 'He beds down at the Temple of the Tirthankers or at Buddh Gaya when he is in from the Road. Then he goes to see the boy at the *madrissah* as we know, for the boy was punished for it twice or thrice. He is quite mad, but a peaceful man. I have met him. The Babu also has had dealings with him. We have watched him for three years. Red Lamas are not so common in Hind that one loses track.'

'Babus are very curious,' said Lurgan meditatively. 'Do you know what Hurree Babu really wants? He wants to be made a member of the Royal Society by taking ethnological notes. I tell you, I tell him about the lama everything that Mahbub and the boy have told me. Hurree Babu goes down to Benares – at his own expense, I think.'

'*I* don't,' said Creighton briefly. He had paid Hurree's travelling expenses, out of a most lively curiosity to learn what the lama might be.

'And he applies to the lama for information on lamaism, and devil dances, and spells and charms, several times in these few years. Holy Virgin! I could have told him all that yee-ars ago. I think Hurree Babu is getting too old for the Road. He likes better to collect manners and customs information. Yes, he wants to be an F. R. S.'

'Hurree thinks well of the boy, doesn't he?'

'Oh, very indeed – we have had some pleasant evenings at my little place – but I think it would be waste to throw him away with Hurree on the ethnological side.'

'Not for a first experience. How does that strike you, Mahbub? Let the boy run with the lama for six months. After that we can see. He will get experience.'

'He has it already, Sahib – as a fish controls the water he swims in; but for every reason it will be well to loose him from the school.'

'Very good, then,' said Creighton, half to himself. 'He can go with the lama, and if Hurree Babu cares to keep an eye on them so much the better. He won't lead the boy into any danger as Mahbub would. Curious – his wish to be an F.R.S. Very human, too. He *is* best on the ethnological side – Hurree.'

No money and no preferment would have drawn Creighton from his work on the Indian Survey, but deep in his heart also lay an ambition to write 'F. R. S.' after his name. Honours of a sort he knew could be obtained by ingenuity and the help of friends, but, to the best of his belief, nothing save work – papers representing a life of it – took a man into the Society which he had bombarded for years with monographs on strange Asiatic cults and unknown customs. Nine men out of ten would flee from a Royal Society soiree in extremity of boredom; but Creighton was the tenth, and at times his soul yearned for the crowded rooms in easy London where silver-haired, bald-headed gentlemen who know nothing of the Army move among spectroscopic experiments, the lesser plants of the frozen tundras, electric flight-measuring machines, and apparatus for slicing into fractional millimetres the left eye of the female mosquito. By all right and reason, it was the Royal Geographical that should have appealed to him, but men are as chancy as children in their choice of playthings. So Creighton smiled, and thought the better of Hurree Babu, moved by like desires.

He dropped the ghost-dagger and looked up at Mahbub.

'How soon can we get the colt from the stable?' said the horse-dealer, reading his eyes.

'Hmm. If I withdraw him by order now – what will he do, think you? I have never before assisted at the teaching of such an one.'

'He will come to me,' said Mahbub promptly. 'Lurgan Sahib and I will prepare him for the Road.'

'So be it, then. For six months he shall run at his choice: but who will be his sponsor?'

Lurgan slightly inclined his head. 'He will not tell anything, if that is what you are afraid of, Colonel Creighton.'

'It's only a boy, after all.'

'Ye-es; but first, he has nothing to tell; and secondly, he knows what would happen. Also, he is very fond of Mahbub, and of me a little.'

'Will he draw pay?' demanded the practical horse-dealer.

'Food and water allowance only. Twenty rupees a month.'

One advantage of the Secret Service is that it has no worrying audit. The service is ludicrously starved, of course, but the funds are administered by a few men who do not call for vouchers or present itemised accounts. Mahbub's eyes lighted with almost a Sikh's love of money. Even Lurgan's impassive face changed. He considered the years to come when Kim would have been entered and made to the Great Game that never ceases day and night, throughout India. He foresaw honour and credit in the mouths of a chosen few, coming to him from his pupil. Lurgan Sahib had made E.23 what E.23 was, out of a bewildered, impertinent, lying, little North-West Province man.

But the joy of these masters was pale and smoky beside the joy of Kim when St. Xavier's Head called him aside, with word that Colonel Creighton had sent for him.

'I understand, O'Hara, that he has found you a place as an assistant chain-man in the Canal Department: that comes of taking up mathematics. It is great luck for you, for you are only seventeen; but of course you understand that you do not become *pukka* (permanent) till you have passed the autumn examination. So you must not think you are going out into the world to enjoy yourself, or that your fortune is made. There is a great deal of hard work before you. Only, if you in becoming *pukka*, you can rise, you know, to four hundred and fifty a month.' Whereat the Principal gave him much good advice as to his conduct, and his manners, and his morals; and others, his elders, who had not been wafted into billets, talked, as only Anglo-Indian lads can, of favouritism and corruption. Indeed, young Cazalet, whose father was a pensioner at Chunar, hinted very broadly that Colonel Creighton's interest in Kim was directly paternal; and Kim, instead of retaliating, did not even use language. He was thinking of the immense fun to come, of Mahbub's letter of the day before, all neatly written in English, making appointment for that afternoon in a house the very name of which would have crisped the Principal's hair with horror. . . .

Said Kim to Mahbub in Lucknow railway station that evening, above the luggage-scales – 'I feared lest, at the last, the roof would fall upon me and cheat me. Is it indeed all finished, O my father?'

Mahbub snapped his fingers to show the utterness of that end, and his eyes blazed like red coals.

'Then where is the pistol that I may wear it?'

'Softly! A half-year, to run without heel-ropes. I begged that much from Colonel Creighton Sahib. At twenty rupees a month. Old Red Hat knows that thou art coming.'

'I will pay thee *dustoorie* (commission) on my pay for three months,' said Kim gravely. 'Yea, two rupees a month. But first we must get rid of these.' He plucked his thin linen trousers and dragged at his collar. 'I have brought with me all that I need on the Road. My trunk has gone up to Lurgan Sahib's.'

'Who sends his salaams to thee – Sahib.'

'Lurgan Sahib is a very clever man. But what dost thou do?'

'I go North again, upon the Great Game. What else? Is thy mind still set on following old Red Hat?'

'Do not forget he made me what I am – though he did not know it. Year by year, he sent the money that taught me.'

'I would have done as much – had it struck my thick head,' Mahbub growled. 'Come away. The lamps are lit now, and none will mark thee in the bazar. We go to Huneefa's house.'

On the way thither, Mahbub gave him much the same sort of advice as his mother gave to Lemuel, and curiously enough, Mahbub was exact to point out how Huneefa and her likes destroyed kings.

'And I remember,' he quoted maliciously, 'one who said, "Trust a snake before a harlot and a harlot before a Pathan, Mahbub Ali." Now, excepting as to Pathans, of whom I am one, all that is true. Most true is it in the Great Game, for it is by means of woman that all plans come to ruin and we lie out in dawning with our throats cut. So it happened to such a one' – he gave the reddest particulars.

'Then why – ?' Kim paused before a filthy staircase that climbed to the warm darkness of an upper chamber, in the ward that is behind Azim Ullah's tobacco-shop. Those who know it call it The Bird-cage – it is so full of whisperings and whistlings and chirrupings.

The room, with its dirty cushions and half-smoked hookahs, smelt abominably of stale tobacco. In one corner lay a huge and shapeless woman clad in greenish gauzes, and decked, brow, nose, ear, neck, wrist, arm, waist, and ankle, with heavy native jewellery. When she turned it was like the clashing of copper pots. A lean cat in the balcony outside the window mewed hungrily. Kim checked, bewildered, at the door-curtain.

'Is that the new stuff, Mahbub?' said Huneefa lazily, scarce troubling to remove the mouthpiece from her lips. 'O Buktanoos!' – like most of her kind, she swore by the Djinns – 'O Buktanoos! He is very good to look upon.'

'That is part of the selling of the horse,' Mahbub explained to Kim, who laughed.

'I have heard that talk since my Sixth Day,' he replied, squatting by the light. 'Whither does it lead?'

'To protection. To-night we change thy colour. This sleeping under roofs has blanched thee like an almond. But Huneefa has the secret of a colour that catches. No painting of a day or two. Also, we fortify thee against the chances of the Road. That is *my* gift to thee, my son. Take out all metals on thee and lay them here. Make ready, Huneefa.'

Kim dragged forth his compass, Survey paint-box, and the new-filled medicine-box. They had all accompanied his travels, and boy-like he valued them immensely.

The woman rose slowly and moved with her hands a little spread before her. Then Kim saw that she was blind.

'No, no,' she muttered, 'the Pathan speaks truth – my colour does not go in a week or a month, and those whom I protect are under strong guard.'

'When one is far off and alone, it would not be well to grow blotched and leprous of a sudden,' said Mahbub. 'When thou wast with me I could oversee the matter. Besides, a Pathan is a fair-skin. Strip to the waist now and look how thou art whitened.' Huneefa felt her way back from an inner room. 'It is no matter, she cannot see.' He took a pewter bowl from her ringed hand.

The dye-stuff showed blue and gummy. Kim experimented on the back of his wrist, with a dab of cotton wool; but Huneefa heard him.

'No, no,' she cried, 'the thing is not done thus, but with the proper ceremonies. The colouring is the least part. I give thee the full protection of the Road.'

'*Jadoo?*' (magic), said Kim, with a half start. He did not like the white, sightless eyes. Mahbub's hand on his neck bowed him to the floor, nose within an inch of the boards.

'Be still. No harm comes to thee, my son. I am thy sacrifice!'

He could not see what the woman was about, but heard the clish-clash of her jewellery for many minutes. A match lit up the darkness; he caught the well-known purr and fizzle of grains of incense. Then the room filled with smoke – heavy, aromatic, and stupefying. Through growing drowse he heard the names of devils – of Zulbazan, Son of Eblis, who lives in bazars and *paraos*, making all the sudden lewd wickedness of wayside halts; of Dulhan, invisible about mosques, the dweller among the slippers of the Faithful, who hinders folk from their prayers; and Musboot, Lord of lies and panic. Huneefa, now whispering in his ear, now talking as from an immense distance, touched him with horrible soft fingers, but Mahbub's grip never shifted from his neck till relaxing with a sigh, the boy lost his senses.

'Allah! How he fought! We should never have done it but for the drugs. That was his White blood, I take it,' said Mahbub testily. 'Go on with the dawut (invocation). Give him full Protection.'

'O Hearer! Thou that hearest with ears, be present. Listen, O Hearer!' Huneefa moaned, her dead eyes turned to the west. The dark room filled with moanings and snortings.

From the outer balcony, a ponderous figure raised a round bullet head and coughed nervously.

'Do not interrupt this ventriloquial necromanciss,* my friend,' it said in English. 'I opine that it is very disturbing to you, but no enlightened observer is jolly well upset.'

'. . . . *I will lay a plot for their ruin! O Prophet, bear with the unbelievers. Let them alone awhile!'* Huneefa's face, turned to the northward, worked horribly, and it was as though voices from the ceiling answered her.

Hurree Babu returned to his note-book, balanced on the window-sill, but his hand shook. Huneefa, in some sort of drugged ecstasy, wrenched herself to and fro as she sat cross-legged by Kim's still head, and called upon devil after devil in the ancient order of the ritual, binding them to avoid the boy's every action.

'With Him are the keys of the Secret Things! None knoweth them beside Himself. He knoweth that which is in the dry land and the sea!' in Again broke out the unearthly whistling responses.

* Ventriloqui: Art of 'throwing' one's voice in such a way that the sound seems to come from a source other than the speaker. Necromancy: Conjuration of the spirits of the dead for purposes of magically revealing the future or influencing the course of events.

'I – I apprehend it is not at all malignant in its operation?' said the Babu, watching the throat-muscles quiver and jerk as Huneefa spoke with tongues. 'It – it is not likely that she has killed the boy? If so, I decline to be witness at the trial. . . . What was the last hypothetical devil mentioned?'

'Babuji,' said Mahbub in the vernacular. 'I have no regard for the devils of Hind, but the Sons of Eblis are far otherwise, and whether they be *jumalee* (well-affected) or *jullalee* (terrible) they love not Kafirs.'

'Then you think I had better go?' said Hurree Babu, half rising. 'They are, of course, dematerialised phenomena. Spencer says – '

Huneefa's crisis passed, as these things must, in a paroxysm of howling, with a touch of froth at the lips. She lay spent and motionless beside Kim, and the crazy voices ceased.

'Wah! That work is done. May the boy be better for it; and Huneefa is surely a mistress of *dawut*. Help haul her aside, Babu. Do not be afraid.'

'How am I to fear the absolutely non-existent?' said Hurree Babu, talking English to reassure himself. It is an awful thing still to dread the magic that you contemptuously investigate – to collect folk-lore for the Royal Society with a lively belief in all Powers of Darkness.

Mahbub chuckled. He had been out with Hurree on the Road ere now. 'Let us finish the colouring,' said he. 'The boy is well protected if – if the Lords of the Air have ears to hear. I am a *sufi* (free-thinker), but when one can get blindsides of a woman, a stallion, or a devil, why go round to invite a kick? Set him upon the way, Babu, and see that old Red Hat does not lead him beyond our reach. I must get back to my horses.'

'All raight,' said Hurree Babu. 'He is at present a curious spectacle.'

* * * * *

About third cockcrow, Kim woke after a sleep of thousands of years. Huneefa, in her corner, snored heavily, but Mahbub was gone.

'I hope you were not frightened,' said an oily voice at his elbow. 'I superintended entire operation, which was most interesting from ethnological point of view. It was high-class *dawut*.'

'Huh!' said Kim, recognising Hurree Babu, who smiled ingratiatingly.

'And also I had honour to bring down from Lurgan your present costume. I am not in the habit offeecially of carrying such gauds to subordinates, but' – he giggled – 'your case is noted as exceptional on the books. I hope Mr. Lurgan will note my action.'

Kim yawned and stretched himself. It was good to turn and twist within loose clothes once again.

'What is this?' He looked curiously at the heavy duffle-stuff loaded with the scents of the far North.

'Oho! That is inconspicuous dress of *chela* attached to service of lamaistic lama. *Com*plete in every particular,' said Hurree Babu, rolling into the balcony to clean his teeth at a goglet. 'I am of opeenion it is not your old gentleman's precise religion, but rather sub-variant of same. I have contributed rejected notes to *Asiatic Quarterly Review* on these subjects. Now it is curious that the old gentleman himself is totally devoid of religiosity. He is not a dam particular.'

'Do you know him?'

Hurree Babu held up his hand to show he was engaged in the prescribed rites that accompany tooth-cleaning and such things among decently bred Bengalis. Then he recited in English an Arya-Somaj prayer of a theistical nature, and stuffed his mouth with *pan* and betel.

'Oah yes. I have met him several times at Benares, and also at Buddh Gaya, to interrogate him on religious points and devil-worship. He is pure agnostic – same as me.'

Huneefa stirred in her sleep, and Hurree Babu jumped nervously to the copper incense-burner, all black and discoloured in morning-light, rubbed a finger in the accumulated lampblack, and drew it diagonally across his face.

'Who has died in thy house?' asked Kim in the vernacular.

'None. But she may have the Evil Eye – that sorceress,' the Babu replied.

'What dost thou do now, then?'

'I will set thee on thy way to Benares, if thou goest thither, and tell thee what must be known by Us.'

'I go. At what hour runs the *te-rai*n*?*' He rose to his feet, looked round the desolate chamber and at the yellow-wax face of Huneefa as the low sun stole across the floor. 'Is there money to be paid that witch?'

'No. She has charmed thee against all devils and all dangers – in the name of her devils. It was Mahbub's desire.' In English: 'He is highly obsolete, *I* think, to indulge in such super-steetion. Why, it is all ventri*lo*quy. Belly-speak – eh?'

Kim snapped his fingers mechanically to avert whatever evil – Mahbub, he knew, meditated none – might have crept in through Huneefa's ministrations; and Hurree giggled once more. But as he crossed the room he was careful not to step in Huneefa's blotched, squat shadow on the boards. Witches – when their time is on them – can lay hold of the heels of a man's soul if he does that.

'Now you must well listen,' said the Babu when they were in the fresh air. 'Part of these ceremonies which we witnessed they include supply of effeecient amulet to those of our

Department. If you feel in your neck you will find one small silver amulet, verree cheap. That is *ours*. Do you understand?'

'Oah yes, *hawa-dilli*' (a heart-lifter), said Kim, feeling at his neck.

'Huneefa she makes them for two rupees twelve annas with – oh, all sorts of exorcisms. They are quite common, except they are partially black enamel, and there is a paper inside each one full of names of local saints and such things. *Thatt* is Huneefa's look-out, you see? Huneefa makes them onlee for us, but in case she does not, when we get them we put in, before issue, one small piece of turquoise. Mr. Lurgan, he gives them. There is no other source of supply; but it was me invented all this. It is strictly unoffeecial of course, but convenient for subordinates. Colonel Creighton he does not know. He is European. The turquoise is wrapped in the paper . . . . Yes, that is road to railway station. . . . Now suppose you go with the lama, or with me, I hope, some day, or with Mahbub. Suppose we get into a dam-tight place. I am a fearful man – most fearful – but I tell you I have been in dam-tight places more than hairs on my head. You say: "I am Son of the Charm." Verree good.'

'I do not understand quite. We must not be heard talking English here.'

'That is all raight. I am only Babu showing off my English to you. All we Babus talk English to show off,' said Hurree, flinging his shoulder-cloth jauntily. 'As I was about to say, "Son of the Charm" means that you may be member of the *Sat Bhai* – the Seven Brothers, which is Hindi *and* Tantric. It is popularly supposed to be extinct society, but I have written notes to show it is still extant. You see it is all my invention. Verree good. *Sat Bhai* has many members, and perhaps before they jolly-well-cut-your-throat they may give you just a chance for life. That is useful, anyhow. And, moreover, these fooolish natives – if they are not too excited – they always stop to think before they kill a man who says he belongs to any specific organisation. You see? You say then when you are in tight place, "I am Son of the Charm," and you get – perhaps – ah – your second wind. That is only in extreme instances, or to open negotiations with a stranger. Can you quite see? Verree good. But suppose now, I, or anyone of the Department, come to you dressed quite different. You would not know me at all unless I choose, I bet you. Some day I will prove it. I come as Ladakhi trader – oh anything – and I say to you: "You want to buy precious stones?" You say: "Do I look like a man who buys precious stones?" Then I say: "Even verree poor man can buy a turquoise or *tarkeean*." '

'That is *kichree* – vegetable curry,' said Kim.

'Of course it is. You say: "Let me see the *tarkeean*." Then I say: "It was cooked by a woman, and perhaps it is bad for your caste." Then you say: "There is no caste when men go to – look for *tarkeean*." You stop a little between those words, "to – look." That is thee whole secret. The little stop before the words.'

Kim repeated the test-sentence.

'That is all right. Then I will show you my turquoise if there is time, and then you know who I am, and then we exchange views and documents and those-all things. And so it is with any other man of us. We talk sometimes about turquoises and sometimes about *tarkeean*, but always with that little stop in the words. It is verree easy. First, "Son of the Charm," if you are in a tight place. Perhaps that may help you – perhaps not. Then what I have told you about the *tarkeean*, if you want to transact offeecial business with a strange man. Of course, at present, you have no offeecial business. You are –

ah ha! – Supernumerary on probation. Quite unique specimen. If you were Asiatic of birth you might be employed right off; but this half-year of leave is to make you de-Englishised, you see? The lama, he expects you, because I have demi-offeecially informed him you have passed all your examinations, and will soon obtain Government appointment. Oh ho! You are on acting-allowance you see: so if you are called upon to help Sons of the Charm mind you jolly well try. Now I shall say good-bye, my dear fellow, and I hope you – ah – will come out top-side all raight.'

Hurree Babu stepped back a pace or two into the crowd at the entrance of Lucknow station and – was gone. Kim drew a deep breath and hugged himself all over. The nickel-plated revolver he could feel in the bosom of his sad-coloured robe, the amulet was on his neck; begging-gourd, rosary, and ghost-dagger (Mr. Lurgan had forgotten nothing) were all to hand, with medicine, paint-box, and compass, and in a worn old purse-belt embroidered with porcupine quill-patterns lay a month's pay. Kings could be no richer. He bought sweetmeats in a leaf-cup from a Hindu trader, and ate them with glad rapture till a policeman ordered him off the steps.

CHAPTER 11

Give the man who is not made
    To his trade
Swords to fling and catch again,
Coins to ring and snatch again,
Men to harm and cure again,
Snakes to charm and lure again –
He'll be hurt by his own blade,
By his serpents disobeyed,
By his clumsiness bewrayed
By the people mocked to scorn.
    So 'Tis not with juggler born.
Pinch of dust or withered flower,
    Chance-flung fruit or borrowed staff,
Serve his need and shore his power,
    Bind the spell, or loose the laugh!

But a man who, etc., Op. *15.*

FOLLOWED A sudden natural reaction.

'Now am I alone – all alone,' he thought. 'In all India is no one so alone as I! If I die to-day, who shall bring the news – and to whom? If I live and God is good, there will be a price upon my head, for I am a Son of the Charm – I, Kim.'

A very few white people, but many Asiatics, can throw themselves into amazement as it were by repeating their own names over and over again to themselves, letting the mind go free upon speculation as to what is called personal identity. When one grows older, the power, usually, departs, but while it lasts it may descend upon a man at any moment.

'Who is Kim – Kim – Kim?'

He squatted in a corner of the clanging waiting-room, rapt from all other thoughts; hands folded in lap, and pupils contracted to pin-points. In a minute – in another half second – he felt he would arrive at the solution of the tremendous puzzle; but here, as always happens, his mind dropped away from those heights with the rush of a wounded bird, and passing his hand before his eyes, he shook his head.

A long-haired Hindu *bairagi* (holy man), who had just bought a ticket, halted before him at that moment and stared intently.

'I also have lost it,' he said sadly. 'It is one of the Gates to the Way, but for me it has been shut many years.'

'What is the talk?' said Kim, abashed.

'Thou wast wondering there in thy spirit what manner of thing thy soul might be. The seizure came of a sudden. *I* know. Who should know but I? Whither goest thou?'

'Toward Kashi' (Benares).

'There are no Gods there. I have proved them. I go to Prayag (Allahabad) for the fifth time – seeking the road to Enlightenment. Of what faith art thou?'

'I too am a Seeker,' said Kim, using one of the lama's pet words. 'Though' – he forgot his Northern dress for the moment – 'though Allah alone knoweth what I seek.'

The old fellow slipped the *bairagi's* crutch under his armpit and sat down on a patch of ruddy leopard's skin as Kim rose at the call for the Benares train.

'Go in hope, little brother,' he said. 'It is a long road to the feet of the One; but thither do we all travel.'

Kim did not feel so lonely after this, and ere he had sat out twenty miles in the crowded compartment, was cheering his neighbours with a string of most wonderful yarns about his own and his master's magical gifts.

Benares struck him as a peculiarly filthy city, though it was pleasant to find how his cloth was respected. At least one-third of the population prays eternally to some group or other of the many million deities, and so revere every sort of holy man. Kim was guided to the Temple of the Tirthankers, about a mile outside the city, near Sarnath, by a chance-met Panjabi farmer – a Kamboh from Jullundur-way who had appealed in vain to every God of his homestead to cure his small son, and was trying Benares as a last resort.

'Thou art from the North?' he asked, shouldering through the press of the narrow, stinking streets much like his own pet bull at home.

'Ay, I know the Punjab. My mother was a Pahareen, but my father came from Amritzar – by Jandiala,' said Kim, oiling his ready tongue for the needs of the Road.

'Jandiala – Jullundur? Oho! Then we be neighbours in some sort, as it were.' He nodded tenderly to the wailing child in his arms. 'Whom dost thou serve?'

'A most holy man at the Temple of the Tirthankers.'

'They are all most holy and – most greedy,' said the Jat with bitterness. 'I have walked the pillars and trodden the temples till my feet are flayed, and the child is no whit better. And the mother being sick too. . . . Hush, then, little one. . . . We changed his name when the fever came. We put him into girl's clothes. There was nothing we did not do, except – I said to his mother when she bundled me off to Benares – she should have come with me – I *said* Sakhi Sarwar Sultan would serve us best. We know His generosity, but these down-country Gods are strangers.'

The child turned on the cushion of the huge corded arms and looked at Kim through heavy eyelids.

'And was it all worthless?' Kim asked, with easy interest.

'All worthless – all worthless,' said the child, lips cracking with fever.

'The Gods have given him a good mind, at least,' said the father proudly. 'To think he should have listened so cleverly. Yonder is thy temple. Now I am a poor man – many priests have dealt with me – but my son is my son, and if a gift to thy master can cure him – I am at my very wits' end.'

Kim considered for a while, tingling with pride. Three years ago he would have made prompt profit on the situation and gone his way without a thought; but now, the very respect the Jat paid him proved that he was a man. Moreover, he had tasted fever once or twice already, and knew enough to recognise starvation when he saw it.

'Call him forth and I will give him a bond on my best yoke, so that the child is cured.'

Kim halted at the carved outer door of the temple. A white-clad Oswal banker from Ajmir, his sins of usury new wiped out, asked him what he did.

'I am *chela* to Teshoo Lama, an Holy One from Bhotiyal – within there. He bade me come. I wait. Tell him.'

'Do not forget the child,' cried the importunate Jat over his shoulder, and then bellowed in Punjabi: 'O Holy One – O disciple of the Holy One – O Gods above all the Worlds – behold affliction sitting at the gate!' That cry is so common in Benares that the passers never turned their heads.

The Oswal, at peace with mankind, carried the message into the darkness behind him, and the easy, uncounted Eastern minutes slid by; for the lama was asleep in his cell, and no priest would wake him. When the click of his rosary again broke the hush of the inner court where the calm images of the Arhats stand, a novice whispered, 'Thy *chela* is here,' and the old man strode forth, forgetting the end of that prayer.

Hardly had the tall figure shown in the doorway than the Jat ran before him, and, lifting up the child, cried: 'Look upon this, Holy One; and if the Gods will, he lives – he lives!'

He fumbled in his waist-belt and drew out a small silver coin.

'What is now?' The lama's eyes turned to Kim. It was noticeable he spoke far clearer Urdu than long ago, under Zam-Zammah; but the father would allow no private talk.

'It is no more than a fever,' said Kim. 'The child is not well fed.'

'He sickens at everything, and his mother is not here.'

'If it be permitted, I may cure, Holy One.'

'What! Have they made thee a healer? Wait here,' said the lama, and he sat down by the Jat upon the lowest step of the temple, while Kim, looking out of the corner of his eyes, slowly opened the little betel-box. He had dreamed dreams at school of returning to the lama as a Sahib – of chaffing the old man before he revealed himself – boy's dreams all. There was more drama in this abstracted, brow-puckered search through the tabloid-bottles, with a pause here and there for thought and a muttered invocation between whiles. Quinine he had in tablets, and dark brown meat-lozenges – beef most probably, but that was not *his* business. The little thing would not eat, but it sucked at a lozenge greedily, and said it liked the salt taste.

'Take then these six.' Kim handed them to the man. 'Praise the Gods, and boil three in milk; other three in water. After he has drunk the milk give him this (it was the half of a quinine pill), and wrap him warm. Give him the water of the other three, and the other half of this white pill when he wakes. Meantime, here is another brown medicine that he may suck at on the way home.'

'Gods, what wisdom!' said the Kamboh, snatching.

It was as much as Kim could remember of his own treatment in a bout of autumn malaria – if you except the patter that he added to impress the lama.

'Now go! Come again in the morning.'

'But the price – the price,' said the Jat, and threw back his sturdy shoulders. 'My son is my son. Now that he will be whole again, how shall I go back to his mother and say I took help by the wayside and did not even give a bowl of curds in return?'

'They are alike, these Jats,' said Kim softly. 'The Jat stood on his dunghill and the King's elephants went by. "O driver," said he, "what will you sell those little donkeys for?" '

The Jat burst into a roar of laughter, stifled with apologies to the lama. 'It is the saying of my own country – the very talk of it. So are we Jats all. I will come to-morrow with the child; and the blessing of the Gods of the Homesteads – who are good little Gods – be on you both. . . . Now, son, we grow strong again. Do not spit it out, little Princeling! King of my Heart, do not spit it out, and we shall be strong men, wrestlers and club-wielders, by morning.'

He moved away, crooning and mumbling. The lama turned to Kim, and all the loving old soul of him looked out through his narrow eyes.

'To heal the sick is to acquire merit; but first one gets knowledge. That was wisely done, O Friend of all the World.'

'I was made wise by thee, Holy One,' said Kim, forgetting the little play just ended; forgetting St. Xavier's; forgetting his white blood; forgetting even the Great Game as he stooped, Mohammedan fashion, to touch his master's feet in the dust of the Jain temple. 'My teaching I owe to thee. I have eaten thy bread three years. My time is finished. I am loosed from the schools. I come to thee.'

'Herein is my reward. Enter! Enter! And is all well?' They passed to the inner court, where the afternoon sun sloped golden across. 'Stand that I may see. So!' He peered critically. 'It is no longer a child, but a man, ripened in wisdom, walking as a physician. I did well – I did well when I gave thee up to the armed men on that black night. Dost thou remember our first day under Zam-Zammah?'

'Ay.' said Kim. 'Dost thou remember when I leapt off the carriage the first day I went to – '

'The Gates of Learning? Truly. And the day that we ate the cakes together at the back of the river by Nucklao. Aha! Many times hast thou begged for me, but that day I begged for thee.'

'Good reason,' quoth Kim. 'I was then a scholar in the Gates of Learning, and attired as a Sahib. Do not forget, Holy One,' he went on playfully, 'I am still a Sahib – by thy favour.'

'True. And a Sahib in most high esteem. Come to my cell, *chela*.'

'How is that known to thee?'

The lama smiled. 'First by means of letters from the kindly priest whom we met in the camp of armed men; but he is now gone to his own country, and I sent the money to his brother.' Colonel Creighton, who had succeeded to the trusteeship when Father Victor went to England with the Mavericks, was hardly the chaplain's brother. 'But I do not well understand Sahibs' letters. They must be interpreted to me. I chose a surer way. Many times when I returned from my Search to this temple, which has always been a nest to me, there came one seeking Enlightenment – a man from Leh – that had been, he said, a Hindu, but wearied of all those Gods.' The lama pointed to the Arhats.

'A fat man?' said Kim, a twinkle in his eye.

'Very fat; but I perceived in a little his mind was wholly given up to useless things – such as devils and charms and the form and fashion of our tea-drinkings in the monasteries, and by what road we initiated the novices. A man abounding in questions; but he was a friend of thine, *chela*. He told me that thou wast on the road to much honour as a scribe. And I see thou art a physician.'

'Yes, that am I – a scribe, when I am a Sahib, but it is set aside when I come as thy disciple. I have accomplished the years appointed for a Sahib.'

'As it were a novice?' said the lama, nodding his head. 'Art thou freed from the schools? I would not have thee unripe.'

'I am all free. In due time I take service under the Government as a scribe –'

'Not as a warrior. That is well.'

'But first I come to wander – with thee. Therefore I am here. Who begs for thee, these days?' he went on quickly. The ice was thin.

'Very often I beg myself; but, as thou knowest, I am seldom here, except when I come to look again at my disciple. From one end to another of Hind have I travelled afoot and in the *te-rain*. A great and a wonderful land! But here, when I put in, is as though I were in my own Bhotiyal.'

He looked round the little clean cell complacently. A low cushion gave him a seat, on which he had disposed himself in the cross-legged attitude of the Bodhisat emerging from meditation; a black *teak-wood* table, not twenty inches high, set with copper tea-cups, was before him. In one corner stood a tiny altar, also of heavily carved teak, bearing a copper-gilt image of the seated Buddha and fronted by a lamp, an incense-holder, and a pair of copper flowerpots.

'The Keeper of the Images in the Wonder House acquired merit by giving me these a year since,' he said, following Kim's eyes. 'When one is far from one's own land such things carry remembrance; and we must reverence the Lord for that He showed the Way. See!' He pointed to a curiously-built mound of coloured rice crowned with a fantastic metal ornament. 'When I was abbot in my own place – before I came to better knowledge – I made that offering daily. It is the Sacrifice of the Universe to the Lord. Thus do we of Bhotiyal offer all the world daily to the Excellent Law. And I do it even now, though I know that the Excellent One is beyond all pinchings and pattings.' He snuffed from his gourd.

'It is well done, Holy One,' Kim murmured, sinking at ease on the cushions, very happy and rather tired.

'And also,' the old man chuckled, 'I write pictures of the Wheel of Life. Three days to a picture. I was busied on it – or it may be I shut my eyes a little – when they brought word of thee. It is good to have thee here: I will show thee my art – not for pride's sake, but because thou must learn. The Sahibs have not *all* this world's wisdom.'

He drew from under the table a sheet of strangely scented yellow Chinese paper, the brushes, and slab of India ink. In cleanest, severest outline he had traced the Great Wheel with its six spokes, whose centre is the conjoined Hog, Snake, and Dove (Ignorance, Anger, and Lust), and whose compartments are all the heavens and hells, and all the chances of human life.

Men say that the Bodhisat Himself first drew it with grains of rice upon dust, to teach His disciples the cause of things. Many ages have crystalized it into a most wonderful convention crowded with hundreds of little figures whose every line carries a meaning. Few can translate the picture-parable; there are not twenty in all the world who can draw it surely without a copy: of those who can both draw and expound are but three.

'I have a little learned to draw,' said Kim. 'But this is a marvel beyond marvels.'

'I have written it for many years,' said the lama. 'Time was when I could write it all between one lamp-lighting and the next. I will teach thee the art – after due preparation; and I will show thee the meaning of the Wheel.'

'We take the Road, then?'

'The Road and our Search. I was but waiting for thee. It was made plain to me in a hundred dreams – notably one that came upon the night of the day that the Gates of Learning first shut – that without thee I should never find my River. Again and again, as thou knowest, I put this from me, fearing an illusion. Therefore I would not take thee with me that day at Lucknow, when we ate the cakes. I would not take thee till the time was ripe and auspicious. From the Hills to the Sea, from the Sea to the Hills have I gone, but it was vain. Then I remembered the *Jâtaka*.'

He told Kim the story of the elephant with the leg-iron, as he had told it so often to the Jain priests.

'Further testimony is not needed,' he ended serenely. 'Thou wast sent for an aid. That aid removed, my Search came to naught. Therefore we will go out again together, and our Search is sure.'

'Whither go we?'

'What matters, Friend of all the World? The Search, I say, is sure. If need be, the River will break from the ground before us. I acquired merit when I sent thee to the Gates of Learning, and gave thee the jewel that is Wisdom. Thou didst return, I saw even now, a follower of Sakyamuni, the Physician, whose altars are many in Bhotiyal. It is sufficient. We are together, and all things are as they were – Friend of all the World – Friend of the Stars – my *chela!*'

Then they talked of matters secular; but it was noticeable that the lama never demanded any details of life at St. Xavier's, nor showed the faintest curiosity as to the manners and customs of Sahibs. His mind moved all in the past, and he revived every step of their wonderful first journey together, rubbing his hands and chuckling, till it pleased him to curl himself up into the sudden sleep of old age.

Kim watched the last dusty sunshine fade out of the court, and played with his ghost-dagger and rosary. The clamour of Benares, oldest of all earth's cities awake before the Gods, day and night, beat round the walls as the sea's roar round a breakwater. Now and again, a Jain priest crossed the court, with some small offering to the images, and swept the path about him lest by chance he should take the life of a living thing. A lamp twinkled, and there followed the sound of a prayer. Kim watched the stars as they rose one after another in the still, sticky dark, till he fell asleep at the foot of the altar. That night he dreamed in Hindustanee, with never an English word. . . .

'Holy One, there is the child to whom we gave the medicine,' he said, about three o'clock in the morning, when the lama, also waking from dreams, would have fared forth on pilgrimage. 'The Jat will be here at the light.'

'I am well answered. In my haste I would have done a wrong.' He sat down on the cushions and returned to his rosary. 'Surely old folk are as children,' he said pathetically. 'They desire a matter – behold, it must be done at once, or they fret and weep! Many times when I was upon the Road I have been ready to stamp with my feet at the hindrance of an ox-cart in the way, or a mere cloud of dust. It was not so when I was a man – a long time ago. None the less it is wrongful .... '

'But thou art indeed old, Holy One.'

'The thing was done. A Cause was put out into the world, and, old or young, sick or sound, knowing or unknowing, who can rein in the effect of that Cause? Does the Wheel hang still if a child spin it – or a drunkard? *Chela*, this is a great and a terrible world.'

'I think it good,' Kim yawned. 'What is there to eat? I have not eaten since yesterday even.'

'I had forgotten thy need. Yonder is good Bhotiyal tea and cold rice.'

'We cannot walk far on such stuff.' Kim felt all the European's lust for flesh-meat, which is not accessible in a Jain temple. Yet, instead of going out at once with the begging-bowl, he stayed his stomach on slabs of cold rice till the full dawn. It brought the farmer, voluble, stuttering with gratitude.

'In the night the fever broke and the sweat came,' he cried. 'Feel here – his skin is fresh and new! He esteemed the salt lozenges, and took milk with greed.' He drew the cloth from the child's face, and it smiled sleepily at Kim. A little knot of Jain priests, silent but all-observant, gathered by the temple door. They knew, and Kim knew that they knew, how the old lama had met his disciple. Being courteous folk, they had not obtruded themselves overnight by presence, word, or gesture. Wherefore Kim repaid them as the sun rose.

'Thank the Gods of the Jains, brother,' he said, not knowing how those Gods were named. 'The fever is indeed broken.'

'Look! See!' The lama beamed in the background upon his hosts of three years. 'Was there ever such a *chela*? He follows our Lord the Healer.'

Now the Jains officially recognise all the Gods of the Hindu creed, as well as the Lingam and the Snake. They wear the Brahminical thread; they adhere to every claim of Hindu caste-law. But, because they knew and loved the lama, because he was an old man, because he sought the Way, because he was their guest, and because he collogued long of nights with the head-priest – as free-thinking a metaphysician as ever split one hair into seventy – they murmured assent.

'Remember' – Kim bent over the child – 'this trouble may come again.'

'Not if thou hast the proper spell,' said the father.

'But in a little while we go away.'

'True,' said the lama to all the Jains. 'We go now together upon the Search whereof I have often spoken. I waited till my *chela* was ripe. Behold him! We go North. Never again shall I look upon this place of my rest, O people of good will.'

'But I am not a beggar.' The cultivator rose to his feet, clutching the child.

'Be still. Do not trouble the Holy One,' a priest cried.

'Go,' Kim whispered. Meet us again under the big railway bridge, and for the sake of all the Gods of our Punjab, bring food – curry, pulse, cakes fried in fat, and sweetmeats. Specially sweetmeats. Be swift!'

The pallor of hunger suited Kim very well as he stood, tall and slim, in his sad-coloured, sweeping robes, one hand on his rosary and the other in the attitude of benediction, faithfully copied from the lama. An English observer might have said that he looked rather like the young saint of a stained-glass window, whereas he was but a growing lad faint with emptiness.

Long and formal were the farewells, thrice ended and thrice renewed. The Seeker – he who had invited the lama to that haven from far-away Tibet, a silver-faced, hairless ascetic – took no part in it, but meditated, as always, alone among the images. The others were very human; pressing small comforts upon the old man – a betel-box, a fine new iron pen-case, a food-bag, and such like, – warning him against the dangers of the world without, and prophesying a happy end to the Search. Meantime Kim, lonelier than ever, squatted on the steps, and swore to himself in the language of St. Xavier's.

'But it is my own fault,' he concluded. 'With Mahbub, I ate Mahbub's bread, or Lurgan Sahib's. At St. Xavier's, three meals a day. Here I must jolly well look out for myself. Besides, I am not in good training. *How* I could eat a plate of beef now!. . . . Is it finished, Holy One?'

The lama, both hands raised, intoned a final blessing in ornate Chinese. 'I must lean on thy shoulder,' said he, as the temple-gates closed. 'We grow stiff, I think.'

The weight of a six-foot man is not light to steady through miles of crowded streets, and Kim, loaded down with bundles and packages for the way, was glad to reach the shadow of the railway bridge.

'Here we eat,' he said resolutely, as the Kamboh, blue-robed and smiling, hove in sight, a basket in one hand and the child on the other.

'Fall to, Holy Ones!' he cried from fifty yards. (They were by the shoal under the first bridge-span, out of sight of hungry priests.) 'Rice and good curry, cakes all warm and well scented with *hing* (asafoetida), curds and sugar. King of my fields,' this to the small son, 'let us show these holy men that we Jats of Jullundur can pay a service. . . . I had heard the Jains would eat nothing that they had not cooked, but truly' – he looked away politely over the broad river – 'where there is no eye there is no caste.'

'And we,' said Kim, turning his back and heaping a leaf-platter for the lama, 'are beyond all castes.'

They gorged themselves on the good food in silence. Nor till he had licked the last of the sticky sweet-stuff from his little finger did Kim note that the Kamboh too was girt for travel.

'If our roads lie together,' he said roughly, 'I go with thee. One does not often find a worker of miracles, and the child is still weak. But I am not altogether a reed.' He picked up his *lathi* – a five-foot male-bamboo ringed with bands of polished iron – and flourished it in the air. 'The Jats are called quarrelsome, but that is not true. Except when we are crossed we are like our own buffaloes.'

'So be it,' said Kim. 'A good stick is a good reason.'

The lama gazed placidly up-stream, where in long, smudged perspective the ceaseless columns of smoke go up from the burning-ghats by the river. Now and again, despite all municipal regulations, the fragment of a half-burned body bobbed by on the full current.

'But for thee,' said the Kamboh, drawing his child into his hairy breast, 'I might to-day have gone thither – with this one. The priests tell us that Benares is holy – which none doubt – and desirable to die in. But I do not know their Gods, and they ask for money; and when one has done one worship a shaved-head vows it is of none effect except one do another. Wash here! Wash there! Pour, drink, lave, and scatter flowers – but always pay the priests. No, the Punjab for me, and the soil of the Jullundur-*doab* for the best soil in it.'

'I have said many times – in the temple I think – that if need be, the River will open at our feet. We will therefore go North,' said the lama, rising. 'I remember a pleasant place, set about with fruit-trees, where one can walk in meditation – and the air is cooler there. It comes from the Hills and the snow of the Hills.'

'What is the name?' said Kim.

'How should I know? Didst thou not – no, that was after the Army rose out of the earth and took thee away. I abode there in meditation in a room against the dovecot – except when she talked eternally.'

'Oho! the woman from Kulu. That is by Saharunpore,' Kim laughed.

'How does the spirit move thy master? Does he go afoot, for the sake of past sins?' the Jat demanded cautiously. 'It is a far cry to Delhi.'

'No,' said Kim. 'I will beg a *tikkut* for the *te-rain*.' One does not own to the possession of money in India.

'Then in the name of the Gods, let us take the fire-carriage. My son is best in his mother's arms. The Government has brought on us many taxes, but it gives us one good thing – the *te-rain* that joins friends and unites the anxious. A wonderful matter is the *te-rain*.'

They all piled into it a couple of hours later, and slept through the heat of the day. The Kamboh plied Kim with ten thousand questions as to the lama's walk and work in life, and received some curious answers. Kim was content to be where he was, to look out upon the flat North-Western landscape, and to talk to the changing mob of fellow-passengers. Even to-day, tickets and ticket-clipping are dark oppression to Indian rustics. They do not understand why, when they have paid for a magic piece of paper, strangers should punch great pieces out of the charm. So, long and furious are the debates between travellers and Eurasian ticket-collectors. Kim assisted at two or three with grave advice, meant to darken council and to show off his wisdom before the lama and the admiring Kamboh. But at Somna Road the Fates sent him a matter to think upon. There tumbled into the compartment, as the train was moving off, a mean, lean little person – a Mahratta, so far as Kim could judge by the cock of the tight turban. His face was cut, his muslin upper-garment was badly torn, and one leg was bandaged. He told them that a country-cart had upset and nearly slain him: he was going to Delhi, where his son lived. Kim watched him closely. If, as he asserted, he had been rolled over and over on the earth, there should have been signs of gravel-rash on the skin. But all his injuries seemed clean cuts, and a mere fall from a cart could not cast a man into such extremity of terror. As, with shaking fingers, he knotted up the torn cloth about his neck he laid bare an amulet of the kind called a keeper-up of the heart. Now, amulets are common enough, but they are not generally strung on square-plaited copper wire, and still fewer amulets bear black enamel on silver. There were none except the Kamboh and the lama in the compartment, which, luckily, was of an old type with solid ends. Kim made as to scratch in his bosom, and thereby lifted his own amulet. The Mahratta's face changed altogether at the sight, and he disposed the amulet fairly on his breast.

'Yes,' he went on to the Kamboh, 'I was in haste, and the cart, driven by a bastard, bound its wheel in a water-cut, and besides the harm done to me there was lost a full dish of *tarkeean*. I was not a Son of the Charm (a lucky man) that day.'

'That was a great loss,' said Kamboh, withdrawing interest. His experience of Benares had made him suspicious.

'Who cooked it?' said Kim.

'A woman.' The Mahratta raised his eyes.

'But all women can cook *tarkeean*,' said the Kamboh. 'It is a good curry, as I know.'

'Oh, yes, it is a good curry,' said the Mahratta.

'And cheap,' said Kim. 'But what about caste?'

'Oh, there is no caste where men go to – look for *tarkeean*,' the Mahratta replied, in the prescribed cadence. 'Of whose service art thou?'

'Of the service of this Holy One.' Kim pointed to the happy, drowsy lama, who woke with a jerk at the well-loved word.

'Ah, he was sent from Heaven to aid me. He is called the Friend of all the World. He is also called the Friend of the Stars. He walks as a physician – his time being ripe. Great is his wisdom.'

'And a Son of the Charm,'said Kim under his breath, as the Kamboh made haste to prepare a pipe lest the Mahratta should beg.

'And who is *that?*' the Mahratta asked, glancing sideways nervously.

'One whose child I – we have cured, who lies under great debt to us. Sit by the window, man from Jullundur. Here is a sick one.'

'Humph! *I* have no desire to mix with chance-met wastrels. *My* ears are not long. *I* am not a woman wishing to overhear secrets.' The Jat slid himself heavily into a far corner.

'Art thou anything of a healer? I am ten leagues deep in calamity,' cried the Mahratta, picking up the cue.

'The man is cut and bruised all over. I go about to cure him,' Kim retorted. 'None interfered between thy babe and me.'

'I am rebuked,' said the Kamboh meekly. 'I am thy debtor for the life of my son. Thou art a miracle-worker – I know it.'

'Show me the cuts.' Kim bent over the Mahratta's neck, his heart nearly choking him; for this was the Great Game with a vengeance. 'Now, tell thy tale swiftly, brother, while I say a charm.'

'I come from the South, where my work lay. One of us they slew by the roadside. Hast thou heard?' Kim shook his head. He, of course, knew nothing of E.23's predecessor, slain down South in the habit of an Arab trader. 'Having found a certain letter which I was sent to seek, I came away. I escaped from the city and ran to Mhow. So sure was I that none knew, I did not change my face. At Mhow a woman brought charge against me of theft of jewellery in that city which I had left. Then I saw the cry was out against me. I ran from Mhow by night, bribing the police, who had been bribed to hand me over without question to my enemies in the South. Then I lay in old Chitor city a week, a penitent in a temple, but I could not get rid of the letter which was my charge. I buried it under the Queen's Stone, at Chitor, in the place known to us all.'

Kim did not know, but not for worlds would he have broken the thread.

'At Chitor, look you, I was all in Kings' country; for Kotah to the east is beyond the Queen's law, and east again lie Jeypur and Gwalior. Neither love spies, and there is no justice. I was hunted like a wet jackal; but I broke through at Bandakui, where I heard there was a charge against me of murder in the city I had left – of the murder of a boy. They have both the corpse and the witnesses waiting.'

'But cannot the Government protect?'

'We of the Game are beyond protection. If we die, we die. Our names are blotted from the book. That is all. At Bandakui, where lives one of us, I thought to slip the scent by changing my face, and so made me a Mahratta. Then I came to Agra, and would have turned back to Chitor to recover the letter. So sure I was I had slipped them. Therefore I did not send a *tar* (telegram) to anyone saying where the letter lay. I wished the credit of it all.'

Kim nodded. He understood that feeling well.

'But at Agra, walking in the streets, a man cried a debt against me, and approaching with many witnesses, would hale me to the courts then and there. Oh, they are clever in the South! He recognised me as his agent for cotton. May he burn in Hell for it!'

'And wast thou?'

'O fool! I was the man they sought for the matter of the letter! I ran into the Fleshers' Ward and came out by the House of the Jew, who feared a riot and pushed me forth. I came afoot to Somna Road – I had only money for my *tikkut* to Delhi – and there, while I lay in a ditch with a fever, one sprang out of the bushes and beat me and cut me and searched me from head to foot. Within earshot of the *te-rain* it was!'

'Why did he not slay thee out of hand?'

'They are not so foolish. If I am taken in Delhi at the instance of lawyers, upon a proven charge of murder, my body is handed over to the State that desires it. I go back guarded, and then – I die slowly for an example to the rest of us. The South is not my country. I run in circles – like a goat with one eye. I have not eaten for two days. I am marked' – he touched the filthy bandage on his leg – 'so that they will know me at Delhi.'

'Thou art safe in the te-*rain*, at least.'

'Live a year at the Great Game and tell me that again! The wires will be out against me at Delhi, describing every tear and rag upon me. Twenty – a hundred, if need be – will have seen me slay that boy. And thou art useless!'

Kim knew enough of native methods of attack not to doubt that the case would be deadly complete – even to the corpse. The Mahratta twitched his fingers with pain from time to time. The Kamboh in his corner glared sullenly; the lama was busy over his beads; and Kim, fumbling doctor-fashion at the man's neck, thought out his plan between invocations.

'Hast thou a charm to change my shape? Else I am dead. Five – ten minutes alone, if I had not been so pressed, and I might – '

'Is he cured yet, miracle-worker?' said the Kamboh jealously. 'Thou hast chanted long enough.'

'Nay. There is no cure for his hurts, as I see, except he sit for three days in the habit of a *bairagi*.' This is a common penance, often imposed on a fat trader by his spiritual teacher.

'One priest always goes about to make another priest,' was the retort. Like most grossly superstitious folk, the Kamboh could not keep his tongue from deriding his Church.

'Will thy son be a priest, then? It is time he took more of my quinine.'

'We Jats are all buffaloes,' said the Kamboh, softening anew.

Kim rubbed a finger-tip of bitterness on the child's trusting little lips. 'I have asked for nothing,' he said sternly to the father, 'except food. Dost thou grudge me that? I go to heal another man. Have I thy leave – Prince?'

Up flew the man's huge paws in supplication. 'Nay – nay. Do not mock me thus.'

'It pleases me to cure this sick one. Thou shalt acquire merit by aiding. What colour ash is there in thy pipe-bowl? White. That is auspicious. Was there raw turmeric among thy food-stuffs?'

'I – I – '

'Open thy bundle!'

It was the usual collection of small oddments: bits of cloth, quack medicines, cheap fairings, a clothful of *atta* – grayish, rough-ground native flour, – twists of down-country tobacco, tawdry pipe-stems, and a packet of curry-stuff, all wrapped in a quilt. Kim turned it over with the air of a wise warlock, muttering a Mohammedan invocation.

'This is wisdom I learned from the Sahibs,' he whispered to the lama; and here, when one thinks of his training at Lurgan's, he spoke no more than the truth. 'There is a great evil in this man's fortune, as shown by the stars, which – which troubles him. Shall I take it away?'

'Friend of the Stars, thou hast done well in all things. Let it be at thy pleasure. Is it another healing?'

'Quick! Be quick!' gasped the Mahratta. 'The train may stop.'

'A healing against the shadow of death,' said Kim, mixing the Kamboh's flour with the mingled charcoal and tobacco ash in the red-earth bowl of the pipe. E.23, without a word, slipped off his turban and shook down his long black hair.

'That is my food – priest,' the Jat growled.

'A buffalo in the temple! Hast thou dared to look even thus far?' said Kim. 'I must do mysteries before fools; but have a care for thy eyes. Is there a film before them already? I save the babe, and for return thou – oh, shameless!' The man flinched at the direct gaze, for Kim was wholly in earnest. 'Shall I curse thee, or shall I – ' He picked up the outer cloth of the bundle and threw it over the bowed head. 'Dare so much as to think a wish to see, and – and – even I cannot save thee. Sit! Be dumb!'

'I am blind – dumb. Forbear to curse! Co-come, child; we will play a game of hiding. Do not, for my sake, look from under the cloth.'

'I see hope,' said E.23. 'What is thy scheme?'

'This comes next,' said Kim, plucking the thin body-shirt. E.23 hesitated, with all a Norssth-West man's dislike of baring his body.

'What is caste to a cut throat?' said Kim, rending it to the waist. 'We must make thee a yellow Saddhu all over. Strip – strip swiftly, and shake thy hair over thy eyes while I scatter the ash. Now, a caste-mark on thy forehead.' He drew from his bosom the little Survey paint-box and a cake of crimson lake.

'Art thou only a beginner?' said E.23, labouring literally for the dear life, as he slid out of his body-wrappings and stood clear in the loin-cloth while Kim splashed in a noble caste-mark on the ash-smeared brow.

'But two days entered to the Game, brother,' Kim replied. 'Smear more ash on the bosom.'

'Hast thou met – a physician of sick pearls?' He switched out his long, tight-rolled turban-cloth and, with swiftest hands, rolled it over and under about his loins into the intricate devices of a Saddhu's cincture.

'Hah! Dost thou know his touch, then? He was my teacher for a while. We must bar thy legs. Ash cures wounds. Smear it again.'

'I was his pride once, but thou art almost better. The Gods are kind to us! Give me *that*.'

It was a tin box of opium pills among the rubbish of the Jat's bundle. E.23 gulped down a half handful. 'They are good against hunger, fear, and chill. And they make the eyes red too,' he explained. 'Now I shall have heart to play the Game. We lack only a Saddhu's tongs. What of the old clothes?'

Kim rolled them small, and stuffed them into the slack folds of his tunic. With a yellow-ochre paint cake he smeared the legs and breast, great streaks against the background of flour, ash, and turmeric.

'The blood on them is enough to hang thee, brother.'

'May be; but no need to throw them out of the window. . . . It is finished.' His voice thrilled with a boy's pure delight in the Game. 'Turn and look, O Jat!'

'The Gods protect us,' said the hooded Kamboh, emerging like a buffalo from the reeds. 'But – whither went the Mahratta? What hast thou done?'

Kim had been trained by Lurgan Sahib; and E.23, by virtue of his business, was no bad actor. In place of the tremulous, shrinking trader there lolled against the corner an all but naked, ash-smeared, ochre-barred, dusty-haired Saddhu, his swollen eyes – opium takes quick effect on an empty stomach – luminous with insolence and bestial lust, his legs crossed under him, Kim's brown rosary round his neck, and a scant yard of worn, flowered chintz on his shoulders. The child buried his face in his amazed father's arms.

'Look up, Princeling! We travel with warlocks, but they will not hurt thee. Oh, do not cry. . . . What is the sense of curing a child one day and killing him with fright the next?'

'The child will be fortunate all his life. He has seen a great healing. When I was a child I made clay men and horses.'

'I have made them too. Sir Banas, he comes in the night and makes them all alive at the back of our kitchen-midden,' piped the child.

'And so thou art not frightened at anything. Eh, Prince?'

'I was frightened because my father was frightened. I felt his arms shake.'

'Oh, chicken-man,' said Kim, and even the abashed Jat laughed. 'I have done a healing on this poor trader. He must forsake his gains and his account-books, and sit by the wayside three nights to overcome the malignity of his enemies. The Stars are against him.'

'The fewer money-lenders the better, say I; but, Saddhu or no Saddhu, he should pay for my stuff on his shoulders.'

'So? But that is thy child on thy shoulder – given over to the burning-ghat not two days ago. There remains one thing more. I did this charm in thy presence because need was great. I changed his shape and his soul. None the less, if, by any chance, O man from Jullundur, thou rememberest what thou hast seen, either among the elders sitting under the village tree, or in thy own house, or in company of thy priest when he blesses thy cattle, a murrain will come among the buffaloes, and a fire in thy thatch, and rats in the corn-bin, and the curse of our Gods upon thy fields that they may be barren before thy feet and after thy ploughshare.' This was part of an old curse picked up from a *faquir* by the Taksali Gate in the days of Kim's innocence. It lost nothing by repetition.

'Cease, Holy One! In mercy, cease!' cried the Jat. 'Do not curse the household. I saw nothing! I heard nothing! I am thy cow!' and he made to grab at Kim's bare foot beating rhythmically on the carriage floor.

'But since thou hast been permitted to aid me in the matter of a pinch of flour and a little opium and such trifles as I have honoured by using in my art, so will the Gods return a blessing,' and he gave it at length, to the man's immense relief. It was one that he had learned from Lurgan Sahib.

The lama stared through his spectacles as he had not stared at the business of disguisement.

'Friend of the Stars,' he said at last, 'thou hast acquired great wisdom. Beware that it do not give birth to pride. No man having the Law before his eyes speaks hastily of any matter which he has seen or encountered.'

'No – no – no indeed,' cried the farmer, fearful lest the master should be minded to improve on the pupil. E.23, with relaxed mouth, gave himself up to the opium that is meat, tobacco, and medicine to the spent Asiatic.

So, in a silence of awe and great miscomprehension, they slid into Delhi about lamp-lighting time.

CHAPTER 12

Who hath desired the Sea – the sight of salt-water
unbounded?
The heave and the halt and the hurl and the crash of
the comber wind-hounded?
The sleek-barrelled swell before storm – gray,
foamless, enormous, and growing?
Stark calm on the lap of the Line – or the crazy-eyed
hurricane blowing?
His Sea in no showing the same – his Sea and the
same 'neath all showing – '
His Sea that his being fulfils?
So and no otherwise – so and no otherwise Hill-men
desire their Hills!

'I HAVE found my heart again,' said E.23, under cover of the platform's tumult. 'Hunger and fear make men dazed, or I might have thought of this escape before. I was right. They come to hunt for me. Thou hast saved my head.'

A group of yellow-trousered Punjab policemen, headed by a hot and perspiring young Englishman, parted the crowd about the carriages. Behind them, inconspicuous as a cat, ambled a small fat person who looked like a lawyer's tout.

'See the young Sahib reading from a paper. My description is in his hand,' said E.23. 'They go carriage by carriage, like fisher-folk netting a pool.'

When the procession reached their compartment, E.23 was counting his beads with a steady jerk of the wrist; while Kim jeered at him for being so drugged as to have lost the ringed fire-tongs which are the Saddhu's distinguishing mark. The lama, deep in meditation, stared straight before him; and the farmer, glancing furtively, gathered up his belongings.

'Nothing here but a parcel of holy-bolies,' said the Englishman aloud, and passed on amid a ripple of uneasiness; for native police mean extortion to the native all India over.

'The trouble now,' whispered E.23, 'lies in sending a wire as to the place where I hid that letter I was sent to find. I cannot go to the *tar*-office in this guise.'

'Is it not enough I have saved thy neck?'

'Not if the work be left unfinished. Did never the healer of sick pearls tell thee so? Comes another Sahib! Ah!'

This was a tallish, sallowish District Superintendent of Police – belt, helmet, polished spurs and all – strutting and twirling his dark moustache.

'What fools are these Police Sahibs!' said Kim genially.

E.23 glanced up under his eyelids. 'It is well said,' he muttered in a changed voice. 'I go to drink water. Keep my place.'

He blundered out almost into the Englishman's arms, and was bad-worded in clumsy Urdu.

'*Tum mut*? You drunk? You mustn't bang about as though Delhi station belonged to you, my friend.'

E.23, not moving a muscle of his countenance, answered with a stream of the filthiest abuse, at which Kim naturally rejoiced. It reminded him of the drummer-boys and the barrack-sweepers at Umballa in the terrible time of his first schooling.

'My good fool,' the Englishman drawled. '*Nickle-jao!* Go back to your carriage.'

Step by step, withdrawing deferentially, and dropping his voice, the yellow Saddhu clomb back to the carriage, cursing the D. S. P. to remotest posterity by – here Kim almost jumped – by the curse of the Queen's Stone, by the writing under the Queen's Stone, and by an assortment of Gods with wholly new names.

'I don't know what you're saying' – the Englishman flushed angrily – 'but it's some piece of blasted impertinence. Come out of that!'

E.23, affecting to misunderstand, gravely produced his ticket, which the Englishman wrenched angrily from his hand.

'Oh *zoolum*! What oppression!' growled the Jat from his corner. 'All for the sake of a jest too.' He had been grinning at the freedom of the Saddhu's tongue. 'Thy charms do not work well to-day, Holy One!'

The Saddhu followed the policeman, fawning and supplicating. The ruck of passengers, busy with their babies and their bundles, had not noticed the affair. Kim slipped out behind him; for it flashed through his head that he had heard this angry, stupid Sahib discoursing loud personalities to an old lady near Umballa three years ago.

'It is well,' the Saddhu whispered, jammed in the calling, shouting, bewildered press – a Persian greyhound between his feet and a cadgeful of yelling hawks under charge of a Rajput falconer in the small of his back. 'He has gone now to send word of the letter which I hid. They told me he was in Peshawur. I might have known that he is like the crocodile – always at the other ford. He has saved me from present calamity, but I owe my life to thee.'

'Is he also one of Us?' Kim ducked under a Mewar camel-driver's greasy armpit and cannoned off a covey of jabbering Sikh matrons.

'Not less than the greatest. We are both fortunate! I will make report to him of what thou hast done. I am safe under his protection.'

He bored through the edge of the crowd besieging the carriages, and squatted by the bench near the telegraph-office.

'Return, or they take thy place! Have no fear for the work, brother – or my life. Thou hast given me breathing-space, and Strickland Sahib has pulled me to land. We may work together at the Game yet. Farewell!'

Kim hurried to his carriage: elated, bewildered, but a little nettled in that he had no key to the secrets about him.

'I am only a beginner at the Game, that is sure. *I* could not have leaped into safety as did the Saddhu. He knew it was darkest under the lamp. *I* could not have thought to tell news under pretence of cursing. . . . and how clever was the Sahib! No matter, I saved the life of one. . . . Where is the Kamboh gone, Holy One?' he whispered, as he took his seat in the now crowded compartment.

'A fear gripped him,' the lama replied, with a touch of tender malice. 'He saw thee change the Mahratta to a Saddhu in the twinkling of an eye, as a protection against evil. That shook him. Then he saw the Saddhu fall sheer into the hands of the *polis* – all the effect of thy art. Then he gathered up his son and fled; for he said that thou didst change a quiet trader into an impudent bandier of words with the Sahibs, and he feared a like fate. Where is the Saddhu?'

'With the *polis*,' said Kim.... 'Yet I saved the Kamboh's child.'

The lama snuffed blandly.

'Ah, *chela,* see how thou art overtaken! Thou didst cure the Kamboh's child solely to acquire merit. But thou didst put a spell on the Mahratta with prideful workings – I watched thee – and with side-long glances to bewilder an old old man and a foolish farmer: whence calamity and suspicion.'

Kim controlled himself with an effort beyond his years. Not more than any other youngster did he like to eat dirt or to be misjudged, but he saw himself in a cleft stick. The train rolled out of Delhi into the night.

'It is true,' he murmured. 'Where I have offended thee I have done wrong.'

'It is more, *chela.* Thou hast loosed an Act upon the world, and as a stone thrown into a pool so spread the consequences thou canst not tell how far.'

This ignorance was well both for Kim's vanity and for the lama's peace of mind, when we think that there was then being handed in at Simla a code-wire reporting the arrival of E.23 at Delhi, and, more important, the whereabouts of a letter he had been commissioned to – abstract. Incidentally, an over-zealous policeman had arrested, on charge of murder done in a far southern State, a horribly indignant Ajmir cotton-broker, who was explaining himself to a Mr. Strickland on Delhi platform, while E.23 was paddling through by-ways into the locked heart of Delhi city. In two hours several telegrams had reached the angry minister of a southern State reporting that all trace of a somewhat bruised Mahratta had been lost; and by the time the leisurely train halted at Saharunpore the last ripple of the stone Kim had helped to heave was lapping against the steps of a mosque in far-away Roum – where it disturbed a pious man at prayers.

The lama made his in ample form near the dewy bougainvillea-trellis near the platform, cheered by the clear sunshine and the presence of his disciple. 'We will put these things behind us,' he said, indicating the brazen engine and the gleaming track. 'The jolting of the *te-rain* – though a wonderful thing – has turned my bones to water. We will use clean air henceforward.'

'Let us go to the Kulu woman's house,' said Kim, and stepped forth cheerily under the bundles. Early morning Saharunpore-way is clean and well scented. He thought of the other mornings at St. Xavier's, and it topped his already thrice-heaped contentment.

'Where is this new haste born from? Wise men do not run about like chickens in the sun. We have come hundreds upon hundreds of *kôs* already, and, till now, I have scarcely been alone with thee an instant. How canst thou receive instruction all jostled of crowds? How can I, whelmed by a flux of talk, meditate upon the Way?'

'Her tongue grows no shorter with the years, then?' The disciple smiled.

'Nor her desire for charms. I remember once when I spoke of the Wheel of Life' – the lama fumbled in his bosom for his latest copy – 'she was only curious about the devils that besiege children. She shall acquire merit by entertaining us – in a little while – at an after-occasion – softly, softly. Now we will wander loose-foot, waiting upon the Chain of Things. The Search is sure.'

So they travelled very easily across and among the broad bloomful fruit-gardens – by way of Aminabad, Sahaigunge, Akrola of the Ford, and little Phulesa – the line of the Sewaliks always to the north, and behind them again the snows. After long, sweet sleep under the dry stars came the lordly, leisurely passage through a waking village – begging-bowl held forth in silence, but eyes roving in defiance of the Law from sky's edge to sky's edge. Then would Kim return soft-footed through the soft dust to his master under the shadow of a mango tree or the thinner shade of a white Doon *siris*, to eat and drink at ease. At mid-day, after talk and a little wayfaring, they slept; meeting the world refreshed when the air was cooler. Night found them adventuring into new territory – some chosen village spied three hours before across the fat land, and much discussed upon the road.

There they told their tale, – a new one each evening so far as Kim was concerned, – and there were they made welcome, either by priest or headman, after the custom of the kindly East.

When the shadows shortened and the lama leaned more heavily upon Kim, there was always the Wheel of Life to draw forth, to hold flat under wiped stones, and with a long straw to expound cycle by cycle. Here sat the Gods on high – and they were dreams of dreams. Here was our Heaven and the world of the demi-Gods – horsemen fighting among the hills. Here were the agonies done upon the beasts, souls ascending or descending the ladder and therefore not to be interfered with. Here were the Hells, hot and cold, and the abodes of tormented ghosts. Let the *chela* study the troubles that come from over-eating – bloated stomach and burning bowels. Obediently then, with bowed head and brown finger alert to follow the pointer, did the *chela* study; but when they came to the Human World, busy and profitless, that is just above the Hells, his mind was distracted; for by the roadside trundled the very Wheel itself, eating, drinking, trading, marrying, and quarrelling – all warmly alive. Often the lama made the living pictures the matter of his text, bidding Kim – too ready – note how the flesh takes a thousand thousand shapes, desirable or detestable as men reckon, but in truth of no account either way; and how the stupid spirit, bond-slave to the Hog, the Dove, and the Serpent – lusting after betel-nut, a new yoke of oxen, women, or the favour of kings – is bound to follow the body through all the Heavens and all the Hells, and strictly round again. Some-times a woman or a poor man, watching the ritual – it was nothing less – when the great yellow chart was unfolded, would throw a few flowers or a handful of cowries upon its edge. It sufficed these humble ones that they had met a Holy One who might be moved to remember them in his prayers.

'Cure them if they are sick,' said the lama, when Kim's sporting instincts woke. 'Cure them if they have fever, but by no means work charms. Remember what befell the Mahratta.'

'Then all Doing is evil?' Kim replied, lying out under a big tree at the fork of the Doon road, watching the little ants run over his hand.

'To abstain from action is well – except to acquire merit.'

'At the Gates of Learning we were taught that to abstain from action was unbefitting a Sahib. And I am a Sahib.'

'Friend of all the World,'– the lama looked directly at Kim, – 'I am an old man – pleased with shows as are children. To those who follow the Way there is neither black nor white, Hind nor Bhotiyal. We be all souls seeking escape. No matter what thy wisdom learned among Sahibs, when we come to my River thou wilt be freed from all illusion – at my side. Hai! my bones ache for that River, as they ached in the *te-rain*; but my spirit sits above my bones, waiting. The Search is sure!'

'I am answered. Is it permitted to ask a question?'

The lama inclined his stately head.

'I ate thy bread for three years – as thou knowest. Holy One, whence came –?'

'There is much wealth, as men count it, in Bhotiyal,' the lama returned with composure. 'In my own place I have the illusion of honour. I ask for that I need. I am not concerned with the account. That is for my monastery. Ai! The black high seats in the monastery, and the novices all in order!'

And he told stories, tracing with a finger in the dust, of the immense and sumptuous ritual of avalanche-guarded cathedrals; of processions and devil-dances; of the changing of monks and nuns into swine; of holy cities fifteen thousand feet in the air; of intrigue between monastery and monastery;

of voices among the hills, and of that mysterious mirage that dances on dry snow. He spoke even of Lhassa and of the Dalai Lama, whom he had seen and adored.

Each long, perfect day rose behind Kim for a barrier to cut him off from his race and his mother-tongue. He slipped back to thinking and dreaming in the vernacular, and mechanically followed the lama's ceremonial observances at eating, drinking, and the like. The old man's mind turned more and more to his monastery as his eyes turned to the steadfast snows. His River troubled him nothing. Now and again, indeed, he would gaze long and long at a tuft or a twig, expecting, he said, the earth to cleave and deliver its blessing; but he was content to be with his disciple, at ease in the temperate wind that comes down from the Doon. This was not Ceylon, nor Buddh Gaya, nor Bombay, nor some grass-tangled ruins that he seemed to have stumbled upon two years ago. He spoke of those places as a scholar removed from vanity, as a Seeker walking in humility, as an old man, wise and temperate, illumining knowledge with brilliant insight. Bit by bit, disconnectedly, each tale called up by some wayside thing, he spoke of all his wanderings up and down Hind; till Kim, who had loved him without reason, now loved him for fifty good reasons. So they enjoyed themselves in high felicity, abstaining, as the Rule demands, from evil words, covetous desires; not over-eating, not lying on high beds, nor wearing rich clothes. Their stomachs told them the time, and the people brought them their food, as the saying is. They were lords of the villages of Aminabad, Sahaigunge, Akrola of the Ford, and little Phulesa, where Kim gave the soulless woman a blessing.

But news travels fast in India, and too soon shuffled across the crop-land, bearing a basket of fruits with a box of Kabul grapes and gilt oranges, a white-whiskered servitor – a lean, dry Oorya – begging them to bring the honour of their presence to his mistress, distressed in her mind that the lama had neglected her so long.

'Now do I remember' – the lama spoke as though it were a wholly new proposition. 'She is virtuous, but an inordinate talker.'

Kim was sitting on the edge of a cow's manger, telling stories to a village smith's children.

'She will only ask for another son for her daughter. I have not forgotten her,' he said. 'Let her acquire merit. Send word that we will come.'

'They covered eleven miles through the fields in two days, and were overwhelmed with attentions at the end; for the old lady held a fine tradition of hospitality, to which she forced her son-in-law, who was under the thumb of his women-folk and brought peace by borrowing of the money-lender. Age had not weakened her tongue or her memory, and from a discreetly barred upper window, in the hearing of not less than a dozen servants, she paid Kim compliments that would have flung European audiences into unclean dismay.

'But thou art still the shameless beggar-brat of the *parao*,' she shrilled. 'I have not forgotten thee. Wash ye and eat. The father of my daughter's son is gone away awhile. So we poor women are dumb and useless.'

For proof, she harangued the entire household unsparingly till food and drink were brought; and in the evening – the smoke-scented evening, copper-dun and turquoise across the fields – it pleased her to order her palanquin to be set down in the untidy forecourt by smoky torch-light; and there, behind not too closely drawn curtains, she gossiped.

'Had the Holy One come alone, I should have received him otherwise; but with this rogue, who can be too careful?'

'Maharanee,' said Kim, choosing as always the amplest title, 'is it my fault that none other than a Sahib – a *polis*-sahib – called the Maharanee whose face he – '

'Chitt! That was on the pilgrimage. When we travel – thou knowest the proverb.'

'Called the Maharanee a Breaker of Hearts and a Dispenser of Delights?'

'To remember that! It was true. So he did. That was in the time of the bloom of my beauty.' She chuckled like a contented parrot above the sugar lump. 'Now tell me of thy goings and comings – as much as may be without shame. How many maids, and whose wives, hang upon thy eyelashes? Ye hail from Benares? I would have gone there again this year, but my daughter – we have only two sons. Phaii! Such is the effect of these low plains. Now in Kulu men are elephants. But I would ask thy Holy One – stand aside, rogue – a charm against most lamentable windy colics that in mango-time overtake my daughter's eldest. Two years back he gave me a powerful spell.'

'Oh, Holy One!' said Kim, bubbling with mirth at the lama's rueful face.

'It is true. I gave her one against wind.'

'Teeth – teeth – teeth,' snapped the old woman.

'Cure them when they are sick,' Kim quoted relishingly, 'but by no means work charms. Remember what befell the Mahratta.'

'That was two Rains ago; she wearied me with her continual importunity.' The lama groaned as the Unjust Judge had groaned before him. 'Thus it comes – take note, my *chela* – that even those who would follow the Way are thrust aside by idle women. Three days through, when the child was sick, she talked to me.'

'Arré! and to whom else should I talk? The boy's mother knew nothing, and the father – in the nights of the cold weather it was – "Pray to the Gods," said he, forsooth, and turning over, snored!'

'I gave her the charm. What is an old man to do?'

' "To abstain from action is well – except when we acquire merit." '

'Ah, *chela*, if thou desertest me, I am all alone.'

'He found his milk-teeth easily at any rate,' said the old lady. 'But all priests are alike.'

Kim coughed severely. Being young, he did not approve of her flippancy. 'To importune the wise out of season is to invite calamity.'

'There is a talking *mynah*' – the thrust came back with the well-remembered snap of the jewelled fore-finger – 'over the stables which has picked up the very tone of the family-priest. Maybe I forget honour to my guests, but if ye had seen *him* double his fists into his belly, which was like a half-grown gourd, and cry: "Here is the pain!" ye would forgive. I am half minded to take the *hakim*'s medicine. He sells it cheap, and certainly it makes him fat as Shiv's own bull. *He* does not deny remedies, but I doubted for the child because of the inauspicious colour of the bottles.'

The lama, under cover of the monologue, had faded out into the darkness towards the room prepared.

'Thou hast angered him, belike,' said Kim.

'Not he. He is wearied, and I forgot, being a grandmother. (None but a grandmother should ever oversee a child. Mothers are only fit for bearing.) To-morrow, when he sees how my daughter's son is grown, he will write the charm. Then, too, he can judge of the new *hakim*'s drugs.'

'Who is the *hakim*, Maharanee?'

'A wanderer, as thou art, but a most sober Bengali from Dacca – a master of medicine. He relieved me of an oppression after meat by means of a small pill that wrought like a devil unchained. He travels about now, vending preparations of great value. He has even papers, printed in Angrezi, telling what things he has done for weak-backed men and slack women. He has been here four days; but hearing ye were coming (*hakims* and priests are snake and tiger the world over) he has, as I take it, gone to cover.'

While she drew breath after this volley, the ancient servant, sitting unrebuked on the edge of the torch-light, muttered: – 'This house is a cattle-pound, as it were, for all charlatans and – priests. Let the boy stop eating mangoes. . . . but who can argue with a grandmother?' He raised his voice respectfully: 'Sahiba, the *hakim* sleeps after his meat. He is in the quarters behind the dovecot.'

Kim bristled like an expectant terrier. To outface and down-talk a Calcutta-taught Bengali, a voluble Dacca drug-vendor, would be a good game. It was not seemly that the lama, and incidentally himself, should be thrown aside for such an one. He knew those curious bastard English advertisements at the backs of native newspapers. St. Xavier's boys sometimes brought them in by stealth to snigger over among their mates; for the language of the grateful patient recounting his symptoms is most simple and revealing. The Oorya, not unanxious to play off one parasite against the other, slunk away towards the dovecot.

'Yes,' said Kim, with measured scorn. 'Their stock-in-trade is a little coloured water and a very great shamelessness. Their prey are broken-down kings and overfed Bengalis. Their profit is in children – who are not born.'

The old lady chuckled. 'Do not be envious. Charms are better, eh? *I* never gainsaid it. See that thy Holy One writes me a good amulet by the morning.'

'None but the ignorant deny' – a thick, heavy voice boomed through the darkness, as a figure came to rest squatting – 'None but the ignorant deny the value of charms. None but the ignorant deny the value of medicines.'

'A rat found a piece of turmeric. Said he: "I will open a grocer's shop," ' Kim retorted.

Battle was fairly joined now, and they heard the old lady stiffen to attention.

'The priest's son knows the names of his nurse and three Gods. Says he: "Hear me, or I will curse you by the three million Great Ones." ' Decidedly this invisible had an arrow or two in his quiver. He went on: 'I am but a teacher of the alphabet. I have learned all the wisdom of the Sahibs.'

'The Sahibs never grow old. They dance and they play like children when they are grandfathers. A strong-backed breed,' piped the voice inside the palanquin.

'I have, too, our drugs which loosen humours of the head in hot and angry men. *Siná* well compounded when the moon stands in the proper House; yellow earths I have – *arplan* from China that makes a man to renew his youth and astonish his household; saffron from Kashmir, and the best salep of Cabul. Many people have died before – '

'That I surely believe,' said Kim.

'They knew the value of my drugs. I do not give *my* sick the mere ink in which a charm is written, but hot and rending drugs which descend and wrestle with the evil.'

'Very mightily they do so,' sighed the old lady.

The voice launched into an immense tale of misfortune and bankruptcy, studded with plentiful petitions to the Government. 'But for my fate, which overrules all, I had been now in Government employ. I bear a degree from the great school at Calcutta – whither, maybe, the son of this house shall go.'

'He shall indeed. If our neighbour's brat can in a few years be made an F.A.' (First Arts – she used the English word, of which she had heard so often), 'how much more shall children clever as some that I know bear away prizes at rich Calcutta.'

'Never,' said the voice, 'have I seen such a child! Born in an auspicious hour, and – but for that colic which, alas! turning into black cholers, may carry him off like a pigeon – destined to many years, he is enviable.'

'*Hai mai*!' said the old lady. 'To praise children is inauspicious, or I could listen to this talk. But the back of the house is unguarded, and even in this soft air men think themselves to be men and women we know. . . . The child's father is away too, and I must be *chowkedar* (watchman) in my old age. Up! Up! Take up the palanquin. Let the *hakim* and the young priest settle between them whether charms or medicine most avail. Ho! worthless people, fetch tobacco for the guests, and – round the homestead go I!'

The palanquin reeled off, followed by straggling torches and a horde of dogs. Twenty villages knew the Sahiba – her failings, her tongue, and her large charity. Twenty villages cheated her after immemorial custom, but no man would have stolen or robbed within her jurisdiction for any gift under Heaven. None the less, she made great parade of her formal inspections, the riot of which could be heard half-way to Mussoorie.

Kim relaxed, as one augur must when he meets another. The *hakim*, still squatting, slid over his hookah with a friendly foot, and Kim pulled at the good weed. The hangers-on expected grave professional debate, and perhaps a little free doctoring.

'To discuss medicine before the ignorant is of one piece with teaching the peacock to sing,' said the *hakim*.

'True courtesy,' Kim echoed, 'is very often inattention.'

These, be it understood, were company-manners, designed to impress.

'Hi! I have an ulcer on my leg,' cried a scullion. 'Look at it!'

'Get hence! Remove!' said the hakim. 'Is it the habit of the place to pester honoured guests? Ye crowd in like buffaloes.'

'If the Sahiba knew – ' Kim began.

'Ai! Ai! Come away. They are meat for our mistress. When her young Shaitan's colics are cured perhaps we poor people may be suffered to – '

'The mistress fed thy wife when thou wast in jail for breaking the money-lender's head. Who speaks against her?' The old servitor curled his white moustaches savagely in the young moonlight. '*I* am responsible for the honour of this house. Go!' and he drove the underlings before him.

Said the *hakim*, hardly more than shaping the words with his lips: 'How do you do, Mr. O'Hara? I am jolly glad to see you again.'

Kim's hand clenched about the pipe-stem. Anywhere on the open road, perhaps, he would not have been astonished; but here, in this quiet backwater of life, he was not prepared for Hurree Babu. It annoyed him, too, that he had been hoodwinked.

'Ah ha! I told you at Lucknow – *resurgam* – I shall rise again and you shall not know me. How much did you bet – eh?'

He chewed leisurely upon a few cardamom seeds, but he breathed uneasily.

'But why come here, Babuji?'

'Ah! *Thatt* is the question, as Shakespeare hath said. I come to congratulate you on your extraordinary effeecient performance at Delhi. Oah! I tell you we are all proud of you. It was verree neat and handy. Our mutual friend, he is old friend of mine. He has been in some dam-tight places. Now he will be in some more. He told me; I tell Mr. Lurgan; and he is pleased you graduate so nicely. All the Department is pleased.'

For the first time in his life, Kim thrilled to the clean pride (it can be a deadly pitfall, none the less) of Departmental praise – ensnaring praise from an equal of work appreciated by fellow-workers. Earth has nothing on the same plane to compare with it. But, cried the Oriental in him, Babus do not travel far to retail compliments.

'Tell thy tale, Babu,' he said authoritatively.

'Oah, it is nothing. Onlee I was at Simla when the wire came in about what our mutual friend said he had hidden, and old Creighton – ' He looked to see how Kim would take this piece of audacity.

'The Colonel Sahib,' the boy from St. Xavier's corrected.

'*Of* course. He found me at a loose string, and I had to go down to Chitor to find that beastly letter. I do not like the South – too much railway travel; but I drew good travelling allowance. Ha! Ha! I meet our mutual at Delhi on the way back. He lies quiett just now, and says Saddhu-disguise suits him to the ground. Well, there I hear what you have done so well, so quickly, upon the instantaneous spur of the moment. I tell our mutual friend you take the bally bun, by Jove! It was splendid. I come to tell you so.'

'Umm!'

The frogs were busy in the ditches, and the moon slid to her setting. Some happy servant had gone out to commune with the night and to beat upon a drum. Kim's next sentence was in the vernacular.

'How didst thou follow us?'

'Oah. Thatt was nothing. I know from our mutual friend you go to Saharunpore. So I come on. Red lamas are not inconspicuous persons. I buy myself my drug-box, and I am very good doctor really. I go to Akrola by the Ford, and hear all about you, and I talk here and talk there. All the common people know what you do. I know when the hospitable old lady sent the *dooli*. They have great recollections of the old lama's visits here. I know old ladies cannot keep their hands from medicines. So I am a doctor, and – you hear my talk? *I* think it is verree good. My word, Mister O'Hara, they know about you and the lama for fifty miles – the common people. So I come. Do you mind?'

'Babuji,' said Kim, looking up at the broad, grinning face, 'I am a Sahib.'

'My dear Mister O'Hara – '

'And I hope to play the Great Game.'

'You are subordinate to me departmentally at present.'

'Then why talk like an ape up in a tree? Men do not come after one from Simla and change their dress, for the sake of a few sweet words. I am not a child. Talk Hindi and let us get to the yolk of the egg. Thou art here – speaking not one word of truth in ten. Why art thou here? Give a straight answer.'

'That is so verree disconcerting of the European, Mister O'Hara. *You* should know a heap better at your time of life.'

'But I want to know,' said Kim, laughing. If it is the Game, I may help. How can I do anything if you *bukh* (babble) all round the shop.'

Hurree Babu reached for the pipe, and sucked it till it guggled again.

'Now I will speak vernacular. You sit tight, Mister O'Hara. . . . It concerns the pedigree of a white stallion.'

'Still? That was finished long ago.'

'When every one is dead the Great Game is finished. Not before. Listen to me till the end. There were Five Kings who prepared a sudden war three years ago, when thou wast given the stallion's pedigree by Mahbub Ali. Upon them, because of that news, and ere they were ready, fell our Army.'

'Ay – eight thousand men with guns. I remember that night.'

'But the war was not pushed. That is the Government custom. The troops were recalled because the Government believed the Five Kings were cowed; and it is not cheap to feed men among the high Passes. Hilás and Bunár – Rajahs with guns – undertook for a price to guard the passes against all coming from the North. They protested both fear and friendship.' He broke off with a giggle into English: 'Of course, I tell you this unoffeecially to elucidate political situation, Mister O'Hara. Offeecially, I am debarred from criticising any action of superior. Now I go on. – This pleased the Government, anxious to avoid expense, and a bond was made for so many rupees a month that Hilás and Bunár should guard the Passes as soon as the State's troops were withdrawn. At that time – it was after we two met – I, who had been selling tea in Leh, became a clerk of accounts in the Army. When the troops were withdrawn, I was left behind to pay the coolies who made new roads in the Hills. This road-making was part of the bond between Bunár, Hilás, and the Government.'

'So; and then?'

'I tell you, it was jolly beastly cold up there too, after summer,' said Hurree Babu confidentially. 'I was afraid these Bunár men would cut my throat every night for thee pay-chest. My native sepoy-guard, they laughed at me! By Jove! I was such a fearful man! Nevar mind thatt. I go on colloquially. . . . I send word many times that these two Kings were sold to the North; and Mahbub Ali, who was yet farther north, amply confirmed it. Nothing was done. Only my feet were frozen, and a toe dropped off. I sent word that the roads for which I was paying money to the diggers were being made for the feet of strangers and enemies.'

'For?'

'For the Russians. The thing was an open jest among the coolies. Then I was called down to tell what I knew by speech of tongue. Mahbub came South too. See the end! Over the Passes this year after snow-melting' – he shivered afresh – 'come two strangers under cover of shooting wild goats. They bear guns, but they bear also chains and levels and compasses.'

'Oho! The thing gets clearer.'

'They are well received by Hilás and Bunár. They make great promises; they speak as the mouthpiece of a Kaisar, with gifts. Up the valleys, down the valleys go they, saying, "Here is a place to build a breastwork; here can ye pitch a fort. Here can ye hold the road against an army" – the very roads for which I paid out the rupees monthly. The Government knows, but does nothing. The three other Kings, who were *not* paid for guarding the Passes, tell them by runner of the bad faith of Bunár and Hilás. When all the evil is done, look you – when these two strangers with the levels and the compasses make the Five Kings to believe that a great army will sweep the Passes to-morrow or the next day – Hill-people are all fools – comes the order to me, Hurree Babu "Go North and see what those strangers do." I say to Creighton Sahib, "This is not a lawsuit, that we go about to collect evidence." ' Hurree returned to his English with a jerk: ' "By Jove," I said, "why the dooce do you not issue demi-offeecial orders to some brave man to poison them, for an example? It is, if you permit the observation, most reprehensible laxity on your part." And Colonel Creighton, he laughed at me! It is all your beastly English pride. You think no one dare conspire! That is all tommy-rott.'

Kim smoked slowly, revolving the business, so far as he understood it, in his quick mind.

'Then thou goest forth to follow the strangers?'

'No; to meet them. They are coming in to Simla to send down their horns and heads to be dressed at Calcutta. They are exclusively sporting gentlemen, and they are allowed special faceelities by the Government. Of course, we always do that. It is our British pride.'

'Then what is to fear from them?'

'By Jove, they are not black people. I can do all sorts of things with black people, of course. They are Russians, and highly unscrupulous people. I – I do not want to consort with them without a witness.'

'Will they kill thee?'

'Oah, thatt is nothing. I am good enough Herbert Spencerian, I trust, to meet little thing like death, which is all in my fate, you know. But – but they may beat me.'

'Why?'

Hurree Babu snapped his fingers with irritation. 'Of *course* I shall affeeliate myself to their camp in supernumerary capacity as perhaps interpreter, or person mentally impotent and hungree, or some such thing. And then I must pick up what I can, I suppose. That is as easy for me as playing Mister Doctor to the old lady. Onlee – onlee – you see, Mister O'Hara, I am unfortunately Asiatic, which is serious detrimnent in some respects. And *all*so I am Bengali – a fearful man.'

'God made the Hare and the Bengali. What shame?' said Kim, quoting the proverb.

'It was process of Evolution, *I* think, from Primal Necessity, but the fact remains in all its *cui bono*.* I am, oh, awfully fearful! – I remember once they wanted to cut off my head on the road to Lhassa. (No, I have never reached to Lhassa.) I sat down and cried, Mister O'Hara, anticipating Chinese tortures. I do not suppose these two gentlemen will torture me, but I like to provide for possible contingency with European assistance in emergency.' He coughed and spat out his cardamoms. 'It is purely unoffeecial indent, to which you can say, "No, Babu." If you have no pressing engagement with your old man – perhaps you might divert him; perhaps I can seduce his fancies – I should like you to keep in Departmental touch with me till I find those sporting coves. I have great opeenion of you since I met my friend at Delhi. And also I will embody your name in my offeecial report when matter is finally adjudicated. It will be a great feather in your cap. That is why I come really.'

'Humph! The end of the tale, I think, is true; but what of the fore-part?'

'About the Five Kings? Oah! there is ever so much truth in it. A lots more than you would suppose,' said Hurree earnestly. 'You come – eh? I go from here straight into the Doon. It is verree verdant and painted meads. I shall go to Mussoorie – to good old Mussoorie Pahar, as the gentlemen and ladies say. Then by Rampur into Chini. That is the only way they can come. I do not like waiting in the cold, but we must wait for them. I want to walk with them to Simla. You see, one Russian is a Frenchman, and I know my French pretty well. I have friends in Chandernagore.'

* A principle that the responsibility for an act or event possibly lies with the one having something to gain.

'*He* would certainly rejoice to see the Hills again,' said Kim meditatively. "All his speech these ten days past has been of little else. If we go together – '

'Oah! We can be quite strangers on the road, if your lama prefers. I shall just be four or five miles ahead. There is no hurry for Hurree. That is an Europe pun, ha! ha! – and you come after. There is plenty of time; they will plot and survey and map of course. I shall go to-morrow, and you the next day, if you choose. Eh? You go think on it till morning. By Jove, it is near morning now.' He yawned ponderously, and with never a civil word lumbered off to his sleeping-place. But Kim slept little, and his thoughts ran in Hindustanee:

'Well is the Game called great! I was four days a scullion at Quetta, waiting on the wife of the man whose book I stole. And that was part of the Great Game! From the South – God knows how far – came up the Mahratta, playing the Great Game in fear of his life. Now I shall go far and far into the North playing the Great Game. Truly, it runs like a shuttle throughout all Hind. And my share and my joy' – he smiled to the darkness – 'I owe to the lama here. Also to Mahbub Ali – also to Creighton Sahib, but chiefly to the Holy One. He is right – a great and a wonderful world – and I am Kim – Kim – Kim – alone – one person – in the middle of it all. But I will see these strangers with their levels and chains. . . .'

'What was the upshot of last night's babble?' said the lama, after his orisons.

'There came a strolling seller of drugs – a hanger-on of the Sahiba's. Him I abolished by arguments and prayers, proving that our charms are worthier than his coloured waters.'

'Alas! my charms. Is the virtuous woman still bent upon a new one?'

'Very strictly.'

'Then it must be written, or she will deafen me with her clamour.' He fumbled at his pen-case.

'In the Plains,' said Kim, 'are always too many people. In the Hills, as I understand, there are fewer.'

'Oh! the Hills, and the snow upon the Hills.' The lama tore off a tiny square of paper fit to go in an amulet. 'But what dost thou know of the Hills?'

'They are very close.' Kim thrust open the door and looked at the long, peaceful line of the Himalayas flushed in morning-gold. 'Except in the dress of a Sahib, I have never set foot among them.'

The lama snuffed the wind wistfully.

'If we go north,' – Kim put the question to the waking sunrise, – 'would not much mid-day heat be avoided by walking among the lower hills at least?. . . . Is the charm made, Holy One?'

'I have written the names of seven silly devils – not one of whom is worth a grain of dust in the eye. Thus do foolish women drag us from the Way!'

Hurree Babu come out from behind the dovecot, washing his teeth with ostentatious ritual. Full-fleshed, heavy-haunched, bull-necked, and deep-voiced, he did not look like 'a fearful man.' Kim signed almost imperceptibly that matters were in good train, and when the morning toilet was over Hurree Babu, in flowery speech, came to do honour to the lama. They ate, of course, apart, and afterwards the old lady, more or less veiled behind a window, returned to the vital business of green-mango colics in the young. The lama's knowledge of medicine was of course sympathetic only. He believed that the dung of a black horse, mixed with sulphur, and carried in a snake-skin, was a sound remedy for cholera;

but the symbolism interested him far more than the science. Hurree Babu deferred to these views with enchanting politeness, so that the lama called him a courteous physician. Hurree Babu replied that he was no more than an inexpert dabbler in the mysteries; but at least – he thanked the Gods therefore – he knew when he sat in the presence of a master. He himself had been taught by the Sahibs, who do not consider expense, in the lordly halls of Calcutta; but, as be was ever first to acknowledge, there lay a wisdom behind earthly wisdom – the high and lonely lore of meditation. Kim looked on with envy. The Hurree Babu of his knowledge – oily, effusive, and nervous – was gone; gone too was the brazen drug-vendor of overnight. There remained – polished, polite, attentive – a sober, learned son of experience and adversity, gathering wisdom from the lama's lips. The old lady confided to Kim that these rare levels were beyond her. She liked charms with plenty of ink that one could wash off in water, swallow, and be done with. Else what was the use of the Gods? She liked men and women, and she spoke of them – of kinglets she had known in the past; of her own youth and beauty; of the depredations of leopards and the eccentricities of love Asiatic; of the incidence of taxation, rack-renting, funeral ceremonies, her son-in-law (this by allusion, easy to be followed), the care of the young, and the age's lack of decency. And Kim, as interested in the life of this world as she soon to leave it, squatted with his feet under the hem of his robe, drinking all in, while the lama demolished one after another every theory of body-curing put forward by Hurree Babu.

At noon the Babu strapped up his brass-bound drug-box, took his patent-leather shoes of ceremony in one hand, a gay blue and white umbrella in the other, and set off northwards to the Doon, where, he said, he was in demand among the lesser kings of those parts.

'We will go in the cool of the evening, *chela,*' said the lama. 'That doctor, learned in physic and courtesy, affirms that the people among these lower hills are devout, generous, and much in need of a teacher. In a very short time – so says the *hakim* – we come to cool air and the smell of pines.'

'Ye go to the Hills. And by Kulu-road? Ah, thrice happy!' shrilled the old lady. 'But that I am a little pressed with the care of the homestead I would take palanquin. . . . but that would be shameless, and my reputation would be cracked. Ho! Ho! I know the road – every march of the road I know. Ye will find charity throughout – it is not denied to the well-looking. I will give orders for provision. A servant to set you forth upon your journey? No. . . . Then I will at least cook ye good food.'

'What a woman is the Sahiba!' said the white-bearded Oorya, when a tumult rose by the kitchen quarters. 'She has never forgotten a friend: she has never forgotten an enemy in all her years. And her cookery – wah!' He rubbed his slim stomach.

There were cakes, there were sweetmeats, there was cold fowl stewed to rags with rice and prunes – enough to burden Kim like a mule.

'I am old and useless,' she said. 'None now love me – and none respect – but there are few to compare with me when I call on the Gods and squat to my cooking-pots. Come again, O people of good will! Holy One and disciple, come again! The room is always prepared; the welcome is always ready. . . . See the women do not follow thy *chela* too openly. *I* know the women of Kulu. Take heed, *chela,* lest he run away when he smells his Hills again. . . . Hai! Do not tilt the rice-bag upside down. . . . Bless the household, Holy One, and forgive thy servant her stupidities.'

She wiped her red old eyes on a corner of her veil, and clucked throatily.

'Women talk,' said the lama at last, 'but that is a woman's infirmity. I gave her a charm. She is upon the Wheel and wholly given over to the shows of this life, but none the less, *chela*, she is virtuous, kindly, hospitable – of a whole and zealous heart. Who shall say she does not acquire merit?'

'Not I, Holy One,' said Kim, re-slinging the bountiful provision on his shoulders. 'In my mind – behind my eyes – I have tried to picture such an one altogether freed from the Wheel – desiring nothing, causing nothing – a nun, as it were.'

'And, O imp?' The lama almost laughed aloud.

'I cannot make the picture.'

'Nor I. But there are many, many millions of lives before her. She will get wisdom a little, it may be, in each one.'

'And will she forget how to make stews with saffron upon that road?'

'Thy mind is set on things unworthy. But she has skill. I am refreshed all over. When we reach the lower hills I shall be yet stronger. The *hakim* spoke truly to me this morn when he said a breath from the snows blows away twenty years from the life of a man. We will go up into the Hills – the high hills – up to the sound of snow-water and the sound of the trees – for a little while. The *hakim* said that at any time we may return to the Plains, for we do no more than skirt the pleasant places. The *hakim* is full of learning; but he is in no way proud. I spoke to him – when thou wast talking to the Sahiba – of a certain dizziness that lays hold upon the back of my neck in the night, and he said it rose from excessive heat – to be cured by cool air. Upon consideration, I marvelled that I had not thought of such a simple remedy.'

'Didst thou tell him of thy Search?' said Kim, a little jealously. He preferred to sway the lama by his own speech – not through the wiles of Hurree Babu.

'Assuredly. I told him of my dream, and of the manner by which I had acquired merit by causing thee to be taught wisdom.'

'Thou didst not say I was a Sahib?'

'What need? I have told thee many times we be but two souls seeking escape. He said – and he is just herein – that the River of Healing will break forth even as I dreamed – at my feet if need be. Having found the Way, seest thou, that shall free me from the Wheel, need I trouble to find a way about the mere fields of earth – which are illusion? That were senseless. I have my dreams, night upon night repeated; I have the *Jâtaka;* and I have thee, Friend of all the World. It was written in thy horoscope that a Red Bull on a green field – I have not forgotten – should bring thee to honour. Who but I saw that prophecy accomplished? Indeed, I was the instrument. Thou shalt find me my River, being in return the instrument. The Search is sure!'

He set his ivory-yellow face, serene and untroubled, towards the beckoning Hills; his shadow shouldering far before him in the dust.

CHAPTER 13

Who hath desired the Sea – the immense and
    contemptuous surges?
The shudder, the stumble, the swerve ere the
    star-stabbing bow-sprit emerges –
The orderly clouds of the Trades and the ridged
    roaring sapphire thereunder –
Unheralded cliff-lurking flaws and the head-
    sails' low-volleying thunder?
His Sea in no wonder the same – his Sea and the
    same in each wonder –
His Sea that his being fulfils?
So and no otherwise – so and no otherwise
    Hill-men desire their Hills!

'WHO GOES to the hills goes to his mother.'

They had crossed the Sewaliks and the half-tropical Doon, left Mussoorie behind them, and headed north along the narrow hill-roads. Day after day they struck deeper into the huddled mountains, and day after day Kim watched the lama return to a man's strength. Among the terraces of the Doon he had leaned on the boy's shoulder, ready to profit by wayside halts. Under the great ramp to Mussoorie he drew himself together as an old hunter faces a well-remembered bank, and where he should have sunk exhausted swung his long draperies about him, drew a deep double-lungful of the diamond air, and walked as only a hillman can. Kim, plains-bred and plains-fed, sweated and panted astonished. 'This is *my* country,' said the lama. 'Besides Such-zen, this is flatter than a rice-field;' and with steady, driving strokes from the loins he strode upwards. But it was on the steep downhill marches, three thousand feet in three hours, that he went utterly away from Kim, whose back ached with holding back, and whose big toe was nigh cut off by his grass sandal-string. Through the speckled shadow of the great deodar-forests; through oak feathered and plumed with ferns; birch, ilex, rhododendron, and pine, out on to the bare hillsides' slippery sunburnt grass, and back into the woodlands' coolth again, till oak gave way to bamboo and palm of the valley, he swung untiring.

Glancing back in the twilight at the huge ridges behind him and the faint, thin line of the road whereby they had come, he would lay out, with a hillman's generous breadth of vision, fresh marches for the morrow; or, halting in the neck of some uplifted pass that gave on Spiti and Kulu, would stretch out his hands yearningly towards the high snows of the horizon. In the dawns they flared windy-red above stark blue, as Kedarnath and Badrinath – kings of that wilderness – took the first sunlight. All day long they lay like molten silver under the sun, and at evening put on their jewels again. At first they breathed temperately upon the travellers, winds good to meet when one crawled over some gigantic hogback; but in a few days, at a height of nine or ten thousand feet, those breezes bit; and Kim kindly allowed a village of hillmen to acquire merit by giving him a rough blanket-coat. The lama was mildly surprised that anyone should object to the knife-edged breezes which had cut the years off his shoulders.

'These are but the lower hills, *chela.* There is no cold till we come to the true Hills.'

'Air and water are good, and the people are devout enough, but the food is very bad,' Kim growled; 'and we walk as though we were mad – or English. It freezes at night, too.'

'A little, maybe; but only enough to make old bones rejoice in the sun. We must not always delight in the soft beds and rich food.'

'We might at the least keep to the road.'

Kim had all a plains-man's affection for the well-trodden track, not six feet wide, that snaked among the mountains; but the lama, being Tibetan, could not refrain from short cuts over spurs and the rims of gravel-strewn slopes. As he explained to his limping disciple, a man bred among mountains can prophesy the course of a mountain-road, and though low-lying clouds might be a hindrance to a short-cutting stranger, they made no earthly difference to a thoughtful man. Thus, after long hours of what would be reckoned very fair mountaineering in civilised countries, they would pant over a saddle-back, sidle past a few landslips, and drop through forest at an angle of forty-five on to the road again. Along their track lay the villages of the hill-folk – mud and earth huts, the timbers now and then rudely carved with an axe – clinging like swallows' nests against the steeps, huddled on tiny flats half-way down a three-thousand-foot glissade; jammed into a corner between cliffs that funnelled and focused every wandering blast; or, for the sake of summer pasture, cowering down on a neck that in winter would be ten feet deep in snow. And the people – the sallow, greasy, duffle-clad people, with short bare legs and faces almost Esquimaux – would flock out and adore. The Plains – kindly and gentle – had treated the lama as a holy man among holy men. But the Hills worshipped him as one in the confidence of all the devils. Theirs was an almost obliterated Buddhism, overlaid with a nature-worship fantastic as their own landscapes, elaborate as the terracing of their tiny fields; but they recognised the big hat, the clicking rosary, and the rare Chinese texts for great authority; and they respected the man under the hat.

'We saw thee come down over the black Breasts of Eua,' said a Betah who gave them cheese, sour milk, and stone-hard bread one evening. 'We do not use that often – except when calving cows stray in summer. There is a sudden wind among those stones that casts men down on the stillest day. But what should such folk care for the Devil of Eua!'

Then did Kim, aching in every fibre, dizzy with looking down, footsore with cramping desperate toes into inadequate crannies, take joy in the day's march – such joy as a boy of St. Xavier's who had won the quarter-mile on the flat might take in the praises of his friends. The hills sweated the *ghi* and sugar suet off his bones; the dry air, taken sobbingly at the head of cruel passes, firmed and built out his upper ribs; and tilted levels put new hard muscles into calf and thigh.

They meditated often on the Wheel of Life – the more so since, as the lama said, they were freed from its visible temptations. Except the gray eagle and an occasional far-seen bear grubbing and rooting on the hillside, the vision of a furious painted leopard met at dawn in a still valley devouring a goat, and now and again a bright-coloured bird, they were alone with the winds and the grass singing under the wind. The women of the smoky huts over whose roofs the two walked as they descended the mountains, were unlovely and unclean, wives of many husbands, and afflicted with goitre. The men were wood-cutters when they were not farmers – meek, and of an incredible simplicity. But that suitable discourse might not fail, Fate sent them, overtaking and overtaken upon the road, the courteous Dacca physician, who paid for his food in ointments good for goitre and councils that restore peace between men and women. He seemed to know these hills as well as he knew the hill dialects, and gave the lama the lie of the land towards Ladakh and Tibet. He said they could return to the Plains at any moment. Meantime, for such as loved mountains, yonder road might amuse. This was not all revealed in a breath, but at evening encounters on the stone threshing-floors, when, patients disposed of, the doctor would smoke and the lama snuff, while Kim watched the wee cows grazing on the house-tops, or threw his soul after his eye across the deep blue gulfs between range and range. And there were talks apart in the dark woods, when the doctor would seek herbs, and Kim, as budding physician, must accompany him.

'You see, Mister O'Hara, I do not know what the deuce-an'-all I shall do when I find our sporting friends; but if you will kindly keep within sight of my umbrella, which is fine fixed point for cadastral survey, I feel much better.'

Kim looked out across the jungle of peaks. 'This is not my country, *hakim*. Easier, I think, to find one louse in a bearskin.'

'Oah, thatt is my strong points. There is no hurry for Hurree. They were at Leh not so long ago. They said they had come down from the Kara Korum with their heads and horns and all. I am onlee afraid they will have sent back all their letters and compromising things from Leh into Russian territoree. Of course they will walk away as far to the East as possible – just to show that they were never among the Western States. You do not know the Hills?' He scratched with a twig on the earth. 'Look! They should have come in by Srinagar or Abbottabad. *Thatt* is their short road – down the river by Bunji and Astor. But they have made mischief in the West. So' – he drew a furrow from left to right – 'they march and they march away East to Leh (ah! it is cold there), and down the Indus to Han-lé (I know that road), and then down, you see, to Bushahr and Chini valley. That is ascertained by process of elimination, and also by asking questions from people that I cure so well. Our friends have been a long time playing about and producing impressions. So they are well known from far off. You will see me catch them somewhere in Chini valley. Please keep your eye on the umbrella.'

It nodded like a wind-blown harebell down the valleys and round the mountain sides, and in due time the lama and Kim, who steered by compass, would overhaul it, vending ointments and powders at eventide. 'We came by such and such a way!' The lama would throw a careless finger backward at the ridges, and the umbrella would expend itself in compliments.

They crossed a snowy pass in cold moonlight, when the lama, mildly chaffing Kim, went through up to his knees, like a Bactrian camel – the snow-bred, shag-haired sort that come into the Kashmir Serai. They dipped across beds of light snow and snow-powdered shale, where they took refuge from a gale in a camp of Tibetans hurrying down tiny sheep, each laden with a bag of borax. They came out upon grassy shoulders still snow-speckled, and through forest, to grass anew. For all their marchings, Kedarnath and Badrinath were not impressed; and it was only after days of travel that Kim, uplifted upon some insignificant ten-thousand-foot hummock, could see that a shoulder-knot or horn of the two great lords had – ever so slightly – changed outline.

At last they entered a world within a world – a valley of leagues where the high hills were fashioned of the mere rubble and refuse from off the knees of the mountains. Here one day's march carried them no farther, it seemed, than a dreamer's clogged pace bears him in a nightmare. They skirted a shoulder painfully for hours, and, behold, it was but an outlying boss in an outlying buttress of the main pile! A rounded meadow revealed itself, when they had reached it, for a vast tableland running far into the valley. Three days later, it was a dim fold in the earth to southward.

'Surely the Gods live here,' said Kim, beaten down by the silence and the appalling sweep and dispersal of the cloud-shadows after rain. 'This is no place for men!'

'Long and long ago,' said the lama, as to himself, 'it was asked of the Lord whether the world were everlasting. To this the Excellent One returned no answer. . . . When I was in Ceylon, a wise Seeker confirmed that from the gospel which is written in Pali. Certainly, since we know the way to Freedom, the question were unprofitable, but – look, and know illusion, *chela*! These are the true Hills! They are like my hills by Such-zen. Never were such hills!'

Above them, still enormously above them, earth towered away towards the snow-line, where from east to west across hundreds of miles, ruled as with a ruler, the last of the bold birches stopped. Above that, in scarps and blocks upheaved, the rocks strove to fight their heads above the white smother. Above these again, changeless since the world's beginning, but changing to every mood of sun and cloud, lay out the eternal snow. They could see blots and blurs on its face where storm and wandering wullie-wa got up to dance. Below them, as they stood, the forest slid away in a sheet of blue-green for mile upon mile; below the forest was a village in its sprinkle of terraced fields and steep grazing-grounds; below the village they knew, though a thunderstorm worried and growled there for the moment, a pitch of twelve or fifteen hundred feet gave to the moist valley where the streams gather that are the mothers of young Sutluj.

As usual, the lama had led Kim by cow-track and byroad, far from the main route along which Hurree Babu, that 'fearful man,' had bucketed three days before through a storm to which nine Englishmen out of ten would have given full right of way. Hurree was no game-shot, – the snick of a trigger made him change colour, – but, as he himself would have said, he was 'fairly effeecient stalker,' and he had raked the huge valley with a pair of cheap binoculars to some purpose. Moreover, the white of worn canvas tents against green carries far. Hurree Babu had seen all he wanted to see when he sat on the threshing-floor of Ziglaur, twenty miles away as the eagle flies, and forty by road – that is to say, two small dots which one day were just below the snow-line, and the next had moved downward perhaps six inches on the hillside. Once cleaned out and set to the work, his fat bare legs could cover a surprising amount of ground, and this was the reason why, while Kim and the lama lay in a leaky hut at Ziglaur till the storm should be overpassed, an oily, wet, but always smiling Bengali, talking the best of English with the vilest of phrases, was ingratiating himself with two sodden and rather rheumatic foreigners. He had arrived, revolving many wild schemes, on the heels of a thunderstorm which had split a pine over against their camp, and so convinced a dozen or two forcibly impressed baggage-coolies the day was inauspicious for further travel that with one accord they had thrown down their loads and jibbed. They were subjects of a Hill-Rajah who farmed out their services, as is the custom, for his private gain; and, to add to their personal distresses, the strange Sahibs had already threatened them with rifles. The most of them knew rifles and Sahibs of old; they were trackers and *shikarris* of the Northern valleys keen after bear and wild goat; but they had never been thus treated in their lives. So the forest took them to her bosom, and, for all oaths and clamour, refused to restore. There was no need to feign madness or – the Babu had thought of another means of securing a welcome. He wrung out his wet clothes, slipped on his patent-leather shoes, opened the blue and white umbrella, and with mincing gait and a heart beating against his tonsils appeared as 'agent for His Royal Highness, the Rajah of Rampur, gentlemen. What can I do for you, please?'

The gentlemen were delighted. One was visibly French, the other Russian, but they spoke English not much inferior to the Babu's. They begged his kind offices. Their native servants had gone sick at Leh. They had hurried on because they were anxious to bring the spoils of the chase to Simla ere the skins grew moth-eaten. They bore a general letter of introduction (the Babu salaamed to it orientally) to all Government officials. No, they had not met any other shooting-parties *en route*. They did for themselves. They had plenty of supplies. They only wished to push on as soon as might be. At this he waylaid a cowering hillman among the trees, and after three minutes' talk and a little silver (one cannot be economical upon State service, though Hurree's heart bled at the waste) the eleven coolies and the three hangers-on reappeared. At least the Babu would be a witness to oppression.

'My royal master, he will be much annoyed, but these people are onlee common people and grossly ignorant. If your honours will kindly overlook unfortunate affair, I shall be much pleased. In a little while rain will stop and we can then proceed. You have been shooting, eh? That is fine performance!'

He skipped nimbly from one *kilta** to the next, making pretence to adjust each conical basket. The Englishman is not, as a rule, familiar with the Asiatic, but he would not strike across the wrist a kindly Babu who had accidentally upset a *kilta* with a red oilskin top. On the other hand, he would not press drink upon a Babu were he never so friendly, nor would he invite him to meat. The strangers did all these things, and asked many questions, – about women mostly, – to which Hurree returned gay and unstudied answers. They gave him a glass of whitish fluid like to gin, and then more; and in a little time his gravity departed from him. He became thickly treasonous, and spoke in terms of sweeping indecency of a Government which had forced upon him a white man's education and neglected to supply him with a white man's salary. He babbled tales of oppression and wrong till the tears ran down his cheeks for the miseries of his land. Then he

* A large carry-pack with a flap.

staggered off, singing love-songs of Lower Bengal, and collapsed upon a wet tree-trunk. Never was so unfortunate a product of English rule in India more unhappily thrust upon aliens.

'They are all just of that pattern,' said one sportsman to the other in French. 'When we get into India proper thou wilt see. I should like to visit his Rajah. One might speak the good word there. It is possible that he has heard of us and wishes to signify his goodwill.'

'We have not time. We must get into Simla as soon as may be,' his companion replied. 'For my own part, I wish our reports had been sent back from Hilas, or even Leh.'

'The English post is better and safer. Remember we are given all facilities – and name of God! – they give them to us too! Is it unbelievable stupidity?'

'It is pride – pride that deserves and will receive punishment.'

'Yes! To fight a fellow-Continental in our game is something. There is a risk attached, but these people – bah! It is too easy.'

'Pride – all pride, my friend.'

'Now what the deuce is good of Chandernagore being so close to Calcutta and all,' said Hurree, snoring open-mouthed on the sodden moss, 'if I cannot understand their French. They talk so particularly fast! It would have been much better to cut their beastly throats.'

When he presented himself again he was racked with a headache – penitent, and volubly afraid that in his drunkenness he might have been indiscreet. He loved the British Government – it was the source of all prosperity and honour, and his master at Rampur held the very same opinion. Upon this the men began to deride him and to quote past words, till step by step, with deprecating smirks, oily grins, and leers of infinite cunning, the poor Babu was beaten out of his defences and forced to speak – truth. When Lurgan was told the tale later, he mourned aloud that he could not have been in the place of the stubborn, inattentive coolies, who with grass mats over their heads and the raindrops puddling in their foot-prints, waited on the weather. All the Sahibs of their acquaintance – rough-clad men joyously returning year after year to their chosen gullies – had servants and cooks and orderlies, very often hillmen. These Sahibs travelled without any retinue. Therefore they were poor Sahibs, and ignorant; for no Sahib in his senses would follow a Bengali's advice. But the Bengali, appearing from somewhere, had given them money, and would make shift with their dialect. Used to comprehensive ill-treatment from their own colour, they suspected a trap somewhere, and stood by to run if occasion offered.

Then through the new-washed air, steaming with delicious earth-smells, the Babu led the way down the slopes – walking ahead of the coolies in pride; walking behind the foreigners in humility. His thoughts were many and various. The least of them would have interested his companions beyond words. But he was an agreeable guide, ever keen to point out the beauties of his royal master's domain. He peopled the hills with anything they had a mind to slay – thar, ibex, or markhor, and bear by Elisha's allowance. He discoursed of botany and ethnology with unimpeachable inaccuracy, and his store of local legends – he had been a trusted agent of the State for fifteen years, remember – was inexhaustible.

'Decidedly this fellow is an original,' said the taller of the two foreigners. 'He is like the nightmare of a Viennese courier.'

'He represents *in petto** India in transition – the monstrous hybridism of East and West,' the Russian replied. 'It is we who can deal with Orientals.'

* In private, secretly.

'He has lost his own country and has not acquired any other. But he has a most complete hatred of his conquerors. Listen. He confides to me last night,' etc.

Under the striped umbrella Hurree Babu was straining ear and brain to follow the quick-poured French, and keeping both eyes on a *kilta* full of maps and documents – an extra large one with a double red oilskin cover. He did not wish to steal anything. He only desired to know what to steal, and, incidentally, how to get away when he had stolen it. He thanked all the Gods of Hindustan, and Herbert Spencer, that there remained some valuables to steal.

On the second day the road rose steeply to a grass spur above the forest; and it was here, about sunset, that they came across an aged lama – but they called him a bonze – sitting cross-legged above a mysterious chart held down by stones, which he was explaining to a young man, evidently a neophyte, of singular, though unwashen, beauty. The striped umbrella had been sighted half a march away, and Kim had suggested a halt till it came up to them.

'Ha!' said Hurree Babu, resourceful as Puss-in-Boots. 'That is eminent local holy man. Probably subject of my royal master.'

'What is he doing? It is very curious.'

'He is expounding holy picture – *all* hand-worked.'

The two men stood bare-headed in the wash of the afternoon sunlight low across the gold-coloured grass. The sullen coolies, glad of the check, halted and slid down their loads.

'Look!' said the Frenchman. 'It is like a picture for the birth of a religion – the first teacher and the first disciple. Is he a Buddhist?'

'Of some debased kind,' the other answered. 'There are no true Buddhists among the Hills. But look at the folds of the drapery. Look at his eyes – how insolent! Why does this make one feel that we are so young a people?' The speaker struck passionately at a tall weed. 'We have nowhere left our mark yet. Nowhere! *That*, do you understand, is what disquiets me.' He scowled at the placid face, and the monumental calm of the pose.

'Have patience. We shall make your mark together – we and you young people. Meantime, draw his picture.'

The Babu advanced loftily; his back out of all keeping with his deferential speech, or his wink towards Kim.

'Holy One, these be Sahibs. My medicines cured one of a flux, and I go into Simla to oversee his recovery. They wish to see thy picture – '

'To heal the sick is always good. This is the Wheel of Life,' said the lama, 'the same I showed thee in the hut at Ziglaur when the rain fell.'

'And to hear thee expound it.'

The lama's eyes lighted at the prospect of new listeners. 'To expound the Most Excellent Way is good. Have they any knowledge of Hindi, such as had the Keeper of Images?'

'A little, maybe.'

Hereat, simply as a child engrossed with a new game, the lama threw back his head and began the full-throated invocation of the Doctor of Divinity ere he opens the full doctrine. The strangers leaned on their alpen-stocks and listened. Kim, squatting humbly, watched the red sunlight on their faces, and the blend and parting of their long shadows. They wore un-English leggings and curious girt-in belts that reminded him hazily of the pictures in a book at St. Xavier's library: *The Adventures of a Young Naturalist in Mexico* was its name. Yes, they looked very like the wonderful

M. Sumichrast of that tale, and very unlike the 'highly unscrupulous folk' of Hurree Babu's imagining. The coolies, earth-coloured and mute, crouched reverently some twenty or thirty yards away, and the Babu, the slack of his thin gear snapping like a marking-flag in the chill breeze, stood by with an air of happy proprietorship.

'These are the men,' Hurree whispered, as the ritual went on and the two whites followed the grass blade sweeping from Hell to Heaven and back again. 'All their books are in the large *kilta* with the reddish top, – books and reports and maps, – and I have seen a King's letter that either Hilás or Bunár has written. They guard it most carefully. They have sent nothing back from Hilás or Leh. That is sure.'

'Who is with them?'

'Only the *beggar*-coolies. They have no servants. They are so close they cook their own food.'

'But what am I to do?'

'Wait and see. Only if any chance comes to me thou wilt know where to seek for the papers.'

'This were better in Mahbub Ali's hands than a Bengali's,' said Kim scornfully.

'There are more ways of getting to a sweetheart than butting down a wall.'

'See here the Hell appointed for avarice and greed. Flanked upon the one side by Desire and on the other by Weariness.' The lama warmed to his work, and one of the strangers sketched him in the quick-fading light.

'That is enough,' the man said at last brusquely. 'I cannot understand him, but I want that picture. He is a better artist than I. Ask him if he will sell it.'

'He says "No, sar," ' the Babu replied. The lama, of course, would no more have parted with his chart to a casual wayfarer than an archbishop would pawn the holy vessels of a cathedral. All Tibet is full of cheap reproductions of the Wheel; but the lama was an artist, as well as a wealthy abbot in his own place.

'Perhaps in three days, or four, or ten, if I perceive that the Sahib is a Seeker and of good understanding, I may myself draw him another. But *this* was used for the initiation of a novice. Tell him so, *hakim*.'

'He wishes it now – for money.'

The lama shook his head slowly and began to fold up the Wheel. The Russian, on his side, saw no more than an unclean old man haggling over a dirty piece of paper. He drew out a handful of rupees, and snatched half-jestingly at the chart, which tore in the lama's grip. A low murmur of horror went up from the coolies – some of whom were Spiti men and, by their lights, good Buddhists. The lama rose at the insult; his hand went to the heavy iron pen-case that is the priest's weapon, and the Babu danced in agony.

'Now you see – you see why I wanted witnesses. They are highly unscrupulous people. Oh Sar! Sar! You must *not* hit holy man!'

'*Chela*! He has defiled the Written Word!'

It was too late. Before Kim could ward him off, the Russian struck the old man full on the face. Next instant he was rolling over and over down hill with Kim at his throat. The blow had waked every unknown Irish devil in the boy's blood, and the sudden fall of his enemy did the rest. The lama dropped to his knees, half-stunned; the coolies under their loads fled up the hill as fast as plainsmen run across the level. They had seen sacrilege unspeakable, and it behoved them to get away before the Gods and devils of the hills took vengeance. The Frenchman ran towards the lama, fumbling at his revolver with some notion of making him a hostage for his companion. A shower of cutting stones – hillmen are very straight shots – drove him away, and a coolie from Ao-chung snatched the lama into the stampede. All came about as swiftly as the sudden mountain-darkness.

'They have taken the baggage and all the guns,' yelled the Frenchman, firing blindly into the twilight.

'All right, Sar! All right! Don't shoot. I go to rescue,' and Hurree, pounding down the slope, cast himself bodily upon the delighted and astonished Kim, who was banging his breathless foe's head against a boulder.

'Go back to the coolies,' whispered the Babu in his ear. 'They have the baggage. The papers are in the *kilta* with the red top, but look through all. Take their papers, and specially the *murasla* (King's letter). Go! The other man comes!'

Kim tore up hill. A revolver-bullet rang on a rock by his side, and he cowered partridge-wise.

'If you shoot,' shouted Hurree, 'they will descend and annihilate us. I have rescued the gentleman, Sar. This is par*tic*ularly dangerous.'

'By Jove!' Kim was thinking hard in English. 'This is dam-tight place, but *I* think it is self-defence.' He felt in his bosom for Mahbub's gift, and uncertainly – save for a few practice shots in the Bikaner desert, he had never used the little gun – pulled trigger.

'What did I say, Sar!' The Babu seemed to be in tears. 'Come down here and assist to resuscitate. We are all up a tree, I tell you.'

The shots ceased. There was a sound of stumbling feet, and Kim hurried upward through the gloom, swearing like a cat – or a country-bred.

'Did they wound thee, *chela*?' called the lama above him.

'No. And thou?' He dived into a clump of stunted firs.

'Unhurt. Come away. We go with these folk to Shamlegh-under-the-Snow.'

'But not before we have done justice,' a voice cried. 'I have got the Sahibs' guns – all four. Let us go down.'

'He struck the Holy One – we saw it! Our cattle will be barren – our wives will cease to bear! The snows will slide upon us as we go home. . . . Atop of all other oppression too!'

The little fir-clump filled with clamouring coolies – panic-stricken, and in their terror capable of anything. The man from Ao-chung clicked the breech-bolt of his gun impatiently, and made as to go down hill.

'Wait a little, Holy One; they cannot go far: wait till I return.'

'It is this person who has suffered wrong,' said the lama, his hand over his brow.

'For that very reason,' was the reply.

'If this person overlooks it, your hands are clean. Moreover, ye acquire merit by obedience.'

'Wait, and we will all go to Shamlegh together,' the man insisted.

For a moment, for just so long as it needs to stuff a cartridge into a breech-loader, the lama hesitated. Then he rose to his feet, and laid a finger on the man's shoulder.

'Hast thou heard? *I* say there shall be no killing – I who was Abbot of Such-zen. Is it any lust of thine to be re-born as a rat, or a snake under the eaves – a worm in the belly of the most mean beast? Is it thy wish to – '

The man from Ao-chung fell to his knees, for the voice boomed like a Tibetan devil-gong.

'Ai! ai!' cried the Spiti men. 'Do not curse us – do not curse him. It was but his zeal, Holy One!. . . . Put down the rifle, fool!'

'Anger on anger! Evil on evil! There will be no killing. Let the priest-beaters go in bondage to their own acts. Just and sure is the Wheel, swerving not a hair! They will be born many times – in torment.' His head drooped, and he leaned heavily on Kim's shoulder.

'I have come near to great evil, *chela*,' he whispered in that dead hush under the pines. 'I was tempted to loose the bullet; and truly, in Tibet there would have been a heavy and a slow death for them. . . . He struck me across the face. . . . upon the flesh. . . .' He slid to the ground, breathing heavily, and Kim could hear the over-driven heart bump and check.

'Have they hurt him to the death?' said the Ao-chung man, while the others stood mute.

Kim knelt over the body in deadly fear. 'Nay,' he cried passionately, 'this is only a weakness.' Then he remembered that he was a white man, with a white man's camp-fittings at his service. 'Open the *kiltas*! The Sahibs may have a medicine.'

'Oho! Then I know it,' said the Ao-chung man with a laugh. 'Not for five years was I Yankling Sahib's *shikarri* without knowing that medicine. I too have tasted it. Behold!'

He drew from his breast a bottle of cheap whisky – such as is sold to explorers at Leh – and cleverly forced a little between the lama's teeth.

'So I did when Yankling Sahib twisted his foot beyond Astor. Aha! I have already looked into their baskets – but we will make fair division at Shamlegh. Give him a little more. It is good medicine. Feel! His heart goes better now. Lay his head down and rub a little on the chest. If he had waited quietly while I accounted for the Sahibs this would never have come. But perhaps the Sahibs may chase us here. Then it would not be wrong to shoot them with their own guns, heh?'

'One is paid, I think, already,' said Kim between his teeth. 'I kicked him in the groin as we went down hill. Would I had killed him!'

'It is well to be brave when one does not live in Rampur,' said one whose hut lay within a few miles of the Rajah's rickety palace. 'If we get a bad name among the Sahibs, none will employ us as *shikarris* any more.'

'Oh, but these are not Angrezi Sahibs – not merry-minded men like Fostum Sahib or Yankling Sahib. They are foreigners – they cannot speak Angrezi as do Sahibs.'

Here the lama coughed and sat up, groping for the rosary.

'There shall be no killing,' he murmured. 'Just is the Wheel! Evil on evil – '

'Nay, Holy One. We are all here.' The Ao-chung man timidly patted his feet. 'Except by thy order, no one shall be slain. Rest awhile. We will make a little camp here, and later, as the moon rises, we go to Shamlegh-under-the-Snow.'

'After a blow,' said a Spiti man sententiously, 'it is best to sleep.'

'There is, as it were, a dizziness at the back of my neck, and a pinching in it. Let me lay my head on thy lap, *chela*. I am an old man, but not free from passion. . . . We must think of the Cause of Things.'

'Give him a blanket. We dare not light a fire lest the Sahibs see.'

'Better get away to Shamlegh. None will follow us to Shamlegh.'

This was the nervous Rampur man.

'I have been Fostum Sahib's *shikarri,* and I am Yankling Sahib's *shikarri.* I should have been with Yankling Sahib now but for this cursed *beegar* (the *corvée*). Let two men watch below with the guns lest the Sahibs do more foolishness. I shall not leave this Holy One.'

They sat down a little apart from the lama, and, after listening awhile, passed round a water-pipe whose receiver was an old Day and Martin blacking-bottle. The glow of the red charcoal as it went from hand to hand lit up the narrow, blinking eyes, the high Chinese cheek-bones, and the bull-throats that melted away into the dark duffle folds round the shoulders. They looked like kobolds from some magic mine – gnomes of the hills in conclave. And while they talked, the voices of the snow-waters round them diminished one by one as the night-frost choked and clogged the runnels.

'How he stood up against us!' said a Spiti man admiring. 'I remember an old ibex, out Ladakh-way, that Dupont Sahib missed on a shoulder-shot, seven seasons back, standing up just like him. Dupont Sahib was a good *shikarri.*'

'Not as good as Yankling Sahib.' The Ao-chung man took a pull at the whisky-bottle and passed it over. 'Now hear me – unless any other man thinks he knows more.'

The challenge was not taken up.

'We go to Shamlegh when the moon rises. There we will fairly divide the baggage between us. I am content with this new little rifle and all its cartridges.'

'Are the bears only bad on thy holding?' said a mate, sucking at the pipe.

'No; but musk-pods are worth six rupees apiece now, and thy women can have the canvas of the tents and some of the cooking-gear. We will do all that at Shamlegh before dawn. Then we all go our ways, remembering that we have never seen or taken service with these Sahibs, who may, indeed, say that we have stolen their baggage.'

'That is well for thee, but what will our Rajah say?'

'Who is to tell him? Those Sahibs, who cannot speak our talk, or the Babu, who for his own ends gave us money? Will *he* lead an army against us? What evidence will remain? That we do not need we shall throw on Shamlegh midden, where no man has yet set foot.'

'Who is at Shamlegh this summer?' The place was only a grazing centre of three or four huts.

'The Woman of Shamlegh. *She* has no love for Sahibs, as we know. The others can be pleased with little presents; and here is enough for us all.' He patted the fat sides of the nearest basket.

'But – but – '

'I have said they are not true Sahibs. All their skins and heads were bought in the bazar at Leh. *I* know the marks. I showed them to ye last march.'

'True. They were all bought skins and heads. Some had even the moth in them.'

That was a shrewd argument, and the Ao-chung man knew his fellows.

'If the worst comes to the worst, I shall tell Yankling Sahib, who is a man of a merry mind, and he will laugh. We are not doing any wrong to any Sahibs whom we know. *They* are priest-beaters. They frightened us. We fled! Who knows where we dropped the baggage? Do ye think Yankling Sahib will permit down-country police to wander all over the hills, disturbing his game? It is a far cry from Simla to Chini, and farther from Shamlegh to Shamlegh midden.'

'So be it, but I carry the big *kilta*. The basket with the red top that the Sahibs pack themselves every morning.'

'Thus it is proved,' said the Shamlegh man adroitly, 'that they are Sahibs of no account. Who ever heard of Fostum Sahib, or Yankling Sahib, or even the little Peel Sahib that sits up of nights to shoot serow – I say, who ever heard of these Sahibs coming into the hills without a down-country cook, and a bearer, and – and all manner of well-paid, high-handed and oppressive folk in their tail? How can they make trouble? What of the *kilta*?'

'Nothing, but that it is full of the Written Word – books and papers in which they wrote, and strange instruments, as of worship.'

'Shamlegh midden will take them all.'

'True! But how if we insult the Sahibs' Gods thereby? I do not like to handle the Written Word in that fashion. And their brass idols are beyond my comprehension. It is no plunder for simple hill-folk.'

'The old man still sleeps. Hst! We will ask his *chela*.' The Ao-chung man refreshed himself, and swelled with pride of leadership.

'We have here,' he whispered, 'a *kilta* whose nature we do not know.

'But I do,' said Kim cautiously. The lama drew breath in natural, easy sleep, and Kim had been thinking of Hurree's last words. As a player of the Great Game, he was disposed just then to reverence the Babu. 'It is a *kilta* with a red top full of very wonderful things, not to be handled by fools.'

'I said it; I said it,' cried the bearer of that burden. 'Thinkest thou it will betray us?'

'Not if it be given to me. I will draw out its magic. Otherwise it will do great harm.'

'A priest always takes his share.' Whisky was demoralising the Ao-chung man.

'It is no matter to me,' Kim answered, with the craft of his mother-country. 'Share it among you, and see what comes!'

'Not I. I was only jesting. Give the order. There is more than enough for us all. We go our way from Shamlegh in the dawn.'

They arranged and re-arranged their artless little plans for another hour, while Kim shivered with cold and pride. The humour of the situation tickled the Irish and the Oriental in his soul. Here were the emissaries of the dread Power of the North, very possibly as great in their own land as Mahbub or Colonel Creighton, suddenly smitten helpless. One of them, he privately knew, would be lame for a time. They had made promises to Kings. To-night they lay out somewhere below him, chartless, foodless, tentless, gunless – except for Hurree Babu, guideless. And this collapse of their Great Game (Kim wondered to whom they would report it), this panicky bolt into the night, had come about through no craft of Hurree's or contrivance of Kim's, but simply, beautifully, and inevitably as the capture of Mahbub's *faquir*-friends by the zealous young policeman at Umballa.

'They are there – with nothing; and, by Jove, it is cold! I am here with all their things. Oh, they will be angry! I am sorry for Hurree Babu.'

Kim might have saved his pity, for though at that moment the Bengali suffered acutely in the flesh, his soul was puffed and lofty. A mile down the hill, on the edge of the pine-forest, two half-frozen men – one powerfully sick at intervals – were varying mutual recriminations with the most poignant abuse of the Babu, who seemed distraught with terror. They demanded a plan of action. He explained that they were very lucky to be alive; that their coolies, if not then stalking them, had passed beyond recall; that the Rajah, his master, was ninety miles away, and, so far from lending them money and a retinue for the Simla journey, would surely cast them into prison if he heard that they had hit a priest. He enlarged on this sin and its consequences till they bade him change the subject. Their one hope, said he, was unostentatious flight from village to village till they reached civilisation; and, for the hundredth time dissolved in tears, he demanded of the high stars why the Sahibs 'had beaten holy man.'

Ten steps would have taken Hurree into the creaking gloom utterly beyond their reach – to the shelter and food of the nearest village, where glib-tongued doctors were scarce. But he preferred to endure cold, belly-pinch, bad words, and occasional blows in the company of his honoured employers. Crouched against a tree-trunk, he sniffed dolefully.

'And have you thought,' said the uninjured man hotly, 'what sort of spectacle we shall present wandering through these hills among these aborigines?'

Hurree Babu had thought of little else for some hours, but the remark was not to his address.

We cannot wander! I can hardly walk,' groaned Kim's victim.

'Perhaps the holy man will be merciful in loving-kindness, Sar, otherwise – '

'I promise myself a peculiar pleasure in emptying my revolver into that young bonze when next we meet,' was the unchristian answer.

'Revolvers! Vengeance! Bonzes!' Hurree crouched lower. The war was breaking out afresh. 'Have you no consideration for our loss? The baggage! The baggage!' He could hear the speaker literally dancing on the grass. 'Everything we bore! Everything we have secured! Our gains! Eight months' work! Do you know what that means? "Decidedly it is we who can deal with Orientals!" Oh, you have done well.'

They fell to it in several tongues, and Hurree smiled. Kim was with the *kiltas*, and in the *kiltas* lay eight months of good diplomacy. There was no means of communicating with the boy, but he could be trusted. For the rest, he could so stage-manage the journey through the hills that Hilas, Bunar, and four hundred miles of hill-roads should tell the tale for a generation. Men who cannot control their own coolies are little respected in the Hills, and the hillman has a very keen sense of humour.

'If I had done it myself,' thought Hurree, 'it would not have been better; and, by Jove, now I think of it, of course I arranged it myself. How quick I have been! Just when I ran down hill I thought it! Thee outrage was accidental but onlee me could have worked it – ah – for all it was dam-well worth. Consider the moral effect upon these ignorant peoples! No treaties – no papers – no written documents at all – and *me* to interpret for them. How I shall laugh with the Colonel! I wish I had their papers also: but you cannot occupy two places in space simultaneously. That is axiomatic.'

CHAPTER 14

My brother kneels (so saith Kabir)
To stone and brass in heathen-wise,
But in my brother's voice I hear
My own unanswered agonies.
His God is as his Fates assign –
His prayer is all the world's – and mine.

– *Kabir*

AT MOONRISE the cautious coolies got under way. The lama, refreshed by his sleep and the spirit, needed no more than Kim's shoulder to bear him along – a silent, swift-striding man. They held the shale-sprinkled grass for an hour, swept round the shoulder of an immortal cliff, and climbed into a new country entirely blocked off from all sight of Chini valley. A huge pasture-ground ran up fan-shaped to the living snow. At its base was perhaps half an acre of flat land, on which stood a few soil and timber huts. Behind them – for, hill-fashion, they were perched on the edge of all things – the ground fell sheer two thousand feet to Shamlegh midden, where never yet man has set foot.

The men made no motion to divide the plunder till they had seen the lama bedded down in the best room of the place, with Kim shampooing his feet, Mohammedan fashion.

'We will send food,' said the Ao-chung man, 'and the red-topped *kilta*. By dawn there will be none to give evidence, one way or the other. If anything is not needed in the *kilta* – see here!'

He pointed through the window – opening into space that was filled with moonlight reflected from the snow – and threw out an empty whisky-bottle.

'No need to listen for the fall. This is the world's end,' he said, and swung off. The lama looked forth, a hand on either sill, with eyes that shone like yellow opals. From the enormous pit before him white peaks lifted themselves yearning to the moonlight. The rest was as the darkness of interstellar space.

'These,' he said slowly, 'are indeed my Hills. Thus should a man abide, perched above the world, separated from delights, considering vast matters.'

'Yes; if he has a *chela* to prepare tea for him, and to fold a blanket for his head, and to chase out calving cows.'

A smoky lamp burned in a niche, but the full moonlight beat it down; and by the mixed light, stooping above the food-bag and cups, Kim moved like a tall ghost.

'Ai! But now I have let the blood cool my head still beats and drums, and there is a cord round the back of my neck.'

'No wonder. It was a strong blow. May he who dealt it – '

'But for my own passions there would have been no evil.'

'What evil? Thou hast saved the Sahibs from death they deserved a hundred times.'

'The lesson is not well learnt, *chela*.' The lama came to rest on a folded blanket, as Kim went forward with his evening routine. 'The blow was but a shadow upon a shadow. Evil in itself – my legs weary apace these latter days! – it met evil in me – anger, rage, and a lust to return evil. These wrought in my blood, woke tumult in my stomach, and dazzled my ears.' Here he drank scalding black-tea ceremonially, taking the hot cup from Kim's hand. 'Had I been passionless, the evil blow would have done only bodily evil – a scar, or a bruise – which is illusion. But my mind was *not* abstracted, for rushed in straightway a lust to let the Spiti men kill. In fighting that lust, my soul was torn and wrenched beyond a thousand blows.

Not till I had repeated the Blessings (he meant the Buddhist Beatitudes) did I achieve calm. But the evil planted in me by that moment's carelessness works out to its end. Just is the Wheel, swerving not a hair! Learn the lesson, *chela*.'

'It is too high for me,' Kim muttered. 'I am still all shaken. I am glad I hurt the man.'

'I felt that sleeping upon thy knees, in the wood below. It disquieted me in my dreams – the evil in thy soul working through to mine. Yet on the other hand' – he loosed his rosary – 'I have acquired merit by saving two lives – the lives of those that wronged me. Now I must see into the Cause of Things. The boat of my soul staggers.'

'Sleep, and be strong. That is wisest.'

'I meditate: there is a need greater than thou knowest.'

Till the dawn, hour after hour, as the moonlight paled on the high peaks, and that which had been belted blackness on the sides of the far hills showed as tender green forest, the lama stared fixedly at the wall. From time to time he groaned. Outside the barred door, where discomfited kine came to ask for their old stable, Shamlegh and the coolies gave itself up to plunder and riotous living. The Ao-chung man was their leader, and once they had opened the Sahibs' tinned foods and found that they were very good they dared not turn back. Shamlegh kitchen-midden took the dunnage.

When Kim, after a night of bad dreams, stole forth to brush his teeth in the morning chill a fair-coloured woman with turquoise-studded head-gear drew him aside.

'The others have gone. They left thee this *kilta* as the promise was. I do not love Sahibs, but thou wilt make us a charm in return for it. We do not wish little Shamlegh to get a bad name on account of the – accident. I am the Woman of

Shamlegh.' She looked him over with bold, bright eyes, unlike the usual furtive glance of hillwomen.

'Assuredly. But it must be done in secret.'

She raised the heavy *kilta* like a toy and slung it into her own hut.

'Out and bar the door! Let none come near till it is finished.'

'But afterwards – we may talk?'

Kim tilted the *kilta* on the floor – a cascade of Survey-instruments, books, diaries, letters, maps, and queerly scented native correspondence. At the very bottom was an embroidered bag covering a sealed, gilded, and illuminated document such as one King sends to another. Kim caught his breath with delight, and reviewed the situation from a Sahib's point of view.

'The books I do not want. Besides, they are logarithms – Survey, I suppose.' He laid them aside. 'The letters I do not understand, but Colonel Creighton will. They must all be kept. The maps – they draw better maps than me – *of* course. All the native letters – oho! – and particularly the *murasla*.' He sniffed the embroidered bag. 'That must be from Hilas or Bunar, and Hurree Babu spoke truth. By Jove! It is a fine haul. I wish Hurree could know. . . . The rest must go out of the window.' He fingered a superb prismatic compass and the shiny top of a theodolite. But after all, a Sahib cannot very well steal, and the things might be inconvenient evidence later. He sorted out every scrap of manuscript, every map, and the native letters. They made one softish slab. The three locked ferril-backed books, with five worn pocketbooks, he put aside.

'The letters and the *murasla* I must carry inside my coat and under my belt, and the hand-written books I must put into the food-bag. It will be very heavy. No. I do not think there is anything more. If there is, the coolies have thrown it down the *khud*, so *thatt* is all right. Now you go too.' He repacked the *kilta* with all he meant to lose, and hove it up on to the window-sill. A thousand feet below lay a long, lazy, round-shouldered bank of mist, as yet untouched by the morning sun. A thousand feet below that was an hundred-year-old pine-forest. He could see the green tops looking like a bed of moss when a wind-eddy thinned the cloud.

'No! I don't think any one will go after *you*!'

The wheeling basket vomited its contents as it dropped. The theodolite hit a jutting cliff-ledge and exploded like a shell; the books, inkstand, paint-boxes, compasses, and rulers showed for a few seconds like a swarm of bees. Then they vanished; and, though Kim, hanging half out of window, strained his young ears, never a sound came up from the gulf.

'Five hundred – a thousand rupees could not buy them,' he thought sorrowfully. 'It was verree wasteful, but I have all their other stuff – everything they did – I hope. Now how the deuce am I to tell Hurree Babu, and *whatt* the deuce am I to do? And my old man is sick. I must tie up the letters in oilcloth. That is something to do first – else they will get all sweated. . . . And I am all alone!' He bound them into a neat packet, swedging down the stiff, sticky oilcloth at the corners, for his roving life had made him as methodical as an old hunter in matters of the road. Then with double care he packed away the books at the bottom of the food-bag.

The woman rapped at the door.

'But thou hast made no charm,' she said, looking about.

'There is no need.' Kim had completely overlooked the necessity for a little patter-talk. The woman laughed at his confusion irreverently.

'None – for thee. Thou canst cast a spell by the mere winking of an eye. But think of us poor people when thou art gone! They were all too drunk last night to hear a woman. Thou art not drunk?'

'I am a priest.' Kim had recovered himself, and, the woman being aught but unlovely, thought best to stand on his office.

'I warned them that the Sahibs will be angry and will make an inquisition and a report to the Rajah. There is also the Babu with them. Clerks have long tongues.'

'Is that all thy trouble?' The plan rose fully formed in Kim's mind, and he smiled ravishingly.

'Not all,' quoth the woman, putting out a hard brown hand all covered with turquoises set in silver.

'I can finish that in a breath,' he went on quickly. 'The Babu is the very *hakim* (thou hast heard of him?) who was wandering among the hills by Ziglaur. I know him.'

'He will tell for the sake of a reward. Sahibs cannot distinguish one hillman from another, but Babus have eyes for men – and women.'

'Carry a word to him from me.'

'There is nothing I would not do for thee.'

He accepted the compliment calmly, as men must in lands where women make the love, tore a leaf from a note-book, and with a patent indelible pencil wrote in gross Shikast – the script that bad little boys use when they write dirt on walls: '*I have everything that they have written*: *their pictures* of *the country*, *and many letters. Especially the murasla. Tell me what to do. I am at Shamlegh-under-the-Snow. The old man is sick.*'

'Take this to him. It will altogether shut his mouth. He cannot have gone far.'

'Indeed no. They are still in the forest across the spur. Our children went to watch them when the light came, and have cried the news as they moved.'

Kim looked his astonishment; but from the edge of the sheep-pasture floated a shrill, kite-like trill. A child tending cattle had picked it up from a brother or sister on the far side of the slope that commanded Chini valley.

'My husbands are also out there gathering wood.' She drew a handful of walnuts from her bosom, split one neatly, and began to eat. Kim affected blank ignorance.

'Dost thou not know the meaning of the walnut-priest?' she said coyly, and handed him the half-shells.

'Well thought of.' He slipped the piece of paper between them quickly. 'Hast thou a little wax to close them on this letter?'

The woman sighed aloud, and Kim relented.

'There is no payment till service has been rendered. Carry this to the Babu, and say it was sent by the Son of the Charm.'

'Ai! Truly! Truly! By a magician – who is like a Sahib.'

'Nay, Son of the Charm: and ask if there be any answer.'

'But if he offer a rudeness? I – I am afraid.'

Kim laughed. 'He is, I have no doubt, very tired and very hungry. The Hills make cold bedfellows. Hai, my' – it was on the tip of his tongue to say Mother, but he turned it to Sister – 'thou art a wise and witty woman. By this time all the villages know what has befallen the Sahibs – eh?'

'True. News was at Ziglaur by midnight, and by to-morrow should be at Kotgarh. The villages are both afraid and angry.'

'No need. Tell the villages to feed the Sahibs and pass them on, in peace. We must get them quietly away from our valleys. To steal is one thing – to kill another. The Babu will understand, and there will be no after-complaints. Be swift. I must tend my master when he wakes.'

'So be it. After service – thou hast said? – comes the reward. I am the Woman of Shamlegh, and I hold from the Rajah. I am no common bearer of babes. Shamlegh is thine: hoof and horn and hide, milk and butter. Take or leave.'

She turned resolutely uphill, her silver necklaces clicking on her broad breast, to meet the morning sun fifteen hundred feet above them. This time Kim thought in the vernacular as he waxed down the oilskin edges of the packets.

'How can a man follow the Way or the Great Game when he is eternally pestered by women? There was that girl at Akrola by the Ford; and there was the scullion's wife behind the dovecot – not counting the others – and now comes this one! When I was a child it was well enough, but now I am a man and they will not regard me as a man. Walnuts indeed! Ho! ho! It is almonds in the Plains!'

He went out to levy on the village – not with a begging-bowl, which might do for down-country, but in the manner of a prince. Shamlegh's summer population is only three families – four women and eight or nine men. They were all full of tinned meats and mixed drinks, from ammoniated quinine to white vodka, for they had taken their full share in the overnight loot. The neat Continental tents had been cut up and shared long ago, and there were patent aluminum saucepans abroad.

But they considered the lama's presence a perfect safeguard against all consequences, and impenitently brought Kim of their best – even to a drink of *chang* – the barley-beer that comes from Ladakh-way. Then they thawed out in the sun, and sat with their legs hanging over infinite abysses, chattering, laughing, and smoking. They judged India and its Government solely from their experience of wandering

Sahibs who had employed them or their friends as *shikarris*. Kim heard tales of shots missed upon ibex, serow, or markhor, by Sahibs twenty years in their graves – every detail lighted from behind like twigs on tree-tops seen against lightning. They told him of their little diseases, and, more important, the diseases of their tiny, sure-footed cattle; of trips as far as Kotgarh, where the strange missionaries live, and beyond even to marvellous Simla, where the streets are paved with silver, and anyone, look you, can get service with the Sahibs, who ride about in two-wheeled carts and spend money with a spade. Presently, grave and aloof, walking very heavily, the lama joined himself to the chatter under the eaves, and they gave him great room. The thin air refreshed him, and he sat on the edge of precipices with the best of them, and, when talk languished, flung pebbles into the void. Thirty miles away, as the eagle flies, lay the next range, seamed and channelled and pitted with little patches of brush – forests, each a day's dark march. Behind the village, Shamlegh hill itself cut off all view to southward. It was like sitting in a swallow's nest under the eaves of the roof of the world.

From time to time the lama stretched out his hand, and with a little, low-voiced prompting would point out the road to Spiti and north across the Parungla.

'Beyond, where the hills lie thickest, lies De-ch'en' (he meant Han-lé), 'the great Monastery.' Tag-stan-ras-ch'en built it, and of him there runs this tale.' Whereupon he told it: a fantastic piled narrative of bewitchment and miracles that set Shamlegh agasping. Turning west a little, he speered for the green hills of Kulu, and sought Kailung under the glaciers. 'For thither came I in the old, old days. From Leh I came, over the Baralachi.'

'Yes, yes; we know it,' said the far-faring people of Shamlegh.

'And I slept two nights with the priests of Kailung. These are the hills of my delight! Shadows blessed above all other shadows! There my eyes opened on this world; there my eyes were opened to this world; there I found Enlightenment; and there I girt my loins for my Search. Out of the Hills I came – the high Hills and the strong winds. Oh, just is the Wheel!' He blessed them in detail – the great glaciers, the naked rocks, the piled moraines and tumbled shale; dry upland, hidden salt-lake, age-old timber and fruitful water-shot valley one after the other, as a dying man blesses his folk, and Kim marvelled at his passion.

'Yes – yes. There is no place like our Hills,' said the people of Shamlegh. And they fell to wondering how a man could live in the hot terrible Plains where the cattle run as big as elephants, unfit to plough on a hillside; where village touches village, they had heard, for a hundred miles; where folk went about stealing in gangs, and what the robbers spared the Police carried utterly away.

So the still forenoon wore through, and at the end of it Kim's messenger dropped from the steep pasture as unbreathed as when she had set out.

'I sent a word to the *hakim*,' Kim explained, while she made reverence.

'He joined himself to the idolaters? Nay, I remember he did a healing upon one of them. He has acquired merit, though the healed employed his strength for evil. Just is the Wheel! What of the *hakim*?'

'I feared that thou hadst been bruised and – and I knew he was wise.' Kim took the waxed walnut-shell and read in English on the back of his note: *Your favour received. Cannot get away from present company at present, but shall take them into Simla. After which, hope to rejoin you. Inexpedient to follow angry gentlemen. Return by same road you came, and will overtake. Highly gratified about correspondence due to my forethought.'* He says, Holy One, that he will escape from the idolaters, and will return to us. Shall we wait awhile at Shamlegh, then?'

The lama looked long and lovingly upon the hills and shook his head.

'That may not be, *chela.* From my bones outward I do desire it, but it is forbidden. I have seen the Cause of Things.'

'Why? When the Hills give thee back thy strength day by day? Remember we were weak and fainting down below there in the Doon.'

'I became strong to do evil and to forget. A brawler and a swashbuckler upon the hillsides was I.' Kim bit back a smile. 'Just and perfect is the Wheel, swerving not a hair. When I was a man – a long time ago – I did pilgrimage to Guru Ch'wan among the poplars' (he pointed Bhotanwards), 'where they keep the Sacred Horse.'

'Quiet, be quiet!' said Shamlegh, all arow. 'He speaks of Jamlin-nin-k'or, The Horse That Can Go Round The World In a Day.'

'I speak to my *chela* only,' said the lama, in gentle reproof, and they scattered like frost on south eaves of a morning. 'I did not seek truth in those days, but the talk of doctrine. All illusion! I drank the beer and ate the bread of Guru Ch'wan. Next day one said: "We go out to fight Sangor Gutok down the valley to discover (mark again how Lust is tied to Anger!) which abbot shall bear rule in the valley, and take the profit of the prayers they print at Sangor Gutok." I went, and we fought a day.'

'But how, Holy One?'

'With our long pen-cases as I could have shown. . . . I say, we fought under the poplars, both abbots and all the monks, and one laid open my forehead to the bone. See!' He tilted back his cap and showed a puckered silvery scar. 'Just and perfect is the Wheel! Yesterday the scar itched, and after fifty years I recalled how it was dealt and the face of him who dealt it; dwelling a little in illusion. Followed that which thou didst see – strife and stupidity. Just is the Wheel! The idolater's blow fell upon the scar. Then I was shaken in my soul: my soul was darkened, and the boat of my soul rocked upon the waters of illusion. Not till I came to Shamlegh could I meditate upon the Cause of Things, or trace the running grass-roots of Evil. I strove all the long night.'

'But, Holy One, thou art innocent of all evil. May I be thy sacrifice!'

Kim was genuinely distressed at the old man's sorrow, and Mahbub Ali's phrase slipped out unawares.

'In the dawn,' he went on more gravely, ready rosary clicking between the slow sentences, 'came enlightenment. It is here. . . . I am an old man. . . . hill-bred, hill-fed, never to sit down among my Hills. Three years I travelled through Hind, but – can earth be stronger than Mother Earth? My stupid body yearned to the Hills and the snow of the Hills, from below there. I said, and it is true, my Search is sure. So, at the Kulu woman's house I turned hillward, over-persuaded by myself. There is no blame to the *hakim*. He – following Desire – foretold that the Hills would make me strong. They strengthened me to do evil to forget my Search. I delighted in life and the lust of life. I desired strong slopes to climb. I cast about to find them. I measured the strength of my body, which is evil, against the high hills. I made a mock of thee when thy breath came short under Jamnotri. I jested when thou wouldst not face the snow of the pass.'

'But what harm? I *was* afraid. It was just. I am not a hillman; and I loved thee for thy new strength.'

'More than once I remember,' he rested his cheek dolefully on his hand, 'I sought thy praise and the *hakim's* for the mere strength of my legs. Thus evil followed evil till the cup was full. Just is the Wheel! All Hind for three years did me all honour. From the Fountain of Wisdom in the Wonder House to' – he smiled – 'a little child playing by a big gun – the world prepared my road. And why?'

'Because we loved thee. It is only the fever of the blow. I myself am still sick and shaken.'

'No! It was because I was upon the Way – tuned as are *sinen* (cymbals) to the purpose of the Law. I departed from that ordinance. The tune was broken: followed the punishment. In my own Hills, on the edge of my own country, in the very place of my evil desire, comes the buffet – here!' (He touched his brow.) 'As a novice is beaten when he misplaces the cups, so am I beaten, who was Abbot of Such-zen. No word, look you, but a blow, *chela.*'

'But the Sahibs did not know thee, Holy One?'

'We were well matched. Ignorance and Lust met Ignorance and Lust upon the road, and they begat Anger. The blow was a sign to me, who am no better than a strayed yak, that my place is not here. Who can read the Cause of an act is half-way to Freedom! "Back to the path," says the Blow. "The Hills are not for thee. Thou canst not choose Freedom and go in bondage to the delight of life." '

'If we had never met that thrice-cursed Russian!'

'Our Lord Himself cannot make the Wheel swing backward. And for my merit that I had acquired I gain yet another sign.' He put his hand in his bosom, and drew forth the

Wheel of Life. 'Look! I considered this after I had meditated. There remains untorn by the idolater no more than the breadth of my finger-nail.'

'I see.'

'So much, then, is the span of my life in this body. I have served the Wheel all my days. Now the Wheel serves me. But for the merit I have acquired in guiding thee upon the Way, there would have been added to me yet another life ere I had found my River. Is it plain, *chela*?'

Kim stared at the brutally disfigured chart. From left to right diagonally the rent ran – from the Eleventh House where Desire gives birth to the Child (as it is drawn by Tibetans) – across the human and animal worlds, to the Fifth House – the empty House of the Senses. The logic was unanswerable.

'Before our Lord won enlightenment,' the lama folded all away with reverence, 'He was tempted. I too have been tempted, but it is finished. The Arrow fell in the Plains – not in the Hills. Therefore, what make we here?'

'Shall we at least wait for the *hakim*?'

'I know how long I live in this body. What can a *hakim* do?'

'But thou art all sick and shaken. Thou canst not walk.'

'How can I be sick if I see Freedom?' He rose unsteadily to his feet.

'Then I must get food from the village. Oh, the weary Road!' Kim felt that he too needed rest.

'That is lawful. Let us eat and go. The Arrow fell in Plains. . . . but I yielded to Desire. Make ready, chela.'

Kim turned to the woman with the turquoise head-gear who had been idly pitching pebbles over the cliff. She smiled very kindly.

'I found him like a strayed buffalo in a corn-field – the Babu; snorting and sneezing with cold. He was so hungry that he forgot his dignity and gave me sweet words. The Sahibs have nothing.' She flung out an empty palm. 'One is very sick about the stomach. Thy work?'

Kim nodded, with a bright eye.

'I spoke to the Bengali first – and to the people of a near-by village after. The Sahibs will be given food as they need it – nor will the people ask money. The plunder is already distributed. That makes lying speeches to the Sahibs. Why does he not leave them?'

'Out of the greatness of his heart.'

' 'Was never a Bengali yet had one bigger than a dried walnut. But it is no matter. . . . Now as to walnuts. After service comes reward. I have said the village is thine.'

'It is my loss,' Kim began. 'Even now I had planned desirable things in my heart which' – there is no need to go through the compliments proper to these occasions. He sighed deeply. . . . 'But my master, led by a vision – '

'Huh! What can old eyes see except a full begging-bowl?'

' – turns from this village to the Plains again.'

'Bid him stay.'

Kim shook his head. 'I know my Holy One, and his rage if he be crossed,' he replied impressively. 'His curses shake the Hills.'

'Pity they did not save him from a broken head! I heard that thou wast the tiger-hearted one who smote the Sahib. Let him dream a little longer. Stay!'

'Hillwoman,' said Kim, with austerity that could not harden the outlines of his young oval face, 'these matters are too high for thee.'

'The Gods be good to us! Since when have men and women been other than men and women?'

'A priest is a priest. He says he will go upon this hour. I am his *chela,* and I go with him. We need food for the Road. He is an honoured guest in all the villages, but' – he broke into a pure boy's grin – 'the food here is good. Give me some.'

'What if I do not give it thee? I am the woman of this village.'

'Then I curse thee – a little – not greatly, but enough to remember.' He could not help smiling.

'Thou hast cursed me already by the down-dropped eyelash and the uplifted chin. Curses? What should I care for mere words?' She clenched her hands upon her bosom. . . . 'But I would not have thee to go in anger, thinking hardly of me – a gatherer of cow-dung and grass at Shamlegh, but still a woman of substance.'

'I think nothing,' said Kim, 'but that I am grieved to go, for I am very tired, and that we need food. Here is the bag.'

The woman snatched it angrily. 'I was foolish,' said she. 'Who is thy woman in the Plains? Fair or black? I was fair once. Laughest thou? Once, long ago, if thou canst believe, a Sahib looked on me with favour. Once, long ago, I wore European clothes at the Mission-house yonder.' She pointed towards Kotgarh. 'Once, long ago, I was *Ker-lis-ti-an* and spoke English – as the Sahibs speak it. Yes. My Sahib said he would return and wed me – yes, wed me. He went away – I had nursed him when he was sick – but he never returned. Then I saw that the Gods of the Kerlistians lied, and I went back to my own people. . . . I have never set eyes on a Sahib since. (Do not laugh at me. The fit is past, little priestling.) Thy face and thy walk and thy fashion of speech put me in mind of my Sahib, though thou art only a wandering mendicant to whom I give a dole. Curse me? Thou canst neither curse nor bless!' She set her hands on her hips and laughed bitterly. 'Thy Gods are lies; thy works are lies; thy words are lies. There are no Gods under all the heavens. I know it. . . . But for a while I thought it was my Sahib come back, and he was my God. Yes, once I made music on a *pianno* in the Mission-house at Kotgarh. Now I give alms to priests who are *heatthen*.' She wound up with the English word, and tied the mouth of the brimming bag.

'I wait for thee, *chela*,' said the lama, leaning against the door-post.

The woman swept the tall figure with her eyes. 'He walk! He cannot cover half a mile. Whither would old bones go?'

At this Kim, already perplexed by the lama's collapse, and foreseeing the weight of the bag, fairly lost his temper.

'What is it to thee, woman of ill-omen, where he goes?'

'Nothing – but something to thee, priest with a Sahib's face. Wilt thou carry him on thy shoulders?'

'I go to the Plains. None must hinder my return. I have wrestled with my soul till I am strengthless. The stupid body is spent, and we are far from the Plains.'

'Behold!' she said simply, and drew aside to let Kim see his own utter helplessness. 'Curse me. May be it will give him strength. Make a charm! Call on thy great God. Thou art a priest.' She turned away.

The lama had squatted limply, still holding by the door-post. One cannot strike down an old man that he recovers again like a boy in a night. Weakness bowed him to the earth, but his eyes that hung on Kim were alive and imploring.

'It is all well,' said Kim. 'It is the thin air that weakens thee. In a little while we go! It is the mountain-sickness I too am a little while at stomach,' . . . . and he knelt and comforted with such poor words as came first to his lips. Then the woman returned, more erect than ever.

'Thy Gods useless, heh? Try mine. *I* am the Woman of Shamlegh.' She hailed hoarsely, and there came out of a cow-pen her two husbands and three others with a *dooli,* the rude native litter of the Hills, that they use for carrying the sick and for visits of state. 'These cattle,' she did not condescend to look at them, 'are thine for so long as thou shalt need.'

'But we will not go Simla-way. We will not go near the Sahibs!' cried the first husband.

'They will not run away as the others did, nor will they steal baggage. Two I know for weaklings. Stand to the rear-pole, Sonoo and Taree.' They obeyed swiftly. 'Lower now, and lift in that holy man. I will see to the village and your virtuous wives till ye return.'

'When will that be?'

'Ask the priests. Do not pester me. Lay the food-bag at the foot, it balances better so.'

'Oh, Holy One, thy Hills are kinder than our Plains!' cried Kim, relieved, as the lama tottered to the litter. 'It is a very king's bed – a place of honour and ease. And we owe it to – '

'A woman of ill-omen. I need thy blessings as much as I do thy curses. It is *my* order and none of thine. Lift and away! Here! Hast thou money for the road?'

She beckoned Kim to her hut, and stooped above a battered English cash-box under her cot.

'I do not need anything,' said Kim, angered when he should have been grateful. 'I am already rudely loaded with favours.'

She looked up with a curious smile and laid a hand on his shoulder. 'At least, thank me. I am foul-faced and a hillwoman, but, as thy talk goes, I have acquired merit. Shall I show thee how the Sahibs render thanks?' and her hard eyes softened.

'I am but a wandering priest,' said Kim, his eyes lighting in answer. 'Thou needest neither my blessings nor my curses.'

'Nay. But for one little moment – thou canst overtake the *dooli* in ten strides – *if* thou wast a Sahib, shall I show thee what thou wouldst do?'

'How if I guess, though?' said Kim, and putting his arm round her waist, he kissed her on the cheek, adding in English: 'Thank you verree much, my dear.'

Kissing is practically unknown among Asiatics, which may have been the reason that she leaned back with wide-open eyes and a face of panic.

'Next time,' Kim went on, 'you must not be so sure of your heathen priests. Now I say good-bye.' He held out his hand English-fashion. She took it mechanically. 'Good-bye, my dear.'

'Good-bye, and – and' – she was remembering her English words one by one – 'you will come back again? Good-bye, and – thee God bless you.'

Half an hour later, as the creaking litter jolted up the hill path that leads south-easterly from Shamlegh, Kim saw a tiny figure at the hut door waving a white rag.

'She has acquired merit beyond all others,' said the lama. 'For to set a man upon the way to Freedom is half as great as though she had herself found it.'

'Umm,' said Kim thoughtfully, considering the past. 'It may be that I have acquired merit also. . . . At least she did not treat me like a child.' He hitched the front of his robe, where lay the slab of documents and maps, restowed the precious food-bag at the lama's feet, laid his hand on the litter edge, and buckled down to the slow pace of the grunting husbands.

'These also acquire merit,' said the lama, after three miles.

'More than that, they shall be paid in silver,' quoth Kim. The Woman of Shamlegh had given it to him; and it was only fair, he argued, that her men should earn it back again.

CHAPTER 15

I'd not give room for an Emperor –
  I'd hold my road for a King.
To the Triple Crown I'd not bow down –
  But this is a different thing!
I'll not fight with the Powers of Air –
  Sentries pass him through!
Drawbridge let fall – He's the Lord of us all –
  The Dreamer whose dream came true!

– *The Siege of the Fairies*

TWO HUNDRED miles north of Chini, on the blue shale of Ladakh, lies Yankling Sahib, the merry-minded man, spy-glassing wrathfully across the ridges for some sign of his pet tracker – a man from Ao-chung. But that renegade, with a new Mannlicher rifle and two hundred cartridges, is elsewhere, shooting musk-deer for the market, and Yankling Sahib will learn next season how very ill he has been.

Up the valleys of Bushahr – the far-beholding eagles of the Himalayas swerve at his new blue-and-white gored umbrella – hurries a Bengali, once fat and well-looking, now lean and weather-worn. He has received the thanks of two foreigners of distinction, piloted not unskilfully to Mashobra tunnel which leads to the great and gay capital of India. It was not his fault that, blanketed by wet mists, he conveyed them past the telegraph-station and European colony of Kotgarh. It was not his fault, but that of the Gods, of whom he discoursed so engagingly, that he led them into the borders of Nahan, where the Rajah of that state mistook them for deserting British soldiery. Hurree Babu explained the greatness and glory, in their own country, of his companions, till the drowsy kinglet smiled. He explained it to every one who asked – many times – aloud – variously. He begged food, arranged accommodation, proved a skilful leech for an injury of the groin – such a blow as one may receive rolling down a rock-covered hillside in the dark – and in all things indispensable. The reason of his friendliness did him credit. With millions of fellow-serfs, he had learned to look upon Russia as the great deliverer from the North. He was a fearful man. He had been afraid that he could not save his illustrious employers from the anger of an excited peasantry. He himself would just as lief hit a holy man as not, but. . . . He was deeply grateful and sincerely rejoiced that he had done his 'little possible' towards bringing their venture to – barring the lost baggage – a successful issue. He had forgotten the blows; denied that any blows had been dealt that unseemly first night under the pines. He asked neither pension nor retaining fee, but, if they deemed him worthy, would they write him a testimonial? It might be useful to him later, if others, their friends, came over the Passes. He begged them to remember him in their future greatnesses, for he 'opined subtly' that he, even he, Mohendro Lal Dutt, M.A. of Calcutta, had 'done the state some service.'

They gave him a certificate praising his courtesy, helpfulness, and unerring skill as a guide. He put it in his waist-belt and sobbed with emotion; they had endured so many dangers together. He led them at high noon along crowded Simla Mall to the Alliance Bank of Simla, where they wished to establish their identity. Thence he vanished like a dawn-cloud on Jakko.

Behold him, too fine drawn to sweat, too pressed to vaunt the drugs in his little brass-bound box, ascending Shamlegh slope, a just man made perfect. Watch him, all Babudom laid aside, smoking at noon on a cot, while a woman with turquoise-studded head-gear points south-easterly across the bare grass. Litters, she says, do not travel as fast as single men, but his birds should now be in the Plains. The holy man would not stay though Lispeth pressed him. The Babu groans heavily, girds up his huge loins, and is off again. He does not care to travel after dusk; but his days' marches – there is none to enter them in a book – would astonish folk who mock at his race. Kindly villagers, remembering the Dacca drug-vendor of two months ago, give him shelter against evil spirits of the wood. He dreams of Bengali Gods, University text-books of education, and the Royal Society, London, England. Next dawn the bobbing blue-and-white umbrella goes forward.

On the edge of the Doon, Mussoorie well behind them and the Plains spread out in golden dust before, rests a worn litter in which – all the Hills know it – lies a sick lama who seeks a River for his healing. Villages have almost come to blows over the honour of bearing it, for not only has the lama given them blessings, but his disciple good money – full one-third Sahibs' prices. Twelve miles a day has the *dooli* travelled, as the greasy, rubbed pole-ends show, and by roads that few Sahibs use. Over the Nilang Pass in storm when the driven snow-dust filled every fold of the impassive lama's drapery; between the black horns of Raieng where they heard the whistle of the wild goats through the clouds; pitching and strained on the shale below; hard-held between shoulder and clenched jaw when they rounded the hideous curves of the Cut Road under

Bhagirati; swinging and creaking to the steady jog-trot of the descent into the Valley of the Waters; pressed along the steamy levels of that locked valley; up, up and out again, to meet the roaring gusts off Kedarnath; set down of mid-days in the dun gloom of kindly oak-forests; passed from village to village in dawn-chill, when even devotees may be forgiven for swearing at impatient holy men; or by torchlight, when the least fearful think of ghosts – the *dooli* has reached her last stage. The little hill-folk sweat in the modified heat of the lower Sewaliks, and gather round the priests for their blessing and their wage.

'Ye have acquired merit,' says the lama. 'Merit greater than your knowing. And ye will return to the Hills,' he sighs.

'Surely. The high hills as soon as may be.' The bearer rubs his shoulder, drinks water, spits it out again, and readjusts his grass sandal. Kim – his face is drawn and tired – pays very small silver from his belt, heaves out the food-bag, crams an oilskin packet – they are holy writings – into his bosom, and helps the lama to his feet. The peace has come again into the old man's eyes, and he does not look for the hills to fall down and crush him as he did that terrible night when they were delayed by the flooded river.

The men pick up the *dooli* and swing out of sight between the scrub clumps.

The lama raises a hand toward the rampart of the Himalayas. 'Not with you, O blessed among all hills, fell the Arrow of Our Lord! And never shall I breathe your air again!'

'But thou art ten times the stronger man in this good air,' say Kim, for to his wearied soul appeal the well-cropped, kindly plains. 'Here, or hereabouts, fell the Arrow, yes. We will go very softly, perhaps a *kôs* a day, for the Search is sure. But the bag weighs heavy.'

'Ay, our Search is sure. I have come out of great temptation.'

* * * * *

It was never more than a couple of miles a day now, and Kim's shoulders bore all the weight of it – the burden of an old man, the burden of the heavy food-bag with the locked books, the load of the writings on his heart, and the details of the daily routine. He begged in the dawn, set blankets for the lama's meditation, held the weary head on his lap through the noon-day heats, fanning away the flies till his wrist ached, begged again in the evenings, and rubbed the lama's feet, who rewarded him with promise of Freedom – to-day, to-morrow, or, at furthest, the next day.

'Never was such a *chela*. I doubt at times whether Ananda more faithfully nursed Our Lord. And thou art a Sahib? When I was a man – a long time ago – I forgot that. Now I look upon thee often, and every time I remember that thou art a Sahib. It is strange.'

'Thou hast said there is neither black nor white. Why plague me with this talk, Holy One? Let me rub the other foot. It vexes me. I am *not* a Sahib. I am thy *chela*, and my head is heavy on my shoulders.'

'Patience a little! We reach Freedom together. Then thou and I, upon the far bank of the River, will look back upon our lives as in the Hills we saw our days' marches laid out behind us. Perhaps I was once a Sahib.'

' 'Was never a Sahib like thee, I swear it.'

'I am certain the Keeper of the Images in the Wonder House was in past life a very wise abbot. But even his spectacles do not make my eyes see. There fall shadows when I would look steadily. No matter – we know the tricks of the poor stupid carcass – shadow changing to another shadow. I am bound by the illusion of Time and Space. How far came we to-day in the flesh?'

'Perhaps half a *kôs*.' Three-quarters of a mile, and it was a weary march.

'Half a *kôs*. Ha! I went ten thousand thousand in the spirit. How we are all lapped and swathed and swaddled in these senseless things.' He looked at his thin blue-veined hand that found the beads so heavy. '*Chela*, hast thou never a wish to leave me?'

Kim thought of the oilskin packet and the books in the food-bag. If some one duly authorised would only take delivery of them the Great Game might play itself for aught he then cared. He was tired and hot in his head, and a cough that came from the stomach worried him.

'No,' he said almost sternly. 'I am not a dog or a snake to bite when I have learned to love.'

'Thou art too tender for me.'

'Not that either. I have moved in one matter without consulting thee. I have sent a message to the Kulu woman by that woman who gave us the goat's milk this morn, saying that thou wast a little feeble and would need a litter. I beat myself in my mind that I did not do it when we entered the Doon. We stay in this place till the litter returns.'

'I am content. She is a woman with a heart of gold, as thou sayest, but a talker – something of a talker.'

'She will not weary thee. I have looked to that also. Holy One, my heart is very heavy for my many carelessnesses towards thee.' An hysterical catch rose in his throat. 'I have walked thee too far; I have not picked good food always for thee; I have not considered the heat; I have talked to people on the road and left thee alone. . . . I have – I have. . . . *Hai mai*! But I love thee. . . . and it is all too late. . . . I was a child. . . . Oh why was I not a man!. . . .' Overborne by strain, fatigue, and the weight beyond his years, Kim broke down and sobbed at the lama's feet.

'What a to-do is here,' said the old man gently. 'Thou has never stepped a hair's breadth from the Way of Obedience. Neglect me? Child, I have lived on thy strength as an old tree lives on the lime of a new wall. Day by day since Shamlegh down, I have stolen strength from thee. *Therefore*, not through any sin of thine art thou weakened. It is the Body – the silly, stupid Body – that speaks now. Not the assured Soul. Be comforted! Know at least the devils that thou fightest. They are earth-born – children of illusion. We will go to the woman from Kulu. She shall acquire merit in housing us, and specially in tending me. Thou shalt run free till strength returns. I had forgotten the stupid Body. If there be any blame, I bear it. But we are too close to the Gates of Deliverance to weigh blame. I could praise thee, but what need? In a little – in a very little – we shall sit beyond all needs.

And so he petted and comforted Kim with wise saws and grave texts on that little-understood beast, our Body, who, being but a delusion, insists on posing as the Soul, to the darkening of the Way, and the immense multiplication of unnecessary devils.

'Hai! hai! Let us talk of the woman from Kulu. Think you she will ask another charm for her grandsons? When I was a young man, a very long time ago, I was plagued with these vapours – and some others – and I went to an abbot – a very holy man and a seeker after Truth, though then I knew it not. Sit up and listen, child of my soul! My tale was told. Said he to me, "*Chela*, know this. There are many lies in the world, and not a few liars, but there are no liars like our bodies, except it be the sensations of our bodies." Considering this I was comforted, and of his great favour he suffered me to drink tea in his presence. Suffer me now to drink tea, for I am thirsty.'

With a laugh above his tears, Kim kissed the lama's feet, and went about tea-making.

'Thou leanest on me in the body, Holy One, but I lean on thee for some other things. Dost know it?'

'I have guessed maybe,' and the lama's eyes twinkled. 'We must change that.'

So, when with scufflings and scrapings and a hot air of importance, paddled up nothing less than the Sahiba's pet palanquin sent twenty miles, with that same grizzled old Oorya servant in charge, and when they reached the disorderly order of the long white rambling house behind Saharunpore, the lama took his own measures.

Said the Sahiba cheerily from an upper window, after compliments: 'What is the good of an old woman's advice to an old man? I told thee – I *told* thee, Holy One, to keep an eye upon the *chela*. How didst thou do it? Never answer me! *I* know. He has been running among the women. Look at his eyes – hollow and sunk – and the Betraying Line from the nose down! He has been sifted out! Fie! Fie! And a priest, too!'

Kim looked up over-weary to smile, shaking his head in denial.

'Do not jest,' said the lama. 'That time is done. We are here upon great matters. A sickness of soul took me in the Hills, and him a sickness of the body. Since then I have lived upon his strength – eating him.'

'Children together – young and old,' she sniffed, but forbore to make any new jokes. 'May this present hospitality restore ye. Hold awhile and I will come to gossip of the high good Hills.'

At evening time – her son-in-law was returned, so she did not need to go on inspection round the farm – she won to the meat of the matter, explained low-voicedly by the lama. The two old heads nodded wisely together. Kim had reeled to a room with a cot in it, and was dozing soddenly. The lama had forbidden him to set blankets or get food.

'I know – I know. Who but I?' she cackled. 'We who go down to the burning-ghats clutch at the hands of those coming up from the River of Life with full water-jars – yes, brimming water-jars. I did the boy wrong. He lent thee his strength? It is true that the old eat the young daily. 'Stands now we must restore him.'

'Thou hast many times acquired merit – '

'*My* merit. What is it? Old bag of bones making curries for men who do not ask "Who cooked this?" Now if it were stored up for my grandson – '

'He that had the belly-pain?'

'To think the Holy One remembers *that!* I must tell his mother. It is most singular honour! "He that had the belly-pain" – straightway the Holy One remembered. She will be proud.'

'My *chela* is to me as a son to the unenlightened.'

'Say grandson, rather. Mothers have not the wisdom of our years. If a child cries they say the heavens are falling. Now a grandmother is far enough separated from the pain of bearing and the pleasure of giving the breast to consider whether a cry is wickedness pure or the wind. And since thou speakest once again of wind, when last the Holy One was here, maybe I offended in pressing for charms.'

'Sister,' said the lama, using that form of address a Buddhist monk may sometimes employ towards a nun, 'if charms comfort thee – '

'They are better than ten thousand doctors.'

'I say, if they comfort thee, I who was Abbot of Such-zen will make as many as thou mayest desire. I have never seen thy face – '

'*That* even the monkeys who steal our loquats count for a gain. Hee! hee!'

'But as he who sleeps there said,' he nodded at the shut door of the guest-chamber across the forecourt, 'thou hast a heart of gold.... And he is in the spirit my very "grandson" to me.'

'Good! I am the Holy One's cow.' This was pure Hinduism, but the lama never heeded. 'I am old. I have borne sons in the body. Oh, once I could please men! Now I can cure them.' He heard her armlets tinkle as though she bared arms for action. 'I will take over the boy and dose him, and stuff him, and make him all whole. Hai! hai! We old people know something yet.'

Wherefore when Kim, aching in every bone, opened his eyes, and would go to the cook-house to get his master's food, he found strong coercion about him, and a veiled old figure at the door, flanked by the grizzled manservant, who told him precisely the very things that he was on no account to do.

'Thou must have – Thou shalt have nothing. What? A locked box in which to keep holy books? Oh, that is another matter. Heavens forbid I should come between a priest and his prayers! It shall be brought, and thou shalt keep the key.'

They pushed the coffer under his cot, and Kim shut away Mahbub's pistol, the oilskin packet of letters, and the locked books and diaries, with a groan of relief. For some absurd reason their weight on his shoulders was nothing to their weight on his poor mind. His neck ached under it of nights.

'Thine is a sickness uncommon in youth these days: since young folk have given up tending their betters. The remedy is sleep, and certain drugs,' said the Sahiba; and he was glad to give himself up to the blankness that half menaced and half soothed him.

She brewed drinks, in some mysterious Asiatic equivalent to the still-room – drenches that smelt pestilently and tasted worse. She stood over Kim till they went down, and inquired exhaustively after they had come up. She laid a taboo upon the forecourt, and enforced it by means of an armed man. It is true he was seventy odd, that his scabbarded sword ceased at the hilt; but he represented the authority of the Sahiba, and loaded wains, chattering servants, calves, dogs, hens, and the like, fetched a wide compass by those parts. Best of all, when the body was cleared, she cut out from the mass of poor relations that crowded the back of the buildings – household dogs, we name them – a cousin's widow, skilled in what Europeans, who know nothing about it, call massage. And the two of them, laying him east and west, that the mysterious earth-currents which thrill the clay of our bodies might help and not hinder, took him to pieces all one long afternoon – bone by bone, muscle by muscle, ligament by ligament, and lastly, nerve by nerve. Kneaded to irresponsible pulp, half hypnotised by the perpetual flick and readjustment of the uneasy *chudders* that veiled their eyes, Kim slid ten thousand miles into slumber – thirty-six hours of it – sleep that soaked like rain after drought.

Then she fed him, and the house spun to her clamour. She caused fowls to be slain; she sent for vegetables, and the sober, slow-thinking gardener, nigh as old as she, sweated for it; she took spices, and milk, and onion, with little fish from the brooks – anon limes for sherbets, fat quails of the pit, then chicken-livers upon a skewer, with sliced ginger between.

'I have seen something of this world,' she said over the crowded trays, 'and there are but two sorts of women in it – those who take the strength out of a man and those who put it back. Once I was that one, and now I am this. Nay – do not play the priestling with me. Mine was but a jest. If it does not hold good now, it will when thou takest the road again. Cousin'

– this to the poor relation, never wearied of extolling her patroness's charity – 'he is getting a bloom on the skin of a new-curried horse. Our work is like polishing jewels to be thrown to a dance-girl – eh?'

Kim sat up and smiled. The terrible weakness had dropped from him like an old shoe. His tongue itched for free speech again, and but a week back the lightest word clogged it like ashes. The pain in his neck (he must have caught it from the lama) had gone with the heavy dengue-aches and the evil taste in the mouth. The two old women, a little, but not much, more careful about their veils now, clucked as merrily as the hens that had entered pecking through the open door.

'Where is my Holy One?' he demanded.

'Hear him! Thy Holy One is well,' she snapped viciously. 'Though that is none of *his* merit. Knew I a charm to make him wise, I'd sell my jewels and buy it. To refuse good food that I cooked myself – and go roving into the fields for two nights on an empty belly – and to tumble into a brook at the end of it – call you *that* holiness? Then, when he has nearly broken what thou hast left of my heart with anxiety, he tells me that he has acquired merit. Oh how like are all men! No, that was not it – he tells me that he is freed from all sin. *I* could have told him that before he wetted himself all over. He is well now – this happened a week ago – but burn me such holiness! A babe of three would do better. Do not fret thyself for the Holy One. He keeps both eyes on thee when he is not wading our brooks.'

'I do not remember to have seen him. I remember that the days and nights passed like bars of white and black, opening and shutting. I was not sick: I was only tired.'

'A lethargy that comes by right some few score years later. But it is all done now.'

'Maharanee,' Kim began, but led by the look in her eye, changed it to the title of plain love – 'Mother, I owe my life to thee. How shall I make thanks? Ten thousand blessings upon thy house and – '

'The house be unblessed.' (It is impossible to give exactly the old lady's word.) 'Thank the Gods as a priest if thou wilt, but thank me if thou carest as a son. Heavens above! Have I shifted thee and lifted thee and slapped and twisted thy ten toes to find texts flung at my head? Somewhere a mother must have borne thee to break her heart. What used thou to her – son?'

'I had no mother, my mother,' said Kim. 'She died, they tell me, when I was young.'

'*Hai mai*! Then none can say I have robbed her of any right if – when thou takest the road again and this house is but one of a thousand used for shelter and forgotten, after an easy-flung blessing. No matter. I need no blessings, but – but – ' She stamped her foot at the poor relation: 'Take up the trays to the house. What is the good of stale food in the room, oh woman of ill-omen?'

'I ha – have borne a son in my time too, but he died,' whimpered the bowed sister-figure behind the *chudder*. 'Thou knowest he died! I only waited for the order to take away the tray.'

'It is I that am the woman of ill-omen,' cried the old lady penitently. 'We that go down to the *chattris* (the big umbrellas above the burning-ghats where the priests take their last dues) clutch hard at the bearers of the *chattis* (water-jars – young folk full of the pride of life, she meant; but the pun is clumsy). When one cannot dance in the festival one must e'en look out of the window, and grandmothering takes all a woman's time. Thy master gives me all the charms I now desire for my daughter's eldest, by reason – is it? – that he is wholly free from sin. The *hakim* is brought very low these days. He goes about poisoning my servants for lack of their betters.'

'What *hakim*, mother?'

'That very Dacca man who gave me the pill which rent me in three pieces. He cast up like a strayed camel a week ago, vowing that he and thou had been blood-brothers together up Kulu-way, and feigning great anxiety for thy health. He was very thin and hungry, so I gave orders to have him stuffed too – him and his anxiety!'

'I would see him if he is here.'

'He eats five times a day, and lances boils for my hinds to save himself from an apoplexy. He is so full of anxiety for thy health that he sticks to the cook-house door and stays himself with scraps. He will keep. We shall never get rid of him.'

'Send him here, mother' – the twinkle returned to Kim's eye for a flash – 'and I will try.'

'I'll send him, but to chase him off is an ill turn. At least he had the sense to fish the Holy One out of the brook; thus, as the Holy One did *not* say, acquiring merit.'

'He is a very wise *hakim*. Send him, mother.'

'Priest praising priest? A miracle! If he is any friend of thine (ye squabbled at your last meeting) I'll hale him here with horse-ropes and – and give him a caste-dinner afterwards, my son. . . . Get up and see the world! This lying abed is the mother of seventy devils. . . . my son!'

She trotted forth to raise a typhoon off the cook-house, and almost on her shadow rolled in the Babu, robed as to the shoulders like a Roman emperor, jowled like Titus, bareheaded, with new patent-leather shoes, in highest condition of fat, exuding joy and salutations.

'By Jove, Mister O'Hara, but I *am* jolly glad to see you. I will kindly shut the door. It is a pity you are sick. Are you very sick?'

'The papers – the papers from the *kilta*. The maps and the *murasla*!' He held out the key impatiently; for the present need on his soul was to get rid of the loot.

'You are quite right. That is correct departmental view to take. You have got everything?'

'All was handwritten in the *kilta* I took. The rest I threw down the hill.' He could hear the key's grate in the lock, the sticky pull of the slow-rending oil-cloth, and a quick shuffling of papers. He had been annoyed out of all reason by the knowledge that they lay below him through the sick idle days – a burden incommunicable. For that reason the blood tingled through his body, when Hurree, skipping elephantinely, shook hands again.

'This is fine! This is finest! Mister O'Hara! You have – ha! ha! – swiped the whole bag of tricks – locks, stocks, and barrels. They told me it was eight months' work gone up the spouts! By Jove, how they beat me!. . . . Look, here is the letter from Hilás!' He intoned a line or two of Court Persian, which is the language of authorised and unauthorised diplomacy. 'Mister Rajah Sahib has just about put his foot in the holes. He will have to explain offeecially how the deuce-an'-all he is writing love-letters to the Czar. And they are very clever maps. . . . and there is three or four Prime Ministers of these parts implicated by the correspondence. By Gad, Sar! The British Government will change the succession in Hilás and Bunár, and nominate new heirs to the throne. "Treason most base". . . . but you do not understand? Eh?'

'Are they in thy hands?' said Kim. It was all he cared for.

'Just you jolly well bet yourself they are.' He stowed the entire trove about his body, as only Orientals can. 'They are going up to the office, too. The old lady thinks I am permanent fixture here, but I shall go away with these straight off – immediately. Mr. Lurgan will be proud man. You are offeecially subordinate to me, but I shall embody your name in my verbal report. It is a pity we are not allowed written reports. We Bengalis excel in thee exact science.' He tossed back the key and showed the box empty.

'Good. That is good. I was very tired. My Holy One was sick, too. And did he fall into – '

'Oah yess. I am his good friend, I tell you. He was behaving very strange when I came down after you, and I thought perhaps he might have the papers. I followed him on his meditations, and to discuss ethnological points also. You see, I am verree small person here nowadays, in comparison with all his charms. By Jove, O'Hara, do you know, he is afflicted with infirmity of fits. Yess, I tell you. Cataleptic, too, if not also epileptic. I found him in such a state under a tree *in articulo mortem*,[1] and he jumped up and walked into a brook and he was nearly drowned but for me. I pulled him out.'

'Because I was not there!' said Kim. 'He might have died.'

'Yes, he might have died, but he is dry now, and asserts he has undergone transfiguration.' The Babu tapped his forehead knowingly. 'I took notes of his statements for Royal Society – *in posse*.[2] You must make haste and be quite well and come back to Simla, and I will tell you all my tale at Lurgan's. It was splendid. The bottoms of their trousers were quite torn, and old Nahan Rajah, he thought they were European soldiers deserting.'

'Oh, the Russians? How long were they with thee?'

1 (Lat.) At the point of death.
2 (Lat.) In possible existence.

'One was a Frenchman. Oh, days and days and days! Now all the hill-people believe all Russians are all beggars. By Jove! they had not one dam-thing that I did not get them. And I told the common people – oah, such tales and anecdotes! I will tell you at old Lurgan's when you come up. We will have – ah – a night out! It is feather in both our caps! Yess, and they gave me a certificate. That is creaming joke. You should have seen them at the Alliance Bank identifying themselves! And thank Almighty God you got their papers so well! You do not laugh verree much, but you shall laugh when you are well. Now I will go straight to the railway and get out. You shall have all sorts of credits for your game. When do you come along? We are very proud of you, though you gave us great frights. And especially Mahbub.'

'Ay, Mahbub. And where is he?'

'Selling horses in this vi-cinity, of course.'

'Here! Why? Speak slowly. There is a thickness in my head still.'

The Babu looked shyly down his nose. 'Well, you see, I am fearful man, and I do not like responsibility. You were sick, you see, and I did not know where deuce-an'-all the papers were, and if so, how many. So when I had come down here I slipped in private wire to Mahbub – he was at Meerut for races – and I tell him how case stands. He comes up with his men and he consorts with the lama, and then he calls me a fool, and is very rude – '

'But wherefore – wherefore?'

'That is what *I* ask. I only suggest that if anyone steals the papers I should like some good strong, brave men to rob them back again. You see they are vitally important, and Mahbub Ali he did not know where you were.'

'Mahbub Ali to rob the Sahiba's house? Thou art mad, Babu,' said Kim with indignation.

'I wanted the papers. Suppose she had stole them? It was only practical suggestion, *I* think. You are not pleased, eh?'

A native proverb – unquotable – showed the blackness of Kim's disapproval.

'Well,' – Hurree shrugged his shoulders, – 'there is no accounting for thee taste. Mahbub was angry too. He has sold horses all about here, and he says old lady is *pukka* (thorough) old lady and would not condescend to such ungentlemanly things. *I* do not care. I have got the papers, and I was very glad of moral support from Mahbub. I tell you I am fearful man, but, somehow or other, the more fearful I am the more damtight places I get into. So I was glad you came with me to Chini, and I am glad Mahbub was close by. The old lady she is sometimes very rude to me and my beautiful pills.'

'Allah be merciful,' said Kim on his elbow, rejoicing. 'What a beast of wonder is a Babu! And that man walked alone – if he did walk – with robbed and angry foreigners!'

'Oah, thatt was nothing, after they had done beating me; but if I lost the papers it was pretty jolly serious. Mahbub he nearly beat me too, and he went and consorted with the lama no end. I shall stick to ethnological investigations henceforwards. Now good-bye, Mister O'Hara. I can catch 4.25 P.M. to Umballa if I am quick. It will be good times when we all tell thee tale up at Mister Lurgan's. I shall report you offeecially better. Good-bye, my dear fallow, and when next you are under thee emotions please do not use the Mohammedan terms with the Tibetan dress.'

He shook hands twice – a Babu to his boot-heels – and opened the door. With the fall of the sunlight upon his still triumphant face he returned to the humble Dacca quack.

'He robbed them,' thought Kim, forgetting his own share in the game. 'He tricked them. He lied to them like a Bengali. They give him a *chit* (a testimonial). He makes them a mock at the risk of his life – *I* never would have gone down to them after the pistol-shots – and then he says he is a fearful man. . . . And he *is* a fearful man. I must get into the world again.'

At first his legs bent like bad pipe-stems, and the flood and rush of the sunlit air dazzled him. He squatted by the white wall, the mind rummaging among the incidents of the long *dooli* journey, the lama's weaknesses, and, now that the stimulus of talk was removed, his own self-pity, of which, like the sick, he had great store. The unnerved brain edged away from all the outside, as a raw horse, once rowelled, sidles from the spur. It was enough, amply enough, that the spoil of the *kilta* was away – off his hands – out of his possession. He tried to think of the lama, – to wonder why he had tumbled into a brook, – but the bigness of the world, seen between the forecourt gates, swept linked thought aside. Then he looked upon the trees and the broad fields, with the thatched huts hidden among crops – looked with strange eyes unable to take up the size and proportion and use of things – stared for a still half-hour. All that while he felt, though he could not put it into words, that his soul was out of gear with its surroundings – a cog-wheel unconnected with any machinery, just like the idle cog-wheel of a cheap Beheea sugar-crusher laid by in a corner. The breezes fanned over him, the parrots shrieked at him, the noises of the populated house behind – squabbles, orders, and reproofs – hit on dead ears.

'I am Kim. I am Kim. And what is Kim?' His soul repeated it again and again.

He did not want to cry, – had never felt less like crying in his life, – but of a sudden easy, stupid tears trickled down his nose, and with an almost audible click he felt the wheels of his being lock up anew on the world without. Things that rode meaningless on the eyeball an instant before slid into proper proportion. Roads were meant to be walked upon, houses to be lived in, cattle to be driven, fields to be tilled, and men and women to be talked to. They were all real and true – solidly planted upon the feet – perfectly comprehensible – clay of his clay, neither more nor less. He shook himself like a dog with a flea in his ear, and rambled out of the gate. Said the Sahiba, to whom watchful eyes reported this move: 'Let him go. I have done my share. Mother Earth must do the rest. When the Holy One comes back from meditation, tell him.'

There stood an empty bullock-cart on a little knoll half a mile away, with a young banian tree behind – a look-out, as it were, above some new-ploughed levels; and his eyelids, bathed in soft air, grew heavy as he neared it. The ground was good clean dust – no new herbage that, living, is halfway to death already, but the hopeful dust that holds the seed of all life. He felt it between his toes, patted it with his palms, and joint by joint, sighing luxuriously, laid him down full length along in the shadow of the wooden-pinned cart. And Mother Earth was as faithful as the Sahiba. She breathed through him to restore the poise he had lost lying so long on a cot cut off from her good currents. His head lay powerless upon her breast, and his opened hands surrendered to her strength. The many-rooted tree above him, and even the dead man-handled wood beside, knew what he sought, as he himself did not know. Hour upon hour he lay deeper than sleep.

Towards evening, when the dust of returning kine made all the horizons smoke, came the lama and Mahbub Ali, both afoot, walking cautiously, for the house had told them where he had gone.

'Allah! What a fool's trick to play in open country,' muttered the horse-dealer. 'He could be shot a hundred times – but this is not the Border.'

'And,' said the lama, repeating a many-times-told tale, 'never was such a *chela*. Temperate, kindly, wise, of ungrudging disposition, a merry heart upon the road, never forgetting, learned, truthful, courteous. Great is his reward!'

'I know the boy – as I have said.'

'And he was all those things?'

'Some of them – but I have not yet found a Red Hat's charm for making him overly truthful. He has certainly been well nursed.'

'The Sahiba is a heart of gold,' said the lama earnestly. 'She looks upon him as her son.'

'Hmph! Half Hind seems that-way disposed. I only wished to see that the boy had come to no harm and was a free agent. As thou knowest, he and I were old friends in the first days of your pilgrimage together.'

'That is a bond between us.' The lama sat down. 'We are at the end of the pilgrimage.'

'No thanks to thee thine was not cut off for good and all a week back. I heard what the Sahiba said to thee when we bore thee up on the cot.' Mahbub laughed, and tugged his newly-dyed beard.

'I was meditating upon other matters that tide. It was the *hakim* from Dacca broke my meditations.'

'Otherwise!' – this was in Pashtu for decency's sake – 'thou wouldst have ended thy meditations upon the sultry side of Hell – being an unbeliever and an idolater for all thy child's simplicity. But now, Red Hat, what is to be done?'

'This very night" – the words came slowly, vibrating with triumph – "this very night he will be as free as I am from all taint of sin – assured as I am when he quits this body of Freedom from the Wheel of Things. I have a sign,' he laid his hand above the torn chart in his bosom, 'that my time is short; but I shall have safe-guarded him throughout the years. Remember, I have reached Knowledge, as I told thee only three nights back.'

'It must be true, as the Tirah priest said when I stole his cousin's wife, that I am a *sufi* (a freethinker); for here I sit,' said Mahbub to himself, 'drinking in blasphemy unthinkable. . . . I remember the tale. On that, then, he goes to *Jannatu l'Adn* (the Gardens of Eden). But how? Wilt thou slay him or drown him in that wonderful river from which the Babu dragged thee?'

'I was dragged from no river,' said the lama simply. 'Thou hast forgotten what befell. I found it by Knowledge.'

'Oh, aye. True,' stammered Mahbub, divided between high indignation and enormous mirth. 'I had forgotten the exact run of what happened. Thou didst find it knowingly.'

'And to say that I would take life is – not a sin, but a madness simple. My *chela* aided me to the River. It is his right to be cleansed from sin – with me.'

'Ay, he needs cleansing. But afterwards, old man – afterwards?'

'What matter under all the heavens? He is sure of Nibban – enlightened – as I am.'

'Well said. I had a fear he might mount Mohammed's Horse and fly away.'

'Nay – he must go forth as a teacher.'

'Aha! Now I see! That is the right gait for the colt. Certainly he must go forth as a teacher. He is somewhat urgently needed as a scribe by the State, for instance.'

'To that end he was prepared. I acquired merit in that I gave alms for his sake. A good deed does not die. He aided me in my Search. I aided him in his. Just is the Wheel, O horse-seller from the North. Let him be a teacher; let him be a scribe – what matter? He will have attained Freedom at the end. The rest is illusion.'

'What matter? When I must have him with me beyond Balkh in six months! I come up with ten lame horses and three strong-backed men – thanks to that chicken of a Babu – to break a sick boy by force out of an old trot's house. It seems that I stand by while a young Sahib is hoisted into Allah knows what of an idolater's heaven by means of old Red Hat. And I am reckoned something of a player of the Game myself! But the madman is fond of the boy; and I must be very reasonably mad too.'

'What is the prayer?' said the lama, as the rough Pashtu rumbled into the red beard.

'No matter at all; but now I understand that the boy, sure of Paradise, can yet enter Government service, my mind is easier. I must get to my horses. It grows dark. Do not wake him. I have no wish to hear him call thee master.'

'But he *is* my disciple. What else?'

'He has told me.' Mahbub choked down his touch of spleen and rose laughing. 'I am not altogether of thy faith, Red Hat – if so small a matter concern thee.'

'It is nothing,' said the lama.

'I thought not. Therefore it will not move thee sinless, new-washed and three parts drowned to boot, when I call thee a good man – a very good man. We have talked together some four or five evenings now, and for all I am a horse-coper I can still, as the saying is, see holiness beyond the legs of a horse. Yea, can see, too, how our Friend of all the World put his hand in thine at the first. Use him well, and suffer him to return to the world as a teacher, when thou hast – bathed his legs, if that be the proper medicine for the colt.'

'Why not follow the Way thyself, and so accompany the boy?'

Mahbub stared stupefied at the magnificent insolence of the demand, which across the Border he would have paid with more than a blow. Then the humour of it touched his worldly soul.

'Softly – softly – one foot at a time, as the lame gelding went over the Umballa jumps. I may come to Paradise later – I have workings that way – great motions – and I owe them to thy simplicity. Thou hast never lied?'

'What need?'

'O Allah, hear him! "What need" in this Thy world! Nor ever harmed a man?'

'Once – with a pen-case – before I was wise.'

'So? I think the better of thee. Thy teachings are good. Thou hast turned one man that I know from the path of strife.' He laughed immensely. 'He came here open-minded to commit a *dacoity* (a house-robbery with violence). Yes, to cut, rob, kill, and carry off what he desired.'

'A great foolishness!'

'Oh! black shame too. So he thought after he had seen thee – and a few others, male and female. So he abandoned it; and now he goes to beat a big fat Babu man.'

'I do not understand.'

'Allah forbid it! Some men are strong in knowledge, Red Hat. Thy strength is stronger still. Keep it – I think thou wilt. If the boy be not a good servant, pull his ears off.'

With a hitch of his broad Bokhariot belt the Pathan swaggered off into the gloaming, and the lama came down from his clouds so far as to look at the broad back.

'That person lacks courtesy, and is deceived by the shadow of appearances. But he spoke well of my *chela*, who now enters upon his reward. Let me make the prayer!... Wake, O fortunate above all born of women. Wake! It is found!'

Kim came up from those deep wells, and the lama attended his yawning pleasure; duly snapping fingers to head off evil spirits.

'I have slept a hundred years. Where –? Holy One, hast *thou* been here long? I went out to look for thee, but' – he laughed drowsily – 'I slept by the way. I am all well now. Hast thou eaten? Let us go to the house. It is many days since I tended thee. And the Sahiba fed thee well? Who shampooed thy legs? What of the weaknesses – the belly and the neck, and the beating in the ears?'

'Gone – all gone. Dost thou not know?'

'I know nothing, but that I have not seen thee in a monkey's age. Know what?'

'Strange the knowledge did not reach out to thee, when all my thoughts were theeward.'

'I cannot see the face, but the voice is like a gong. Has the Sahiba made a young man of thee by her cookery?'

He peered at the cross-legged figure, outlined jet-black against the lemon-coloured drift of light. So does the stone

Bodhisat sit who looks down upon the patent self-registering turnstiles of the Lahore Museum.

The lama held his peace. Except for the click of the rosary and a faint *clop-clop* of Mahbub's retreating feet, the soft, smoky silence of evening in India wrapped them close.

'Hear me! I bring news.'

'But let us – '

Out shot the long yellow hand compelling silence. Kim tucked his feet under his robe-edge obediently.

'Hear me! I bring news! The Search is finished. Comes now the Reward. . . . Thus. When we were among the Hills, I lived on thy strength till the young branch bowed and nigh broke. When we came out of the Hills, I was troubled for thee and for other matters which I held in my heart. The boat of my soul lacked direction; I could not see into the Cause of Things. So I gave thee over to the virtuous woman altogether. I took no food. I drank no water. Still I saw not the Way. They pressed food upon me and cried at my shut door. So I removed myself to a hollow under a tree. I took no food. I took no water. I sat in meditation two days and two nights, abstracting my mind; inbreathing and out-breathing in the required manner. . . . Upon the second night – so great was my reward – the wise Soul loosed itself from the silly Body and went free. This I have never before attained, though I have stood on the threshold of it. Consider, for it is a marvel!'

'A marvel indeed. Two days and two nights without food! Where was the Sahiba?' said Kim under his breath.

'Yea, my Soul went free, and, wheeling like an eagle, saw indeed that there was no Teshoo Lama nor any other soul. As a drop draws to water, so my soul drew near to the Great Soul which is beyond all things. At that point, exalted in contemplation, I saw all Hind, from Ceylon in the sea to the Hills, and my own Painted Rocks at Such-zen; I saw every camp and village, to the least, where we have ever rested. I saw them at one time and in one place; for they were within the Soul. By this I knew the Soul had passed beyond the illusion of Time and Space and of Things. By this I knew that I was free. I saw thee lying in thy cot, and I saw thee falling down hill under the idolater – at one time, in one place, in my Soul, which, as I say, had touched the Great Soul. Also I saw the stupid body of Teshoo Lama lying down, and the *hakim* from Dacca kneeled beside, shouting in its ear. Then my Soul was all alone, and I saw nothing, for I was all things, having reached the Great Soul. And I meditated a thousand thousand years, passionless, well aware of the Causes of all Things. Then a voice cried: "What shall come to the boy if thou art dead?" and I was shaken back and forth in myself with pity for thee; and I said: "I will return to my *chela*, lest he miss the Way." Upon this my Soul, which is the soul of Teshoo Lama, withdrew itself from the Great Soul with strivings and yearnings and retchings and agonies not to be told. As the egg from the fish, as the fish from the water, as the water from the cloud, as the cloud from the thick air; so put forth, so leaped out, so drew away, so fumed up the soul of Teshoo Lama from the Great Soul. Then a voice cried: "The River! Take heed to the River!" and I looked down upon all the world, which was as I had seen it before – one in time, one in place – and I saw plainly the River of the Arrow at my feet. At that hour my Soul was hampered by some evil or other whereof I was not wholly cleansed, and it lay upon my arms and coiled round my waist; but I put it aside, and I cast forth as an eagle in my flight for the very place of the River. I pushed aside world upon world for thy sake. I saw the River below me – the River of the Arrow – and, descending, the waters of it closed over me; and behold I was again in the body of Teshoo Lama, but free from sin, and the *hakim* from Dacca bore up my head in the waters of the River. It is here! It is behind the mango-tope here – even here!'

'Allah Karim! Oh, well that the Babu was by! Wast thou very wet?'

'Why should I regard? I remember the *hakim* was concerned for the body of Teshoo Lama. He haled it out of the holy water in his hands, and there came afterwards thy horse-seller from the North with a cot and men, and they put the body on the cot and bore it up to the Sahiba's house.'

'What said the Sahiba?'

'I was meditating in that body, and did not hear. So thus the Search is ended. For the merit that I have acquired, the River of the Arrow is here. It broke forth at our feet, as I have said. I have found it. Son of my Soul, I have wrenched my Soul back from the Threshold of Freedom to free thee from all sin – as I am free, and sinless. Just is the Wheel! Certain is our deliverance. Come!'

He crossed his hands on his lap and smiled, as a man may who has won Salvation for himself and his beloved.

THE END